AUTHOR NOTES

This book includes triggers like – Alcohol use for coping, death of a minor, death of loved ones, thoughts of suicide, mental health struggles/depression, imprisonment, grief, violence, blood, torture, death, decapitation, dismemberment, forced orgasms, mention of sexual assault and physical abuse, explicit language, sexually explicit scenes. This book does end on a cliffhanger.

There are also bonus chapters at the end of the book. You don't want to miss those hidden gems.

The next book in the Dark Curse series will be coming out in 2025.
Stay in the know.

Last warning: I am not responsible for your therapy bills. Only my own for writing this beast.
Enjoy!

Pronunciation Guide

Davyna/Dy: Duh-veen-a/Die
Kadeyan: Kade-E-an
Drystan: Dr-i-stin
Eryx: Eric-x
Sahar: Sa-har
Levanna: Leh-van-a
Calix: Cal-i-x
Nyna: Neen-a
Akari: Uh-car-e
Zaryk: Zar-ick
Alyahiia: Al-ah-he-a
Arcadyus: Ar-kade-e-us
Valyner: Val-i-ner
Armaros: Arm-a-rose
Qeles: Key-les
Gelmyra: Gel-meer-a
Anawyn: Uh-nah-win
Solyus: Soul-e-us
Lunavas: Lu-na-vas
Saawyn: saw-win
Waar Sairini: War-suh-reen-e

Gelmyra
Mortal Realm
Armaros
Qeles
Cursed lands

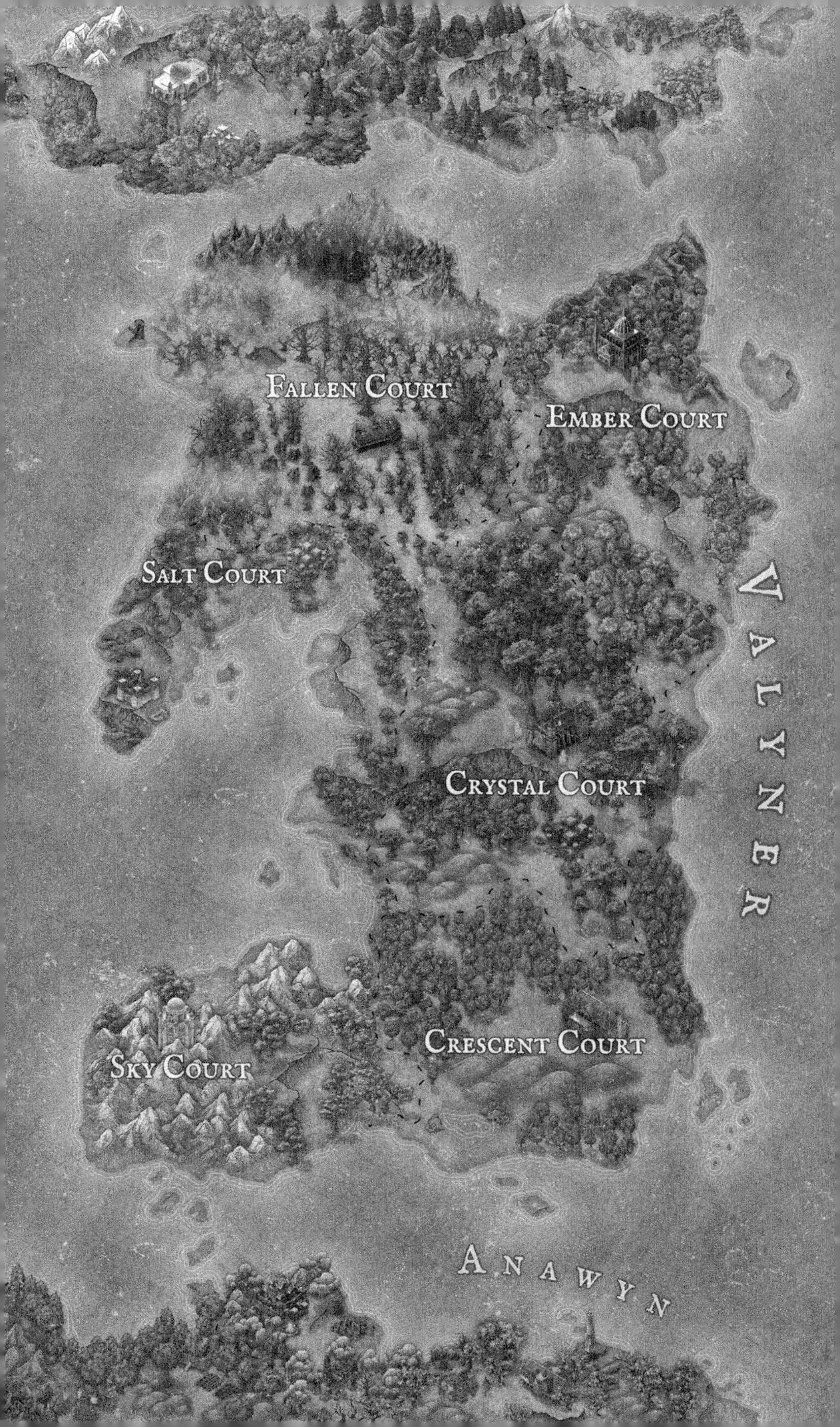
Fallen Court
Ember Court
Salt Court
Valyner
Crystal Court
Crescent Court
Sky Court
Anawyn

Previously in Hidden Beneath the Embers

In Mortal Lands, Davyna sought freedom from her adoptive mother, Hera, and a new start with her sister, Evren. A letter led her to a red stone necklace left by her father but was lost during the ball when her fire power came out. That night, she found herself a Realm away, in a land called Valyner with the fae.

After time with Alastair, Lord of the Crescent Court, she came to trust him, and they both opened up about life and loss. While with him, Davyna read about the fae Realms, and how Valyner was made by the gods: Obsidian, the god of darkness, and Tanith, the goddess of light.

Davyna agreed to bind her powers to avoid the dangers of being a known Ember but discovered the binding curse was meant to kill her. She escaped and was taken to the Lord of the Fallen Court: Kadeyan. They struck a deal: she unlocks her powers in exchange for information about her father.

While traveling to the Courts with Kadeyan and his friends, Davyna's powers emerged, revealing her true lineage as the daughter of former King Ezekiel Ember and her mother, Nyna; a cursed fae from the Mortal Realm whom Persephone had killed.

Captured by Queen Persephone, she learned of Alastair's betrayal and Persephone's plans for becoming more god-like using her father's stone, the one hidden in her necklace. Escaping with Kadeyan, they found themselves caught in a war in the Mortal Realm between the humans and the Cursed. Persephone killed Davyna, leading her to confront her father in the void he created for her.

Upon returning from the void, she then killed Persephone, while undoing her father's curse on the fae in the Mortal Realm. But Persephone left her with one last warning: that "he" would come for her.

With freedom achieved for so many, including Davyna, she struggled to accept her new life and Kadeyan's declaration of their mating bond. The book concludes with Davyna being acknowledged as Queen by the Lords and Ladies of Valyner in the throne room but ultimately does not take it, and burns the throne out of anger for what it took from her. A family.

And that one choice…would change everything…

Even when things are not okay, and you're breaking...
you are still strong.

Don't underestimate the allure of the darkness...
Even the purest hearts are drawn to it.
-Klaus Mikaelson

CHAPTER 1
DAVYNA

All I wanted were answers that would bring me peace in who I was. But somehow, I ended up with fate's hands wrapped around my throat, robbing me of that simple pleasure.

Flames thrashed behind my eyes as I moved down the hollow halls of my father's castle, the dark grey stone blurring around the edges of my vision. This was his legacy, not mine. I felt nothing but wrath towards that godsforsaken throne and what it took from me.

A family...

The tension from the throne room slithered behind me, meeting my pace as I took in their shock and worry about what I did. The distance I was putting between me and them wasn't enough to dull the erratic emotions slamming against my psyche.

The past two months were playing on repeat within my mind. The deception. The secrets. The loss I witnessed before my eyes, and the fear of losing any more people. And something I hadn't let myself deal with yet: dying.

After everything, this still wasn't the life I wanted, nor the title I searched for.

I was not their Queen.

Pressing my hands into the copper steel doors, I pushed them out as sparks sizzled against them. The sensation forced me to look down to see my skin burning a dark red. I tried to steady my breathing as I stepped out, closing the doors behind me before I rested my head against the thick metal. After settling the raging power within, I stepped onto the terrace and overlooked the lush lands painted in autumn.

The wind brushed against my skin, making me turn to follow its course. How freeing it would be to become like the breeze. Here one moment and gone the next, like a gentle gust was promising to take you to the sanctuary you craved. My power roared within me, forcing me to squeeze my eyes closed. What the hell was happening? I couldn't shut anything out right now.

When I said I wanted to stay in the light, I meant it, but that was only because I thought it would bring me peace and reveal what was hidden from me. And while it did, I felt as if I would never be able to move on from the reality of what the blinding light showed me.

I was the Cursed Queen's and the fae King's daughter... Their heir. I was bound and shackled by blood without being permitted to learn more about this new version of myself. There wouldn't be peace within these four walls. Only the constant reminder of the ones who hurt my family, and the secrets kept from me...

I. Was. Done.

My hands shook as I raised them to my face, the sob building up in my throat. Raking my fingers through my hair, I pulled strands free from my braid and took a few deep breaths.

A broken melody rang out within, coursing through my veins. It was like my own power was mourning in anguish with me, with the dull ache growing into something more ferocious. My ears began to ring, and the world around me fell silent as I stepped forward. Even with trying to take a few cleansing breaths, the power within was growing like uncontrolled vines climbing a stone structure. And it was determined to swallow me whole.

Turning around, I faintly heard boots echoing off the stone within the castle before picking up the scent: pine and leathers.

Kade.

My heart began to slam against my ribs as his emotions filtered in with the chaos challenging me. He was concerned, but I didn't want to see him or anyone else right now. I needed a minute to calm down.

Closing my eyes, I turned away and thought of being anywhere but here. The wind spiraled around me, like it was reminding me of its promise of a peaceful shelter. And without permission, my power soared to life and billowed out around me.

Fire blazed through my veins as I let out a silent yell. Everything inside me beat against a glass wall, chipping away until it shattered into a million pieces. I didn't want him or anyone else to see it because they already saw enough of me breaking down and struggling up to this point.

For a moment, I swore I heard him call out to me before he said, *"Where the hell did you go?"*

But then, it was gone... The distance between us gave me the relief of silence I desperately craved.

Opening my eyes, I let the exhale from my lungs drag out as I took in the gap surrounding me. It was as dark as ever; its onyx mixing with the shimmers of blue and purple, hugging close to me like a friend. I realized the raging thoughts and power within were muted now, allowing me to take a full breath.

Maybe I was wrong when I first perceived the dark because, in here--away from everything--I could tell that the darkness was always promising you some type of reprieve. It gave you a void that erased the world around you. Was it the right choice right now? Probably not, but it was a shelter from the glaring light of the future that was expected of me.

My mind still flashed with images of what I'd been through since arriving in Valyner, along with the warped childhood I lived. And I realized I didn't need to fight in here or hold up the walls around myself to protect the broken girl who lived within.

My eyes started to burn as tears filled them because I didn't need to be strong right now. There was a freedom in here, allowing me to fall deeper into the bliss of being hidden, and to embrace all the brokenness within.

I could shatter.

Tears began streaming down my cheeks as I closed my eyes, hearing the soft sobs barely echo within the void. I wanted my dad... I wanted more time with him to tell me what being a fae in Valyner would be like. I wanted my mom to explain what it was like to be this unique being with multiple abilities. But those dreams of having them here with me were just that—dreams.

Opening my eyes, I took in the void, watching the colors shift. The blues and purples within the onyx abyss gained more hues, swirling together with an iridescent white, copper, and crimson. The colors encircled me, causing me to turn and furrow my brows. This wasn't normal.

Sucking in a sharp breath, my body began to free fall through the gap, and fear pricked at my skin. My stomach rose and the world around me glowed bright, forcing me to gaze at the ground, which was fast approaching.

Bracing myself, I dug my feet into the ground, causing the dirt to shoot up and rain down around me. The force of it pulled me down, making me drop to one knee as my hands went out, stopping me from falling forward. Taking a few shallow breaths, I saw each finger coated in what felt like soil, but instead of it being a dark brown, it was onyx with silver specks throughout.

Furrowing my brows, I pulled them back and inspected them. My mind changed its pace quickly, wondering what ripped me out of the gap.

Did Kade pull me out...? And if so, where was he?

I waited for his voice to vibrate my bones and force my fires to rise, but as I looked at my surroundings, the opposite happened. My bones turned to stone, and the flames within froze over while I took in the world around me. It was like nothing I'd ever seen before.

Desolate grounds...and void of colors any land would be painted in.

Closing my eyes, I tried to steady myself as a wave of dizziness took hold. I dropped to my other knee, waiting for it to pass, but the world began spinning and nausea bloomed in my core.

After a few minutes, the effects began to fade and my chest

expanded, taking in more air. It was thicker here, coating my lungs with its weighted embrace before I sensed it...an overwhelming force of power.

Clutching my father's stone, an undeniable sense of security washed over me, as if his presence still lingered inside. Despite the emptiness it held, it brought me strength, reminding me of our connection as I scanned over the lands again. This didn't look like the Mortal Realm or anywhere in Valyner. So, where was I?

The bleached sky was striking. It took a moment for my eyes to adjust to its assaulting rays. Squinting, I took in the vast void above with blackened stars speckled throughout, matching the massive half-moon beaming onto the land.

Glancing over my shoulder, I assessed the grounds again for anything that would give me an answer to what this place was when I spotted the blinding sun. My eyes widened as I took it in. It was painted in the same iridescent hues that were in the gap, but was surrounded by a gloomy ring. It blazed onto the lands, obliterating any shadows that tried to hide from it.

Standing up, a sense of confusion crept in like tendrils of smoke holding me in its haze. I brushed my hands together, removing the soil from my skin before glancing down. Tilting my head, I took in my flesh stained with a deep inky soot. It was strange, and I traced the blotches on each digit. My lips parted, wonder taking over because soil normally wouldn't do that.

Glancing around, my ears strained to listen beyond for any signs of life, but it was as silent as a crypt, forcing an unnerving quake to pass through me. The brush and trees in the distance barely moved with the breeze and none of them held color either. My heart was beating like a drum, incessantly pounding in my chest like an urgent warning.

Where the fuck was I?

Shaking off the chills crawling up my spine, I moved forward through the dense, opaque growth before me and every sense in my body heightened. The eerie ambiance grew with each step as I scanned and strained my hearing to find someone. Although, the silence was deafening, like no one had lived here for thousands of years, only adding to its haunted vitality.

Another shudder ran down my spine as I pulled for my Crystal power and changed from my gown to my fighting leathers.

My power began to hum within, screaming for me to leave and return to Valyner. However, I couldn't ignore that with each step, my power matched the weight of energy in the air, brushing against mine. A recognition that I'd never felt before.

Climbing over some rocks, I ascended a steep hill, determined to figure out why these lands gave off a bizarre mystery that spoke out to my soul.

This was my problem...I couldn't leave things alone. I always wanted to get answers.

I paused, my thoughts raging back and forth. But how could I ignore something that was instinctual? Something that no one else possessed in Valyner, and that matched the same energy I expelled on the throne.

The real question, though, was: Was this power something I needed to embrace? Or fear?

I pressed on, letting my stubbornness win once again as I reached the top of the hill. My jaw fell slack when I took in the dazzling white castle before me, melding up as it climbed into black stone. Heavy clouds sat over it, blocking how tall the structure was.

A shadowy aura radiated around it, and I could tell it was stained in darkness, pulling an icy quake from me as its power caressed my skin. It was beautiful, but a distant feeling pushed me to believe something about it promised death...

Shaking my head, I dropped my gaze to the onyx lake covering the grounds of the west side. The water barely moved, giving the appearance that it was as thick as blood and unable to circulate. A breeze whipped from the side, sending my hair in its current. I tucked the loose strands behind my ear, sensing...something that smeared my skin with unease.

I should leave, but I physically couldn't.

I felt pulled to understand the unknown essence flowing within the lake. Picking up my feet, I began moving forward to investigate it further, unsure what I was hoping to find. Maybe I'd discover something in there about where I was, or a person willing to explain this world to me.

I needed to stop *seeking* answers.

Ignoring my intuition, I moved towards the archway and took in the two massive doors. One was painted in the richest white, making snow appear dull in comparison. While the other was coated in the darkest night, threatening to never show the light of day again. Each one held a shimmer of colors within, but it was subtle.

The soft blues reminded me of Lana's and Drystan's eyes, while the purples swaying within matched the color of the gown I made for Marta. Reds and oranges swirled, dancing like my fires before I caught sight of the black and white, reminding me of the void I was in with my father.

Each hue was hypnotizing, and slowly, it hit me. These were the same colors each court possessed in Valyner. What did that mean?

The door was ajar, but it did nothing to hide the large dagger carved into it, holding the opposite color in the blade. And I couldn't help but wonder what that stood for.

A strong urge ran through my veins, and my body betrayed me as I veered off course from the castle to go towards the gloomy lake. Wonder flooded my mind as I moved closer to it. Its unwavering power danced out and brushed against my flesh. My body began to buzz with an intensity that I never felt before, and it was almost painful with the need to get closer to it.

It was a spell... It was coming from the lake.

I needed to stop, but I didn't want to. The closer I got to the dark water, I could feel it wanting to draw me into its endless depths, and it actually sounded nice. Serene... Peaceful.

Go on...you know you want to...

Confusion seeped in as the voice in my mind spoke; it was my own but distorted. It quickly turned to mist as I took a few steps forward, and the curiosity fell away with it. My stomach tightened and my lungs even began to ache. Panic bubbled up inside of me, breaking its hold as my body stiffened along the edge.

I needed to snap out of it...and get out of here.

The still lake began to sway and let out sweet music that besought me to obey and fall to my knees in reverence before it. I resisted its perfect melody as the waves grew wilder, trying to make sense of what magic it possessed.

Pulling for my power, I pushed back on its enchantment and its control broke, allowing me to step back. My head spun as I looked up in time to see a wave shoot out and wrap around my foot. Jerked to the ground, the air ripped from my lungs, causing me to cough violently. I tried to kick myself free, but it was no use. It had sunk its invisible claws into me and it was going to take what it wanted.

I kicked and yelled, but it was enjoying the fight, pulling me in inch by inch, like I stepped into quicksand. To my ankles first, then to my knees, taunting and promising one thing: to devour me after it had its fun.

My body started to heat as I called forth everything within to fight. My skin began to glow, but the water pulled me in faster, like it knew my power was building. It kept dragging me until I was chest-deep in its hold, pushing my own power away from me.

Flashes of back home with my sister, my friends, and...Kade slammed into my chest, and my power returned to me, smeared in a primal indignation. I let my voice roar to life and released the firestorm blazing within. The beautiful melody emanating from the water faded and turned into a bloodcurdling scream, piercing my ears. My body engulfed in searing flames, causing the water to move away and the slick hands to fall from my legs.

Pushing myself up, I turned and grabbed onto the edge of the ground and pulled my body out of the lake, but I could still feel its smothering hold on me. What was down there? And how did I miss their firm embrace pressing to my skin?

Glancing back, my lungs twisted, cutting off my next breath as I took in the great wave crawling up into the air. The onyx hands with long, claw-like nails were fighting to break free, with the thick water dripping from each digit. Through the dense lake, I heard hissing, sending a shudder down my body.

I yelled as I pushed my fire out again, breaking the spell's grip on my body, and rolled to the ground. Drawing in ragged breaths, I looked over at the lake again and watched as the hands fell back into the safety of the water. It came crashing down, forcing my eyes to widen as it began rushing towards me. They were furious and hell-bent on their revenge to take what I denied them: to make me their captive.

Rising, wrath bloomed inside, and I extended my hands out with intense fervor. The sea of flames I unleashed smothered the murky water, and the screams from within the wave fell silent. I backed away, keeping my eyes on my crimson and apricot blaze and taking comfort in the colors contrasting against this world.

My chest rose and fell rapidly from the adrenaline pumping through my veins, but my entire body froze to the ground. An inferno of black flames grew from the lake's surface, towering over my own before swallowing them whole. Where did that come from? And why did it have shimmery hues throughout, like the doors on the castle? Like the gap?

Anxiety blanketed me, causing me to stagger back and get farther away from whatever that was.

Was I going crazy? Or was it this place?

My body slammed into something...

No, *someone.*

CHAPTER 2
DAVYNA

I turned, dragging my feet through the dense dirt as my blood ran cold. The spinning in my head returned...because I knew her. Every feature from her dark brown hair to the leathers she wore, and the piercing silver eyes staring back at me. It was like I was standing in a mirror, seeing my own reflection.

"Who are you, little fae?" Even her voice was a reflection of my own, making my jaw fall open.

She showed no sign of being fazed by the fact that we were identical in every way. Staring at me with impatience captivating her eyes, she waited for my response, but I was stunned. Unsure of what to make of her or what *little fae* meant...

"Who are you?" I asked after a long minute before stepping away from her and the lake.

The woman in front of me didn't speak. She only tilted her head to the side with a twisted smile, looking me over.

"H–how is this possible?" My thoughts turned into a frenzy, confused by everything I'd ever learned about myself. I didn't have a twin sister. I was pretty sure my father would have told me that.

A lump formed in my throat as I looked her up and down again, still trying to understand how this was possible.

She moved in a wide circle around me, causing me to feel more uneasy as I tried to stop the shudder skating down my spine.

"How did you get here?" she asked as she came back into view, tilting her head again and allowing one brow to rise.

"I used the gap. Where are we?" I blinked before allowing my gaze to take in the lands again. Was this all real, or was this all an illusion toying with me? "Are we related?" I turned to face her head-on, unable to stop the questions from rolling off my tongue.

She gave me a smile, but the kindness didn't reach her eyes. They were cynical—practically plotting something—and it made my heart rate increase. "Wouldn't you like to know... But I will tell you this: you are in a place you shouldn't be."

"Why?" I asked, stealing a glance at her ears that came to a point as she tucked her dark brown waves behind it.

We were similar. In our appearance, yes, but it was something more. It was like her power called to mine, weaving together as if they were the same. And I couldn't ignore the apprehension growing in my bones, warning me something was off with her.

As we stood there in the eerie silence, I focused on her power and could tell it was similar to mine. It danced around our bodies, aggravated, and challenged the other like they wanted to clash into war. My heart doubled over from how fast it was beating, and she took a step closer to me.

"Are you me?" I asked.

"No, sweet...little...fae. I'm not. I'm better than you."

My eyes narrowed, and something in her words lit the match within. "I don't know what game you're playing here, but I want answers. Now!" I shouted, and she chuckled.

"Come now. I asked you first, and you have rudely ignored my questions." My fighter instinct told me deep down to not give her anything, and I obeyed its command. "How did you leave Valyner and break through the veil?"

"I'm not telling you shit!" How did she know I was from Valyner? The veil? What the hell was that? But more importantly, how did I break through it?

My chest began to ache, like it was bruised from my heart slamming against my ribs. I buried down the ache that was growing more intense, along with apprehension, before placing my walls up to create a fortress of protection against the person before me.

She watched me intently as her power brushed up against my walls, pushing on them before she stopped.

"What are you?" She laughed, shaking her head. I retreated a step, watching her every move. "Mm, very interesting."

"What?" I asked, my emotions swaying before I realized that I couldn't feel hers at all. The only thing I could make sense of was her expression, which was apparent... She was just as much puzzled as I was.

"How are you fighting my power? It's not possible..." She took another step towards me, her face losing all soft edges as her anger became evident. Her eyes glowed a brighter silver, almost like that would convince me to talk.

"Listen, I didn't mean to come here. So, I'll just leave."

"I can't let you do that..." She tilted her head up to the castle, forcing my eyes to follow as I took in a figure standing behind sheer black curtains. I couldn't see their face, only their build, which was a male's. And based on that alone, it made me swallow the trepidation crawling up my throat. "I think my mate would like a word with you."

Fuck that! I wasn't staying around to meet anyone else, let alone anything mated to her.

I summoned my power, smelling the ashes as they built around me to fall into the gap. Before I could even blink, her hand darted out and grabbed my wrist in a death grip. Searing pain rushed up my arm, traveling through my veins and muscles with vengeance before stabbing into my skull.

A broken scream fell from my lips, echoing beyond as I tried to stay upright. Her power was much like my own. My own body recognized it and gave up its fight at the intrusion.

My walls shattered, and she dove into my mind. I winced from her invasion, gritting my teeth as the pain doubled. Looking back at her, my throat locked up and the cries stopped, regardless of the pain. Because what was staring back at me now shook me to my very core.

Her eyes were beaming an iridescent hue, extinguishing the silver that was there a moment ago, but that wasn't all. Her skin also matched, glowing with different hues of color that shifted when she pulled me closer.

"What are you?" she asked again as ferocity tainted her voice, but I could still discern the confusion marking every little feature. Her brows pulled down, looking me over and trying to find an explanation for what stood before her.

I closed my eyes and pulled for every line of my power again. The heat of my skin doubled in a matter of seconds and overpowered the agony she was still inflicting on me.

I pushed everything out, breaking her hold.

My power spiraled through the air with no remorse, and I watched as the flames aimed for her. She put up a similar glittering shield that matched her skin and eyes, stopping my flames from devouring her. Each flare of my power feathered off her protection barrier until they became mere embers floating around us, losing their color to match the world beyond.

When I dropped my hands, my breathing was heavy. I could feel the fire licking behind my eyes before I narrowed my gaze into her. I wanted to kill her...to rip out her throat and wear her ribcage as a—

What? Why was I thinking like that?

She dropped the shield and straightened before me as her skin beamed brighter. I'd never seen anything like that back home. So, what kind of power was this? I steeled my spine, waiting for her next move and willing my power to grow within.

Did I want an answer to any of this? Did I want to learn about this world or who she was? And I knew, right now, the answer was clear and unequivocal: no.

"You can leave now, Davyna." I was taken aback by the use of my name, but her vile smile only grew wider. She found what she wanted in my mind... "We will be seeing each other again...soon."

My jaw fell open as I pulled my brows down. See her again? My power built around me, eager to get away from her and these lands.

I pictured the Fallen Court, my friends, Kadeyan...and I prayed up to the gods that they would guide me back home.

My breathing became shorter and shorter as I fell through the void, hoping that I'd never step foot in that place again.

CHAPTER 3
UNKNOWN

My eyes lingered on the spot near the black water where she stood moments ago as footsteps approached from behind. The door swung open, and I already sensed her annoyance.

"We're going to need to take care of that."

I chuckled, still unable to draw my gaze away. How could something so young and so naive to what power she contained hold me in this spot, longing to learn everything about her?

"I know..." I turned, locking my gaze on my *mate,* no longer wearing the face of the fae who was still captivating my attention. Waxen eyes seared into me as I brushed a piece of ivory blonde strands off her shoulder. "But I will decide when...where...and how *I* will kill her. Do you understand?"

She nodded before retreating back through the door. I walked over to the vase of black and white roses and took in the contrast between them. Picking up a white rose, I sneered and wrapped my fingers around the petals until they were ripped off the stem. She knew better than to test my patience. Especially after this.

No one from the other realms had ever broken through the veil... So, how did she do it? And was it tied to what just happened in Valyner? I could still feel the stain of magic coming from their Lands, forcing my own to surge.

Throwing the white rose to the ground, I picked up a black one, studying its beauty held in the opaque petals. The best things in this world were found in the darkness, embodying an onyx soul, and embracing what they truly were.

Was *she* one of them?

Like a moth to a flame, my body turned back to the window to look at the place where Davyna stood.

Ah, Davyna. You have no idea what you started.

She was going to be a problem that crawled beneath my skin, irritating and impossible to rid myself of... However, I welcomed the challenge. I always had.

For now, I'd stay close by...watching, waiting, and relishing in how I was going to break her.

By the time I was done with her...

I laughed, running my tongue over my bottom lip.

She would beg for death.

CHAPTER 4
DAVYNA

The gap evaporated around me and my legs trembled as my feet made contact with the ground. Losing my balance, I fell onto my ass and my heart pressed up in my throat. Was I back in Valyner? Was *she* here? Fae moved past me, their eyes narrowing in confusion as they took in my delirious state.

Pressing the heels of my boots into the cobblestone, I pushed myself out of the road, until my back pressed into the uneven stone wall. My eyes darted back and forth, barely registering the world, when the familiar energy of the realm washed over me.

I was back...

A long, shuddered breath passed my lips as I rested my head against the wall and closed my eyes. It took a few minutes to calm down, but once I did, I took in the Court.

Everything was painted in darkness, and the trees peeking through the establishments held no life. The Fallen Court. An ounce of security fell over me, washing away the horrors enough for me to pick myself up off the ground.

I could feel Kade in the distance. His fury pulsed in waves that slammed into my chest, causing my skin to pebble. I traced it back, guessing he was probably at his castle on the outskirts of town. It made me nervous as I tried to take a step forward, wary that his anger was probably directed at me for leaving...for denying him.

I stalled, looking around, and realized I'd never been down here. I'd never seen the Fallen in their own element.

And maybe giving him some time to cool off was what he

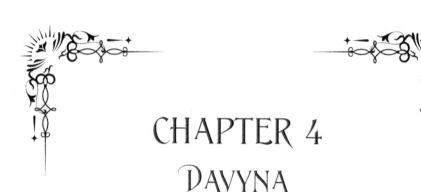

needed… While I figured out how to bury my fear that was still seeping out through my pores.

I began moving through the town, observing the fae and the buildings around me. Much like the people, the town mirrored a haunted place, with dead trees bent and twisted in unnatural ways, scattered throughout the square. The darkness adorned every detail of the streets and the structures of homes and shops. Even windows contained smoke as if shadows lived within them.

It made sense why people feared this Court. But, to me, it felt like home. And after being in that unknown place, this was like paradise in comparison.

Pushing the thoughts aside, I came to an opening in the square and looked up as three fae flew over, their wings forcing the wind to throw my loose strands into the breeze. A blur of darkness shrouded them, causing me to see the image of the lake again as I blinked. The invisible touch of the hands within the thick, inky water wrapped around my legs and my breathing began to shorten. A chill ran down my body, and I looked up, searching for that familiar power because…it felt like it was watching me.

So, maybe this wasn't my safe haven anymore… But did I ever really have one? Because the security of home was finite. It could be there one second, then you blink, and your world would be forever changed. I should understand that better than anyone by now. And yet, even with all that I had been through, I still hoped for a place that would offer the solace my soul craved.

I think it always would.

Turning back, I looked over the large opening with shops creating a wide circle. It reminded me of back home in Armaros, but in the middle of the square was a large fountain of three tiers flowing with thick crimson water.

Iron invaded my nostrils, making my blood heat as I watched someone fill a cup and bring it to his lips. Stepping forward, I watched the male turn and every desire to have some for myself faded as I took in his hand. It was grey…almost like he was desiccating. The energy and emotions flowing off him wrapped around me and it physically hurt to bear it.

As our eyes met, I averted my gaze, but I couldn't deny that I sensed his pain in that fleeting moment. His tough demeanor kept it buried away, showing me just how strong he was for hiding the agony flowing through him. Was he sick? How would that even be possible? Fae didn't get sick, and we didn't age. Maybe someone cursed him. That would make sense...right?

Picking up my pace, I pressed on until a sign for a pub where fae were entering caught my gaze. Glancing down the road, I saw the Dead Forest that led towards the castle, but the scent of whiskey wafting out of the bar had me moving towards it.

I'd say after today, whiskey was needed.

Moving around some people, I got to the door and paused as a couple of males stumbled out, singing a song...poorly. It brought a smile to my face. Lifting my arm, I grabbed the edge of the blackened door and stalled as I took in my hand. Dropping it, I heard a man curse when the door hit him, but it faded away as my eyes zeroed in on the scars moving up my hand...where she touched me.

"What the fuck?" I whispered, but it was barely audible.

Iridescent scars branched out over the top of my hand like veins, and as I moved my hand, I could see the light hues of color shimmering within. The sound of the world around me faded, until the only thing that remained was a piercing ring that forced panic to take over.

I looked into the window, nausea returning as I saw the extent of what she left me with. My hair remained unchanged, as it had always been—dark brown—but there was something new. On the right side, a good portion of my strands were a pale blonde—almost void of any pigment. Undoing my braid with shaking hands, I looked back to the window and took it in again.

No...this wasn't happening.

Yes, it is...

I turned, looking for that voice, but I realized it wasn't anyone near me. It was the same one I heard near the onyx lake, matching my own with a mangled tone. Was this her?

Rolling up my sleeve, I looked at the scars again and saw how they branched out over my flesh like the mangled tree branches of this Court. The shimmering hues through each mark she left behind reminded me of her power and the way her skin glowed. Whatever magic she used must have done this and I didn't understand what it meant.

The world slowed, along with my heart in my chest as tears threatened to spill over. Steadying myself against the building, I took a few shaky breaths and closed my eyes. The cyclone of fear smothered me, offering no reprieve from its torment, and it made me want to leave my own body.

I don't know how much time passed, but when I opened my eyes, they locked on the sign for the pub. I decided I needed a drink more than I did before finding this. I needed to drown this chaos out, even if it was for five fucking minutes.

I needed to not think...or feel...anything.

Burying the mayhem within, I pushed my body forward and walked into the bar as the world around me stood in a blur. The establishment was large—larger than Lana's bar. It was painted in darkness, with soft red orbs glowing down from above, giving the bar a sinister appeal. I moved forward, taking in the details of the black leather booths that lined the walls and were all filled in with fae.

A loud thud broke me out of my trance, and I looked at the male yelling at his friend. "Bullshit! You weren't even there. You should have seen this thing, though. It was fucking huge! And I killed it!"

The men around him began laughing, calling him a liar. I averted my gaze to the bar, seeing there was one more seat open. I moved swiftly through the tables and pulled myself up into the chair, feeling each tremor more intensely than the last.

I waited for the nostalgia to hit me because I sat in a similar spot in Lana's bar, with a sweet, woodsy aroma mixing with the potent liquors. That life felt so far away...like I never truly lived it.

Running my hands through my hair, I let out a disrupted breath by the chills rushing through me. *That* feeling was here again, along with something else coming off of the fae in here... They seemed off. Turning, I looked them over, sensing the pain, panic, grief, and even anger enveloping them.

A heavy weight fell onto my shoulders, taking all their anguish as if it was my own, and I turned back around. It was similar to my own, though. Broken, shattered, lost in fury, and above all else, fear. So, maybe I was projecting; maybe this was my emotions smothering all of them.

After a minute, I tilted my head up to make eye contact with the bartender.

He smiled at me before calling out, "Give me a minute, love!"

I forced my lips into a tight, thin line that barely resembled a smile. The corners of my mouth struggled to turn upward, but it was all I could muster. His silver hair glowed under the warmth of the orbs, giving it a fiery haze as he served the two males before him. Pulling my eyes back to the bottles before me, I caught my reflection in them and couldn't pull my gaze away. I wanted to scream.

I wanted to run...

"What will it be, hon?" the male asked as he gave me a gentle smile, bringing me back to his forest-green eyes. His expression changed as he took in the fear plastered to my face.

Fuck. I couldn't show weakness.

His worry wrapped around me, making me feel weak, and I didn't need that right now. I needed to not break...

Concealing my feelings—similar to the countless occasions with Hera and the disappointment of every failed lead to find my father—I forced a smile. "Give me five of whatever is your strongest."

His eyes widened in a playful way before he laughed. "Bad day?" he asked, turning to look over the bottles before using his shadows to pull one from the top shelf.

"You have no idea."

I watched him as he grabbed the shot glasses, laying them before me while his shadows undid the top of the bottle. The black tendrils of smoke picked up and poured out the amber-brown liquor, filling each glass. After the last glass was filled, the liquid rippled until it became as still as the onyx lake.

Swallowing hard, I looked up. "Thanks."

"Hey…" he said, forcing me to meet his gaze again. "First two are on me." He winked. A chuckle fell from my lips and he walked away, keeping his eyes on me.

Picking up one glass, I tipped it in his direction before he fell back into taking orders. Bringing it to my lips, I drank down every drop as fast as I could, before picking up the second glass and doing the same. With no food in my stomach, the numbing effect blazed through my system, and I welcomed it more than ever before as each minute passed.

I took in the bar and the people within again, recognizing that same weighted sensation as before. I grabbed the third glass and tried to let the alcohol help ebb the emotions that kept taking hold.

Rubbing my temple with my other hand, I thought about how in one hour of being gone—at least, that was how long it felt—it made me never want to leave again. And that meant…I was going to have to face what I did to the throne.

You don't have to… We could leave it all behind.

I shook my head, hearing that vile tone matching my own voice again. What was it? I drank down the whiskey, ignoring the snickering echo in my mind as if it was white noise. I'd feel better when I was back home…with my sister, my friends…and Kade.

A smile graced my face before it began to fall, tears rushing to invade my eyes. How was I going to face him like this? Kadeyan never gave me a reason not to trust him with my pain or fears, and yet I was hurting him like he had. How was I supposed to tell him about what happened? Or why I burned the throne…or denied him?

I was such a fucking coward.

I needed to let things be. I needed to not go searching for

anything else and learn how to live a life after being...killed? Human? I got what I wanted: a new life. But sitting here now, I realized there was no plan for what came next because I was always focused on being free.

Sniffling, I turned the empty glass on the counter, my gaze becoming more vacant to my surroundings as I stared at the wall. I couldn't wrap my head around all this--that this was my life now. And I couldn't tell if I walked out of one prison just to walk into another.

Wiping my eyes, I shoved down the thought and tried to find the silver lining to all this. I found my father and was out of Hera's grasp. And if that bitch with my face showed up, I wouldn't hesitate like I did before. I would kill her. Because I needed to find some peace in this new life I was living.

I closed my eyes again, taking as much air into my lungs as I could to calm the unease still clinging to me.

A lump formed in my throat, so I grabbed the fourth glass and kicked it back. Was this always destined to be my life? To be in a constant state of wonder and determination to find the truth? My magic hummed within as if it was agreeing with my thoughts, and I rolled my eyes.

All I wanted to do right now was fade into an alternate reality where life was simple.

Where I had parents who raised me to know what I was.

Where there was no taking a throne.

Where I wasn't refusing my own mate out of fear.

Where I didn't meet creatures who looked like me.

Where I wasn't stabbed in the heart by an evil Queen.

Where I didn't watch people I loved die...

Where I didn't always feel so alone and forced to be strong.

My shaking hand reached out one final time for the fifth glass as a tear escaped, trailing down my cheek. Drinking it down, I felt the sob battling to rise as I brought the glass down on the bar, pleading the whiskey would take me to that place faster. Before my *real* life caught up and forced me to face what came next.

CHAPTER 5
KADEYAN

I walked back and forth through my destroyed study, allowing my boots to crunch down on the shattered glass and torn books. None of it mattered anymore...

One thousand five hundred years on this earth, and that felt like I blinked it away compared to this. Time never moved this slow, but when you were waiting on the only thing worth living for to return to you...eternity was what you endured.

And an eternity without them had no meaning.

Spinning the dark obsidian blade between my fingers, I drank down blood laced with whiskey, hoping it would calm me down. Although, it wasn't working. Nothing was.

It felt like a rope was around my neck with a weight at the other end, dragging me into the deepest parts of the ocean. At some point, you had to decide whether you'd cut yourself free and go up for air, or die in those depths. The latter was the only option I would choose because oxygen would only taste of acid. Colors would never be vibrant again, and nothing else in this world would bring me to life like she did.

Why hadn't she reached out through our bond? Why couldn't I feel her?

My eyes fixated on the base of the glass, my fingers clenching around it with such force that it began to fracture. With a fierce snarl, I hurled it into the fireplace and my chest heaved, trying to tame the rage taking over. The glass melted into nothing, matching what was happening to my soul without her.

Where the fuck did she go? Or was she...

I flipped the dagger again, letting the flesh of my palm catch the blade. The sharp edge bit into my skin until iron filled my senses. I looked down, watching my blood pool up and drip to the ground on a page titled: *Ember Court.* The dark obsidian would keep me from healing, and that was exactly what I wanted right now. I wanted to feel something other than this...void.

A soft knock sounded at the door and I straightened myself, not caring to hide the agony. I didn't have the strength anymore...

"What is it?" I barked out from over my shoulder, tightening my grip on the blade until the burning made me grit my teeth together. The door opened softly and I could already sense who it was, but I kept my eyes on the flames before me.

"Do you want to talk?" Levanna's voice was soft, nurturing even.

"Does it look like I want to talk about it?" I spat out, the blood rushing to my eyes as I looked over to my friend.

She dropped her head, and her black and grey hair covered most of her face. I could feel the sting of my words hit her because, like me, they all weren't the same without her here. She left an imprint on us all that would never be removed or masked by another.

"Kade...this isn't the way to deal with—"

"Oh, please, tell me how I am supposed to deal with it, then? Because, last time I checked, you burned your family home to the ground because they killed Silas. And you still haven't moved on. It's been over a hundred years." His name burned on my lips because I hadn't spoken his name since his death, and guilt flooded through me.

"Don't...because we both know *you* aren't over it either!" she yelled, and I bit my tongue.

She was right; I'd never get over his loss. Not even after her parents paid for what they did with their own blood, and justice was served. I promised my father I would play it smart until the time presented itself.

"And I've trusted you this long with helping me... Do you think I would give up in helping you get your mate back?"

"I'm sorry, Lev..." I said, turning away from her. "Is there anything to update on?"

"We tried some new spells, but with our powers being affected, it's depleting us all faster." I dropped my head, my shoulders falling an inch, and defeat seared into me. "Maeve keeps pushing into her visions, but she can't see Davyna. And Faelynn has been in meditation, but told us not to disturb her while she filters through the last 1,500 years of information."

My eyes started to sting as I turned to face her. "She's out there... She has to be." My voice broke as I said the last word before moving over to the couch. Numbness closed in as I looked down at the obsidian blade still clutched in my hand.

Levanna moved into the room, making her way around the couch before sitting by my side. Her eyes took in the blade and I could hear her heartbeat pick up. I didn't want to talk about why I took it out of the weapons room or what thoughts were racing through my head at the realization that she may never come back to me.

"You are allowed to grieve...to feel pain, Kade."

"I've been living in grief and pain since she was killed..."

"Kade, I told you she wasn't ready for the throne. It might be in her blood to rule, but after everything she went through...she needed time."

"Yeah, and I should have known that. But I thought it would help her feel a connection to her father, and it would make her feel whole here...since she didn't want me."

"Gods, Kadeyan." I looked up, taking in the broken chuckle that escaped Levanna's lips. "She needed to feel whole first." Moving her hand, she pulled my fingers from the blade and I allowed her. "She died, saving all of us...and you." Wiping the blood off the dagger with her arm, she sheathed it back into my holder at my thigh before looking into my gaze. "She loves you. Even Faelynn can *see* that."

I laughed as a sob crawled up my throat.

"I'm going to tell her you said that just so she uses her power on you for a change. You won't sleep for a year with the scary shit she'll show you."

She laughed, but it sounded broken as she leaned back into the couch. "What's another year..."

I nodded, the moment passing as fast as it arrived. Standing up, I took one last look into the flames, before moving towards the door. "I'm going to go for a walk. Get some rest."

I didn't give her the opportunity to lecture me on doing the same before I jumped into the gap and landed outside near the Dead Forest. The chilled night air did little to my already frozen body as I began walking down towards the trees, seeing her silver orbs every time I blinked.

"*Come back to me, Dearest... Please.*"

I was met with silence again, but I refused to give up, trying over and over as the plea began to fall from my lips.

After an hour of walking through the woods, I began moving back towards the castle, but a familiar scent in the distance caused me to stall. Turning, my breath hitched in my throat. It was like my soul came home, entering me and giving me life. I prayed to the gods above that it wasn't a cruel trick.

Blood roses and ash invaded my nostrils even though the bond did nothing to alert me of her. However, I knew it was her, and my eyes welled up with tears.

The broken side of me unwillingly closed in, embodying rage because she wasn't anywhere to be seen through the lifeless trees. A low, guttural growl passed my lips as I focused on her scent and followed after it.

"Come out, come out wherever you are, Dearest... I want to play *my* game now."

CHAPTER 6
DAVYNA

Fuck me. How many drinks had I added to this order? Another five? I almost pulled Levanna here to pay the tab, but when the owner asked me who I was and I said I was with the castle, he told me the tab was covered. I guess he figured it out—that I was either the crazy bitch who burned the throne or that I was with Kadeyan. Either way, I drank more.

But now, I couldn't feel my hands...

The thought of going to Kade to talk about everything sent me deeper into the intoxication, melting away...well, everything. And it felt good. It was like a soft lullaby being sung to me as I swayed back and forth into oblivion. And oblivion could keep me.

A male with golden hair and piercing turquoise eyes sat down next to me about a half hour ago. He was talking my ear off, but I had no fucking clue what he was saying.

I finished my last drink and stood up, my body swaying as I fell through the air.

"Shit. You okay, Princess?" he asked as he caught me, keeping me from hitting my head against the table behind us. Shit, I told him that, didn't I? Why would I do that? It was my title, but did I even consider myself one? The answer was clear, even in this state.

No.

"Alllll good." I laughed as I forced my legs to move forward, catching enraged glares from a couple of males sitting in their booths. It looked like they were directed at me... Probably because I was a drunken mess. Letting out a long breath, I turned my gaze back to the man by my side. "I'll be finnne. I'm fine, Drystan."

He laughed. "My name is Tallen. But you can call me whatever you want, Princess. Just please let me walk you home."

I looked at him with wide eyes. "Okay, Tallllen... But, you knoow, you do look a little like Drystan. He was the first guy I *fucked*." I waved my finger in his face, getting another chuckle from him.

"Lucky man." He moved us through the bar as I rambled on, barely understanding myself as I laughed. "Where do you live?"

"Mmmm. Let me see... Where do I live...? Where do I live...? Oh, right! With that sarcastic asshole who made me come harder than I ever had with Drystan." I laughed, hanging my arm over his shoulder as we stepped outside.

"Okay, come on, hon. Think."

I pursed my lips together, not feeling them as I pointed in the direction of the woods in the distance. It was shrouded in dense fog, blanketing the path before us like a beacon. "Up there. In the castle...because I'm a forking princess... Forking? Fucking?" I laughed again as he moved us down the path into the woods. "Did you know they wanted me to be Queen? Do you think I'd make a good Queen? I don't...I got problems. Like big proooblems."

"I mean, you look like a queen to me," Tallen stated, giving me a smile. "Just one who is hurting."

"Nooooo... I'm strooong!" I said as I let my head fall back, giggling and letting it echo out between the trees around us. "I neeed to be strong for everyone and hide weaknesss. Because if it comes in...I won't be strong anymore. And I'll be that girl again...on the floor, crying as my *not* mother beats me, or sends me to a whore house to be almost raped and beaten by men."

His eyes widened and I chuckled.

"True story." I let out a long sigh as I looked back at his face, watching his eyes scan the trees. "And don't forget...that I died and came back. If that doesn't make you strong... OOH! Or getting marked by a twin who isn't your twin!" I showed him my hand with the scars, but he looked unimpressed now. "I'm drunk..."

"Yeah, I can see that, Princess." His tone sounded a bit harsh as it spilled from his lips, but I tried to pay it no mind.

Looking forward, I saw tombs scattered below the hill and felt my stomach twist.

Shit...I was going to puke.

"Where is the castle?" I asked as my skin heated and saliva built in the back of my throat.

"It's right here." Tossing me to the ground, I rolled down the hill, the world spinning out of control and picking up speed. Dirt shot up, coating my skin and leathers as small rocks and branches assaulted my body on the way down.

My back slammed into one of the edges of the tomb and I cried out as I coughed. Pushing my body up, dirt embedded under my nails as I looked up to where Tallen had been, but he was gone.

What an ass!

Before I could sit up all the way, my head was knocked back, cracking against the stone as I fell over. Peering up through hazy eyes, I saw Tallen standing there with three...or five men? I couldn't tell.

"What are you doing?" I choked out as his hand wrapped around my throat and lifted me off the ground.

"This is all your fault! None of this would be happening if you didn't exist!"

I went to speak again, but his other hand balled into a fist, connecting with my cheek and sending me back down to the ground. The alcohol in my system burned away as my fires came to life within, sobering me up almost instantly.

As I went to put my hands out, boots connected with my ribs, and I heard a sickening crack before it stole the air from my lungs. Coughing, I glanced up to see the boot right before it slammed into my face, forcing the world around me to blur again.

Another voice I didn't recognize sounded. "My family would

still be here!" Confusion filtered in as I took each blow, crying out while the pain grew all over.

"Fucking abomination!" another screamed at me as he got down on his knees before punching me.

Pain bloomed over every inch of my body and I wanted to curl inward, away from it all. A violent cough ripped from my lungs, and blood trickled out of my mouth, coating my cheek.

Tallen grabbed me by my hair and started pulling me back. I shouted, "Let me go! Or I will fucking kill you!" I took in my surroundings. Tombs decorated the lands and bare tree branches obscured the dark sky above as the fog grew thicker. This was the Dead Forest that was near Kadeyan's castle, but I'd never been out this far.

Looking forward, I took in the other two males walking towards me. One had long black hair, and his eyes were so dark that I couldn't make out the color. The other had rich copper curls and piercing green eyes. I saw them...in the bar. Those were the same men who looked at me with rage, and it clearly wasn't about me being drunk. Did they plan this while I was getting lost in each drink?

"You already did...Princess." He pulled a blade out of his sheath as the other men surrounded us. The two I saw shifted into wolves, meaning they were Crescents.

Another came around from behind me, summoning a purple mist to his fingers—a Crystal. His eyes glowed a deep purple and malice graced every feature.

Tallen leaned down, with his blade running against my cheek. "My mate died... Desiccated in my arms because of you. Because of what you unleashed on the throne! And I died that day." His voice broke and my stomach twisted into a knot.

"I...I..." I looked up in his once turquoise eyes that were now beaming red while I tried to process what he was saying. I burned it... How was the death of his mate my fault?

"Hold her down."

The two wolves jumped out towards me, burrowing their teeth

into my legs. The scream that ripped through me was violent, filling the forest and echoing out beyond. I could feel their sharp teeth slicing into each muscle and each tendon as they locked their jaws on me.

The other male threw out purple mist, holding down my arms as I thrashed and screamed louder. Pain seared through me and I pulled my eyes closed, wondering how I was going to get free of this. With my blood pooling around me, I felt weak, and my own fires sizzled out below my skin. Looking down, I ground my teeth as I took in the damage the wolves were causing, and my body refused me my next breath at the sight.

It wasn't red...

Grey blood flowed from my wounds. It resembled melted iron, giving off a sheen that dressed the brown dirt below. My entire body froze in shock, trying to understand why this was happening. Was I delirious?

"You aren't one of us, and you never will be." He pulled the dagger back from my cheek, forcing me to wince.

I looked up at Tallen, seeing the obsidian dagger hanging in the air above my heart. And something inside came to life, snaking its way through my veins until it corrupted my blood with its venom. My vision flickered for a moment, and the pain, the fear...it was gone.

I smiled up at him with a demonic glare, making him falter. Closing my eyes, the power within surged without permission until it imploded, pushing the males off me and shaking the ground below.

Everything went black for about a minute before my eyes fluttered open, and the pain they inflicted was already fading away. Sitting up, I ignored the bodies around me as their wrath grew wilder, pulsing off in waves until it slammed against my flesh. Pulling themselves up, they were prepared to finish what they started, but I didn't care... Not anymore.

Because everything within me burned, sensing the male in the distance before I even saw him. My fires spun within as I took the cleansing breath I needed after today. It was short-lived as something shifted between us, and it became clear.

He was furious.

One by one, the males turned to look at him, and I knew Tallen was also aware of his presence by the way his breathing stalled behind me.

His eyes beamed red as his shadows poured out with vengeance. The tendrils shot through the air without pause, holding each male in place.

“Which one of you fuckers wants to die first?”

CHAPTER 7
DAVYNA

My heart raced as my eyes locked on my calves again, seeing the deep lacerations through my shredded leathers. They were healing quickly as if they were never there. Although, the evidence of the grey blood remained painted to my flesh. A silent reminder that I wasn't seeing things... It was real. My body began to shake as I lowered my hand, grazing the thick liquid and thought about that place I was in. When she touched me...did she do this, too?

A deep, guttural sound ripped from the Crescent males, forcing me to look up as Kade moved in. His shadows ripped their hearts out with one swift movement, before walking towards the male from the Crystal Court.

He cried out, asking to be spared. His purple eyes so wide that they were on full display. Kade ignored him as he unsheathed his dagger from his hip that matched the darkness of the sky above. He moved with inhuman speed, burying the dagger into the male's eye socket. His victim let out a half scream before his body went limp.

When he turned to me, I looked at the blood painting his face and leathers. His fury brushed against me before he averted his gaze to Tallen. I moved my body out of the way as he made quick strides towards the male, sizing him up.

"Kadeyan. It needed to be done!" he yelled, pushing against his Lord's shadows.

"You're right...it does." Kadeyan pressed his fingers into the male's eyes. Tallen cried out as I heard the crunching of bone. A shudder racked through my body as the screams echoed far beyond, and their words sunk in.

Abomination... This is your fault... What you unleashed on the throne.

In one swift move, Kadeyan twisted Tallen's head, removing it from his body as his shadows tore him to pieces. He stepped back, spitting on his remains.

Silence blanketed us, aside from both of our heavy breathing. Kadeyan turned, his wholly amber eyes still nowhere to be found as he stalked up towards me. His hand wrapped around my jaw as he pulled me to my feet and looked me over. His emotions warred around us in relief, shock––but most of all––fury.

"Kade?" I asked, but our bodies rushed through the air until my back slammed against one of the tombs.

"Where the fuck did you go?"

Anger began taking over me as I pulled at his hand and threw it down by his side. "I was only gone for a few hours, Kade... What the fuck is going on here?" I yelled, my blood boiling as I stepped closer to him.

He stepped forward, his deep, guttural emotions penetrating every fiber of my being. It caused me to retreat until my back was flush with the stone again. His voice dropped as he growled. "You've been gone for six fucking months, Davyna!"

Running his hand through his hair, he turned away from me and allowed his pain to surface. After a long minute passed, he turned back to look at me, but I was frozen in place.

My mouth went dry as he moved in again, each step making me fall further into myself. "No... I was gone for about an hour...and then...a few more at the bar... It hasn't been six months, Kade. It can't be."

"I would know... I've been the one here, searching for you!" he yelled. "Where did you go?"

Words failed me as I thought about what the males were saying as they beat me, everyone in the bar with worry drenching them, and the man with the grey skin near the blood fountain.

"Fuck, Davyna... Tell me!"

"I DON'T KNOW!" I screamed, the tears threatening to burst free.

He took a moment to collect himself as he scanned his eyes over my body again, noticing the scars on my hand. "Who did this to you?"

"I don't know..." I said again. It came out small, holding a hollowness that made my body feel cold.

Moving in, he grabbed my face and rested his forehead against mine as his thumb brushed over my skin. "Why is your blood..." His voice trailed off, his own wonder and worry mixing together.

"I don't know..." I looked into his eyes, my world collapsing around me as his amber gaze held me tethered to the ground. "What did I do?" I whispered, but he shook his head, shushing me.

"You did what you needed to do." My fires spun inside me as his scent mixed with mine. "But if you ever walk away from me again...I will fucking make you pay in blood and agony." His fingers brushed along my arm, sending sparks off into the dead of night as my breath hitched in my throat.

"Fuck, Dy..." His tongue swiped over his bottom lip as he pressed into my body, letting me feel the length of him. "What do you want now?" His other hand came up and wrapped around my nape, forcing my gaze to lock on his. "Do you want to go home?"

I couldn't speak because looking into those eyes made the world obsolete. How could one person make you forget everything in an instant? It felt like time stood still as my jaw fell open, sensing the bond between us that demanded more.

Before I even had a chance to move in to take the only thing I wanted in this moment, Kadeyan's hands gripped onto my thighs and swept me off my feet.

My back slammed into the tomb again as his mouth crashed down on mine, devouring my moan before it could pass my lips. Heat bloomed over every inch of my body as his kiss turned feral, bruising my lips and causing me to fall deeper into this twisted moment with him. It was our sweet dance of darkness and passion, always molding and capturing the other until they became one. It was bliss. It was torture...but it was never enough.

I always wanted more.

Pulling back, Kade's hands darted up and ripped at my leather jacket, splitting it down the center and exposing my skin to the chilled air. My nipples hardened as I looked down, seeing both of his hands were decorated with new ink. Black roses covered the tops of his hands, and I watched them as they ran up my stomach and gripped onto my breasts, forcing a small moan to fall from my lips.

"When did you get those?" I asked between shuddered breaths.

"The day after you left." He growled as he looked up into my eyes, but unlike the impenetrable walls he once held to hide his emotions, it was evident in his gaze. Like I was looking through the clearest glass, seeing everything, and the main emotion on display... was pain.

Holding me to his body, he moved over to a tomb's gate and threw it open with his shadows. My body spun in a blur until I was laying down on my stomach. My skin heated to ward off the chill of the stone slab I was on.

"I told you once, you could try to run..." His hands pulled off my leather top before pressing my body into the rough surface. "But there is no escaping this, Davyna..." His words swirled in my mind as his hands ripped down my leather slacks.

"Fuck!" I screamed as his hand slammed against my ass, causing my nails to dig into the stone before I let out a moan. The sting blazed and I turned back to look at him. A wide grin was on his face and his hand came back down harder, forcing me to jolt forward.

"You have no idea how much I missed those sounds."

His shadows curled up my legs, feathering against my skin. The heat within faded, being replaced with the sweet chills only he could inflict. They worked over my clit in slow strokes, bringing a haze to my mind and forcing me to forget the world around us. It was sweeter than any intoxication one could search for in this world.

"All I want to do is punish you... Make you scream out for mercy." There was no humor in his voice, not even the playfulness I was used to. It was raw, unhinged. And as much as his tone sent fear into my blood, the excitement chased along with it, making me want it.

"Do your worst," I breathed out as my muscles tensed with the building pleasure his shadows were inflicting.

"You're such a little whore for me, aren't you?" He laughed as I tried to push myself up from the stone, but his shadows lashed out. They wrapped around my wrists, pressing into my flesh and keeping me from moving an inch. More sheer, black wisps of smoke poured out, darkening the edges of the tomb until all I could see was him.

Backing away with his gaze fastened to me, he leaned against the wall. "Answer me," he growled.

I titled my head up to gaze into his beautiful crimson pools. "Yes..."

"That's my good girl." His shadows moved between my legs, entering me as I gasped from each inch filling my pussy. He moved back, smiling with the hint of mischief in his eyes. He crossed his hands over his chest, and without pause, he forced his shadows in, pulling a cry from my lips. Yet, the feeling of his dark tendrils in me...it only intensified the pleasure he was causing.

My eyes rolled back as he began working them in and out, building the sensation in my core as my arousal seeped down my inner thighs. Glowing embers flew off my skin as moans and curses fell from my lips, and I fell deeper into our insanity.

As my release began to crest its horizon, his phantom hand wrapped into my hair. Pulling me up, he growled. "Eyes on me." My gaze widened as my breathing became shorter, unable to handle every nerve burning within. "I want to see what goes through those eyes as I make you come without even touching you."

I got lost in his gaze and my lower stomach tightened, chasing my release until all I saw was flames firing off with a ferocity that would burn anything in its wake. A scream ripped from my lungs as I tumbled over the edge, his shadows refusing to slow and making me feel every pulse with more force.

"Again," he demanded, holding my gaze on him.

His shadows thickened inside me, moving faster as the small tendrils continued to circle around my throbbing clit. Before I knew it, I was falling all over again, screaming curses as my body lit up the tomb.

"Again," he demanded.

I could barely catch my breath as his shadows snaked back to my ass, pressing into me, meeting the same pace of the others. Claws pierced through my hands, digging into the stone. My flesh began to glow, burning a deep apricot hue.

Panting, I watched him stand as still as stone with little expression, but I could sense his arousal...his need to be inside me. And I wanted that; I wanted to feel *him*.

My body succumbed to his will three more times within a matter of minutes. And I collapsed onto the stone slab as he worked his shadows within me, forcing my core to tighten again. My power was raging inside, causing the stone around us to shake as he looked at me.

"Again..."

"Please..." I begged, looking up at him. "I can't..."

A twisted smile grazed his face. "Oh, but you will..."

My head dropped and anger flared inside me, knowing now that this was punishment for leaving him. Joy radiated off him, and something cold from deep within rumbled, begging to be set free. It was an odd feeling, and fear surrounded it. Although, it felt strong... unwavering in its energy. Like the power I used when I pushed those men off me.

Without my command, it took on its own life, breaking the shadows around us. The tomb began to crumble as I sat up and threw out streams of shimmering onyx shadows towards Kade. They wrapped around him, pulling him onto the stone before I climbed up to straddle him.

I could hurt him...and I wanted to, which made unease rise inside me. Looking into his amber pools, it was clear he saw the moment rage bubbled up and welcomed whatever I deemed to inflict.

As fast as the power came, it faded. Fear crept in, forcing a quake to skate down my spine. My shadows were grey. So, why were they black, like his? But also, why did they glimmer with hues of the colors from each Court?

His breathing was heavy as he studied my face before pulling me down to his mouth. Our tongues collided in a war, battling for one more lick, one more nip, and I basked in the distraction from what just came over me.

Biting his bottom lip, I silently chanted the spell to remove his clothes and his shaft pressed into my center. The trepidation was gone and all I wanted was to feel him—all over me and deep within.

"Use me, Dearest. Do as you wish," he begged.

I sat up, taking in the sky veiled in dense clouds. I began rocking my hips against him, feeling my arousal slick against his skin. His hands traveled down my body before resting on my hips, grinding me harder over the length of him.

Grey shadows darted out of my hands, holding him to my will. They were their normal hue again, matching thick smoke as the smell of ash invaded my nostrils. Maybe I was seeing things from him making me come so many times.

"No touching," I said as I lifted my body, lining his cock up with my entrance. I lowered, letting out a moan that vibrated through every fiber of my being.

Kadeyan groaned, pulling against my restraints. It was no use as I forced more out, keeping him still. I sank down, working him in and out as I brought my face to his chest. I bit down hard, his blood coating my lips as he hissed. I began to fall into the frenzy of needing more, biting and drinking deeply because it was mine to take.

"If you want to burn everything else down, Davyna...I'll help you. But don't burn my heart along with it." I looked up into his eyes. They were soft and pleading with me.

The weight of his earlier statement pulled at my heart as I licked my lips and I sat up, realizing that we lost six months.

That time slipped through our fingers like loose sand, taking away the chance to explore the depths of our connection. Or how it would look and feel to have my soul tethered to his for eternity. I lost that time...and put him through hell. He was the last person I wanted to hurt in this world...and yet...

"Kade...what di—"

"Not right now... All I want in this moment is to feel alive." His words shot into my chest, freezing over my heart as I realized I did too. I wanted to live in this moment with him before reality swept it away.

I began moving my hips over him, dropping my shadows from his body. He sat up, wrapping his arms around my waist as we both fell into a perfect rhythm. Each thrust had us unraveling together as my skin beamed in the darkened forest.

My fingers ran through his hair, gripping hard as every muscle locked and my orgasm racked through my body. Kadeyan held onto me as he rode out each wave of pleasure before cursing and spilling inside me.

My body went slack in his arms as the world around me flickered in and out... It was like something was lurking within, waiting for its perfect time to surface and consume me. My stomach spun as I pinched my eyes closed, trying to push it away, but it was no use...

I'm not going anywhere.

My breathing slowed and I looked up at Kade. The exhaustion was pulling me under, laced with the horrors of that voice.

"Take...me...home..." Everything went black, but I heard a voice in the distance. One that would always have a hold on my life, my heart, my soul...whether I was ready for it or not.

"I got you, Dy... I will always have you."

CHAPTER 8
DAVYNA

I don't know how long I was out for, but when my eyes began to open, it felt like my bones and muscles were made of rock. They protested at even the smallest movement.

Looking over, I groaned, taking in the muted greys of the sky illuminating the room. Taking a deep breath I rolled to my side, ignoring the aches and my eyelids softly closed.

What a strange nightmare...

Laughing sounded from within my mind, forcing my eyes to snap open.

It wasn't a nightmare... This is our life now, and we are going to have so much fun together.

Jumping up, my chest tightened as I looked around, but I knew the voice was inside me, continuing to laugh in the deepest corners of my psyche. My stomach turned as I pulled my eyes shut. After the laughing within ceased, I looked down at my right hand. My gaze traveled up my arm to my shoulder, where the scars stopped.

"Good morning, beautiful."

I sucked in a sharp breath as I looked to my right, seeing Kadeyan in a chair with a book resting in his lap. He was shirtless, and his muscles looked more defined below his inked skin than before. I took in his room painted in darkness before moving the covers. My body was all cleaned up, and a black silk nightgown pressed against my skin.

"What are you reading?"

He smiled, looking down at the book. "It's about a winged, half-shifted dragon whose cock swells every time the princess he should hate enters the room..." Dropping his head back, he let out a low hum and a grin graced his face. "I know the feeling." He smiled at me as I sat up, shaking my head. Pain shot through it, causing me to wince.

"How long was I asleep for?" I asked, turning to face those amber orbs. He grabbed his bookmark and placed it on his page, before putting it on the side table.

"Three days," he said, gently.

I was out for three days?

Kade rose from his chair, moved over to the bed, sitting on the edge, and took me in with his concerned gaze. He reached for my hand, and I slightly jumped as our eyes connected again. "Please, Dy...tell me what happened to you." He moved in closer.

His voice dropped an octave as he looked down at my scars, memorizing each one before looking up into my eyes. "I'll kill them."

I know he would in a heartbeat, and if I was being honest, at this point, I'd do the same. "I'm fine, Kade. I'm not sure what happened anyway." The lie burned on my tongue, and I wasn't sure why I even did it.

No...that wasn't it. I was scared to give that creature or place more life. Scared that if I started talking about it, I'd only be able to feel the fear still coursing through my body at an accelerated rate that would shatter me. I needed to focus on being back here and what was happening.

"Then show me."

"What?" I stared back at him, confused. "Kade. It's over...okay? I'm back."

"No!" His voice rose as he stood from the bed and began pacing. "I've spent six months not knowing whether you were dead or alive." His head fell as he came to a stop, and his agonizing grief slammed into me like sharp daggers.

For a moment, I wanted to rip apart anything making him feel that way, knowing it was our bond compelling me to do so. It was strange...the connection I felt.

But how did you truly know it was real or being forced by the stars above? Humans didn't have this type of connection with one another. It was simple: you met, fell in love, got married. But here, with the fae, it was something entirely different--something more. And while I did love him, I still felt like I couldn't give myself over fully. I'd never been able to with anyone, and with everything going on now...I wasn't ready.

Shaking the thought away, I realized it didn't matter, though. If I was going to rip anyone apart for hurting him, it would have to be myself... And maybe I deserved that.

However, he deserved to know where I was, didn't he? I could give him that. Taking a deep breath, I let the walls around my mind fall. Piece by piece, they crumbled around me until I emerged back into the memories of leaving my father's castle. I could feel the power again, growing as I fell into the void before everything I faced there started flashing before my eyes.

Wincing, the phantom pain returned in my hand, traveling up my arm until it plunged into my skull. I buried down the pain, hoping he wouldn't think it hurt me. He didn't need to know that.

As my eyes opened, I looked at Kadeyan, who sat back on the bed, confused. "I don't understand..."

"Neither do I," I said as I fiddled with the inky sheets still covering my legs.

"No... All I saw was...darkness." Kadeyan looked down at my arm before looking at me. A puzzled expression consumed his features. "Try again," he begged as he moved in, grabbing both my hands. "Make sure you aren't holding anything back."

I swallowed hard, and my eyes closed again as it all rushed in. It took everything in me to not cry, to not break. There had been too much between us, and I refused to be another burden with what was going on here.

"What the fuck?" he said, breaking me out of the memories as I glanced up at him. "Davyna, I can't read your mind. I can't even feel you anymore... Everything is just...dark."

I pulled my hands back and proceeded to move off the bed. The cool stone traveled through my body. "This doesn't make sense. What did she do?"

"She? She who?" Kadeyan's voice was deep, laced with concern and fury.

I paused, my throat closing as if an invisible hand wrapped around it.

You shouldn't be scared of her... You should be more scared of who we truly are, the voice snickered within.

Panic bubbled up.

Turning, I looked into his vengeful eyes. "That's the thing: I have no idea. But Kade..." I paused, steadying the slight shake racking through my hands. "She was like me... She *was* me..."

"What do you mean by that?" he asked, closing the distance between us.

I shook my head as the presence of that power returned, bringing back the paranoia I felt on those lands. She said we would be seeing each other again—soon. Was this all her, toying with me until I broke? I bit the inside of my cheek, shaking my head. I didn't want to admit it, but it was working.

"I'm not sure how to explain it. I don't have the words other than...our power was similar."

"We will find her, Dy. And make her pay."

"Kadeyan, it's over. Let's just drop it. I want to focus on what's happening here."

He moved in and hugged me tight, causing me to realize I was shaking. "As you wish, but this isn't over. I refuse to let this go." I swallowed hard. His gaze bore into mine as though he was trying to extract the truth from my eyes.

"Get ready. Everyone is downstairs." He kissed the top of my head and began walking towards the door. "Or do I need to stay...? Feel like running again?" He cracked a smile, and my eyes rolled in response. "Are you sure you are okay?"

"Why wouldn't I be?" I gave him a fake smile, knowing neither one of us believed it.

He nodded before heading to the door. As it clicked shut behind him, I let out a shuddered breath, my unease billowing out until it filled the room.

My breathing picked up as I walked back and forth, sensing the tremors intensifying. Letting out another shaky exhale, I ran my fingers through my hair as I questioned everything. Did I know what I was dealing with here in Valyner? Or with my shadow self, back in that place? Did I even understand how to fix the mess I created or how to stop this infliction inside my mind?

I needed to figure it out...before *she* or I caused any more damage.

Ha...we can't ever let things go, can we? You know what can help with that?

My jaw locked up as I narrowed my gaze around the room. All the tension I felt moved to my shoulders as if the weight of the world sat upon them, and the irony was...I think it did at this point. But the plan would remain the same: I'd only deal with her if she showed up. And I would figure out what was happening here and help fix it. After that, this had to end. I had to figure out how to live like this... To be...the *abomination.*

Everything went limp as the words sunk in, reminding me that Persephone once called me that. Maybe she was right.

Pushing the thought aside, I moved to the washroom and turned on the tub before making my way to the armoire. Searching through the clothes, I finally found and pulled out a pair of black leathers embroidered with red stitching to create flames.

As I placed it on the bed, I noticed the sleeves came down to points with loops on them, which would hide my scars. Did Kade have these made for me when I was sleeping, to help me keep this to myself until I was ready to share it? I mean, the hair was already going to be hard to explain, but the scars... I wasn't ready for everyone to see them.

A weak smile turned my lips up as I turned back towards the

bath. The water rushing from the pipes beat against the rising surface, and steam billowed up. It gave the air a warmth that stuck to my skin, soothing me like an embrace.

I let the nightgown slip down my body, pooling at my feet before stepping into the hot water. Sinking down, my muscles started to loosen, and I reveled in the release. If I was being honest... this tension had been with me since the ball. Since I learned I was something else.

Everything was going to be okay... I was strong. I would not break.

The mantra I used to recite to myself as a teenager came flooding back in, giving me the strength I needed.

My body slid down until the water rested at my chin. I took a deep breath, watching the steam rise from the surface. After a few minutes, my eyes closed and I pulled my head under, my ears blocking out the subtle noises throughout the castle. The world around me faded as I took another deep breath, the hot water filling my lungs before pushing it back out, thanks to my Salt magic.

It was serene in here. Maybe I could stay...

A chill ran through my body, turning the water around me to arctic temperatures. My eyes shot open, bracing myself for something--anything—to explain this. But what I took in forced my body into another wave of trembles. The water around me was pitch-black and opaque, reminding me of the void of my nightmares--and worse--the onyx lake.

The world beyond was gone and ice pricked at my skin as I jumped up, breaking the surface while my breathing struggled to settle.

Water sloshed over the edge of the tub, falling to the marble floor below. I focused back on the water around me in the bath, but it was back to normal. I wasn't seeing things... That was real. I looked around the washroom as I rose out of the tub, wrapping my arms around my body, when I felt it.

That power looming close by, watching my every move.

Fury mixed with fear took over, and I reached for a towel lying on the counter. Wrapping it around my body, I threw open the door and looked around.

"Where the fuck are you?" I growled.

My eyes darted to the window and then scanned the bed. Turning to face the floor-length mirror, I stopped dead in my tracks. The scars on my hand were no longer their iridescent white, but wholly consumed with darkness and subtle hues spinning within--just like the doors to the castle in the land.

The world slowed to a stop, freezing me to the ground. I watched the blackened hues creep up my arm, shimmering with subtle tones of red, blue, purple, orange, and white.

Instead of fear...all I felt was rage. Rage that she gave me these to be constant reminders, leaving me with questions I didn't want answered. "Show yourself, you fucking coward," I said a little louder as I looked up, sensing the energy loom closer.

Minutes passed as I stood there, waiting... But nothing came.

I was losing it...

I walked over to the window and took in the land below. The bare trees moved with the gentle breeze, and the mountains in the distance were just as they always were here—dark stone, untouched by the elements surrounding it.

The feeling that flooded my system faded away as if everything was a delusion. I used a lot of power lately, and maybe that caused some strange reaction... But I couldn't shake that I was lying to myself.

Something was different... Something changed within me, and I didn't want to face it.

After a few more minutes of watching the grounds, my heart returned to its normal rhythm.

Turning around, I walked over to the bed and started getting dressed. I moved at a fast pace, eager to see everyone and figure out what was going on. I pulled boots out from the armoire and got them on before looking back into the mirror. I stalled again, the blood leaving my face and turning my flesh a ghostly shade of white.

Staring back at me through my reflection was me...but it wasn't.

I couldn't look away from the black eyes on display, with the silver irises beaming bright.

And I knew... It wasn't her that I felt in the distance; this was coming from me.

We are going to have so much fun soon.

Closing my eyes, I shook my head as the eerie version of my voice laughed within my mind. Confusion racked through me as I glanced back at the mirror, still seeing eyes beaming with darkness. I took a step forward, watching the reflection with trepidation.

I stood still, wondering why this was happening, and my stomach twisted. The head in the mirror began to tilt, smiling wide, and my jaw fell open.

What? Are you afraid of who we are, Davyna? Because this is our true face.

My blood stilled in my body as the mirror began to crack, forcing me to step back, but my reflection stood the same: amused. A laugh sounded off in my head, making me turn to look over the room again.

My shoulders went rigid, sensing that I was being watched again, and bile rose in my throat. The sound of the mirror cracking and the pieces of glass shattering against the floor made me swallow hard. And in that moment, I felt like that was me—splintering and cracking under a pressure I couldn't begin to understand.

Turning to face it one more time, I saw my reflection normal within the spiderweb cracks of the glass, now missing a few pieces that laid on the ground around it. My eyes contained their whites once again and I sighed in relief as I took in the scars on my arm, which was also void of the darkness that was just there.

Moving towards it, I looked down at the sharp, dagger-like piece, before hearing a deep laugh. My body froze as if I was submerged into icy water, stunned by its freezing depths.

"Hello, Davyna..."

Looking up to the mirror, I froze as a distorted shadow cloaked in nightfall appeared. I jumped back and turned, seeing nothing once again. Anger poured out as I shouted, "Leave me alone!" I turned back to the mirror and the figure reappeared right behind me.

"Not until you give us what we want," a male's voice boomed next to my ear.

I stalled as a shadow hand brushed against my face, smelling of fire, brimstone, and...death. Fear gripped onto my soul, crawling to find a place deep enough to hide from this creature.

We... She hadn't been alone, and I knew the shadow touching me was the figure who watched from the window.

"W–what do you want from m–me?"

"I want you...to fix the mess you made...or I'll kill everyone you love," he said with a voice as smooth as silk. His threat ignited the primal urge to protect the ones I loved, blazing away the fear.

"Don't you dare touch a hair on their heads, or I'll––"

He laughed, wrapping the phantom hand around my throat. "And what will you do to stop me?" The invisible fingers gripped tighter, cutting off air to my lungs as the tears built in my eyes.

"This is our secret... You'd be wise to keep it because, if you tell anyone what you saw, I'll know." His voice was deep, and it stole the air from my lungs as I pinched my eyes shut, praying this was a dream. "I will start with your sister...then your friends...and finish with your *mate* before I make you suffer a slow...agonizing...death."

Dropping me, I fell to the ground and gasped for air. I looked back up at the mirror, seeing I was alone. The energy and power that was emanating in the room began fading, leaving me to only feel my own.

My hand went to my throat, still feeling the weight of his grip as I pushed away from the glass on the floor. I took a steadying breath, closing my eyes as the air passed my lips.

Everything was going to be okay... I was strong. I would not break.

But who was I fooling? Because nothing was okay... I didn't feel strong...and I was on the verge of breaking. Something bigger was going on here. In me, and with those creatures I saw, and I couldn't help feel like if there was ever a time to find the truth, it was now.

But what if the greatest threat to this realm, and the people I loved... was me? What if I was capable of destroying so much more?

The horror it provoked was unparalleled, overshadowing any past fears I had ever experienced. I couldn't play a game of chance now...not with their lives. I needed to keep what happened a secret... for now, and carry the weight it would inflict. I'd done it before, and I could do it now.

There was no other option.

Pulling myself off the floor, I crossed my arms over my chest and dug my nails into my leathers, cutting half-moons into them.

"Dearest?" The door opened and I sucked in a harsh breath, burying down the fear. His eyes took me in before glancing at the shards of glass. "What did the mirror do to you?" he asked, jokingly, but the urge to run into his arms and tell him burned my throat.

No...I couldn't. I loved him more than I think I could even comprehend, and I was not going to put his life in jeopardy. Not until I dealt with them; not until I was free of their torment.

I could feel his worry build around me. So, I pulled my shoulders back and started walking towards the door. My hand rose, sending out a spell and repairing each crack as I passed him and entered the hall.

"Nothing. Let's go."

CHAPTER 9
UNKNOWN

I should go back home...but I didn't want to leave the void between our realms. Realms that none of us should be able to cross. And yet, she did. Could she be...

No. It was not possible. *He* wouldn't allow that creature to live if that was the case.

But something within her called out to me. It was deep in my bones and kept me rooted inside the void. I pushed out, sensing her sweet paranoia, and relished in it. My lips pulled up to the side as I savored her fear, wanting to drink down every drop.

She had guts to even attempt threatening me. I kind of enjoyed it.

Kind of.

Oh, my little cinder. You'd be *wise* to take heed of my warning... but I sincerely hope you don't so I could teach you how it feels to be utterly alone.

I just left out one important detail. After she fixed Valyner, I was going to have to kill her, anyway. No one comes to my realm and lives.

How unfortunate...

Such a beautiful waste.

CHAPTER 10
DAVYNA

Each step down the stairs pushed my heart up in my throat, stopping me from pulling more oxygen in. Kadeyan picked up his pace, placing his hand on my lower back, but I kept my eyes forward.

I could sense his emotions, visualizing them as if I was peering through a portal into his soul. He was confused by what happened, and angry with me that I would lie. It was like I was being immersed in his storm, knowing I was the chaos causing it all but I couldn't... Not now.

Not after what that *thing* said.

"Dy?" Evren's sweet voice said as we turned around the spiral stairs, showcasing the foyer where she stood.

My eyes widened, taking in my little sister, and I picked up my feet to move into a run. Her body moved, taking two steps at a time until her welcoming arms wrapped around me in a death grip.

Kadeyan stopped next to us as our hushed sobs broke from our lips, meaning two different things. For her, it was getting her sister back after six months, and for me...it was fear for her life... For all of them. My heart rate increased, bringing on a wave of nausea at the thought.

"I missed you. Don't you ever do that to me again!" She squeezed me harder, her worry melting into me.

I nodded, loosening my grip on her before taking her in. She looked well, and that alone allowed me to take a deep breath.

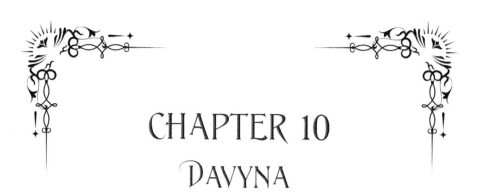

Her red hair shined with a beautiful copper hue, and soft waves tumbled down her chest as she wiped her eyes. Her blue pools softened on me as she smirked.

I reached out, tucking her hair behind her pointed ear. "I won't." Not intentionally, at least. "How have you been? Are you okay?"

"Me? Dy, I'm more concerned with you," she stated, bringing her hand up to grab onto the white strands on the right side of my head. "I mean, you can pull off anything...but what happened? Where were you?"

"Maybe those questions can wait, Evren." Kadeyan stepped down, giving her a stare that said, *not now,* and to be honest...I appreciated it.

Evren softly nodded her head once before giving me a gentle smile. She had a right to the truth. Everyone did, but...

"Let's go get all the welcomes out of the way, shall we?" Kade said, directing us to the hall to the right.

We moved down the hallway until familiar doors came into view for the dining room. The same room I burned in a fit of rage, trying to kill Kade. That memory felt like ages ago now...but in reality—at least for me—it was only a little over a month ago. Shadows poured out as I took in a cleansing breath, watching the onyx mist lift like a curtain and reveal everyone's wide eyes locked on me.

"Davyna!" Levanna screamed as she ran towards me, her beaming blue eyes wide and overpowered with joy. Her small frame slammed into me, and we stayed in our embrace for a long moment before Nesrin began walking towards us. Her green pools were hard, making me crack a smile.

"What the fuck, Dy?" she said, before her face softened and her lips turned up. Letting go of Levanna, Nesrin grabbed me by my shoulder and pulled me in, her icy blonde hair almost matching what I now had.

"You have no idea," I said in her ear, making her laugh. Looking over to Axel and Calix, I moved towards them. They both wrapped their arms around me at the same time, causing me to choke on the air in my lungs. "Guys, I...can't...breathe."

"Too bad! We missed you, Your Grace," Calix said, squeezing tighter.

"It's good to see you again, Dy," Axel said as he stepped back, his storm-grey eyes bouncing from me to the pale blonde strands framing one side of my face.

I looked over to Calix, his golden-brown pools on me as I raised my brow. "Your Grace?"

He laughed as Axel shook his head and Calix pushed him, causing him to join in with a small chuckle. Turning, I saw Kadeyan hold back his own laughter, showing off a genuine smile that made my body heat.

My eyes caught on Sorin and my mouth parted in shock. "You're here?"

He began walking towards me, bowing as he stood in his perfect form of the soldier I knew him to be. "Welcome home, Davyna."

I smiled, moving and wrapping my hands around his waist. "Have you been home?" I asked as I pulled back.

His expression turned to sorrow as he dropped his head to the side, showcasing his tribal tattoo with the moon phases throughout, and I knew the answer.

"No... Alastair banished me from the Crescent lands after..." Anger from within billowed up. "But I don't regret it. It was the right thing to do... To help you."

I pulled my ire back, giving Sorin a small smile. "Well, you'll always have a place here...with us villains," I teased, causing him to chuckle.

I couldn't help but see his eyes shift over to Evren. His emotions surfaced and it was clear he cared for her. It brought me some comfort that she had someone from her Court with her over these past six months.

Maeve walked over, wearing a benevolent smile that made the room glow brighter, before taking both my hands. I looked into her gentle eyes, prepared to tell her how happy I was to see her again, when her gaze shifted. I stared into her once-silver orbs, consumed with a milky-white sheen as she stood as still as stone, causing my stomach to drop.

"Maeve?" I asked, watching her shake her head as she blinked rapidly.

"Sorry, I can't control the visions now." She pulled me in. "I'm glad your back." My blood froze in my veins as I pulled back and studied her gaze. They screamed, telling me she held something within, and didn't want to announce it in front of everyone. Her eyes burrowed into me as if it was a silent message to say, *we will talk about it soon.*

Shaking off the shudder rippling over me, I turned and looked at everyone. "So, what is going on in Valyner?"

Everyone paused, exchanging glances as my gaze caught on the table behind them. It was graced with plates, with steaming food that filled the air with rich and savory scents. Drawing my eyes back to them, I sensed their emotions waver, showing me their hesitation.

"Let's all eat first," Kadeyan finally said, breaking the silence and unease that was filling the room.

Everyone silently took their seats and began eating as I watched them, sensing their worry peak. I took the seat next to Levanna as Kade finally sat down and watched me put food onto my plate.

Ten or so minutes passed, and the silence was driving me crazy as I picked at the food in front of me. Slamming my hand on the table, everyone stopped and looked up. "Okay, enough of this. Will someone please tell me what is going on?"

Kadeyan looked up from his plate, glancing at Sorin for a few seconds before nodding.

"Davyna... In the last six months, there have been many attacks on the realm," Sorin said as he pushed his plate away from him.

"What kind of attacks? Are the Courts fighting?"

"Well...yes, and no. What I mean is, creatures that no one has ever seen or heard of before are showing up in all the Courts and..."

"And what?" I asked.

"Killing..." He took a moment to collect his thoughts as my own swirled, forcing me to drop back in my chair. "We have lost over three thousand fae to date since you went missing. The armies of each Court taking the biggest hits, but some civilians have been caught in the crossfire—either trying to help or didn't see it coming."

Levanna cleared her throat, turning to face me. "And fae seem to be getting sick. It starts out with desiccating skin, and then affecting their minds before they die... There have also been about two-thousand deaths with that alone." The room began to spin as I pictured the man in town and what Tallen said about his mate. "We have been doing barrier spells to block the toxic power and giving herbs to take as a preventive measure...but it doesn't always work."

"Are any of you..." My throat closed up, refusing to finish the sentence.

Levanna placed her hand over mine, making me realize I was digging my nails into the armrest. "No...it seems to be affecting everyone in different ways. And more focused on the younger fae. We think it's because their magic isn't as strong as the older generations."

My heart sank, but the beating intensified, traveling to my ears. "Why is this happening?" I asked, scanning over all my friends' faces, but no one responded. They didn't need to; I already knew. "It's what I did to the throne, isn't it?"

"Dy...it..." Levanna looked to Maeve before turning to face Kade. I glanced over to him, his eyes anchoring on her with a severe gaze.

Fix the mess you made. That was what the shadow figure was talking about, making Tallen's attack warranted. Because this mess was my own creation, affecting them all...

Evren leaned forward, grabbing my attention. "The creatures have mainly been coming in from the Ember Court. We think they are coming through some type of portal. We've been working with the remaining Embers and the former Cursed fae, along with the ones who have been exiled from their Courts, to try to stop the creatures from going any farther into the Land."

"We?" Shock coated my voice, and I could tell my question jabbed into her as her mouth hardened.

"Yes, your sister has been a good little wolf in battle." Calix winked at her, making her cheeks flush slightly.

The worry and fear returned for the one life I promised to always protect. She hated training with Elias. She must have done it a total of five times before quitting, not wanting any part of it. What if she got hurt? Looking back at her, I took in the face that was so familiar, and yet different, holding invisible armor beneath her black leathers that was never there before.

"There are other matters that need to be addressed about the Court Lords and Ladies," Evren stated, glancing at Kade with disdain.

"What? He fucking started it," Kade said, letting out a breathy laugh. My head turned, meeting his amber eyes that were already on me. "Valyner has never been without a ruler. And the Courts are... adjusting."

"What do you mean, adjusting?" I asked, one of my brows lifting in wonder because I felt like there was a lot more to that statement.

Evren leaned forward, her elbows hitting the table as she said, "It means that the Crystals and Crescents teamed up and are refusing to work with any of us on the outside. Especially him." She pointed a finger at Kade, making him laugh as he picked up a berry off his plate and threw it into his mouth.

"What about the Sky Court, Maeve?" I queried and her eyes softened.

"We are a neutral Court. We don't get involved in the politics. I'm only here to listen because we are staying true to the laws that have stood since your father implemented them. Meaning only the Queen can tell us if things will change."

"There isn't one of those here. So, what do we do?" I looked over everyone for a moment, taking in their eyes locked on me.

"Well, what do you want to do, Your Grace?" Calix blurted out, smiling wide. But it only brought unease to the surface now. Hadn't all the death and sickness made them see that they didn't want me ruling this realm? I had already failed at rejecting it.

Standing up, I steeled my spine. "Listen. Let's get one thing straight. I'm not the Queen, nor will I ever be. So, please don't expect me to rule after I fix the shit I caused here." The room fell utterly silent as they exchanged glances.

Kadeyan cleared his throat, before another laugh passed his lips. "Okay, little Ember. But would you want to give some advice on how to handle the current predicament?"

My gaze narrowed on him, showing no humor, but it did little to wipe the grin off his face. Always taunting me to play his games. "My advice...is to get the Courts working together until I figure out how to fix the throne."

Maeve dipped her head. "I will send out a letter to all the Lords and Ladies to meet soon, then," she stated before everyone nodded in agreement.

Evren stood up, her pools beaming with hope. "So, you'll meet with Alastair?"

"What? Why does it have to be me?" I asked, my skin prickling with ice, before being replaced with a raging heat at the thought of being in a room with him.

"Because he still fancies you. And he will listen if you ask." Kade's emotions shifted, and I heard him through his walls in his mind. "*Over my dead, fucking body. That dog will end up hurting her again.*" But he leaned back in his chair, mirroring the perfect picture of ease as he lifted his boots onto the table. He brought his hand up, balling his fist until the knuckles turned white, before releasing it.

"Alastair won't let Crescents back onto the Lands if they leave. Only he and his select few can leave for supplies and to send messages for him. The rest were considered deserters and ended up in the Ember Court," Evren continued. Shaking her head, her disdain grew by the second for the Lord of the wolves.

"What do you think I can do about that, Ev?" I asked as her jaw fell open a fraction, shocked I would say that.

Quickly, she shut her mouth, shaking her head softly as her rage billowed into the air around her. "You don't want to be the Queen..." she stated, but it wasn't coated in ease, only aggravation. "Fine. But you're still a Lady of a Court...just like me." Her anger was growing by the second, her eyes flashing a yellow before returning to blue. "And I think our people deserve better."

"You want to lead a Court now?" I asked in surprise.

"No, it's not a want. It's what I am. It's *my* father's Court." The sting of her words hit me like a ton of bricks, falling onto my chest. The Ember Lands were my father's, ergo mine...but Elias was my father too.

"Evren, you and I have no right to decide anything about a Land that we only learned about recently," I said softly. Sorin moved to Evren's side, placing his hand on her shoulder, and she pulled her anger back in.

"No...I know my Lands. I know my people...because I didn't disappear and throw away what I was. I embraced it..." She looked me up and down, making my stomach sink. "I didn't run away, unlike you." Evren's eyes were cold as they pierced into me, traveling to my heart as if that blow would stop it from beating.

Without a second thought, she began walking towards the door. My jaw was slack, and every emotion within slammed against my walls, begging to be free. Sorin gave me a tight smile before following after her.

She was right: I ran. I screwed up and hurt this realm. And now. I couldn't even share what was happening without having their blood coat my hands. The thought of the fae who were lost in the last six months filtered in. I looked down, turning my palms up and inspecting them.

Their blood was on my hands too... So much blood.

Come on. You know you love it, the voice inside my mind sounded off, giggling with a demonic tone. I swallowed hard.

"Yeah..." Kadeyan said, breaking the silence. Looking over, I saw his hand travel up, smoothing down his short beard. "I should have told you that your sister has taken to her...new form."

"I can see that..." I took a long breath before meeting his gaze. "And what the hell did you do to Alastair?"

I honestly didn't care because he probably deserved it. And after the way we left things in the throne room, I wanted nothing to do with him. Anger bubbled up, reminding me how he took my father's stone to bargain with Persephone. How he tried to kill me in his wolf form before I opened my Ember power... He was a complete and utter asshole who deserved everything coming his way.

I looked Kade over, waiting to see what led to Alastair cutting off the other Courts in a time where they all should be working together.

Kadeyan got more comfortable in his chair and looked down at his hand again, smiling wide. "I might have almost killed the little Lord after you disappeared..." His hand bawled into a fist again—his wrath mixing with his sheer glee in recounting the events. "He said you were better off far away from me." His wicked smile traveled to his eyes, making my stomach tighten, but it slowly faded as he took in everyone. "I think this is enough for Davyna today."

He stood up, looking at his friends. "We will come up with a game plan soon. Until then, Axel and Calix." They both stood. "Fly over the Ember Court and make sure our soldiers aren't fucking around. And if they are..." He gave them a wry smile, placing his hands forward to rest on the table. "Bring them to me."

Their shadows wrapped around their bodies, swallowing them whole as the black mist faded up into the air. At the same time, Levanna rose with Nesrin and they both began walking out, but Maeve made her way over to me.

Hugging me again, she held onto me tighter. "I'm glad you're back, Dy." As she pulled back, she stopped. Bringing her mouth to my ear, she whispered so low that it would be inaudible for anyone but us. "Beware of the throne..." She stepped back as I went to ask why, but her white light circled her, taking her away and leaving me in wonder.

Turning to Kadeyan, the weight of everything I learned tugged my shoulders down. "Tell me one last thing."

"What do you want to know?" he asked.

"Is this all happening because I burned the throne?" I knew the answer, but I wanted someone to say yes. To confirm it.

"I'm not going to say it's your fault, Davyna. But I'll tell you what Maeve told me." He slowly walked towards me. "The magic coming off the throne is more complicated than each Court being merged into one."

"Fuck... What the hell did I do?" Stepping back from him, I shifted my gaze to the expanse of windows, where the dim light struggled to pierce through the thick, grey clouds veiling the sun.

All I could think about was that, four days ago, I burned the throne, and this overwhelming power in my veins came to life. And it was only amplified in that other place, making me see that there was something else within. But it wasn't like my other power; it was unhinged, angry even. Now, I was being forced to feel it every time I blinked, causing me to feel off-kilter.

That's because you need to give in. I can help, Davyna. I can keep you strong.

I shook my head. The distorted voice made me envision a dark void within, lurking and waiting for my surrender. Was this the real reason my father took me away? Did he want to protect the realm from me? Was this why Persephone wanted my power? Was she aware of what I contained too?

Shadows swirled behind me before familiar arms pulled me in. "Shhh, Davyna. This isn't your fault. Your sister had six months to adjust...and no one gave you that." He laid his head on my shoulder. "Forgive me...I shouldn't have pushed you to take your title." His lips touched my neck, causing my eyes to close. "But you know who you are. It's in your blood. So, let it pull you forward."

"But what if it drags me down into the darkness?"

"Then I'll be holding your hand the entire way."

Turning around, I looked in those amber orbs and my heart ached.

"You know I didn't plan any of this, right?" I said, the panic and regret lacing into each word. "I didn't want to lose all that time...to make things..." I wanted to make things right between us. But I couldn't finish that sentence. Not with everything going on. Not when I was still trying to figure out so much, including our bond...

"I know..." Kadeyan lowered his head to mine, taking in a deep breath. "What do you want now?"

My mind began to race, wanting to undo the horrors I inflicted on Valyner. To obey the dark shadow and fix my mess so they would go away. And to make that voice within stop... But was it going to be that simple?

What would happen if my shadow self came back to torment me? Or if the shadow figure killed everyone I love out of spite?

Taking a deep breath, I focused on the problem I could confront today...and prayed to the gods that I could do it.

"Take me to my father's throne..."

CHAPTER 11

EVREN

Throwing the front door open, I jumped out, shifted in the air, and my claws dug into the dead grass. I pushed my body as growls spilled from my lips before sensing Sorin close behind.

I didn't stop, pushing each muscle in my body to its breaking point. My form wove through the trees and the need to hunt something—to feel its flesh being ripped to shreds—overwhelmed me.

"Evren...come on," Sorin shouted into my mind. When we were in wolf form, we could communicate with one another. Another thing I only got to do with a small number of wolves in the Ember Court Lands. Not with my own that were locked in their Court like prisoners.

My body pushed harder, breaking through the tree line into No-Man's-Land, where roses laid throughout. I pushed harder, but Sorin tackled me to the ground, pinning me as his growl echoed into the clearing around us.

Shifting back, we looked into each other's eyes. His hazel ones were drinking me in.

I pushed back and sat up. "I needed a minute."

"I know, but you have to show her some grace."

"You're going to take her side?" I asked as the hurt penetrated my voice.

He laughed, moving to sit by me. "I'm always on your side... But from all that you told me about your life before with Davyna..."

"That's not my sister. My sister wouldn't stand for something like this."

"I don't think she does. I think it's a lot to take in." I shut my mouth before speaking again, knowing he was right. "Think about being in her shoes. She isn't just a wolf. Or a witch... She is everything. And then, coming back to all this..."

"You don't think she knew and decided to stay away? To leave us?" *To leave me.*

He shook his head. "I don't think she did. That girl loves you with every fiber of her being, Evren. And from what Kadeyan told us, she thought she was only gone for a little while."

I let my head fall and pulled my eyes shut as I replayed the last six months. There was an incurable hole left by my sister, but being with the wolves and the other fae... They filled a void in me that I didn't realize I needed nor wanted in my life. But now... "I want to be with them, Sorin. I want to make sure they are all okay and not brainwashed by that fucker."

He chuckled again. "Trust me, I stood by Alastair's side for five hundred years. People might follow orders from their alpha, but it doesn't mean they are brainwashed. Well...not all of them at least." His shoulder tapped mine, pushing me a little as he smiled wide. My lips turned up as I tried to return the gesture, but he barely moved an inch.

"It's just..." I was at a loss for words. Looking up, I took in the crimson sky as the sun began its descent, getting lost in the colors that only reminded me of her.

"It's a lot to take in... I get it."

Silence fell over us as I let out a long breath. I had so much anger buried down, and I didn't know how to let it out after six months. I grieved her. I grieved my father all over again, knowing who he was and how he didn't get to live here with his kind after he was exiled. And I didn't either. It was all-consuming, pulling me down into a dark shell.

And it only got worse as I was forced to witness the former Cursed fae die from this sickness—including the wolves—and wondered why I wasn't affected. And the only reasoning Maeve could give me was because I was descended from an Untouched fae, which made my blood old, even though my body wasn't.

But my own kind, along with so many innocent fae, were dying. They were being attacked, and I couldn't stop it. And I wanted more than anything to protect them. To fight for them.

I wanted Davyna back every day. To help me... To talk to me about all this. To even save me at times, when I was overcome with anger and shifting multiple times a day. Or when the emotions were so strong, I could barely keep my puffy, bloodshot eyes open during training. But in time, I learned I had to stand on my own. And I failed over and over.

The way she looked at me tonight was exactly how she used to look at me—not seeing how much I've grown, or how much I've changed. It was like I was still this fragile, little thing who couldn't handle my own, and it brought back the weakness I felt in the early days she was gone, trying to figure out how to be fae. That version of me was gone, and I wanted Dy to see that I was finally like her. The one I looked up to all my life.

Guilt began coursing through me because maybe I shouldn't have said those things to her...

Fuck.

Laying back, Sorin followed, and our hands brushed together. "Sorry, but I want to know why she is so off... It's like something dug its claws into her, and she is doing everything in her power to hide it."

"She will tell us when she's ready," Sorin said, turning his head to gaze deep into my eyes. "You need to let go of everything in the past...we don't live there. Stand by her side. You both need each other." He smirked and that alone made any bright, warm day dull in comparison. The sight caused my heartbeat to speed up.

"Plus, she is going to need someone to show her the ropes on this whole immortality thing." His fingers brushed against my hand again, making my core flutter.

"Because I understand it so well?" I teased, interlacing my fingers through his.

"You don't give yourself enough credit sometimes." His body turned and his eyes changed from hazel to yellow. "You have come so far, Crescent..."

"I know..." I smirked, glancing down at his full lips. "It's because I had a good teacher." I bit my lower lip as he leaned in.

A loud thud pulled our attention to the male standing before us, his black wings spread wide.

"Ouch. You're not going to even acknowledge me?" Calix spat out, placing his hand over his heart as he grinned.

"Teachers." I smiled, turning away. Rising from the ground, I looked back to Sorin, who was crossing his arms over his knees and glaring at Calix.

Calix moved in, placing one hand on my waist. His light brown hair brushed against my face as he brought his lips to my cheek. Tingles rushed through my body as I kept my eyes locked on Sorin. His eyes watched Calix with disdain...but also longing because I knew he wanted to do the same.

Pulling away slightly, I looked at the two males before me. The awkwardness laid thick against my skin. It still hadn't faded with our *arrangement* that started four months ago.

Sorin silently watched his next move as my protector, and Calix smiled at him, taunting him to try.

After a minute passed, Sorin finally turned to me, smiling. "I'll see you tomorrow." Leaning down, his lips brushed against mine, before pressing deeply and claiming my mouth. My heart jumped as I laid my hands on his chest, savoring his sweet oak and fresh rain scent.

"Okay. I think she gets it," Calix said, causing Sorin to pull back and glare at him one last time before he turned and started walking away. I kept my eyes locked on him as he shifted, running back towards the Fallen castle.

Arms wrapped around my waist, and my breath hitched.

"So, tell me, little wolf..." His hand crept down towards my center. "Where would you like me to fuck you tonight? Under the stars...or somewhere else, where I can make you see the entire universe?”

CHAPTER 12
KADEYAN

My shadows swirled up to the peaks of the ceiling and I turned my head, taking in Davyna staring at the copper doors with flames carved within the metal. My jaw clenched as her blood roses and ash invaded my nose, savoring it more than air itself. I did my best to hide my raging desire to consume her behind my walls, because it wasn't the time.

The longing to read her thoughts—to sense her emotions—was pouring out of me. I had always been able to read her, even back in the Mortal Realm when she was a teenager. But now, it was like being met with a black wall of steel—unwavering and impenetrable.

Did she purposely place a spell on herself to keep me out, or was it unknown to her? I wanted to believe it was the latter, especially with how her eyes screamed in shock when I brought it up. Something in my gut told me it was something much more, and that it was tied to what her eyes looked like before she threw those men off her.

It was like I was staring into a sea of darkness; the whites nowhere to be found with a searing silver ring that shined brighter than the moon itself. It stunned me, along with the power that brushed up against my skin. I'd never known any fae to contain power like that, but I'd also never met anyone like her.

And then there was the darkness running through her scars like corrupted veins as I walked by her to kill Tallen. I usually could feel her warmth brush against me, but it was nonexistent, making my own form feel like I was plunged into a frozen lake.

I might not be able to read her, but those signs alone gave me a glimpse into what happened to her. It made the darkest parts of my soul want to come alive—to kill for her. And when the time came, I would.

Moving around her, I placed one hand on the small of her back before looking down at her eyes that were searing into the door. "Are you ready?"

She didn't answer, but she stood taller. So, I pushed on the doors, throwing them open.

Her eyes widened as she took in the throne, blazing as bright as the day she placed them there. The glow of the flames illuminated her skin as she stepped forward, and I interlaced my hand into hers.

"Gods... It's..."

"Beautiful," I said, and she gazed up at me. I wasn't looking at the throne, I was looking at her. Maybe I was afraid if I turned away now, she would vanish again, leaving me for another six months... Or forever.

I spent anytime I wasn't searching Valyner or the Mortal Realm in here...seeking beyond the flames as if they held the answers I needed. Or that maybe they would show me a glimpse of her, but they never did. The only thing they offered was the heat I craved to thaw my frozen body, reminding me of her touch, her smile...which only shattered me more.

Dy started moving forward, but I stayed rooted. Her hand slowly fell out of mine, and my heart ached from the distance.

"Why is there salt surrounding it?" she asked as she walked the salt border that was laid in a wide circle.

"Some fae got too close...and..." She paused and her shoulders fell low before she turned her gaze away from me.

Minutes passed and I watched her, waiting. Without another word, she lifted her head and placed her hand on the barrier, causing it to ripple. Slowly, a hole appeared, growing larger by the second. My brows furrowed before I realized what she was doing and picked up my feet.

"Dy..." My voice trailed off as everything around me stood still.

She stepped through, closing off the barrier as my hands slammed into it. Everything within woke, prying at me to get her away from it. To protect her...but that was the problem. This was her creation, her magic. What could I really do?

Abandoning the thought, my mind shifted. It was her power, so it couldn't hurt her, right?

"What are you doing?" I asked, forcing her to look over her shoulder.

"Fixing my mess," she stated as she turned back and made her way up the stairs.

My stomach turned, and my shadows raged within, sending off warnings I couldn't ignore. Her hand hovered over the armrest, coating her skin in the blaze, and my heart pounded harder against my ribs.

Slowly, her head fell back as the flames spiraled up her arm like a snake constricting its victim. And then, it hit me. She was trying to take it back—to reabsorb that power.

"Davyna!" I beat on the barrier as the flames twisted down her body with a searing glow. It was blinding, forcing me to turn away from its assaulting rays. The power in the air shifted, which caused the barrier to shake and crack under the pressure.

"Stop!" I yelled and turned back, fearing for her life as the blood refused to move through my veins.

What if I lost her again?

The flames surrounding her flickered black, showing an array of colors within. I stopped, trying to make sense of what I was seeing. Each Court power held its own shade of magic, and somehow, they were all there, swirling together.

The barrier shattered, and my body was thrown back as the walls around us rumbled in protest. The energy of the throne roared to life, like a monster warning you not to touch it. Warning you that it would devour every piece of your soul, and a shudder ripped through me.

My body slammed into the ground, the vibrations of the power on the throne shaking the stone, as my eyes scanned for her.

Looking up, I took in Davyna's limp body and sent my shadows out, wrapping them around her. My eyes darted to the throne. The power filtered back to its home, stopping its pursuit to destroy the room.

I pulled us into the gap, landing in my chambers. My knees slammed into the floor as I held her tighter in my arms. My breath was uneven as I looked down at her. She was dazed, but after a few seconds, she started to focus.

Her gaze locked on mine, no doubt seeing the anger consuming my features, but below that was undeniable worry. Could she see that it was drowning me? "What the fuck was that?" I asked, a harsh tone coating each word.

She sat up, looking around the room before sliding off my lap onto the stone floor. Her eyes became heavy as she avoided my gaze. "I was trying to take it back." Her voice cracked, making the anger within fade with each passing second. She looked so...defeated, broken. Tears gleamed in her eyes when she looked up, but she blinked them away as fast as they appeared. "I'll figure it out. I'll fix it."

I moved over to her, placing both my hands on her face to keep her from looking away. "Do you even know what you did the first time?" A few heavy breaths passed between us before she finally shook her head no. "Then why the hell would you try? What if taking it back hurts you, or worse?"

I tightened my grip as she tried to look away from me. Blood rushed up, invading my eyes as I waited for an answer. One of many I now got to add to the list because she wouldn't give me anything.

A minute passed, and I pulled myself off the ground, running my hands through my hair before pulling the leather strap free. "Maybe you should get some sleep."

She rose, and I couldn't help but notice the small trembles in her hands as she made her way over to the bed. I wanted to give her space, and to allow her time to make sense of all this... But didn't I of all people show her that I would carry every burden, every nightmare as my own? And that I was here for her...

I began walking to my door, giving up the fight to force it out of her. I'd respect her wishes...but I wouldn't be able to do this forever.

"Kade?" she whispered.

I turned and fell into those silver pools. Every stone-cold part of me melted under that look alone, pulling me back in. I sat on the edge of the bed, taking her hand in mine.

"I'm sorry...for everything," she whispered, and nothing else mattered. Not when I could see her, touch her.

Wrapping my hand around her nape, I pulled her up and relished in the way her lips molded to mine. I sent everything in me through that kiss to let her know I would be right here, to hold her, to fight with her, and to love her for eternity.

Because our souls were tethered to one another.

Our souls were the mirrored image of one another... She had no idea about my past, or that I was familiar with the pain she bore because I already lived it...and still lived it every day.

Pulling my head back, I rested my forehead on hers as our breathing filled the silent space around us. "We will get to the bottom of everything, I promise." I let her go, watching her lay back down as her eyes closed.

Rising, I walked back to the door and stole one last glance as a tear fell down her nose onto the silk pillowcase. And my own began to surface...

Leaving the room, my breathing picked up while the door closed behind me. I needed to get out of here... She didn't need to hear me breaking down when it was clear that one more thing on her shoulders—even me—could crush her.

The chilled night air swept past me as my legs hung over the cliff overlooking the mountains beyond. The last six months played on repeat in my mind, reminding me of the agony I endured. Not only because she was gone, but also because Valyner needed someone to take on some type of leadership role. The Fallen Court was always second-in-command to the Ember King. So, it was my duty to uphold my role as best as I could during her absence.

I made sure the armies were equipped for attacks. Which was a challenge because the creatures invading our lands had all different types of abilities.

The first creatures looked like us, with bat-like wings, except their bones were on the outside of their flesh. They were able to release high-pitched blasts from their mouths and stun our soldiers into paralyzed states before they feasted on them. And that was just the start as we dealt with many more creatures, all hell-bent on destroying our people, our world.

Spells and herbs were also provided for all fae to block the sickness from touching them...or at least putting it off as long as possible. I had a group of people to help the orphans who lost their families due to all this, making sure they ended up with families who would care for them and protect them as their own. Much like Elias did for Davyna.

Every move I made was with her in mind, doing what my Dearest would have done. But so many of those days, I struggled to take my next breath.

Thankfully, my friends stood in at certain meetings where I was nothing but a shell, unable to rise from the floor of my bedroom. And when I did, I found myself at the death ring in the Fallen mountains...wishing someone could put me out of my misery. But all it did was add more blood to my hands. No one knew I went there, and I was going to keep it that way. They didn't need to know I was desperate to stop feeling the excruciating pain...to stop breathing.

But I did the best I could, for her. And if tonight proved anything to me it was that, while she might not want to be a leader, she was willing to put herself in harm's way to protect us all. She was always going to be a beacon of light that I could only live in the shadows of. And I'd keep it that way because there would always be darkness that I could vanquish to keep her burning bright.

"Soldiers are all good for tonight's shift." Calix appeared next to me, his shadows spiraling off him as he sat down and dangled his legs over the cliff too.

"Did you check them before or after you and Evren..." My brow lifted, waiting for his response as a big-ass smile spread across his face.

"Both." He laughed, pushing my shoulder. "You didn't tell Davyna, did you?"

I smiled, glancing at him. "What? Are you afraid she'll burn your ass for touching her sister?" I teased.

"Well, she'll have to burn Sorin too. That actually might work out for me perfectly." He stared off, almost as if he was imagining that scenario, and I shook my head. *Unmated fae...* "Shut up. Don't act like you never had multiple partners."

"Not with another guy in the mix. But that was before..." *Before I found her.*

"No, we have rules. Never together." Knowing Evren, if she wanted that...she would get it. She was stubborn when it came to what she wanted, just like her big sister.

Changing the topic, I looked at him. "Do you know if Levanna checked in with Maeve about sending out the message to the Court leaders?"

"As far as I know, she did. But I can check in with her before I crash." A bottle of whiskey appeared in his hand, and he took a long drag before handing it over to me. I drank down a good amount before passing it back, my gaze becoming more vacant as I stared off in the distance. "What's up, man? Why don't you seem happier?"

"I am. But something isn't right...with her," I said before taking a deep breath. I slowly exhaled, the air dancing up into the night sky. "We went to the throne, and she tried to take the magic back from it."

"Isn't that a good thing? From what Maeve told us, that's what caused a tear in the veil and let this toxic magic in...along with those fuckers."

"Yeah...but it threw us both back...and what I felt... It was unsettling." I paused, thinking back to the walls rumbling, and the flames growing wilder as the power shot out and assaulted my flesh. "She doesn't know what she did...and I don't know how to..."

"Kade?" A pregnant pause sat between us as my eyes began to well up.

I turned, looking into my friend's golden-brown eyes. "I'm fucking scared..."

Silence wrapped around us as the breeze hummed in the distance. Calix brought the bottle back to his lips, drinking down more than half, before passing it to me. I placed it between my legs but didn't rip my eyes away from the mountains beyond.

"I can't lose her again."

"Nothing is going to happen to our Queen... Your mate."

I laughed. "She's not the Queen. Or my mate...not really."

Calix turned to face me, forcing my eyes to connect with his. "She can't keep lying to herself. She is both." He placed a hand on my shoulder, tightening his grip for a moment before releasing me. "Try to get some rest. You need it after these last six months." Shadows swallowed him whole, leaving me alone with my thoughts and the midnight sky above.

Closing my eyes, I saw flames dance, twisting and turning to their own melody.

I took a deep breath and my lip quivered as I focused to hear her breathing from within the castle. A broken smile graced my face, but it shattered as the tears lined my eyes. Every emotion I battled with for the last six months rushed in faster than I could handle it. And I was forced to let them fall—to let out the sobs that broke and crushed the walls I kept up in my mind.

How did I make it through each day bleeding into one long nightmare? No colors held life, and no sounds brought joy. Only numbness stitched me together, holding onto a single prayer that she was still out there. That she would come back. And she did... So, why was it hitting me like this now?

I got what I wanted...

And yet, I was still broken.

She broke me.

Through the sobs, I grabbed the bottle and threw it out into the abyss, hearing the faint shatter below a minute later.

I never wanted to lead either... I never wanted to lose my own family... And I never wanted to find someone who would make me fear loss again. But here I was, doing it all.

Pulling my legs up, I rested my head within my palms as I wiped the tears away. Something bigger was going on here, with her...or within her. I didn't know, but I needed to figure out how to get my answers now. To make sure I was ready to defend the last thing in this world worth living for. Because, regardless of the pain she inflicted on me, I knew deep down...pain still had its claws dug into her.

If I couldn't save her from it—and lost her again—then I'd gladly surrender my life and soul to whatever god out there to be by her side and never be parted again.

Pushing down our bond, I stood and looked up to the window of my room, where she was fast asleep. I felt the dark wall block me, but I still said, *"You're not alone, Dearest... I'm right here."*

CHAPTER 13

DAVYNA

Over the past three days, I moved throughout the castle in a daze, avoiding everyone as much as possible. I felt on edge, sensing *that* energy close by, and anxiety smothered me. It knew I failed in my attempt to take the power back off the throne, and I feared the repercussions. Because it wasn't my life on the line...it was theirs.

When I tried, I saw inside the flames...

One long tear revealed two worlds afar, void of color and slightly blurred. Was that what I did by burning the throne? Did I open a door to other worlds? I read about the others once, but nothing described what they looked like. And the books I'd been flipping through also held nothing on them to confirm if that was where I ended up.

Slamming the book in front of me shut, I threw it onto the small table in front of the couch and looked over the rich onyx library. I'd been in here every day at sunrise, and stayed until the sky turned black with dulled stars peering through the clouds.

Kadeyan sat in here with me, watching and picking up the books I tossed aside. It was like he was searching for an explanation as to what I was doing, without asking.

Getting up, I moved a few feet over to stand in the center and changed my focus to the magic on the throne, hoping a book explaining it would come forth. After a long moment, one book flew off the shelf, circling me before I reached out and grabbed it. Opening to the first page, I read the title: *Dark spells and enchantments.*

Why are you even trying? Give up and let me help you now.

Shaking my head, I refused to acknowledge the voice inside my mind as I moved back to the couch, flipping through the pages and scanning the text. Except, the demonic voice in my head giggled louder, forcing a chill to pass through me.

"Davyna..." Kadeyan finally spoke, and I closed my eyes as frustration built.

"What?" I asked. I brought my gaze back to the book and continued to flip through the pages, seeing stuff about sacrifices and relics, but nothing that would explain the power I used. I spelled that throne to burn forever so no one could take it...not even me. What the fuck did I do?

"I'm trying to give you time, but maybe I could help you if you tell me what you are looking for," Kadeyan said, leaning forward and throwing the book in the pile.

"You can't help me... Stop trying." I looked up at him, shocked by my own words. I didn't mean to say that, but the laughs in my head grew louder, making my skull rattle. "I'm sorry..." I said, letting the book go slack in my hands. As I glanced down, I saw the scars on my hand shimmer into a darkening shade.

The door flew open and Evren walked in with Sorin. Their talking came to a pause when Evren looked at the books before glancing at me. "What's going on?" she asked as she sauntered over.

But Kadeyan turned to look at her, stopping her in her tracks.

"Nothing," I said as I placed the book down and began walking towards the door. Evren's hand wrapped around my arm, holding me from taking another step.

"No, it's not nothing. What's going on?" Her eyes glanced down at my hand, seeing the scars before I ripped my arm back.

"Nothing that concerns you." I tried to control my tone, but I couldn't help the hurt that filtered through each syllable. Her words were still carving into me, and it made me feel like a failure.

"Bullshit. It concerns me. You're my sister, Dy!"

Kadeyan rose from the chair as I began moving to the door, but I paused, my body having a different plan in mind. I turned around and walked up to Evren, staring into her blue eyes laced with concern. Yet I could see the anger below, I could feel it...and it was directed at me.

"No...it doesn't. Not anymore. I will take care of it. So, please... drop it. All of you." I scanned over all their faces before landing on Kadeyan, his demeanor showing no emotion as I turned back around and left them.

I felt more like shit with each step. One side wanted to break down and cry for treating them like that, while the other wanted to rain fire. Like it was begging to hurt them.... And I knew I needed to get away from everyone before either side came out. Maybe it was the stress...or maybe it was what was inside me.

Using the void, I fell into Kade's room. My vision flickered, sensing the darkness within crawling up, and I turned to face the mirror. My eyes were black again, matching the scars on my hand. Instead of feeling fear, anger fueled my fires. I let them rain out, setting it ablaze as I yelled. The glass cracked under the heat as the wood started to break down. Shattering, it fell to the floor, one piece slicing into my foot before settling beside it.

I tried to take a deep breath as I walked over to the bed and sat down. Running my hands through my hair while my eyes blurred with tears, I looked down at my foot. The grey blood dripped to the floor below as the wound began to close. I couldn't help but wonder what she did to me, and what magic could change my blood. Did her touch make this voice appear and haunt me too?

Could I stop it? Could I fix myself?

Shhh, Davyna. I am you and I've always been here. You set me free... There is no fixing what we are.

Shaking my head, I let out a frustrated growl. No, that couldn't be true... This wasn't me! As I went to push myself off the bed, my ears picked up on yelling from below, and I focused on it.

"Has she told you anything?" Evren demanded with her own fury laced in her tone.

"And if she did, what makes you think I would tell you without her giving me permission to tell *her* story?" Kadeyan barked.

"She is my family!"

I blocked them out, noticing that there was a privacy spell layered over them, yet it did nothing to keep me out. How was I able to do that?

My eyes narrowed in on the stone floor, getting lost in who I thought I was and the abilities I held.

The agonizing question still remained: How was I able to do these things and cause catastrophic effects on a realm that didn't deserve it? Was my mother this strong? Did she do anything like this with her own power? I couldn't begin to fathom what she was capable of now, and that scared me.

Along with the threat the shadow figure left me with. It made me feel like my only option was to push away the people I loved most in this world. To protect them from something beyond... But also, I think I needed to protect them from me too.

Maybe that was my curse: being the hybrid of all the Courts, destined to be alone because loving me truly was a death sentence.

Laying down, I pulled the covers up and closed my eyes. What if there was a way to give it all up? To just be an Ember... Would I take it? But Maeve's voice flooded back into my mind: *Beware of the throne.*

What did that mean? Was it about the power on it? Was it possible? The gods cursed my father to never bear a child when he took his title and sat upon the throne, yet my mother made it possible for him. Could the gods even free me from this? Free me from the loneliness that was seeping in.

Or was I destined to do this by myself? To push people away to keep them safe? I went from being isolated in my suffering under Hera, to finding these amazing people that gave me hope of a different future. The walls I had built over the years began to fall, until this.

I sniffled, wiping my eyes as I let out a shaky breath. It didn't matter, because I needed to be alone in this, whether I liked it or not.

Except, I wasn't the only one with this power. Those other creatures were like me and probably possessed more knowledge about what I contained. Were they from one of those realms I saw through the tear? Was there more to my mother... More to me? And did we have ties to those Lands?

Cursing under my breath, I tried to seal off the unraveling questions dancing around in my mind. I wanted to feel like me again, and to put all this behind me and start new.

That was all I ever wanted when I was under Hera's rule. And now...I still didn't know what I wanted my life to look like, but I'd find it eventually, right?

I needed to finish this...and soon. Before that thing came back and took a possible future I had with everyone—with him—away from me.

Finding peace was the true fairytale, wasn't it? Or maybe it was for me.

The dark space hugged around my body as I moved through the eerie void, reminding me of being here many times before.

A voice echoed out and I turned as it said, "What are you?"

I knew that voice...

Persephone.

The words echoed around me as I moved through the void, my skin becoming chilled and bumps rose along my arms. Cool smoke passed my lips as the chill settled deep in my bones, feeling death nearby. Panic spiraled through my thoughts. I picked up my feet and moved farther into the darkness, when an opening appeared before me.

I swallowed down the lump growing in my throat, forcing myself to move through the opening and felt the energy change around me. My heartbeat became erratic while my eyes adjusted to the searing light that stole my sight, before screams sounded off.

Turning my head, I saw the throne room in shambles. The ceiling was missing, showcasing the beaming red sky as rain fell down on the stone in heavy droplets. The air was colder now, stealing the warmth within as smoke rose from my next exhale. My eyes narrowed back down, seeing the throne still on fire, unfazed by the element.

The one who stood before it made me suck in a breath.

It was me...with tears streaming down my face as anger captivated every feature. I couldn't hear my voice, and the movements that followed were a blur, causing my mind to think it was all playing a cruel trick on me.

I moved in as I watched this version of myself fall to the ground, but then I felt it again...death.

Turning to the left, I saw the dark shadow looming close by, watching me. Hollowness twisted inside me as the cries of myself in this scenario sounded off, shaking the ground below. I ran in towards the chaos, looking down at what made me scream, and confusion ripped through me.

Crimson blood flowed out in a stream towards my boots, but the face of who laid there was unclear. It could have been Evren, Levanna, Calix, Axel, Sorin...even Maeve. Or...Kade. Nausea took hold of me as I fell down, staring at the figure. I tried to will it to show me who it was, but it refused me.

Until it didn't.

The face became crystal clear, with eyes that were void of life.

My eyes...

What the hell was this?

Trembles racked through me and I slowly looked up, seeing the shadow standing by my side. In one swift moment, the shadow figure grabbed onto me, pulling me off the ground, and we flew through the air until we were back in the void.

Large hands I couldn't see gripped my throat tighter and I pushed out flames, watching them stream out onyx as it absorbed them.

"You failed...such a disappointment." *The voice was deep, piercing into my skull and adding to the fear trying to bubble up. I buried it down, denying him the pleasure of seeing me afraid, and tried to stay focused.*

"Who...the fuck...are you?" *I got through my lips as my lungs protested for more air to enter them.*

"I'm your worst nightmare, little cinder." *He chuckled and my mind flashed back to the large figure in the window of those lands and in Kade's room within the mirror. He was here.* "And I can promise you this: the nightmares I inflict, come true." *He dropped me and my lungs burned as they drank down the air filling them.*

I pushed myself back from the dark form as it watched me.

"Are you from the other fae realms?" *I choked out between coughs as he chuckled, like he was amused by my question.*

Bending down, he got closer to my face, groaning as he took me in. "You are a little fool, aren't you?" *A chuckle coated in acid passed his lips.* "Stop delaying and do as you're told. Or I'll start beheading your precious, little family."

Darkness surged through my body, matching his, and I glared up at him. "Stay away from us!"

He moved back, and though his eyes remained veiled from my view, I sensed them assessing me.

"I'm going to have so much fun breaking you..." *He laughed, and my body quaked.* "You'll be begging for that death soon enough. And I'll give it to you."

Standing up, the flames were already barreling down my arms as I threw them out at the mist of darkness. The echo of my screams were swallowed up by the void as I watched the flames dart through the air.

Before they hit the creature, they were met with his darkened blaze, glistening with the colors I saw in my scars. It pushed me back, causing me to falter.

Screams ripped from my body as I began to fall through the void, my panic swallowing me whole. I continued to plunge deeper into the abyss, realizing there was no escape from this life—this power—until death came for me.

CHAPTER 14
DAVYNA

Sucking in a sharp breath, I jumped up. The sheets wrapped around my legs and constricted my movement like a snake. My hand flew up to my chest, trying to steady my irregular heartbeat as I kicked at the fabric to free myself. I looked around Kadeyan's room, and the air I was holding in my lungs passed my lips. I was alone, and I thanked the gods for the small mercies because the chills running through my body were evident.

Turning to the window, a soft glow illuminated the lands as it crested over the trees and I realized I slept the entire day away.

My heart ached with how fast it was beating and I started to replay everything within my dream. It was too familiar...like my nightmares about the black void before it became my reality. Except, I'd never seen myself in it from a third person... And that voice matched the dark shadow that was behind me a few days ago. Was he prying on my worst fears: that those blurred faces could be people I loved? Or did he only want me to fear my own death?

Would that be the worst thing, though? Me...not here anymore.

Closing my eyes, I dropped my head and took a stilling breath to calm my nerves.

It was nothing. Just a nightmare...not a vision of the future. And that male was not in there with me... It was a bad dream.

Bringing my hand from my chest, I looked down at the black ash coating my skin, thick and glistening. My jaw fell open as I looked around, that power returning to taunt me. Panic shifted into pure horror as the cold reality slammed into my chest and warped my reality.

It wasn't a dream...and that realization prickled the need to protect my friends, my sister, and Kade from that thing. I needed to figure out something that could help me take back that magic on the throne before he came for them.

The power on the throne was dense though, as if it took on a life for itself and grew stronger with each passing day. And it didn't want to leave. So, how was I going to do it?

Jumping up, I ran to the washroom and turned on the sink. I scrubbed at my hands until they burned and went raw, but I couldn't stop. I wanted his touch off my body.

After getting every speck off me, I gripped the cool, metal sink and let my head fall. Was I going to lose them? Were they all going to be another casualty for loving me?

Of course, they are...but you don't have to feel that weight if you don't want to. The demonic voice returned, snickering inside my mind. I crumbled to the ground as I ripped my wet hands through my hair.

"Shut up!" I screamed through a broken sob.

It laughed, clawing at my psyche and making me wince as it tried to penetrate my mind deeper.

"I'm going to fix this! And you're going to leave me alone!"

The voice subsided in my head and I took a few minutes to collect myself as I rose from the floor. When I got to the middle of the room, my veins began to burn, causing me to stop as the little demon within my head spoke again.

You can try...but you will fail because this version of you is weak.

Fury pulsed out in waves around me, filling the room as I balled my hands into fists. I'd burn *their* world down... I'd become their villain if it meant my family and friends got to live.

Get angry and show yourself who you really are.

Fire blazed in my hands and I looked down, seeing the scars shift from their iridescent white to a shimmering onyx as I prepared to burn the room. Ice filtered through my veins, and for the first time in my life...I wanted it. I wanted it to erupt and leave its icy tendrils touching every inch of my body.

Glancing over, my eyes locked on the window and my vision once again flickered. The darkness began to invade the whites, swirling rapidly and making it nonexistent. A knock sounded at the door, jerking me back into the moment.

My chest rose and fell as I realized the power I was summoning to the surface was like nothing I thought I could contain. I didn't feel anything but release from both my pain and worries plaguing me. It was freeing, and I began to bask in its numbing embrace. Although, something about it screamed malice, torment, and death...but not towards me. It was more like what I could inflict on others, and terror rippled through me.

"Dy?" Nesrin opened the door, peeking her head in. Her sea-green eyes assessed me before getting caught on my arm.

Shit... My head fell, seeing they were back to a dazzling white. It did little to comfort me because I didn't want my friends to see this and ask questions.

After a moment, she cleared her throat. "I'm heading to the Ember Court to train with the other fae. I thought you'd like to come with me. Maybe join in."

"Yeah...sounds good. I can check out the throne again after that." Using my magic to change my clothes into the leathers I wore the other day, I pulled the loop over my hand to hide the scars from any more prying eyes.

She moved into the room, taking my hand. I looked up into her piercing green orbs before her lips pulled up to one side. It was almost as if she wanted to say something, no doubt seeing the sadness on my face. I buried it down, giving her a fake smile I had practiced giving others since I was sixteen, but I didn't think she bought it.

Her magic spun around us with a sheer sapphire hue, and I could smell the salt water encase us as everything went black. My heart picked up. A wave of nausea bloomed at the thought of being in the gap again, and I wondered if the shadow figure was here. Before I could even look around, our feet landed on solid ground.

Glancing over my shoulder, I took in the lands dressed in coppers, pale yellows, and crimson that stretched over every inch. This Court lived in fall down to every detail, even giving off the crisp air that held a chill. The forest beyond was coated in leaves, reminding me of a simpler time.

When fall would make its appearance each year, I walked through the forest to savor the beauty of the season. Evren and I would run between the trees for hours with Elias and the kids from town. We were lost in the simplicity of life—as a child should be. But that was before... This was now. I tried to feel for what those memories once gave me—comfort—but it didn't come, no matter how much I craved them in this moment.

Turning, I watched Nesrin walk over to a large stone that overlooked the lands below before sitting down on it. Moving towards her, the sounds from the town became clear before I saw the fae who occupied it. They were sparring with each other, metal ringing into the sky above, along with their power creating a beautiful aura. It caressed my skin, urging me to let my own free, but I resisted, cautious of what I could bring to life.

Sitting down next to Nesrin, we watched the fae train for a little while, before she nudged me.

"Do you want to talk about it?"

I opened my mouth but quickly closed it as my throat constricted. I knew I could trust them all with this. They would drop everything to help, but I wouldn't put them in any more danger. Or chance those creatures making good on their threat. They—along with everyone else in Valyner—had been through enough because of what I inflicted. I wouldn't do it.

I couldn't...

"You know...I have scars like that too..."

I looked over and took in her arms that were bare from the dark blue leather top hugging her torso like a second skin.

"I had Levanna put a spell on me to hide them from people I

didn't want seeing them, which was everyone. But it does allow me to show them if I choose to." She traced her finger down her arm in a jagged path towards her hand. "But while no one else can see them on a regular basis...I do, every day." She took a deep breath. "A constant reminder of what he did to me."

"Nes..." I said softly. She looked over at me, but I didn't have the words. Her tough exterior thinned out as if it became as narrow as a sheet of paper, showing the pain she held. And it was torturous.

"Do you know the stories of how Sahar was viewed as...property?" she asked.

"Yeah, Levanna told me a little bit about it."

"My family was in a lot of debt with her uncle...and they sold me to be a whore." Her gaze fell and she swallowed hard. "They gave me one year to prepare... Every day, I dreaded the thought of what I was going to endure for the rest of my life. And then, I met Aeron."

"Who was he?" I asked, my voice nothing more than a whisper.

"He was from a higher up family in the Salt Court. He was sweet...in the beginning. I didn't believe the rumors the other females told me. He wanted me to spend a few days with him since I was *new.* He wanted me whole...so he could..." Her fear rose and my stomach twisted in response. "He put dark obsidian chains on my wrists and forced himself on me... Beating me until I struggled to breathe..."

She took a deep breath, trying to settle her trauma of the past, but her pain still blanketed me. "I asked him to let me leave so I could get a message to my family to help me. I thought if they knew what I was going through, they would move mountains to come save me. But it was delusional... They knew...and they didn't care."

"Nesrin...I'm so sorry."

Her hand came up, taking mine and squeezing tightly as her eyes gleamed with tears. I glanced down and the glamour began to ripple, exposing the scars covering her arms, her chest, and even one going down her face.

"For an entire year, I was kept in a cell as his plaything while he told me about his third bonding ceremony coming up. I wasn't able to heal properly in there. But I knew, deep down, there was no healing from what he put me through."

"How did you get away?"

A broken laugh passed her lips before her head tilted up to look over the clouds above.

"Something took over. Survival, I guess. I was still in chains, so I couldn't use my magic on him. When he came to blow off some steam that night before the ceremony, I let him beat me a little. Waiting for him to weaken to give me my chance to wrap the chains around his neck." She smiled, looking forward as she relived the memory, and I could feel her undiluted elation surface.

"Everything happened so fast. His head falling from his body. Grabbing the keys from his pocket and removing the cuffs before I undid the lock on the cell. And then killing three guards as I ran up the stairs..."

Glancing over at me, she smiled before turning back to overlook the lands. "I still don't know how I even had it in me to fight...but I did. I entered the gap, coughing up blood when I fell into the Fallen Court. I knew if I could bargain with Osiris—Kadeyan's father—to let me stay...then I would do whatever I could to keep my freedom."

She fell silent and her emotions swirled for a moment, before one that was so recognizable slammed into me. *Love.*

"Kadeyan was there. Osiris said I needed to do nothing but heal, and that it would always be my home. When I walked out of the room, I collapsed, crying so loud, I knew the entire castle heard me... That's when Axel came over... My mate."

"You knew the whole time?"

She shook her head. "Yeah...but I needed to find myself again before I was ready to give him all of me. And he was slower at realizing it...what we were to one another." She laughed, and I joined in, remembering how he was around her before everything happened with Persephone. How I was slow to realize that me and Kade had an unbreakable connection...

"What do I do, Nes? I feel like I'm drowning." My lip trembled as I looked over the lands for a minute.

Looking down at my hand, she pulled the loop off my finger and rolled up my sleeve. She studied the marks before wrapping her hand around my wrist, gently running her finger over it. It was nurturing. Almost like she was trying to say it was okay to be scared, and tears rushed to my eyes as a lump in my throat formed.

"Fuck, Dy... You can breathe underwater, you can't drown." She laughed, but on a deeper level, I understood what she meant by it. "I'm telling you, whatever happened out there, or is happening here, you will come through it. Because you aren't alone in any of this anymore. You have all of us. You have *him*."

She smiled at me, letting go of my wrist before standing up. "Come on, I think some fighting will do you some good."

"Nesrin?"

"Yeah?" she asked, turning to face me.

"I can't tell him..." A breeze flowed past us both, pushing our hair back as the silence fell between us. He knew about my scars, but not the internal ones I was carrying. The ones I battled to keep closed because it wouldn't be my blood flowing...it would be his.

"Then wait until you feel like you can. Now, come on."

Metal chimed through the air as sweat began to form on my head and my breathing became rigid from exhaustion. Nesrin moved with grace. Her sword blocked my strike as she slid to the side, hoping to get a blow to my back. Pivoting out of the way, I threw up a shield before the metal slammed down onto it, and the barrier rippled in response.

No matter how much I trained in my life, the feeling of strength never ceased to be present. And right now, it felt good.

I smiled and watched Nesrin wipe her brow as I let the shield fall.

"Nice one," she said as she stabbed the blade into the ground before I followed suit with my own weapon.

Metal continued to clash together around us as we began moving over to a table where some food and water was laid out. We had been out here for at least a couple of hours without stopping for a single break...and damn, I needed one.

I didn't realize how much I needed to spar with someone to get out the pent-up fear and frustration inside my head. Or to feel some semblance of control right now. I was grateful to Nesrin for asking me to come today, like she knew I needed to detach from the problems floating around in my head.

The looming darkness within seemed to retreat during our time here. Maybe I needed to channel my energy into something else to keep me sane.

As I drank down the entire cup of water, I looked around at the fae. I could feel their determination filling the field, along with their power flying through the air. Turning, I watched as water expelled from a fae's hands. It turned into a great wave before consuming the blaze darting towards them, causing smoke to rise.

Wolves raced by, their fur rich in hues of blacks, greys, reds, and browns. I watched as they took on shadows prowling towards them, doing their best to avoid being captured. Howls sounded as the pack pulled together, protecting the wolf in the back. Fallen Court members subdued each one, but the last wolf got through their line, taking down one of the Fallen members.

Calix.

He laughed as he stared up at the beast on top of him, before she shifted back. Evren smiled down at him. Standing up, she offered her hand. Helping him up, she walked away to talk to the Crescents as Calix kept his eyes on her. I strained my hearing, listening to Evren engrossed in her conversation about how to better their formation and avoid the shadows. She stood tall and the small pack soaked in each word flowing from her lips.

They respected her.

It was strange to see her here, leading even a small pack. In my mind, she was still human. I think I also viewed myself as such.

Nevertheless, those versions of us were gone, and I couldn't ignore that my little sister worked hard to hold the strength she now possessed. I could feel it rolling off her.

A broken smile grazed my face as she glanced up and saw me, but her eyes moved back to her people, like I wasn't even there. A sharp pain of regret stabbed into me, twisting deeper into my gut until I pulled my gaze away from her.

I hated this feeling of being on the outskirts with her. I was at fault for how I treated her in the dining room and the library, but it wasn't my intention to upset her. I was on edge with all of this, teetering on a thin string, just waiting for it to snap. Which was no excuse; I knew that.

We were so different now and I could feel it pulling us apart. Before, all we had was each other. Now, we viewed things from different angles, which placed a barrier between us. Would it ever go away? Would she understand that I needed to push her away to keep her safe? Would she let me explain one day and forgive me? Would I forgive myself if I lost our relationship?

"Princess?" asked someone from beside me.

I turned, taking in the fae next to me. Her honey-blonde hair was cut above her shoulders but faded down to red on the tips. I took in her eyes, seeing a yellow only found in flames, with a red ring in the center. Her neck was covered in beaming tattoos, as if her fires rose to the surface to mark her, traveling down both arms.

Glancing around, I noticed a few other Embers in the distance, matching with the same glowing tattoos beneath their skin.

Turning my gaze back to her, I cleared my throat. "Just Davyna."

Nesrin touched my arm, grabbing my attention. "I'll see you in a little bit." She took off, running into Axel's arms as he wrapped his hands under her thighs and lifted her.

I smiled, shook my head, and looked back to the Ember in front of me. "I'm sorry. Can I help you with anything?" I asked.

She smiled. “No...I wanted to thank you for everything you did for our people.” Her flames spun around my hand as she grabbed it, making me smile. “I’m Ash... I knew your father. I was actually one of his guards.” My throat tightened, trying to resist the urge to ask her everything about him. “If you need anything from me—anything at all—please let me know.”

“Actually...” I said, taking a step forward, “could you train with me?”

She was taken aback for a second before smiling wide. “It would be an honor.”

Following her, we moved off to the side. We found a spot away from the growing magic filtering into the air, along with the echoes of metal clashing.

“What do you want to train with?” she asked, looking over to the weapons rack to our left.

I glanced down at my hands, calling my fires forward until they encased them entirely. My power flowed with ease right now, giving me a peace that I hadn’t felt since I arrived back. I was in control, and I wanted to soak it in and make sure the feeling remained. And I wanted to know what it felt like to work with not only an Ember but someone who was close to my father.

“I haven’t been able to fight an Ember yet.”

She smiled, and her hands ignited before me as she moved a few steps back.

We moved into a similar dance of swords, throwing out a blaze towards each other before blocking each blow. There was something about this—being around the Embers and on the soil of my Court—that made me feel like my father’s presence was here. It was a comfort that I savored, fully immersing myself in my element.

Smoke filled my nostrils, and I savored the scent as I got lost in my magic, feeding it everything I had. Ash began throwing more out and I dodged each one, letting my fire grow with intensity as I propelled it towards her. I fell deeper and deeper into the magic, each instinct coming alive like a new day with the sun obliterating the night.

Shifting to the side, my gaze caught on the fae around us as they stopped what they were doing to take in the dance of battle we were creating. Their eyes pierced into me, transferring their various emotions onto me like a heavy weight. Some were stunned in amazement...while others were scared and disgusted with the power lashing out.

And it had nothing to do with Ash...

The darkness seeped back in, egging me on to find each one and tear their throats out. The cool sensation washed over me as a wall of flames barreled towards my body. I turned in time to throw them back with everything I was feeling. It was as if I held life and death within my palm and it was intoxicating.

My eyes focused on the untamed power as it slammed into Ash's chest, sending her hurling through the air before slamming to the ground.

"Fuck!" I yelled, running towards her, the twisted thoughts vanishing as I took in her still body. I dropped to my knees, looking her over and held my breath.

"Damn!" She coughed, and a laugh passed her lips. "You *are* your father's daughter."

I let out a sigh of relief as she sat up.

"I'm so sorry," I said. Looking down at my hands, I noticed the leathers burned away, exposing half my arm where the scars laid. They were fading back to an iridescent white, and my heart quickened in my chest as I looked back to her. They went dark again... Did anyone see it?

"Don't be. That was badass!"

I tried to laugh it off, but unease cloaked me. Taking her hand, I pulled her up and looked over my shoulder to see the fae dispersing. I could feel— No, hear their thoughts as if they were talking out loud.

"She shouldn't be here."

"She is the reason we have to fight like this."

"She is the reason people are dying."

And one that twisted the words Ash just spoke into a negative light, turning my stomach: "*She is just like her father.*"

Maybe I deserved that... I know the evil my father unleashed; he told me himself.

Fear rose into the air, mixing with my own as I watched the dense smoke lift from me and Ash. Was I viewed by some of Valyner as the next great evil?

I couldn't blame them. Maybe I was... And maybe it was a mistake to tap into my power right now without fully understanding its capabilities.

"I think I'm going to go study the throne a little more today." I started walking away, keeping my head down.

Ash called out, "Hey, Davyna..."

I stalled, turning to face her.

"Don't let them steal your strength. I meant what I said earlier; anything you need, I'm here for you. All the Embers are."

Smiling, I began walking again. Eyes burrowed into me as I made my way through town and towards the castle. I blocked them all out, but there was one that wouldn't stop; that wouldn't give me peace.

The distorted voice within my mind returned, snickering as I took each step, and sent me back into a spiral.

You're a monster, Davyna... Embrace it. And let's burn it all down.

CHAPTER 15
DAVYNA

I sat on the floor for hours, staring at the throne as I tried different spells to trace my own magic. Yet, everything ended with me feeling empty and lost for any explanation that would explain what I did. How was that even possible? It was done by my own hand, and yet nothing connected.

I looked around the room, seeing the new cracks that were left through the walls and floor from the last time I came with Kade. The power was determined to turn this space into rubble in order to stay in its place, but I had more to lose than it did. And I needed it to let me in... Needed it to obey me.

Trying again, I pushed out a barrier to encase the throne and me, and channeled the power until I was psychically intertwined with it. The energy pulsed through my veins, sparking off into thousands of embers as I tried to focus in on the main source.

A force within the throne pushed back as I dug my hands into the stone ground, but it was unrelenting. It threw me back and my body slammed into the stone, ripping the air from my lungs.

Sitting up, I coughed and took in the flames roaring and spinning off the throne in a frenzy. They snaked out, stopping an inch from my face, and its energy brushed against my skin. I could feel the toxic power watching me, and I swallowed hard. I stood still as it slowly made its way back, shooting out embers as it settled back into the blaze.

Taking a breath, I pulled myself to my knees and dropped my head.

It won't come to you until you give yourself over to who you were meant to be.

The voice inside my head didn't laugh or taunt me. Its eerie voice spoke to something deeper within myself, and I paused. Therein lied the question: I no longer knew who I was. I thought I had my answers, but it turned out those were just scratching the surface. So, how would I know who I was meant to be if I still felt lost in what I had become?

Deep down, you know who you are. What you will become: The ruler of death.

A chill ran down my back as I grabbed my father's stone. Heat pulsed off it and into my palm.

Maybe the sickness it was releasing was affecting me too. Anticipation bloomed inside, and my breathing picked up. Maybe this was the reason I was falling into the craze of my own head. Levanna said it was affecting not only the body but the mind.

I stood up and paced as I searched my mind for the protection barrier, a surge of hope filling me for the first time since I arrived back. After locating it, I stopped and began silently chanting the spell. It grew over me, caressing my skin in warmth, and my shoulders started to release. Every muscle in my body began to feel the ease taking over, and I basked in the serenity.

Standing still, I waited for the voice to drag along the walls in my mind, taunting and laughing at me... But it was gone. I sighed in relief as I opened my eyes.

I did it...

A minute passed and the laughter sounded off in my mind, forcing my body to go rigid.

Did you think you could get rid of me that easily? We are one.

Anger flooded out of me as I screamed, the echo ricocheting off the stone walls as I bent over. My fingers scraped against my scalp as I gripped my hair, tugging at the strands until pain was all I felt. I wanted this to stop... I wanted it *all* to stop.

Closing my eyes, I took a few deep breaths, and a lone tear slid down my face. Pulling my hands down, I opened my eyes and took in the throne as a wave of unease prickled my skin. Turning fast, I hoped I wasn't right...but the power didn't lie.

"Did you miss me, little fae?" My shadow self stood in front of me, smiling with wicked intent.

My hands ignited and shot out towards her, and I poured everything I'd been feeling into the flames. Like it was nothing, she lifted her hand, blocking it all as she kept her smile plastered to her face—*our* face.

"Can't we be civilized and just talk?"

I dropped my hands, walking right up to her. "You want to talk... Then tell me, what did you do to me? Why am I hearing voices in my mind?"

She tilted her head, her smile faltering, and I knew whatever was going on inside wasn't by her hand. Which meant...it was all me and the voice wasn't lying. We were one. So, was everything it said to me something I truly wanted? No...I couldn't accept that. I didn't want what it was offering me.

"Why haven't you taken the power back?"

"I've tried." I gritted my teeth, forcing out each word.

"Apparently, not hard enough," she spat out, moving a few steps away from me.

"Why do you even care about what I did?"

"Because you are ruining our plans." She turned and her face was as cold as death.

"What plans?" I asked, my mind spiraling into a million possibilities, but I knew she wouldn't give me answers. Why would she? They were the masters in this situation, and I was their puppet.

But you don't have to be. You could make them pawns in a matter of minutes if you let me out.

Temptation racked through me at the thought, but whatever was lurking below made me hesitant to tap into it. I hurt Ash, I snapped at Kade, and I almost burned his room down. I needed to keep myself in check.

"Oh, Davyna... Now, why would I tell you anything other than it will be glorious? And if you don't do your part, your friends will never get the honor of seeing it."

I rushed up to her, grabbed her hand, and readied myself to demand answers to what she was, where she came from, and what this all meant. But my mind was sucked into hers.

A cabin sat in the woods, and I couldn't shake a sense of familiarity of that place. Soft cries sounded from within...almost like they were coming from a baby.

I turned to see her standing next to me. Her eyes were lost in rage, beaming white with all the hues shining out and onto my face.

She threw me back out of her mind and my body slammed into the ground. Coughing, I looked up as she came over to me, crushing her boot onto my chest.

"What are you?" she asked, her tone laced with venom.

"I'm getting sick of people asking me that!" I growled and let out my shadows, ripping her to the ground. Shifting my body, I straddled her and pressed my forearm into her neck, smelling her flesh burn. She didn't cry out, only gritted her teeth as she stared up at me. "What was that?" I asked, confused by what I saw.

She smiled, and I looked into her eyes, searching for more. "Where it all began."

Where what began?

"Looks like you have a visitor. Fix the throne, or there will be a price to pay." She vanished beneath my hold, leaving me on the ground, blankly staring into the stones.

The power she held began to fade farther away, leaving me to wonder what secrets that cabin held within... I couldn't shake that something beamed through the aged, wooden walls, speaking to a deep part of my soul as if we were familiars. And if that were the case, was the baby inside...me?

"Davyna?"

Everything in my body iced over and my stomach turned because I already knew who was there... My brows furrowed as I rose, turning to narrow my gaze on *him*.

Alastair stood in the doorway. His honey-brown eyes were soft as he looked me over in shock. My vision began tunneling in, while the demon tapped on my brain, begging to shed blood—*his* blood.

"Please. Hear me out..." He placed his hands out, his expression softening as if it was his way of waving a white flag of surrender.

Hear him out? I wanted to laugh at him. "Are you serious?"

He claimed to care for me, but he lied at every turn when it suited him, letting me live in a fantasy that was never going to have a happy ending.

"I have nothing to say to you..." My power heated my skin, which caused a deep itch to rise, begging to be released. "And why are you even here in the Ember Lands?"

"I got a letter requesting a meeting with all the Court fae for this coming week. It said the Ember Court would be in attendance, and I just... I needed to see for myself." He took a step closer, but I backed up, the heat of the throne brushing against my back. "It's been six months, Davyna..."

"For you, not me." I took in his confusion as he ran his hand through his red hair.

"I thought you were dead..." I watched his eyes lock on my hair before trailing down to take in my arm decorated in scars. "Are you okay?"

"What do you think?" My fists tightened as I tried to steady my breathing.

He shut his mouth and I could see his jaw lock for a moment as he tried to hold his emotions back. But I'd seen the beast within. There was no point in hiding it now.

"The last six months have been..."

"I've heard... I've also heard you won't let your own people leave the Court. Why's that?"

He moved in, making me retreat until my boots pressed into the bottom stair that led up to the throne. "You know why..."

"Right, because you and Kadeyan hate each other for no good reason. Your mother and sister were never dead, Alastair. Why are you still at each other's throats?"

He pulled his tunic aside for me to see silver scars surrounding his heart. "Because he tried to rip my fucking heart out." His eyes darkened as he stared me down, before pulling the fabric back in place. Images of Kadeyan flashed in from the other day of how he kept flexing his hand and smiling down at it as he told part of the story. "All because I said you were better off far away from him."

I held no sympathy for Alastair...but something twisted in my gut, thinking that maybe he was right in a way. But it was that Kade was better off without me. Without a shattering mess who only brought more pain...

A deep urge to defend Kade rose, and I looked back into his eyes. "What did you expect? He's my..." The word froze on the tip of my tongue, begging to be said out loud. His eyes softened in realization of what I was about to say, and the words fell away, turning into a mere mist. "You know why he did it."

"Yeah well... Someone needed to say it." He moved, looking over the throne room for a long moment before turning to face me again. "I think you did the right thing. The Courts should be running themselves."

I paused, hearing his words. Regardless of our history right now, I saw it the same way. The Courts could run themselves, but not like this. It would lead to war, and Valyner had enough shit to worry about without fighting from within.

"Yeah, well, it won't work like this. So, it needs to stop," I stated before pausing to wait for him to respond, but then I felt it. His own emotions flared to life, tainted with annoyance.

"Or what? You'll take the throne? I know you don't want it... You made that very clear...just like you have made other things clear."

"What does that mean?"

Silence fell between us as he moved back in.

"It doesn't matter anymore..." Hurt flashed within his eyes before he buried it down. "I will negotiate with Kadeyan. For your sake only."

"Maybe you should consider doing it for Valyner. Not for me, because if you think this is going to change a damn thing between us, you're wrong."

He smiled, letting his head fall for a moment before looking back to meet my gaze. Nodding, he straightened his shirt before he began to walk away. Getting to the throne room doors, he turned, and my fire spun when he opened his mouth again.

"Everything I did was for you. Whether you believe that or not. I wanted to protect you from this."

Holding my breath, my head spun as I looked down.

"I made mistakes, Davyna. I lied, hid things from you...and I'm sorry... For whatever it's worth at this point." Glancing back up, I looked into his eyes laced with regret, holding their own prayer for forgiveness. "But I will always fight to protect you from the darkness that lives within you. Will he do the same?"

When I went to speak, the words failed me, keeping me silent once again in his presence. An orange glow swirled around him, taking him away while I took in the empty room.

My heart began to beat harder in my chest as I let my fists fall open, seeing my nails pierced into my skin. I watched as the flesh began to heal and let my own mist of ashes surround me, pulling me away from this place.

I didn't trust him. But something in his words rang out while I was in the gap, pulling me back to the past to when we talked about my power and how it would be better if I locked it back up. And I couldn't help but wonder if he was right this entire time.

CHAPTER 16
Davyna

Landing in the Fallen Court castle, I moved through the halls until I heard Levanna's voice in the distance. I moved quicker, until I stood in front of a large black door, taking a moment to collect myself before throwing it open. I couldn't tell them anything...but maybe they could help me with one thing.

I paused and took in the room made of glass, overlooking the gloomy mountains beyond with dark clouds surrounding them.

"Hey, how was training?" Levanna asked as Axel stood from the couch.

I turned, closed the door, and tried to think of what to say without giving away too much.

"Good... I saw Alastair. He is going to negotiate the terms with the other Courts." I turned, watching both their eyes meet before Levanna signaled for me to sit. Moving in, I looked out the windows again, before letting my body fall into a chair. "There is something else...I need from you two..." I said, sitting forward, and my fingers trailed over the scars.

"What do you need?" Axel asked, taking a seat and watching me with his storm-grey eyes that matched the sky beyond.

"Can you try to get into my mind, like you did in training before?"

Levanna looked between us. "Dy, what's this about?"

I shook my head slightly. Bringing my gaze to Axel, I said, "Can you at least try?"

He rose from his chair and moved over, kneeling down before

me as his black hair fell into his eyes. He kept his gaze locked on me as his power built within my mind. I longed for him to show me anything to divert my fear away from myself and the turmoil that was thickening like the onyx lake.

I waited for the invasion, but nothing happened. The silence of the room stabbed into my skull as the heavy weight of the truth crushed down on me. Kadeyan wasn't the only one who couldn't get into my mind.

"Sorry, Dy. I can't. It's just...dark," he said, laying his hand over my knee.

I nodded, my eyes stinging as I suppressed my emotions and glanced at Levanna. "What do you know about the throne?" I asked as she moved in, and Axel sat back onto the couch.

"Maeve and I studied it back to its origins. The gods made it for your father, but the magic you placed on it feels...different than anything Crystal witches can do. But you aren't a regular Crystal witch, like me. And Maeve said the magic that was expelled by you... caused a tear in the realm. Like an opening..."

My breathing faltered for a moment. I saw that...the realms beyond. That was how the creatures were getting in. And the magic from those realms was more than likely making them sick, right? Or was it my own power placed on the throne?

"How do we close it?"

"That's the thing. No one from Valyner can. Even if everyone was in perfect health here, it still wouldn't be enough. Do you still not know what you did?"

"No fucking clue. But afterward...something felt different." I recalled the feeling of the day I burned the throne. Feeling off, something else opening up, and then how I ended up in that place.

"Give me your hand..." I looked into her crystal-blue eyes before taking in the grey streaks that framed her face, shimmering through each strand.

I gave her my arm and her fingers traced over the scars in a delicate touch. Ancient words fell from her lips for a long moment.

Slowly, I started to understand what she was doing. She was trying to trace the magic inside me.

I watched her jump back as a spark of fire broke her hold, but I didn't do it.

She's not allowed to know what we are capable of, Davyna... Not until you give over to who you should be.

The walls in my body built without my permission and my eyes widened.

"Shit..." she said, looking down at her hand.

"Are you okay?" Remorse smothered me as I looked from my hand to hers. I didn't mean to hurt her...

"Yeah, you just scared me," she stated, trying to shake off the unease growing within. "I think Maeve and Faelynn might know more."

"Why Faelynn?"

"She came from one of the other Realms, but she hasn't talked about it with anyone since arriving. Maybe she would if it was just you two."

I thought back to when I saw her last, and she said she wanted to tell me the stories lost to time. Maybe they would help.

"Do you think this magic I used was from another realm?"

"No, your father was from here. And even if your mother never lived here, she held our power as one of the Cursed. I think Maeve and Faelynn would be the best people to help since I can't penetrate it," she said.

I nodded my head, looking back out to the sky beyond. "Thanks for trying..." Levanna moved over to the couch where Axel was sitting, making me look back to them. "When was the last attack on the Lands?"

Axel cleared his throat. "About two weeks ago. They haven't been happening as often the last couple of months."

I shook my head, a heavy weight settling in. Something like a warning.

I can change that... A laugh rattled my brain, pulling bile into my throat.

"Are you going to be okay, Dy?"

Glancing back to him, I took in his concern and gave him a smile, hoping to hide the worry building around me. "I mean, I died and came back. What could be worse than that?"

He laughed, making me join in, even if it was fake. Because this felt worse than death. More powerful than life.

I could see it in their eyes, as well as in the fae back in the Ember Court, and even in Kadeyan. They looked at me like I was a fuse about to set off an explosion, and maybe I was.

Rising, I moved through the room, my hands shaking as the dark place inside me began hissing out a laugh. "Levanna, could you ask Maeve and Faelynn if we can come by soon and talk?"

"Absolutely," she said, turning to face me. Worry billowed off her, caressing my skin.

Giving her a small smile, I averted my gaze back to the mountains beyond again. The sky was beginning to darken, promising to conceal the Lands.

I could feel the pressure again, the darkness sinking in deeper as it invaded every marrow and fiber of my being. It was going to drag me down, wasn't it? It was going to hold me there in chains, smothering me until I gave in to what it wanted me to be: a soulless monster.

Twisting the doorknob, I pulled it open as the faint snicker sounded off deep within my mind like a siren call—enchanting...but deadly. And here I was, waiting to see if it would devour me whole before I could make things right.

CHAPTER 17
Davyna

I walked through the woods, trying to catch my breath as everything slammed into me. I knew there was a ticking clock on this all. Before another attack, before someone died from sickness, or worse...they returned to take someone I cared for as payment for not following orders.

I pulled a bottle of whiskey from the castle as I moved on through the trees. Bringing it to my lips, I drank down half of the contents, but it did nothing to settle the taunting within. Coming to a stop after the castle was out of view, I placed one hand on a tree as my other one with the bottle went slack.

I wanted... I needed...

But I couldn't finish those thoughts, not with the giggles within my mind sounding off. Leaning forward, I rested my forehead against the rough bark as I heard branches crack behind me.

"Look who we have here, boys. The bitch who destroyed our realm." Laughs bounced off the trees as the other men joined in, but I didn't cower. Nor did I feel any empathy for them in this moment.

All I felt was rage.

"You need to pay for what you did." Another spat out, and a smile rose on my lips as I glanced down at the bottle in my hands. The scars turned from their light shimmering hue to match the midnight sky above as the darkness within rushed up to invade my eyes.

"Then what are you waiting for?" I whispered.

Multiple boots crunched against the debris on the forest floor as they rushed in. I slammed the glass bottle against the tree, shattering it before I turned and sliced one of the men across the face. Iron filled my senses as I grabbed the other male and dug my teeth into his neck, forcing him to cry out in pain.

Fear rose from them as I threw the corpse to the ground, taking in the other three men hesitant to move in. "What, you don't want to play anymore?" I asked, provoking them.

"What the fuck is wrong with her eyes?" one said.

Another shouted, "You are a fucking monster!"

The power that came forth slithered back to the darkest parts of my psyche, and the laugh within sounded off.

They watched me step back, but I was lost in a daze, looking down at the man whose lifeless eyes stared back up into mine. Blood streamed profusely from his neck, creating a pool of crimson beneath him. My eyes glanced over at the other male, who was knocked out cold with a gushing wound across his face. My own blood ran cold.

I didn't want to hurt them... I didn't mean to...kill.

The other two men didn't hesitate as their dark purple power wrapped around me, pulling me to the ground. It was Crystal magic, tainted with something dark and sacrificial. My seer ability quickly picked up on the dialect they were using, and I knew the spell they were trying to perform.

They were trying to kill me...and hex my soul to never find peace.

I heard my cries as the power ran through my veins, splintering pain into my bones while it passed. I didn't bother fighting them as the guilt washed over me, hurting me more than they ever could. I deserved this. I deserved resentment, pain, agony... I deserved it all. And on a deeper level, I think there was a part of me that was done fighting. I'd been doing it since Elias died, and even more since I became fae.

We fight for love, Elias once said... But what he never told me was what happened when love was fighting you. When it tore you up inside, forcing you to live with the bleak reality that anyone who loved you...was doomed.

I closed my eyes as I continued to cry out, trembling while I dug my nails into the coarse dirt. I welcomed the next wave of splintering pain from their spells, hoping it would numb the soul-crushing agony deeper within.

Their magic began to fade, one by one, until I could take in a full, ragged breath. Glancing up through tear-filled eyes, I saw Kadeyan and Calix standing a few feet away, assessing the area with blood coating their hands. Calix moved in, picking up the male with the wound to his face by his shirt before his hand disappeared into his chest.

Turning away, I heard a rip and the thud of the male's lifeless body returned to the soil. The echoes plunged deep into the forest, bringing it back into its eerie silence.

"Dearest, look at me... Are you hurt?" Kadeyan was in front of me now, with his hand coming to my jaw and forcing me to look at him. How could I tell him I wasn't? Not by these men, but by what was coming for us all...by what lived within.

Well, turn it off and you won't have to feel it, the voice within said in an alluring tone.

"Gods damn it, Davyna... Talk to me! Tell me what's going on!" Kadeyan yelled as Calix came back into view, but he avoided looking our way.

"And say what?" I choked out as my mind traveled down the winding road of despair and complications. "I don't know what you want from me." Did he want me to be honest right now and tell him that I wished they would have finished me off? Or that him being here made me feel unworthy of his love, and all I could do was push him away in hope that it would protect him?

He let go of my face and stood tall. "Calix, leave us." Calix didn't say a word as his shadows shot out and devoured him whole, leaving me and Kade in the woods. "I'm trying to give you space, but that clearly isn't working. So, tell me, what's going on?"

I rose from the ground and began walking. The tears returned, blurring my vision. "I'm not dragging you into my mess. I need to—"

His hand wrapped around my arm, turning me around to face him. His eyes beamed a dark crimson as he leaned in, tightening his grip on me. "You know what I need? The whole damn story!"

For a moment, everything faded as I looked at him. His pupils dilated, fixating on me and I wanted— No, felt pulled to tell him the truth. To free myself from the agony I was carrying. I wanted to, more than anything, because he of all people deserved the story of what happened.

I took a deep breath and battled with myself as the words tried crawling up my throat. His gaze softened, like he could tell I was trying, and I began to open my mouth...

My eyes caught on something in the distance before the weight of that power dragged me back down, silencing me so deep, I became hollow.

Shadows snaked out towards us, and I heard his deep voice penetrate my mind, just like he spoke to me in my nightmare. *"Go ahead, little cinder... Watch how fast I remove his head from his body."*

My stomach turned and I realized I was about to sign his death warrant because I was being selfish. Because I didn't want to carry this weight alone anymore. My mouth closed and I narrowed my eyes on Kadeyan.

"I have no fucking clue what I did to the throne! And maybe everyone is right...I'm the problem here."

"Who fucking said that to you? I'll rip their tongues out of—"

"Stop! Don't you see... I am! I fucked up! Do you think any of this would be happening if I never came to Valyner?" My eyes snapped back to the shadows behind him, slithering back into the tails of night...and I realized Kadeyan never felt them. He never even turned. And that selfish part of me wished he did so I didn't have to be isolated, but I was. And I needed to accept that.

Kade went silent. I pulled my arm free of him and began

walking again, each step breaking my heart a little more. I could feel his frustration and love collide, making this so much harder.

"Why did you deny our bond?" he asked quietly, and it forced me to stop.

I didn't turn, but I knew he would hang on to every word I was going to say next. It didn't help that the shadow figure's threat was echoing in my mind, and I knew I needed to hold onto that to make sure Kade kept on breathing.

Maybe there was an alternate reality where we were happy, had a child of our own, and really got to fall in love with one another... But that wasn't the one we were in. This one came with difficulties, secrets, and never-ending questions. Like, if he ever loved me for me...or because the bond told him to?

With the power looming close by—watching my every move—and my own fatal sorrow building, I snapped.

"You want to know why? Because I didn't choose this! I didn't want this, us... So, drop it." The words darted out, blazing into his chest before snapping back and hitting me. I didn't want to deny him... I just needed time. And now, I was trying to save his life, but it seemed I was going to lose him either way by the end of this. I would rather him hate me and be alive than...

The demonic voice snickered in my mind, and I shook my head.

"You should have left me in the Mortal Realm... Left me human," I whispered.

I went to take another step, but my body was ripped back into his arms, while he held me in a bruising grip. "We're doing this my way now."

We landed on the terrace, the stone arches as I remembered with the dark sky on full display above. Kadeyan walked away to the edge, overlooking the eerie night as I tried to muster the strength to stand taller. The silence between us was palpable, begging to be broken, and it made me recoil.

I never wanted to be alone. I feared it, but maybe that was what I needed in this life. To be utterly alone to protect the ones I loved.

Looking over at him, I readied myself to apologize when I saw a blade flying towards me. I dropped to the ground. The metal pierced into one of the stone arches, sending an echo of cracking rock around us before I looked up. The sword was shaking back and forth from the impact as I heard his boots scuff against the stone ground, coming near me.

"You want to fight? Then let's fight." His voice was threatening, making me turn in time to see another blade in his hands strike down next to me. I pushed to the side, watching the blade cut into the stone where I just was.

"What the fuck, Kade?" I yelled as I backed up more, but he ignored me, moving towards me with the determination of a dark god. He struck again, forcing me to put up a barrier, and I screamed out from the impact.

My heart pounded in my chest as I looked at the anger held in his eyes, along with heartache, but that wasn't all. There was joy, too, swirling around him as he fell into his game of being the predator, and I was his prey. His shadows poured out, pressing down on the barrier until the weight of his power began crushing it.

I couldn't concentrate on him as fragments of the shield started to fracture, granting him entry to my tiny sanctuary from his fury. As the barrier broke, he swung the blade from the side, coming straight for my head, and I sucked in a sharp breath.

Jumping into the gap, I reappeared next to the blade that was stuck in the stone and pulled it free. Fear flooded my body as I felt Kadeyan from behind, completely unhinged. His sword clashed with mine, almost knocking it free from my hands, and I backed away.

"You always did like playing with *your* Devil." He laughed, throwing his shadows out towards me, and I threw up a wall of flames. I watched him move around, looking through the blaze with his wicked grin, and nothing in it promised me peace, only destruction. "Aw, is the poor human girl still in there? Want me to rip her out?"

My eyes narrowed on his. Anger flooded my entire being, and my power rushed to the surface. I pushed the wall of flames towards him, the power booming around us and causing my skin to heat. It was tainted in a darkness celebrating within and telling me to let more out...to end him. His wings pulled him up into the night, before vanishing.

A minute passed as I walked forward and my blood started to boil, waiting... I focused on our bond, sensing him coming near. I turned, pulling my sword out in time to stop his blade. Pushing him back, I hoped to catch him off guard and send him stumbling away, but it did little to move his solid form. It only fueled him, swinging with more power and more determination to break me.

Metal was ringing out and echoing into the mountains beyond the terrace as the sweat formed on my forehead. Although, he continued to move in, giving me little time to recover. He was ruthless in his attack, yet every move was exuding control because he was a seasoned warrior.

Unlike me, who had never been to battle, except for fighting off the Cursed and the humans when I killed Persephone. I might be fast and calculated with my moves, but I didn't fight like him.

I stepped back as he moved in. I went to turn out of the way, but I was too slow and the steel cut into my arm. I hissed, looking at the wound where grey blood flowed down. He paused, taking in the color as his eyes started to beam a deep crimson.

In that moment, I knew my own were doing the same, which caused him to smile. Turning away, that dark part within came alive, relishing in the sting of the wound and wanting more. I threw the blade to the ground, watching it bounce off the stone, before turning back to face him. I knew the smile on my face was twisted, but he didn't retreat... He looked pleased.

"You shouldn't fight with me... Neither one of us knows what I am capable of..." Each word that fell from my lips was laced in a warning, not only to him, but to myself.

He moved in, gripping me by my throat until no air could enter, and lust began to swirl between us. My feet left the ground as I grabbed onto his hand, looking deep into his eyes with a smile.

"Then give me your worst." He smirked, bringing his wicked charm to the surface.

I didn't fight him, allowing my lungs to burn before every emotion and life of power rushed to the surface. Everything within sang out, until the melodies of death led me through their dance of horrors.

My lungs screamed out, but I stayed still as I silently chanted a spell to boil his blood, mouthing the words as I yelled them within my mind. I watched his face turn from wicked joy to agonizing pain as it ripped through him, pulling groans from his lips. His hand began to loosen its grip and I sucked in air.

Pulling my feet up, I pressed out and kicked him in the chest, sending him stumbling back.

I landed on the ground, bringing one knee down as my head shot up to see him regain his footing and fighting the spell. He rushed me and I rolled to the side before lifting my hand. Water filled his lungs, causing him to stall. The demons within praised me, and I sent more power out, until he dropped to his knees with water pouring from his lips.

Getting up, I moved over to him, watching him struggle to breathe when his shadows lashed out and grabbed both of my hands, breaking my hold. His shadows pulled me down to the ground and my face scraped into the stone, drawing blood that made me instantly smell iron.

Kadeyan was quick, gripping me by my hair and pulling me up to face him. His shadows entered my body. Traveling at lightning speed, they surrounded my heart, and I gasped at the pain. The pressure built, making me cough as fear filled my eyes.

"How does it feel to have someone crush your heart?"

"Stop!" I yelled as screams rang out of me, the dark power faltering within as I took in his words.

"Make me!" he growled before squeezing again, causing venom to pulse through my veins. And anger grew within, consuming the pain I felt.

Focusing through the agony, I looked back to him, and he scooted back in...fear? The world blurred around me, and I broke his hold surrounding my heart before shifting into my wolf form. I let out a growl that sounded feral and sent an echo through the Lands.

Kadeyan stopped and braced his body to stay in place, letting his arms widen and welcoming me to devour him. "Let the demons out to play, little Ember. I'll still kick your ass."

CHAPTER 18
KADEYAN

Davyna accepted my challenge and leaped from the ground, colliding with my body. Her eyes that beamed red in her wolf form were gone and were now encased in a chilling darkness. My body slammed into the ground, but I could care less about the impact, or how my bones ached. All I cared about was what she was going through.

I stood still as her teeth snapped at my face and let out a growl that made even my shadows within shake, but I forced them out. They wrapped around her and broke her focus, causing her to shift back. Her hand darted out, grabbed onto my throat, and tightened it with all her strength, and damn, she had a lot more now since she got back home.

Her tendrils of black smoke entered me and I followed, copying her every move as our shadows rushed to each other's hearts. We both paused, holding each other's lives in our hands. Her black and silver eyes stared down at my chest, waiting and smirking as if she was trying to decide if she truly wanted to kill me.

I stood still, not showing her any emotion, even though I couldn't stop wondering why her power was like this now. Even her shadows matched my own when she was in this state. Her eyes flickered back and forth for a moment before her shadows retreated, and I did the same.

Those silver pools looked back at me, but I could see her fear... her regret weighing them down. I lifted my hand, tucking her hair behind her ear as I softened my gaze on her, and she leaned into my touch like it was a safety net pulling her out of the rough seas of her mind. I would always be that for her… Couldn't she see that?

"You were born fae, Dearest. It's who you are. And I never want to hear you say that shit again." I sat up, pulling her closer until her legs settled on each side of me.

"Is this normal though? This raging power…the darkness." She glanced down, taking in the shimmering scars on her hand that were now void of their darkened hues.

I took a moment to study her, holding back the fact that no one had ever shown signs of what she presented, but she wasn't a normal fae. "You are the daughter of an Untouched fae. It comes with the territory."

"You went through this too?" Her eyes widened, and I could hear the hope in her voice, causing me to laugh.

"Of course, in different ways than you…but I've had 1,500 years to control it. You just need time." Her shoulders dropped a few inches and the tension eased in her body.

Her head fell, and I brought my hand up, bringing her gaze back to mine. "I can handle anything you throw at me. Give me all of your darkness. All your pain… Let me fucking drown in it until my black heart gives out."

Her lip quivered before she placed both hands on my face, and my own body relaxed into her touch. "Your heart isn't black… I don't think it ever was." Her forehead met mine and my heart swelled in my chest, beating harder.

"I don't think I can do this without you…" she whispered, and while I wanted to press her for what that was, I soaked in the words she willingly gave. Because I knew with what was to come with fixing the throne, this realm, and beyond…I couldn't do anything without her. I needed her in my life, like I needed blood in my veins. Without it, I was nothing but a shell.

"You will never have to. I'm here…"

Our scents began to swirl around one another, caressing each part of my body. She leaned into me, and at least there was still one thing I could pick up on…her desire. Lifting us off the ground, I held her to my chest as her legs wrapped around me, before I slammed her body against one of the stone arches.

Pulling back, I ripped her top, pulling the air from her lungs, before I dropped to my knees and did the same with her pants. Her skin pebbled up for a moment before the heat within her warded off the chill, but her nipples stood in perfect peaks, causing my mouth to water.

"Watch me, Dy. I want to remind you how much I love worshipping at your altar." Her eyes stayed on me as my tongue slowly dragged up her center, flicking her clit. A moan slipped from her lips, and I did it again, and again, watching her melt into me.

"Fuck... Kadeyan..." she said in a breathy voice, while working her fingers into my hair.

I licked and sucked on her, savoring her taste as my dick swelled past the point of pain. *I needed her.* Nothing else mattered in that moment. It was just her and me.

Glancing up, her head fell back as her eyes closed and I dropped her legs. Her eyes widened, and I knew her pussy was aching for release, but I moved in, taking her by the throat. "Do I need to remind you what happens when you don't listen to me?" She fucking smiled at me, and it took everything in me not to bend her over my knee. I took in her naked body as her small breaths grew heavier. "You're going to regret that."

Shooting into the sky, the rush of wind stabbed into my flesh, but I refused to slow. Davyna wrapped her arms around my neck, shielding her face in my chest as I flew up to the highest peak of the mountains, where an open mine of dark obsidian laid below us. I took a deep breath and glanced down at the darkness, hoping this would help her see that I would always be there for her...no matter the cost to me.

I came to a stop, my wings beating through the air to keep us still. My hand went between her legs, and she willingly parted them, giving me access to do what I pleased.

Slipping two fingers into her wet cunt, I curled them and worked my way in and out, ripping more moans from her lips. I could tell she was getting close as she dug her nails into my chest, cutting right through the leathers. "Do you trust me?"

She looked into my eyes, and for the first time since she came back to me, I saw her... "With my life..."

"Then don't use your magic..." I picked up the pace, forcing her pussy to tighten around my fingers until they could barely move. Curses fell from her lips as she came around me, and I did the hardest thing... I let her go.

Her body fell through the air as I stood still, waiting for those silver eyes to look back at me.

One...two...three...

Her eyes opened and I breathed in, but I kept my cold expression as she realized she was falling. A gasp ripped from her lungs as she turned, seeing the mine below with jagged obsidian waiting for her. It took everything in me to stay still as I felt the bond compelling me to get her out. To keep her realms away from danger, but that was the thing...I couldn't. I couldn't lock her away and keep her safe. I had to show her that I was here and she wasn't alone.

Using the gap, I hovered above the toxic stones and my power faltered from being so close as she fell into my arms. Forcing all the magic within me out before it completely neutralized my abilities, I pulled us into the gap, and landed back on the terrace.

My muscles burned as I recovered, and I glanced at her. "Good fucking girl," I said as I brushed the hair back from her face, but the eyes staring off, void of emotion made me worry. Was she upset that I did that? Or was she upset that I stopped it from happening?

I couldn't help but think it was the latter.

Turning her to face me, I held onto her face until her eyes were solely focused on me. "There is nothing in this world that would keep me from being there for you, Davyna." Her eyes started to glisten in the muted moonlight. "You are not alone anymore."

Before a tear could fall from her eyes, she moved in, capturing my mouth, and I fell into the chaos of her kiss. Death might offer us some semblance of peace, and life might be suffering...but I wouldn't want death without her by my side. Or to suffer in this life without her.

"What's my prize?" she asked, bringing her mouth back down on mine as she rocked her hips into me.

Fuck, this girl... My clothes vanished from my body, and I growled as I slammed her down onto the rough stone. I leaned in, wanting to drink her in, but hesitated... Her blood had changed. What would happen now if I drank from her?

She arched into me, and that was all it took for my fangs to dart out and sink into her neck.

Her blood tasted different, and it shocked me, but I couldn't deny that it was like drinking down life and death at the same time. My blood felt as if it was charged by a bolt of lightning, sending power through my veins in a flash, and it was fucking amazing. So sweet, with a hint of darkness that made my cock pulse and almost come.

Letting go, it took everything in me to not come on her chest as I lowered my body to her entrance. She moaned as I slid into her, and her heat mixed with her blood in my veins made me lose control. I fucked her hard, hearing her skin scrape into the stone, but I was feral, chasing my release. I brought my shadows out, circling her clit as I pinned her arms down above her head, thrusting into her and savoring how my body began to heat.

Davyna's walls tightened, and I watched her melt into the ground as her pussy pulsed. I followed after her, pouring every last drop inside. I fell forward, resting my weight on her as my breathing tried to settle, but fuck, it wouldn't.

Rolling to the side, my back connected with the cold stone, but it did little to bring me down from the high she gave me.

We sat there for a few minutes, taking in the stars above, when Davyna jolted up.

"Fuck!" she yelled, and as I looked her over, any lingering aftereffects dissipated. Her hand darted up to her neck, grasping onto her father's stone.

"What is it?" I asked, tilting my head.

“I don’t know… My necklace…it felt like it burned me.”

Moving my hand in, I went to take it from her hands and cursed myself. It was blazing, even making my own flesh hurt and turn red.

My eyes looked back at her chest, and I stopped breathing. That wasn’t possible. She was burned. A perfect oval seared into her chest, and it wasn’t fading… At least, not quickly. “What the fuck?”

“I thought Embers couldn’t burn?” she asked, turning to face me.

“They can’t…”

We both sat there for a moment in the dead of night, but the concern in her eyes faded as hope filled them.

“Don’t the stones hold secrets from the Untouched fae?” She thought this was a sign from her father, but his essence wasn’t in there anymore. And from what I knew, the secrets within would never try to make themselves known to an offspring… Not like that.

Her chest began to heal, but my stomach was still in a knot. Before she could mutter another word, I picked her up and began walking into the castle. She leaned her head against me and stared into her father’s stone as if it was her deliverance—her answer to something I still had no clue of.

Yet, I experienced no relief, only apprehension for the transformation occurring inside her. Maybe I was overreacting, but something deep within my bones was unleashed the day she disappeared, devouring me in a sea of horror. With everything that was going on inside her now, I couldn’t help but think of the worst-case scenario resulting in me losing her again. And I refused to back down until I knew exactly what this meant.

CHAPTER 19

Davyna

Blinding white light consumed my vision, causing my heart to speed up. It was similar to my doppelganger's power, and every fiber in my body stood on end. Did I accidentally end up back there? Or did they pull me back?

Jumping, I turned to see Nesrin's hand on my shoulder, giving me a gentle smile. "You ready?" she asked, and I swallowed hard before nodding my head.

Turning, I took in the Sky Court's temple, beaming as bright as ever under the searing sun.

Last night, Kade and I went to see Levanna about my father's stone, and like I suspected, it could hold secrets. Secrets that were trying to get my attention. Kadeyan didn't look comforted by all this, but for me, it gave me a sliver of hope. What if my parents knew about this? Did that mean there was more they kept from me?

I tried not to linger on that sting of resentment building in my gut, but I couldn't deny that it was there. Another thing they possibly kept from me...and for what purpose?

"Come on, you two. Maeve and Faelynn are waiting," Levanna shouted back at us as she approached the two enormous doors that began to open and welcome us in.

Picking up my feet, I followed after her, and my eyes scanned over the library. The fae moved around much like they did before—in silence and with books stacked in their hands and veils concealing their faces.

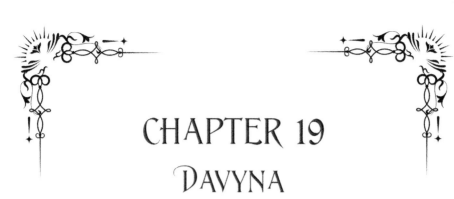

I walked to the banister and looked down, taking in the levels alternating between light and dark, a perfect representation of magic in these lands. A balance. I took a slow breath in and as I began to exhale, my hands started to tingle. The sensation was mild—strange even—reminding me how they buzzed in Elias' office or in the library at the Crescent Court. Yet, it wasn't the same. This felt more distant, as if it was worlds away.

The feeling vanished as Levanna called out, "We have to go up."

I lingered for another moment, taking in the depths below, and got lost in the mystery of what was calling out to me. Was there anything down there or was my power surging within?

Shaking it off, I turned and took wide strides until I caught up with Nesrin and Levanna.

We went up multiple levels, spinning around in a circle as my mind did the same. Last time I came here, we ventured down into the book-filled walls of the library, but this was nothing like that. Each level we passed held luminous white halls with ebony doors, which I assumed were sleeping quarters or rooms used for meetings. The faint sounds emanating from below subsided with every ascending level, eventually leaving nothing but the rhythm of my own heart pounding within.

As we approached the last staircase, I took in the ceiling curving to create the dome of the temple. Before us was a small set of stairs, leading to a door that was half black and the other white. A fusion of light and dark magic. And I couldn't help but stare at them, lost in a trance for a moment.

Climbing the staircase, I pondered the simplicity with which one was labeled good and evil... Or, at least, that was how the humans viewed it. Light would always represent virtuous morals, while darkness would mirror a wicked soul.

In Valyner, there were light Courts and dark ones. So, where did that leave me? Because I was both...and there were no shades of grey here. Unless you counted the blood coursing through my veins...

As we approached the door, it swung open, revealing an Acolyte dressed in all white, with a gold crown holding their veil in place.

"Please, come in," he said as he moved aside, letting his hand go out wide to welcome us.

As I stepped in behind Nesrin and Levanna, I slowed down, taking in the room. It was circular and split down the middle, matching the door we entered through. The left side beamed light, with unblemished bookshelves and a white couch. On the right, it was set up the same, but consumed in shadows.

It was like having day and night in one room.

Looking up, I saw swirls working their way through the ceiling like snakes. Gold glistened down onto the light side as if the sun was captured within, giving a warmth to the air. But as the swirls slithered past the contracting line, they became silver, like the moon softly glowed down on the darkness.

"Thank you, Xorn." Maeve's voice caused me to look down, and I took her in without her veil at the gold desk with Faelynn by her side. Behind them held a breathtaking view of the mountains on full display, and it was hard to pull my gaze from it, basking in the serenity it held.

Maeve grabbed a stack of papers and tapped them against the desk, aligning them before offering them to Xorn. "Could you check in on our newest members to make sure they are ready for the ritual coming up?" She gave him a gentle smile as he took them from her and bowed, before summoning his snowy mist to take him away.

"Well, shall we get started?" Faelynn asked. Her black eyes connected with mine as she moved my way.

The door swung open, slamming into the wall and causing me to jump. Turning, I was met with amber eyes staring back at me.

"Now we can start," he said as he closed the door behind him.

He was gone early this morning, leaving a note by my head that said he had to go deal with some soldiers. I couldn't help but think it had to do with the men that attacked me last night and how they got past the Fallen patrols. This was the second time. Were there more out there, planning their revenge? Or did they think that if they succeeded in killing me, this would stop?

Would it?

I didn't want to fall back into that thought, because if Kade hadn't caught me last night before my body pierced into the obsidian...I felt okay with that fate. A small part of me was glad he couldn't get into my mind right now, because I never wanted to share that with anyone.

But if my death didn't fix this for the fae, I don't think I could find peace in what life came after this. Their blood would continue to stain my hands...and I didn't want any more spilled.

It's so much fun though... You should try doing it more.

Ignoring the demon within, I watched as Kadeyan moved into the room and made himself comfortable in the chair on the dark side.

"Davyna, let me see your father's stone." Maeve moved around her desk.

I gripped the stone in my hand, eager for the answers it held within. I respelled it to my neck after I gave it to Levanna, still wary to be without it. Pulling at the clasp, I whispered the spell until the chain fell from my neck. I placed it in her waiting palm, and her fingers curled around it.

"What do you know about the stones?" I asked.

"The same thing you know...and maybe a little more." My cousin smiled at me as she looked it over. "Faelynn, could you help me?" They both stood in the center of the room, joining hands to encase the stone. They didn't speak, but an ashen glow began wrapping around their hands.

After a few minutes passed, the power ceased to pulse into the room, and they both looked down at it. Faelynn looked at me, her lips slightly parted, and while the darkness in her eyes couldn't show me her emotions, I felt it: shock.

"When the stone is passed down into an offspring's hand and holds something they need, the stones can send out a burst of magic to get their attention." Maeve finally said as she placed it back in my hand. "But it's usually not by harming them. Maybe it had to push harder to break through to you."

"Maybe?" Kadeyan said, rising from the chair, his voice drenched in concern. "What if it decides to..." He paused and Levanna walked over to him, placing her hand on his arm.

"It won't harm her." Faelynn said.

"How do you know that?" He pulled his arm free.

She tilted her head in his direction, smiling. "That stone holds energy I know...from Anawyn." We all stopped, looking at her. She turned and faced me. "I told you once that I wanted to bring the stories lost to time to life again... Would you like to hear about them?" How was that possible? How was the energy in this stone tied to one of the other fae realms?

"Why now?" Levanna asked.

"Because that power is here..." Faelynn claimed and Kadeyan's eyes darkened. "I didn't understand until now. The magic from the creatures coming here was obviously coming in from Anawyn and Gelmyra, but now I think I know why."

"Why?" I asked, my throat tightening.

"I think they want that." She pointed towards the stone. "Maybe the six Untouched fae of their realms are spelling the creatures to pass over and get them all. Valyner is at its most vulnerable state right now, and I think they are taking advantage of it, but I don't think they can pass themselves, or they would have by now," Faelynn said softly as she moved over to the desk. She leaned against it and clasped her hands over her black gown, contrasting against her colorless skin and hair.

Meeting my gaze, she continued. "I was a crone in my world... from the Sage Court. We are made up of a female Court, viewing ourselves as the sisters of sight." She shook her head, grinning. "There are some males, but they don't hold the power like us, and we are expected to procreate to further our Court's magic with more female heirs.

"All my sisters had sight once—to see the world in color and all the beauty it held. But when we became of age, we had to make a choice: To lose our sight and *see* in a new way...or only live with our core ability."

"What are your core abilities?" I asked.

She smiled in amusement as she tilted her head towards Kade. "I can make you feel peace and horror in one thought. I can make you see life in all its beauty or take it away and make you only see death. And, depending on the person's aura, I give them the reality they deserve."

"You know, Faelynn, it's not nice to do that when I'm joking with you." Kadeyan laughed.

"Yes…well, I was hoping it would teach you a lesson. Or maybe I just find it entertaining to watch your aura emulate fear." She winked and turned to face me. "But once we lost our sight, we could see and remember everything in history. Along with anything we learned along the way." She moved in, running her fingers over my hand, and touched the stone again. "I have held this before…"

"You met my father?"

She shook her head. "Yes…but he wasn't the one who brought this to me… It was your mother." She joined her hands together as she stepped back, glancing down for a moment before meeting my gaze.

Stunned and unable to speak, my body went still as I looked into her soulless eyes.

She continued. "She wanted me to search for the strongest protection spell, since I traveled and studied the other Realms prior to the veils going up."

"You were helping my…mother." The room began to spin, and I backed away. Kadeyan moved in, leading me to the chair as I sunk down into it.

"Yes…it was a little over twenty-five human years ago. Actually, almost twenty-six now."

"What happened?" Levanna asked, her voice small. "I mean—"

"I know what you mean, my dear. The veil was placed between our Realms in the early days we were all created because war was brewing between the Realms. After the King here used his power to curse his own kind, it created a ripple effect."

Dropping my head, I tried to steady my breathing as she continued.

"Valyner's power has always been greater. Well, until this happened." Her lips pulled down slightly, her brows furrowing. "It made Gelmyra and Anawyn jealous with rage to conquer them, and to possess the power that was given to them by *their* gods."

"What makes us so different from them?" Kadeyan asked.

"Those stones. They are an energy source that was given to help the Untouched fae, but if they were to fall into the other Realms' hands...they could use that power in other ways."

My mother... She wanted something in this stone to stay hidden...something that only I would see.

"Do you know what's in it? How do I open it?" I asked as I rose, pushing away the spiraling thoughts about how Faelynn was connected to this.

"I do not know what the stone holds. My job was simply to find the spell that could keep what was held within secured."

Maeve crossed her arms over her chest, before moving over to me. "Opening it is usually simple. There is a totem that acts like a key, but for you and the power you hold, I think you could open it yourself. And if your mother was anything like your father, they would have both wanted it that way."

"What do we do about the other Courts' stones?" Levanna asked.

"Inform the Court fae to keep them protected at all costs. Along with this one," Faelynn said as she gestured towards it. "Once the tear in the veil is closed, all of this will stop. Those were gifts to your kind from the gods above. Why they want them, though, is knowledge I don't know... Other than speculating they want information and to possibly channel the power that made them to wipe this realm out of existence."

My stomach turned. This was so much bigger than I thought it could be, but it was at least taking us a step forward. "Faelynn, can you help me channel the magic?" I asked as I stood, holding up the stone.

"That's the thing... The spell that was placed long ago faded when it ended up in your hands, Davyna. It was meant to find you, and only you. I just didn't know it at the time." She turned to face my cousin. "Maybe Maeve could help you channel your power since you are blood."

Agreeing, I moved forward again, wanting what was in there so I could put this to bed. To not have creatures that were from another realm come here and kill us all, or another fae here fall ill to the toxic magic.

Maeve took my hand, and I focused on the stone, begging it to open to me. Maeve's power flowed into my veins, amplifying the energy for me to focus on the beaming red light coming into view. I could feel it working, pulling me further into the stone, but the color fell away and flashes of the world beyond pulled me in. I saw the castle, the onyx lake...and then her. Always my doppelganger.

Maeve's hand gripped my wrist hard, and my eyes shot open, seeing her eyes swirling with a milky sheen. I stood still, hearing Maeve's voice sound off loudly in my mind just outside the walls protecting my psyche.

"*You will fall. You will die.*"

Yelling, images flashed in a blur. They all held pain and suffering, and it cracked something within. I pulled my hand back, dropping the stone, and stared into her eyes that were changing back.

"What the fuck was that?" Kadeyan growled as he looked at her.

"I–I'm not sure..." She swallowed hard as her eyes landed on me before forcing a smile for everyone around us. "Are you okay, Davyna?"

My breathing was uneven as I gazed to the stone and back to her. "I'm fine..."

"Levanna, Nesrin," Faelynn called out. "Would you both accompany me in the library to retrieve some books I need?" They both nodded and moved to the door before looking back at me, Maeve, and Kade. "Kadeyan, you should come too," she said, but he was unmoving.

Turning, I faced him as Maeve walked around her desk, lost in thought. "Go. I'll be right there," I stated.

After a long minute passed, he looked down at me, the concern melting from his eyes.

The room fell silent as the door clicked, and I took in the fear rising from Maeve as she stared out at the mountains. Moving in, I grabbed onto her arm and ripped her into the gap away from any prying ears within the temple. It was clear that whatever she witnessed in her vision made sense to her. And she was going to tell me.

CHAPTER 20

Davyna

Landing on the edge of the mountain, I took in the trees bending over us like a blanket, and I realized this was where Akari took me to tell me about my father. About my mother... But the nostalgia faded as I turned and took in Maeve.

"What just happened?"

"I have no idea... But it was like the magic you used on the throne. Strong, unbreakable."

"What did you see?" I asked, moving closer to her.

"It was strange... The world was void of color. I could see some shimmering hues in the sun...and in a door of maybe a castle. And then you...in pain."

I turned around, running my hands through my hair. How was she able to see it, but Kadeyan couldn't?

"Was that where you were?" she asked with worry coating her tone. My eyes pinched together, still not wanting to give those memories life by speaking it. Or worse...making my cousin a target. And yet, she saw it... So, did that make her one? "Davyna, I'm so sorry..."

My mind began to spin with one main thing glaring at me like the beaming sun above. My mother. "What does this mean? Was my mother from somewhere else and not one of the Cursed? Does that mean part of me isn't from Valyner?"

"This is your home, Davyna," she said, moving over to the bench where her mother sat not too long ago. "My mother's visions of you, your father, and your mother were clear. You were their daughter." I moved over, letting my body fall to the bench.

"What about my mother though? Is it possible she is from one of the other fae realms?"

She stared off into the thick trees lining the walk path, her eyes holding a dense fog for a long moment as if she was scanning through the past. "She had our abilities. She was Cursed. My mother shared what she saw of her with me at a young age so I would know. But maybe her bloodline tied back to one of those Realms... I didn't have a deep connection with her." She turned, her silver eyes colliding with mine. "I saw you mostly...even with my own magic covered."

"Your mother hid you? Why?"

"From Persephone. She was growing more in power, and someone we knew said they overheard her plans to kill all the Court fae to replace them with their children or who she saw fit. My mother had a close friend who stood before Persephone on that day, mirroring herself to look exactly like my mother." She paused, closing her eyes for a moment. "She sacrificed her life so that my mother could live longer to help you find your parents and for me to take my title."

She could mirror someone? Was that the same magic the creature used?

"How was she able to do that?"

"Magic that wasn't from this realm... I'm guessing fae in Anawyn can do it since Faelynn is from there and she helped us with the spell," she said before standing and moving to the railing to overlook the mountains surrounding us.

"Faelynn has never shared anything about her realm until today...and it makes sense. She was the one who told us about that magic. It took ten Sky members to siphon her power and replicate it to make Alysia appear as my mother. And they couldn't break the circle during the spell until they felt Alysia's essence pass on."

The magic she spoke of made me think of all the unknowns still at work in this treacherous game I was playing... I couldn't help but think about how the throne was the centerpiece, at least to those other beings I met. Maybe they wanted the stones, too, but they wanted something else first...

"Tell me about the throne. What have you gathered from it?"

"All I know is the magic you expelled on it is not from here and *is,* all at the same time. You hold every element of our realm, and I think that's what makes it complicated, because no one has ever held this much power."

"My mother did..." I looked down, hesitation coating my tongue because, from what I knew, the Cursed loved my mother... They looked to her as a beacon of hope and followed her. Yet, people feared me.

Maybe it was because I was something more than what my mother was, and I was here—in Valyner—whereas my mother never stepped foot on these lands.

Taking a deep, shaky breath, I looked over at my cousin. "What does that make me?"

"I think it means you are the only one who can seal up the tear. And I have a sense that whatever your father has stored away in that stone will help you with it. Anything else beyond that doesn't change that you are fae...that you are my family."

We don't need family. We need fire and blood... We need to set ourselves free and do as we please.

A chill ran down my spine as I glanced down at my hand, seeing the black creep down through the scars. "*No!*" I yelled back at the voice in my head, hoping to put the demon in its place.

I felt like I was living with a voice of reason and chaos within, pulling me back and forth until one claimed my soul. And it was getting harder each passing day with the vile thoughts blaring inside my mind.

You forget, I am you...and I wouldn't suggest it if you weren't already thinking it. And you are. Deep down in the pit of your soul. A laugh rattled within, making pain bloom against my skull. *I'll break you... You'll see my way is so much better.*

My blood began to boil as I looked over at Maeve, refusing the voice once again because I wouldn't do those things. I wasn't going to break.

"I'll fix it, Maeve... I'll fix it all. No matter what."

CHAPTER 21
DAVYNA

The scent of pine delivered a sense of tranquility as my eyelids slowly lifted, struggling to bring the environment around me into sharp focus. The feeling reminded me of training with Elias in the forest, or when I was protected from Alastair's attack, and being around Kadeyan. Always him.

I rolled over, the rough forest floor scratching into my skin before I shot up. My eyes scanned over the woods holding me captive as brush fell from my arms.

Where was I?

Standing, I wiped the rest of the dirt off my skin and nightgown as I looked around at the trees stretching up into the sky. Something familiar washed over me, like I'd been here so many times before. I picked up my feet and began to move east, looking around at the desolate grounds muted in a dull grey hue.

After a few minutes, I made it onto the path I traveled more times than I could count to go into town and back to the Foster estate. A smile pulled up on my lips for a moment, remembering Elias before the reality of what life became after he was taken by a wolf... The shell of a person I became, hiding behind every wall I constructed from the ground up to keep people out, and to never showcase the brokenness I held. Tears pricked at my eyes at the thought, but I pushed them aside and moved on.

Walking towards the estate, I looked around at the dusty grey ambiance of the Mortal Realm growing with intensity, which wasn't normal. Why did it look like death touched every inch of these lands?

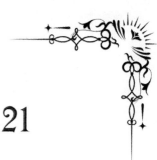

My heart sounded off like a drum, traveling up to my ears as I reminded myself to keep breathing.

Why was I here again?

Was the void my father created calling me back? Was he still in there? No...he was gone. It wasn't possible.

As I got closer to the opening of the forest where my old house was, a faint blue glow appeared before me, creating a silhouette of a body. I paused, every muscle within locking up as the figure turned to face me. Blinking a few times, I tried to make sense of what I was seeing, but my eyes weren't playing tricks on me.

The ghost-like figure had no face.

Nodding its head, it turned back around and began to move deeper into the woods, away from the house. I tried to take in its silhouette, wondering if it was someone I knew, but no one came to mind. However, I could tell based on its form, it was a female.

Pausing, the figure looked over her shoulder once more to see if I was coming. My feet fused to the ground and trembles racked through my body, forcing my gaze to look around again. The air was getting colder by the second with the gloomy lands turning more colorless. We were still alone, but a looming energy nearby told me to follow her. I wanted to fight it, but it felt different as it grew between us. Not feeling of war...but of ease.

"Come..." *said the figure in a soft, distorted tone before rushing through the woods like a bolt of lightning.*

Something in that voice forced me forward. I moved fast through the trees, watching the glow weave its way through the trunks like it knew where each one was placed by heart. Was she from here? Pushing myself to run faster, my breath shortened the closer I got to it, while the cold air coated my lungs like thick smoke.

Stumbling to a stop, I looked around at the opening of the forest, dressed with overgrown vines and bushes holding no color. I kept my distance from her as she moved towards the thicker vined area with such grace, her long, flowing hair touching the small of her back.

I went to speak—to ask her who she was and where we were—but she turned, facing me. The air vanished from my lungs, taking the questions away with the next chilling breeze.

She turned back, walking through the bushes and vines, not moving them an inch. Her hand rose, a blue light pulling them down and exposing an opening to the cave she was nestled in.

Tilting my head, I took a few steps forward, but hesitation held me back from her and the growing urge to figure out this new mystery unfolding before me. She entered the cave, not looking back to see if I would follow. The glow she illuminated vanished, leaving me surrounded by the deathly world I once knew as my home.

Shit...

Before I could talk myself out of it, I picked up my feet. Part of me felt like she wasn't a threat, but the curiosity of what this meant truly drove me forward. I made my way through the brush, the branches scraping into my skin as their dry whispers echoed into the hushed forest.

Hissing through my teeth, I pushed through. Stopping before the opening, my eyes widened. The cave's tunnel was carved out in perfect precision, the stone as smooth as a still lake, drawing me in. I looked back at the forest one more time before I picked up my feet and ran after her.

Getting to the large opening in the cave, my eyes locked on the glowing blue figure standing in the middle. I stopped and looked around, seeing I was surrounded by ruby stone walls etched in symbols I'd never seen before. I moved over to the side, my heart racing as my hand ran over the symbols, and something within rose. They called out to me, shaking me to my core as if an earthquake was taking place within.

Looking back, I fastened my eyes on the faceless ghost. "What is this?"

"Answers, Davyna."

The air pulled from my lungs as I looked over the figure and moved in slowly. I took in her voice, replaying it over in my mind. It was no longer distorted, and I didn't recognize it.

"Who are you?" *Each syllable came out shaky, and I watched the figure before me ripple, letting more of the details of her form become clearer.*

Stepping in closer, my heart stalled in my chest as my jaw fell open. The blue glow shined brighter, making the walls around us illuminate as if fire from within the stone ignited. Standing a few inches from her, I watched as the light began to dull, giving me a crystal clear image of who this was. Someone I had seen before, but only in the visions Akari showed me.

How was this possible?

"Mom?"

CHAPTER 22

DAVYNA

I woke in a panic as I heard a rumble through the castle, before hearing stone fall, crashing to the ground below. My heart doubled over in my chest as I sat up and turned to see Kadeyan appear next to the bed. He was shirtless and covered in glowing crimson blood, with a sword hanging down by his side. I could see the relief in his eyes that I was okay before they hardened again on the window as another quake shook the stone walls. I jumped up, hearing screams from outside and began to focus.

We were under attack.

I used the spell to change us both into fighting leathers layered with armor before he rushed in towards me. I had no clue how many creatures they had faced over the past six months. But from his demeanor, I could have easily been fooled into believing it was the first time. Like it never dulled with time and would always promise anxiety and fear for what the outcome would be.

Kadeyan's hand wrapped around my waist before the gap swallowed us whole. In a heartbeat, we were outside on the edge of the Lands, where it dropped off with the castle to our right. Soldiers were swinging their blades at the creatures while some threw out their shadows, pulling the hearts from what looked like large bobcats.

They all had eyes that glowed an unnatural bright red, their grey fur spotted with black as their own onyx mist spun off them. Some were small, but others were larger than any fae I'd seen in wolf form.

My eyes darted around, seeing fae fall into the clearing on the side of the castle, but it was clear we were outnumbered. There were maybe one hundred of us...and five or six hundred of them.

"Davyna!" Kadeyan yelled as I looked forward, seeing one running towards me.

As it was about to lunge, it stalled for a moment, its claws ripping through the dead grass until it came to a halt. It watched me as its predatorial gaze fell, leaving its eyes blank. It felt as if something passed between us, but before I could decipher it, a blaze to my left turned it into ash. Looking over at the Ember fae with blazing red hair, he nodded before calling out, warning another fae.

Pushing the confusion aside, I ran towards two fae who were surrounded. I threw both of my hands out as grey vapor flowed out, taking down five beasts who were lunging towards them.

Flames blazed from the opposite direction, and I watched as they darted past me before seeing Ash emerge from a cloud of smoke. Her eyes were narrowed on the beasts in the distance, but it did little to hide her irises melting to create the shades of fire.

My eyes started to dart around for Kade, seeing him take on two larger beasts. His shadows crushed their necks as they let out high-pitched screams, mixing with the growls and yells still persisting around us.

Sweat stuck to his skin. His screams filled with anger, and I could feel every emotion he was keeping behind his walls. The fury, the pain, and even his worry. It brushed up against me, giving me a sliver of insight into what he was going through since I left...and returned. He was letting it all go on the battlefield, and I wondered how long until he redirected that at me for keeping the secrets I held.

More yells pulled my attention back to the fight. Just beyond him, I saw my sister. She ran full force, shifting into her wolf form as one beast lunged towards Calix who was on the ground. Sorin, already in wolf form, followed close behind her, his growl vibrating the ground.

My heart slammed against my ribs, causing my chest to tighten out of fear. I began running towards them, throwing my flames out towards the creatures who started to chase them. They darted through the air, devouring their bodies until their remains fell like snow.

Sliding to the ground, my hip dragged along the dead grass as a beast leaped into the air. I unleashed my searing flames, devouring it whole as the smell of burned fur invaded my nostrils. The ashes scattered down like heavy snowflakes, sticking to my face and melding with the beads of sweat. I sprung back up to my feet, my jaw falling open and tasting the bitterness of their remains floating in the air.

Panic surged through me as I frantically searched for my sister through the chaos, unease capturing me with each second that ticked by. A high-pitched cry rang out and I turned, seeing Evren on the ground wrestling with one of them. I readied myself to attack, running towards her.

To protect her...

I was stunned, coming to a complete stop when my sister pinned the beast to the ground, her jaw dripping with glowing red blood as the creature below her laid lifeless. Her eyes narrowed on me for a moment before running back to where Calix and Sorin were, helping them with the herd of beasts coming their way.

I stood in the madness, watching more of them flood in as fae and the creatures' screams rung out in my ears. My breathing was heavy, but the panic laced into my blood made it feel like the oxygen wasn't filling them.

Where were they coming from? Turning, I saw some climbing the walls of the castle, using their razor-sharp teeth to break through the stone.

Broken pieces came cascading down, slamming into the dead grass, and fae moved into the gap to avoid being crushed. I shot my flames out, taking out six of them, while someone else's shadows lashed out, ripping down the rest.

Turning back, I saw all my friends struggling to hold their ground as more continued to flood the lands. There wasn't enough of us to fight. They outnumbered us fifty to ten, at the very least.

I heard the growls and hisses growing as I looked behind me, seeing more crawl over the edge of the mountain that was only about twenty feet away, matching the things of nightmares as they gnashed their teeth. My blood ran cold, and I stumbled back a few steps, trying to think of a plan.

And only one came to mind...

"Kadeyan! Get everyone in the air!" I yelled, hoping whatever was in me would listen to the call and keep the darkness at bay. I looked over my shoulder, watching him kill another before looking to me, his gaze dark. "NOW!"

An understanding passed between us; that I was about to burn them all, and I didn't need anyone getting caught up in the inferno I was going to create.

Or you could stop fighting... Let the beasts do the dirty work for you. It would be so much easier if you stopped caring.

Shaking my head, I looked up at Kade in time to see him shoot up into the air, commanding everyone else to follow suit. The fae without wings were jumping into the gap, but Ash ran next to me. She took my hand and I looked into her gaze as she nodded. Other Embers formed a line next to us and I glanced over at them. Each one of them was coated in luminous blood, their chests rising and falling as they prepared themselves to fight.

Closing my eyes, I dropped Ash's hand and listened to the herd coming directly for us, their claws digging into the stone of the mountain as they climbed.

Power surged to life within, and it was similar to what woke the day I burned the throne. It captivated my attention, forcing my stomach to twist into a knot. It was powered by fear of the other world I was in, what was inside me, and most of all...what would happen if I failed to control it.

My mind traveled to the one place I could cling onto for hope—for determination needed in a fight—and it was centered around protecting the ones I loved. That was the only fuel I needed to focus as I let my fires build around me.

The other Embers followed suit, their hands burning bright, but mine extended past my palms, encasing my entire body. I basked in the sizzling and popping of the flames, their heat only intensifying my drive.

Closing my eyes, I listened beyond for a moment, hearing the claws dig into the dead grass as I felt it. That deep pit inside me opened, ready to unleash hell and fury. It was wild, unhinged as I tried to channel it. Each line of power within vibrated, intertwining itself into the blaze as it circled around me. My eyes snapped open and I smiled, taking in their red eyes as they all began sprinting towards us in perfect formation.

My vision flickered in and out, and the darkness began to creep in. A wicked smile graced my lips as the power within exploded and everything around me slowed. "Now!" Raising my arms, I released the sea of fire on them and the fae near me did the same.

The creatures' ear-piercing screams sang out, but it wasn't a horrid sound—it was poetic. Tainted in raw beauty as it penetrated my ears. The sound danced deep into my bones as I focused back on the flames. Each one licked at the beasts, turning them to ash, while cinders danced in the wind. The inferno fell over the edge of the mountain and continued down to where the beasts came from.

I think we both know by now, the fangs of death are in us...and we want more.

My blood ran cold as I looked around through the thick smoke mixing with the beasts' remains. The high of the kill pulsed through my veins, but also, there was the presence of that energy again from the shadow figure and his mate...my look-alike.

Swallowing down the lump in my throat, I walked over to the edge and saw the flames light up the valley below as the screams continued to sound off.

I'll keep saying it until you understand...we are one.

Growls pulled my attention back as I turned, seeing about another fifty more beasts stalking towards us as I swayed from the power I expelled.

"Drop now! Go!" Kadeyan yelled, dropping with the other Fallen soldiers and my friends. They fell into their attack and showed no mercy as they dodged the blows the beasts attempted, and took their lives one by one.

The smell of death made my blood heat, recharging something in me and causing me to look down. The scars on my hand began wavering between their iridescent white and shimmering black, and panic spiked through me.

No…not now. I fought against it, trying to keep my head clear, but pain radiated through me, stealing my breath. Stabbing agony buried deep into my skull as the voice inside my head laughed, causing me to fall to the charred grass. It was like the demon within was punishing me for not listening, holding more ground within my psyche and forcing me to bend to its will.

Kadeyan's eyes zeroed in on me as I glanced up, holding my head through the blinding pain. His shadows poured out in a wide circle, making the dark night even darker as all the beasts touched by his shadows fell.

Looking up, I took in the five large cats surrounding me, but not one hissed or growled…they just watched. I pushed my body back a few inches through the crisp grass, wincing through the pain.

"Dy!" Kadeyan yelled, running towards me. The beasts in front of me turned, becoming blood-hungry once again as they ran towards him. My eyes connected with Kade, and on instinct, my fire spun off my hands and lashed out towards their hindlegs.

The smell of burned fur assaulted my nose again as the flames consumed their bodies and caused them to fall to the ground. My stomach turned as I pushed my body back more, crying out from the pain. I stalled as my hand fell over the edge of the cliff where the creatures climbed over. I let out another yell, the agony beating against my skull like a symphony of drums.

"Davyna!" Kade yelled.

Black shadows launched out, wrapping around me and pulling me from the edge. Before I could even take my next breath, a sting seared through my shoulder as one of the beasts from below latched on, shaking its head back and forth. Kadeyan snapped its neck with his shadows and my hand darted up to grip my shoulder, my skin instantly coated in grey blood.

Dropping to his knees, he looked me over as I pulled my hand away, watching the iron liquid trail down and disappear below my black leather sleeve. "It's healing! You're going to be okay," he yelled over the dying disarray of the battle.

Two more creatures ran towards us and Kade jumped up, swinging his sword to cut the heads from both of them in one swift movement. Bright crimson flew through the air as their bodies fell, spitting blood from the arteries in their neck.

Pulling myself up, I tried to steady my body and looked over, seeing a beast run right for me. Bracing myself, it quickly halted, its claws digging into the ground. I looked it over as my power rose within to kill it, but resisted, staying still as the mountains beyond.

Our eyes were locked on each other, and something passed between us that felt unknown to me. I went to move forward, to put an end to this night, but it slowly began to lower its head...like it was bowing.

A few cries of beasts filtered through the air before it went quiet, signaling the battle was over as the eerie silence mixed with the heavy breathing of the fae. But this one was unfazed by the world surrounding us, or why they came here in the first place. It was just us. Kadeyan rushed over, lifting his sword when the creature lowered itself more.

"Kade, wait!" I yelled, making him stop his sword mere inches from its neck. Dropping to my knees, the ache in my shoulder pulsed, but I ignored it.

I moved in, hearing whimpering for a moment as if it was scared of...me. Reaching out, I hesitantly touched its fur, running my hand through the coarse hair. And slowly, it relaxed, welcoming the caress. Locking my gaze with Kadeyan's for a moment, I glanced back down at the beast, still frozen under my touch.

Standing, I looked at everyone as they stood a few feet away, shocked, and I felt my own rise into the night sky. What did this mean? "Davyna, what are you doing to it?"

"Nothing..." It came out as a whisper, but it was true.

Slowly, it lifted its head and its red eyes locked with mine again. A purr left its throat, before letting its deep pink tongue dart out, licking the top of my hand. I pulled back, watching it sit, its face no longer vicious or intent on killing us. It was like it was always a fully tamed animal.

"Okay...let me cut its head off," Kade said as the creature got up and walked over to him.

"No, wait..." I said, watching it in amazement. What did I do to make it stop?

It moved around Kadeyan, rubbing its head against his calves as it purred again. Biting back a laugh, I looked into his disapproving glare. I was still unsure what was happening, but it was like this creature and me connected somehow. Which sounded insane... So, why did it feel that way?

"What the fuck?" he said, looking down at the large cat.

Lifting from the ground, I began moving away from everyone, testing this theory to see what would happen. If it turned on me or anyone else, it would be easy to kill since it was alone now...but I didn't think it would. I snapped my fingers as I turned around and the little creature ran to me, taking a seat next to my feet.

Calix took a few steps forward through the crowd of soldiers, looking from me to the cat. "Damn! What else can you do, Your Grace?" he asked, and I instantly narrowed my gaze at him for using that title. The creature next to me hissed in his direction, making everyone still.

"I'm going to put it in one of the cells," I said, but I searched the crowd for Levanna. The grey strands in her hair were stained crimson with the creatures' blood and splatters of it created freckles on her cheeks. "Send word to all the Court leaders about this attack."

Kadeyan nodded and cleared his throat. "And tell them our meeting has been moved up to tomorrow morning. Whoever doesn't show will stand alone from this point on."

She nodded before vanishing from the grounds.

Kadeyan came to my side, wrapping his hand around my waist. My eyes scanned over everyone, especially my friends, and their gazes were locked on my shoulder. I slightly glanced at the grey blood coating my skin where my leathers ripped. The scars that crawled up to my shoulder were on display, vibrant in the gloomy night for all to see. I looked away, seeing Kadeyan's eyes locked on the beaming red orbs staring up at us, awaiting its command.

We began to walk as the furry beast followed after us until it was walking by my side, and my mind launched into wonder. Why did some pause? It wasn't fear that kept them in place, it was something else. So, what was in me that made them do that? Or more importantly, what if I could do it again in other attacks...with more of the creatures?

No one else had to die.

More questions kept piling up, and I was truly beginning to wonder if I would ever be able to make sense of any of this. Maybe our little beast would help, along with the dream I had tonight.

Maybe the real answers didn't lie with my father anymore...but with my mother. And I had a feeling there was more to her...more to me. And whether I liked it or not, I needed to figure it out to put a stop to this, once and for all.

Looking beyond the mountainside, I felt that familiar power for a moment before it vanished, reminding me of my own shadow self and her mate out there. Were they involved in this attack? I wouldn't doubt it, but with what we learned yesterday at the Sky Court, we knew who they were now.

It was what they wanted that was throwing me. They might very well want the Untouched fae's stones, but they also wanted the same thing as us: to extinguish the flames on the throne... Or was there more to this that I couldn't see yet?

Now it was time to get the final pieces to this puzzle and push them back out where they belonged.

Away from all of us.

CHAPTER 23
KADEYAN

Walking down the halls of the Ember castle reminded me of so many memories with my father. The way he walked, how he held himself before everyone in meetings, and how he always saw the potential in me. Even when my mind was elsewhere, wanting to have fun and spend time with... I push the thought away, not allowing myself to feel that right now.

I grew up traveling between our two Courts to stay at my father's side while he stood by the King. I watched them work together to keep the realm in order, and they did it well. And let's face it, a little fear never killed anyone.

A smile tugged my cheeks up as I looked down at Davyna, walking by my side. She was in a crimson gown that cut low to her navel, and part of me didn't know whether I wanted to keep on walking or say fuck the realm and take her against this wall for all the Lords and Ladies to hear. And taste her again... Fuck, that wasn't ever going to be enough.

I wanted to drown in her.

I could tell she was uneasy by the way her hands fidgeted at her sides. Her gaze searched the halls, waiting for something to pop out of the shadows.

She still hadn't told me anything else from what happened to her with the female who scarred her, but it took my focus every time I glanced down. The pale blonde strands were yet another constant reminder. Someone hurt her...and I wanted their blood. Yet she was holding it all in like a dam, refusing to let the raging water behind it flow to freedom. And I wanted to know why.

I hated seeing her like this. Especially when I was right here, willing to carry her burdens. I needed to find a way to get it out of her soon, before it ate her alive. Because even though we were this close, our hands brushing as we walked, it still felt like we were miles apart, living in two different worlds. I wish I could say I was strong enough to endure it, but the distance was crippling me more each day.

I moved forward, pausing at the doors, and turned to face her. "Dearest..."

"Yes?" she asked as the worry melted from her eyes.

Maybe I underestimated how well my little Ember could hide things from me.

"You look beautiful..." I watched the small smile form on her face as I moved in, taking her jaw and tilting it up to look into my eyes. "Ready for some fun?"

Her gaze looked beyond the doors as her body stiffened. "Not sure we can call this fun."

I pressed my lips to hers, claiming her mouth until her body melted into my chest. Biting on her lower lip, my fangs pierced the sensitive flesh, before moving my tongue over the small wound. She was so fucking sweet and bitter all at the same time. Her essence traveled through my veins, rushing straight to my cock.

Then, I felt it. My own body turned to ice...colder than its normal state. A chill racked through me, like something within her blood was warning me to not take another drop. In return, my own power tried to retreat from the silent threat.

I tried to control my reaction as I backed up, but glancing down at her hand, I noticed the scars darkening a shade. A feeling of unease blossomed over me as I turned away from her, not wanting to see if she sensed it too.

What the fuck was that?

"Let's go in, then." I smiled as I placed my arm out. She moved around me and pushed the doors open. Everyone was already sitting at the long table that burned with small flames down the center. I buried down my emotions and walked in after her.

"Davyna!" Sahar rushed over, wrapping her arms around Dy. Her gold tattoos shimmered brighter as she pulled back. "We missed you, sweetie."

Eryx moved over, giving Davyna a gentle hug. "We did... I'm glad you're back," he said to her before wrapping his arm around his mate.

"Missed you guys too..." She smiled before looking over to Alastair, who was standing by Jinx.

My fist balled up as I remembered what it felt like to hold his heart in my hand before the fae witches under Jinx's command stopped me. He didn't deserve another breath, let alone continue to live the last six months. He tried to kill Davyna before she released her power, and that was something I would never forget.

"Can we get started?" Jinx spat out, her annoyance spreading across the room.

I laughed. "Oh, please, let's have another Crystal run this. It went great last time I checked." Moving over to the chair at the head of the table, I sat down and lifted my boots onto the edge with a loud thud. Glancing back up, I watched daggers shoot out of her eyes as her hands balled up into fists by her sides.

The room fell into silence. I looked over at Davyna, her eyes stuck on Alastair and Jinx. She looked angry, making my dick twitch. I always loved seeing that fire come out to play.

"So, why was this meeting moved up?" Alastair asked, looking around the room while he and everyone took their seats.

Making a glass filled with blood appear in front of me, I picked it up and gently spun the contents.

"Are you fucking kidding me? Do you need to drink that here?" Alastair glared at me as I brought the glass to my lips and drank half of it down.

I let it bang against the table, watching some spill over, and looked up to smile at him. Running my finger up the side of the glass, I brought it to my lips and sucked it off.

"It's the blood of my enemies. Don't want it to go to waste." I looked over at Davyna and winked. "Want some?" She shook her head, but I couldn't help but notice the small smile that grazed her lips before she stood.

"There was an attack last night," she said.

"Wait, what do you mean? Why didn't you reach out through the spell Levanna made to notify us? How many casualties?" Eryx asked, leaning forward to rest his elbows on the table as he looked at me.

"There wasn't enough time. We got the people from the Ember Court to help...and we didn't lose anyone," I stated as I leaned back in the chair, ready for their reactions.

Davyna snapped her fingers, and everyone watched, confused by the action. Moments later, the doors whipped open, and I glanced back. Black tendrils of smoke began to fade, and the large cat ran into the room. It was growling loud enough to send echoes into the vaulted ceiling as the doors clicked shut.

Turning, I watched everyone jump back. Their eyes were wide as it jumped on the table and sat before Davyna. *Little fucker.* I still wanted to kill it, but I couldn't deny the mystery here on how she was getting it to obey her.

"What the fuck is that?" Jinx asked as the little beast moved in, growling at her. It dug its long, black claws into the wood of the table, forcing her to lean back.

"It was one of the creatures who attacked last night," Davyna said.

"And you thought to bring it here?" she spat out as her straight black hair fell forward.

Davyna snapped her fingers again and the cat jumped off the table, curling up by her feet. It looked up at me with beaming crimson eyes, purring. It seemed to love Davyna as if she was always its owner... I think it liked me, too, but I still wanted it dead.

"Yes, because I thought it could give us an opportunity to trace what realm it's from and how its magic differs from ours."

"How is it listening to you?" Eryx asked, looking to Davyna before his gaze landed on me.

I shrugged in response. "We don't know why...yet," I spoke up as I looked around the room, taking in everyone on edge, before looking back to Davyna.

"If we would have closed Valyner months ago, none of this would be happening," Jinx said, giving me a disgusted look. It only made me laugh as I averted my gaze back to Dy, seeing her eyes widen.

Davyna looked around, worry pulling her brows down as her gaze snapped back to me. "What does that mean, close Valyner?"

"They wanted to close our realm completely, keeping us from leaving," I said, looking back to Jinx with a death stare. "It would have kept you from returning..." I stood up, looking from Jinx to Alastair, his gaze burning hotter. "That's why you almost got your heart ripped out, remember? Try one more thing...and I'll make sure to finish the job."

"Can we stop bickering for five fucking seconds and find a way to stop this?" Davyna said, with authority elevating her tone, before pushing the chair back to stand before us. Her power entered her hands, making them glow for a moment before fading, and I couldn't help but study her.

I tried to push into her mind again, but I was only met with cold, unbending darkness that pushed me back. It felt like it was her doing it, but I don't think she was aware... Or maybe I wanted to believe that rather than the alternative...

Because that was too gods damn depressing, and the thought alone made my heart ache. She either didn't trust me with what she was going through or was trying to protect me from the painful truth that she didn't want what we had. She said as much.

I didn't believe her then...or even now. The last thing I told her when we were alone before she left still rang true: *Don't underestimate me...if this is the game you want to play, then we are just getting started.* And I had more tricks up my sleeve.

"How can we? You're the reason this all happened... And why

are you even here?" Jinx asked, moving over towards Davyna with fury tainting each feature.

The cat on the floor let out a growl as Jinx closed in, making her slow. I watched Davyna's spine straighten as the little bitch took another step. If she said another fucking word to insult my mate, I'd rip her tongue out.

"Because I'm trying to fix it."

"Well, it wouldn't have needed fixing if you weren't some fucking hybrid mess."

I readied myself to spill blood, but I stalled as I took in Davyna's hand. The black scars slowly traveled up her hand, shimmering with hues that reminded me of each Court.

"Persephone was right about you: an abomination."

Davyna stepped closer to Jinx, their noses almost touching. "Watch yourself, Jinx..." she said in a low tone that made my own body quake.

"Why should I? You aren't my Queen," she spat out.

Davyna turned away, and I moved to her side. The cat hissed as it pounced at Jinx, who moved back and released a sharp breath from her lips.

"Davyna." I placed my hand on her jaw and tilted her head up to look at me and away from everyone else in the room.

I froze, hiding my expression from anyone watching me. Her eyes were black again, with the silver rings burning bright. The smile on her face was vile, longing to tear fear from the deepest parts of a person's soul.

I would know.

While this version of her didn't scare me, it made me concerned because I didn't think she could control it... And in that state, I assumed nothing would be able to stop her. If she wanted blood, she would get it. But would she regret it and hold onto that guilt?

Footsteps sounded from behind us, and I looked back in time to see the doors fly open, exposing Evren. Turning back to Davyna, her eyes shifted back, and I could see fear consuming them.

Her eyes snapped up to her sister, who entered without pause. She ignored the room as her burnt orange gown flowed with each step she took. Davyna pulled back from me, turning her gaze away. Worry consumed me because something in her eyes flashed with terror. Deep down, I knew it had to do with the magic that came forth.

As I moved back to my seat, I could see her eyes become heavier. They hadn't talked since the argument in the library. From sensing Evren's emotions, I knew it was hurting her, and while I couldn't feel Davyna's, I had no doubt it was doing the same to her. I knew how much she loved her sister.

I knew that love for family...and I lost them all.

It was why I used her as bait back in the Mortal Lands. She would have killed to redeem her. I needed her to fight with that love, with that pain. I felt terrible for doing that to her, and to Evren because I'd come to like the baby wolf, but it needed to be done. Davyna deserved her freedom. She deserved to live.

Yet, here she was...living in invisible chains I couldn't free her from.

Evren moved down the long table, sitting directly across from Alastair. "What the fuck are you doing here?" he asked her.

"I'm a Lady. It's my right to be here," Evren said with ease, unbothered by him. I watched the two wolves stare each other down before clearing my throat.

"Let's get back on track, shall we? I think if we can trace the magic in the little creature to Anawyn or Gelmyra, then, we could find a spell to keep other creatures out that are coming from those lands, until Davyna fixes the tear."

"How do you know the names of the other Realms?" Jinx asked, furrowing her brows.

"Faelynn," I stated. "So, let's trace its magic."

"Don't you think we've tried something like that?" Jinx said, rolling her eyes as she moved to the far side of the room. "We had hundreds of Crystal witches trying to trace their power in the first attacks, but our magic isn't the same anymore. It grows weaker every day! And I will not have my Court expel magic that could keep them safe from that sickness she caused."

"Well, if I can't close the tear, what if we go there and spell the creatures within their realm?" Davyna said, looking around the table.

Everyone fell silent, passing glances for a long moment.

I cleared my voice and grabbed her attention. "We can't travel to their realms. We haven't been able to since your father took the throne 1,500 years ago. After the Great War ended."

"Then how are they getting in here? Clearly, they can travel... So, what if I..."

I searched as her gaze went blank, finally understanding that she was there...in another realm. It was why I couldn't feel her, and the time probably moved differently on their plane.

The thought of her leaving again and losing, what? Years? No, I couldn't survive that. Especially if something went wrong and she...

"I'd like to talk about something else," Evren said, breaking the silence. "I want the decree that keeps members off their own Lands destroyed."

"They made a choice to leave..." Jinx lashed back, her eyes narrowing in on Evren, who laughed.

"I don't give a fuck about the Crystals right now. My concern is with my people." Her eyes shifted to Alastair.

"They sided with the Fallen Court. They made their choice," he gritted through his teeth.

I glanced to Eryx and Sahar as they exchanged silent words between them through their bond. Eryx looked at me and shook his head in disapproval of what Alastair was saying. I knew his stance on all of this. Alastair was too lost to holding grudges to ever be civilized.

It was like having a child run a Court...and we were getting tired of dealing with his tantrums. Evren was the rightful leader, and we all knew it. She wouldn't do half the shit he'd been doing. She cared about the wolves, but she also cared about Valyner as a whole, like we all did.

She shook her head, glaring back into Alastair's eyes. "Yes, to fight. To help Valyner. And to get away from a dictator like you."

Alastair threw his chair back. His claws came out as they dug into the table. "Don't test me, wolf. You never test your alpha."

Evren laughed again, but harder this time, before standing. She walked over to him and leaned down until their faces were inches apart. "You aren't even a beta..."

"Can everyone shut the fuck up?!" Davyna yelled, breaking the tension in the room. "Decrees need to be void right now! The only way this all works is if we can work together, regardless of how much some of us hate each other."

Her eyes scanned over to Alastair, before looking back to me. "I'm not going to waste my time here, bitching with you all, when we could be finding the solution we need to bring Valyner some semblance of peace."

I watched Jinx and Alastair, seeing their anger both fade as they took in the power of Davyna's voice. It made me smile as I looked over to Eryx again.

"I agree. What do you need from us, Davyna?" Eryx asked.

"Keep the Untouched fae stones safe under spells and stay on guard. The rest, I need to do myself."

Without waiting for her dismissal, Davyna got up and started making her way to the door.

"What are you doing?" Jinx yelled, her hatred still coating every word.

I narrowed my gaze at her to say, *watch your fucking tone.*

Davyna looked over her shoulder, her silver orbs melting. "Saving your fucking ass." She picked up her feet and began to move down the hall with that damn cat following after her.

I used my shadows to pull me into the void before I fell into step beside her.

"Told you that would be fun..."

CHAPTER 24
UNKNOWN

"I'm growing impatient... The little fae isn't working fast enough," she said with disdain coating each word. "And that fae from Anawyn should be gutted for giving her that information."

I laughed as I whirled the contents of my cup and stared at the swirling mirror on my desk. "It's okay... Receiving parts of the puzzle doesn't mean she will be able to see the full picture." I rose and turned to walk over to her, placing my hands on her waist to calm her agitated body. "We don't move without weighing all the options—all possibilities. That's how you end up dead."

"She can't kill us."

Smiling, I kissed her forehead before releasing her. My naive... *mate* still doesn't understand that even *we* can be killed. Not with obsidian...but in other ways.

"Go and keep an eye on her," I commanded. As she went to move, my hand darted around her throat, pulling her back. "And if you step out of line, there will be consequences. Do you remember the story I told you of the last mate I had?"

She trembled, her eyes showing slight fear come through. *Good.*

Smirking, I released her and waved my hand towards the door. Moving back over to the desk as my door clicked shut, I sat down and looked into the mirror, waiting for my King to summon me.

Within a few minutes, his voice boomed through the mirror. All I could see was darkness beyond, warming my soul. "Tell me about this girl," he demanded.

"She contains all elements of Valyner and has been able to resist even our power."

I heard him growl. "What are your plans for her?"

"Get her to fix the curse she unleashed to stop the Realms from colliding. Then, we'll get the stones, and kill her..." I said, smiling as his anger boomed into the stone room.

"Are you positive she isn't the one we need?"

"Yes." But something within still beckoned me to her, like she was the one who held the power needed to be *his* undoing.

"I can tell you're lying to me...and I won't have that." A chill ran down my spine, and I bowed my head. "We have come this far. Get the stones, kill everyone she loves, and that entire realm for all I care... But make sure you are positive before you take her life."

"I will, Your Grace."

Without another word, he vanished, and the mirror returned to its subtle swirls.

Leaning back in my chair, I took a deep breath before glancing up at the mirror again. I summoned the power within, pulling Davyna into view as she walked down the corridor of her father's castle. Her eyes were heavy, sparking with trepidation, and I couldn't help but smile.

Maybe it was time to play a little game with her.

I needed to see what she was fully capable of...

And I knew exactly what would do it.

CHAPTER 25

DAVYNA

I moved through the Fallen castle, savoring the slowness of the morning. Everything after the gathering with the Court leaders had been flashing before my eyes. Days began to blur into one another as I attempted to get into my father's stone, only for it to burn me over and over again. It made no sense; it got my attention, and now it was denying me. And after barely sleeping the last few nights, I felt drained.

The Courts were clearly going to struggle to work together. Well, maybe not all of them, but the Crescents and Crystals were going to be a headache. While I felt like it was falling on my shoulders now to fix the discord between them, I couldn't help but empathize with the heavy burden that Kade had to carry.

For six months, he dealt with all of this, and held it together for the other Courts, all while trying to find me. Guilt began to creep in again, weighing down each step I took as the dark walls around me became nothing but a blur.

My mind replayed what Jinx said to me and how everything turned into utter darkness. I wanted to rip her heart out and stop it from taking another beat. I wanted to see my hands stained in her blood as the organ turned cold against my flesh.

If Evren didn't walk in when she did, I might have, and I didn't think anyone in there would have stopped me. Guilt still sunk in deeper though, becoming a part of my DNA. It was a permanent reminder that this was all because of me. Like I could forget even if I tried.

After eating something light, I made my way through the castle. Hearing swords clash, I knew exactly who was training. He had been spending most of his time out there, trying to get lost in the next winning blow...and I didn't blame him. There was something freeing about it. At least, it always had been for me when I trained with Elias.

I didn't think that was the real reason he was out there though. His fury bled through the walls with a determination I knew all too well. He wasn't going to stop until he knew everything that was going on with me. And if he figured it out—

I didn't let myself finish that thought as I looked around, swallowing hard.

When I moved closer to the back door leading to the terrace, I heard metal hit the ground next to me. I looked over to see the large bobcat on the table. Its head was lost inside a pitcher... Kadeyan's pitcher. I glanced around, confused, because I put it in the cell downstairs after returning yesterday.

Walking over, its head popped up, and I watched the crimson liquid fall from its jaw as a purr escaped it. I arched a brow, trying to figure out if this was funny or something to be concerned with.

Jumping down, it ran to the door as if waiting for me to let it go outside. "You know...we need a name for you if you are going to be hanging around and not killing us."

Kneeling down, I pet the top of its head, watching it lean into my hand before rolling to its belly. "Well...you're a girl... So, how about Ravyn?" Her red eyes glowed brighter as her gaze locked with mine. Smiling, I gave her one last pet and stood to open the door.

I watched her run off before hearing Kadeyan curse, and I silently chuckled. He really hated her. Walking towards the terrace, I saw Ravyn pouncing at his sword as he pulled it away from her, which only made her want to chase it.

"Davyna, what the hell is your *pet* doing out?"

"Drinking the blood that was in your pitcher, and now, it would seem she is playing." His eyes narrowed as they looked down at her sitting and waiting. "Go run around and stay close... But no killing any fae. Got it?"

She nodded before running off into the fog beyond, leaving us with the soft echo of her paws against the cool ground.

"Is that a good idea?" Kadeyan asked, looking back to me.

"No clue. If she does anything, I promise, you can kill her." Something within me hoped she didn't, because even with the beaming crimson eyes and razor-sharp teeth, I was beginning to like her. "What are you guys doing?"

Calix moved back over, swinging his sword in a circle. "Training because some of us can't stop." He turned his head and looked at Kade with eyes that screamed, *I'm talking about you*. "Want in, Your Grace?"

Kadeyan chuckled, letting his head fall.

"Okay, can you stop that?" I asked, shaking my head slightly.

"Not a chance." Calix laughed. He threw up his sword as Kadeyan brought his down, and they fell back into their sparring match.

I moved over to the side and leaned against the archway, watching them. They both moved with such grace, such fury as they anticipated each other's moves. Nothing was out of their control; it was in sync and beautiful.

I got lost in their movement. I didn't know how much time passed when footsteps came up from behind me. Evren was holding a blade. She was dressed in skin-tight black leathers with the profile of a wolf's head stitched in orange on her right shoulder. We hadn't spoken since the library, and the tension between us was thicker than the stone pillars surrounding us.

I went to speak, but what could I say?

She pulled her hair back and tied it into a low bun before looking at me. "You okay?"

"Yeah, I guess I'm getting there..." It was a lie that I hoped would become my truth soon. Taking a deep breath, I turned to face her. "Evren?"

"Yeah?" she asked, spinning her blade between her fingers. There was a wolf on the top of the dagger's hilt.

"I'm sorry..." Taking in her blue pools, I watched her study my face. After a minute of silence, her walls softened.

"I am, too. But, Davyna, I'm not sorry for calling you out. You needed to hear it because I think you are forgetting we have both been through hell." She fell silent and looked away, taking a few deep breaths.

I wondered what she was thinking about, but I assumed it was everything she had faced since I vanished. What Persephone did to her, leaving her mother, losing fae she knew, fighting to survive, and wanting to be a part of her own Court... All the emotions circling me told the story with some highs, but also severe lows, and my heart hurt for her.

"This is our home, even if we didn't live here our whole lives. Our voices matter, especially for our people."

I nodded, realizing she was right. We both had roles to play in all of this. Seeing her take it so easily made my heart break, thinking something was wrong with me. If I could have accepted this before, none of this would be happening.

Even looking back on that day, I knew the only thing I was sure about was not taking the throne. Something on the throne was engraved in darkness...even if I couldn't explain it, and my power made it more vengeful now. I shouldn't have burned it...but I also know I made the right choice in not taking it.

"You are my sister, and you needed it. Just like I know you feel the need to protect me, but it needs to stop."

"Evren, I love you. But it's my job—"

"No. What are you not getting? It's not your job alone. I have to protect you too. I don't want my sister fighting my battles, pushing me behind her. I want her to stand by my side, fighting with me."

My heart slowed, taking in her words as my eyes locked back on the guys. I shook my head, before glancing back towards her.

"Okay... I'll stand by you." I watched her smile grow as she pulled me into a hug, and I was amazed by the person she had become. And while I'd always see her as my little sister—the one I almost lost—she wasn't weak. She never was.

"Come to play, little wolf?" Calix yelled out, before flashing his perfect white smile.

Evren pulled back, narrowing her eyes at him, and a wicked grin pulled her lips to one side. "Is the vampire scared?" She moved in, falling into the fight.

I watched her, mesmerized by the way she moved. It was like she was with me and Elias during every training, memorizing each move and soaking up every detail he taught. She must have been out here every day since I left. Maybe even twice a day.

"What about you, Dearest?" Kade asked before moving over to me. His eyes swirled with red. "Are you scared of me?"

He threw me his sword and I reached my hand out, taking the handle and tightening my fingers around the leather. I smiled and glanced up at him. "Not even a little bit."

Hours passed and we were all coated in sweat, breathing heavily. We took turns being on each other's teams, working together to undermine the others. And there was something incredible about working with Evren.

We definitely took Kade and Calix by surprise when we both shifted to take them to the ground. Although, being able to push out my own shadows to break theirs probably helped. We couldn't stop laughing, and I realized I couldn't remember the last time I felt this.

Content...maybe even happy.

It was foreign now, to not be concerned with everything beyond for a little while. It felt nice, but as we slowed, it all crept back in, weighing me down more than before. This moment was a glimpse into the future, and I craved more of it. More moments filled with laughter and joy with my friends, and with *him*.

You are delusional if you think that's what you'll get. If you want true happiness, true peace...it's giving up this fight and embracing who we truly are.

Chills ran down my spine as I turned away from everyone. The taunting laugh filled my mind and made my head burn in response.

"Hey, we are going to go down to the hot spring for a little bit." Kadeyan's hands skated across my stomach, before pulling me into him. "I can tell them to fuck off so we can..."

Looking over my shoulder, he lifted his brows twice, and I gave him a forced grin. "I'd like that...just give me a minute."

His hands left my body, but before I could feel that void set in, his hand smacked down on my ass. A soft yelp ripped from my lips as I turned, watching him back away. He was undoing his jacket with a lust-filled grin plastered to his face.

Turning away, I watched Calix and Evren walking towards the castle, and I knew Kadeyan used his ability to get into his head by the look Calix gave me. He draped his arm over Evren's shoulder before turning back. Their laughs filled my ears as I shifted my gaze out over the Lands.

Pulling my arms around my body, I moved off the terrace until I walked onto the dead grass towards the cliff. It was so quiet, as if not a soul existed in this realm except mine. It felt...strange, even eerie. Part of me believed we sometimes craved the silence; for the world around us to fade away so we could just be.

I remembered loving that feeling when I was sewing or reading. My mind would empty, and I could relax. But now, being alone with my thoughts felt more dangerous. Not even an infinite number of distractions would erase what happened.

Walking along the edge, I got to a portion that narrowed, and I stopped to lean against the castle.

I wished I could say I understood my thoughts right now, but they all fused together, brewing their own kind of storm. I let out a breath. My eyes opened to see the cool air smoking up before the tendrils lifted into the sky.

Everything stopped around me as my heart began to hammer

against my ribs. That power was nearby again, watching me. The feeling awakened what lived within, dulling every other sense in my body.

My fires rose to the surface as I went to turn, but they stopped the second I saw Kadeyan standing next to me.

"Fuck!" I yelled, jumping back.

"Did I scare you?" He laughed and I tried to let the unease fall, but I couldn't.

My eyes scanned over the mountains beyond, looking for *them*.

"Yeah...I guess you did." I glanced back into his amber eyes, glistening with wicked intent. Everything inside me was firing off. I pressed my body back into the castle, trying to ground the frantic energy within.

"Good." He moved in front of me, touching my face, and I instantly froze.

What was happening?

Before I could pull away from his touch, he leaned in, drawing my face to his until our lips clashed together. He savored the taste of me, wrapping his hand around the nape of my neck and pulling me in deeper. Although, it didn't feel right. Kissing Kadeyan was like drinking down life itself, but this felt like acid... Like death.

I pushed him away with all my strength and looked him over, feeling utterly lost for a moment. Then, that energy returned. Not only from me, but from who was standing before me.

"Kadeyan?" I asked, my voice shaking.

As my power began to hone in on the bond, I realized he wasn't here... Not this close, anyway. The male before me shook his head back and forth as his vile smile continued to grow.

"Who the hell are you?"

"Come on, little cinder. Did you already forget about me from your nightmare?"

Fury rose and I threw up my hands, letting the flames spiral off. It slammed into his chest, but he was unmoving and unfazed by the blaze. I looked down as he absorbed each one, letting out a moan as if he was enjoying it.

Stopping, I pushed my body into a run. I wanted to call out for Kadeyan, but I couldn't... They would...

Hands dug into my hair, pulling me back, until my body slammed into his form. "I'm always watching, waiting. I've got nothing but time. Remember that the next time you think this is over."

Throwing my head back, my skull crushed into his windpipe, and he released me. Turning, I watched him cough, but through it, he was laughing.

"Go back to your realm! Or I swear to the gods, I will kill you!"

He found my statement hilarious as he placed his hands on his knees, laughing harder.

"You think you can stop me? Stop what's coming? You can try, but I'll gladly put a dagger through your heart after I slaughter your sister...your friends...then your mate." He moved in, and his hand wrapped around my neck before he tossed me through the air.

My vision went black as I fell. Recovering quickly, I sat up and released my fires again, rage coating each one.

But it was pointless... *He* was gone.

My breath shortened as I looked around. I spotted Kadeyan running towards me and my breathing grew heavier. Concern was laced in his eyes, and his chest rose and fell fast as he assessed the grounds.

Pulling myself away, I studied him, making sure it was *my* Kade. I took in his bare, chiseled chest and the ink running through his skin, before looking up into eyes that were slowly turning red. And then, I felt it—our bond circling us.

A sudden realization washed over me that I was exposing my vulnerability, my fear. It was spilling out like a waterfall crashing into a vast lake.

"What the fuck happened?" he asked, taking small steps towards me as I gasped for air.

"It was... It was..."

Kadeyan moved in, dropping to his knees and pulling my face up to meet his gaze.

"Who was it?"

If that answer was easy to give, I would have said it, but the reality was that this creature...was a mystery. My power didn't harm him, and if that was the case, then how was I supposed to protect any of them? They weren't going to stay patient for long, and I needed to repair the damage I created before...

"I don't know..." My eyes scanned every angle of his face, still in disbelief. Without pause, the words fell from my lips in a whisper, and I instantly regretted saying them because I could no longer open up or share the truth without consequences.

"I–it was...you."

CHAPTER 26
KADEYAN

"She fucking saw something, Levanna. She said it was me, but I was in the hot spring, waiting for her, when I heard something going on," I said as I paced back and forth through my office.

"Did she explain what it felt like?" she asked.

I gave her a look to say, *What do you think?*

She placed her hands on her hips and began pacing. "It makes no sense. Why would she keep all this to herself... Unless..."

"Unless what?"

"Unless she was threatened..." I stopped, turning to face my friend, who was staring at me with wide eyes. "That has to be it. They could have threatened her, and with how she is acting, I'd say she could care less about her own life... It has to be someone she cares about."

"You think they threatened Evren?" I asked.

"Or you..."

Her words warmed my heart, but quickly faded as I shook my head. I didn't want her protecting me. I wanted to fight with her, and to destroy this fucking creature before it consumed her.

"I think she was in Gelmyra or Anawyn," I said softly as I sat down in the chair closest to me. "She said something in the meeting with the Court leaders...and I think that's where she was."

"It would make sense why you couldn't feel her with the veils placed between our Realms...and the time loss," she said, moving over to the couch and sitting down. "But it doesn't explain how these things are only coming for her. Unless..." She stopped, biting her tongue, but her thoughts were loud enough.

"She is not fucking linked to one of them!"

"Kade...it could be possible."

Nowhere in our history showed that one could be linked or bonded to two people. And I saw it in her eyes; she was scared of this thing. I knew Davyna more than anyone here. Fear was not something she liked to show, let alone feel. She always wanted to show her strength—that she could handle herself.

But with the darkness that kept flickering in and out, the paranoia in her body language, and the secrets... No, she wasn't linked to those fuckers.

Dropping my head into my hands, I roughly dragged them down, rubbing out the tension in my temples. But if she *was* linked...

"So, if we kill this thing, would it stop everything else from affecting her?"

"In theory, it should. But, Kade, we don't know what we are dealing with. We know nothing about the fae in Anawyn or Gelmyra, other than what Faelynn told us."

"Then Faelynn will have to tell us more," I demanded, standing up.

"No. I think the person who should be telling us more...is Davyna." She stood, moving in towards me. "If there is anyone who can get through to her, it's you..."

Doubt racked through me because, right now, I didn't think my words would make a difference. I buried it down and shook my head. "I'll talk to her again..."

Levanna touched my arm, giving a gentle squeeze before walking towards the door. "I love Davyna...and under other circumstances, I wouldn't condone this. But..." She took a long breath, looking up to the ceiling before glancing back at me. "Do what you do best."

Smiling, I let my mind fall into the dark corners of my soul, thinking of all the ways I could break her and make her sing the only melody I wanted to hear: the truth. “I wouldn’t have it any other way.”

CHAPTER 27
DAVYNA

I picked a different room down the hall from Kade's and spelled the door shut hours ago. I needed to open this fucking stone, get what I needed, and get those creatures out of my life for good!

There was one thing I couldn't make sense of, though. Why would they want me to fix it? If their goal was to eradicate Valyner, then how was closing the veil the way to do it? Why weren't they going after the stones while being here?

Leaning my head back, it hit the footboard of the bed. They had a plan...I knew that. So, maybe this was affecting them, too, in a negative way.

I stopped my spiraling thoughts and brought my head back down to look at my father's stone on the floor.

I could do this. I needed to do this.

Hours passed, and the frustration grew with each tear that slid down my face. Waving my hand over the room, I made sure no one could hear as I broke down, the agony of my failures rooting itself within.

Visions of the throne room dream flashed behind my eyelids. The blurred faces, the shadowed figure, and the blank stare of my own eyes gazing back at me.

My eyes jolted open, pulling a ragged breath from my lips as I wiped my face.

This was a mistake... This was all one big fucking mistake.

Or maybe you trying to live like a saint is the real mistake.

The sobs slowed as I stared off, seeing nothing in focus. Numbness flowed over me as I took in the words from my demon within.

"Maybe you are right..." I sat there, waiting for the laughs, or for some twisted statement to snap back, but it was silent.

I rose from the ground, swiping the stone up as I moved over to the bed. But words from my father's letter filtered back into my mind, causing me to stall. "*You were our biggest blessing and our only reason to fight. You were the light we both needed in the darkness of this world.*"

I looked down at the stone, thinking that had to do with Persephone, but maybe they meant something greater than her. Did he know that his little girl he saw full of light contained just as much darkness?

A book fell off the bookshelf. The pages flipped fast before it stalled, and I jumped back.

What the fuck? I didn't do that.

It settled open to a passage about the Mortal Realm and I looked around. Leaning down, I hesitantly went to pick it up, but as my hand touched it, my vision shifted. My stomach turned. It felt like I was being pulled far away from this world, and I closed my eyes as my body tensed.

When I opened them, my jaw dropped.

The walls surrounding me were red and had different facets that showed myself in all of them. It was like I was inside a ruby, seeing a world through its prism, and it was captivating. I tried to settle my breathing and walked forward, watching my reflection closely as I turned to take it all in.

Panic coursed through me as the walls began closing in. I started looking for a way out, but there wasn't one. Voices chanted beyond, echoing within the ruby walls, and I shuddered in response.

What was going on?

Turning, I looked at every wall, now holding small memories in each reflection of the crystal. I saw my father, my mother... Shock filled me because I did it...

I was in the stone.

Glaring light forced every bone in my body to freeze over, turning me into a statue.

My eyes fastened on a white shadow, showcasing the light shades of the six Courts within...like my shadow self. I forced my body to move, and my back slammed into the wall. It moved closer to me, and the iridescent vapor grew thicker, obscuring the ruby walls around us.

"There are two paths, but only one you need to know," the male's voice boomed, shaking the ground. "When the flames sit upon the throne, light and darkness will rage war until one stands between, able to control both."

I went to speak to the voice, asking what that meant, but the air was ripped from my lungs as I was physically forced out of where I was, and back into the room. The last thing I saw before it pushed me out was the cave my mother showed me in my dream.

My breathing picked up as I looked around, trying to remember if I had ever heard that voice before. No one came to mind, but there was this feeling... I couldn't describe it.

Who was he?

I looked down at my hand, where I was gripping my father's stone so hard that blood was coating it and dripping to the floor. Wiping the lingering tears from my face, I took a needed breath and pushed away the dark cloud that was hanging over my head moments ago.

Something was in that cave. Something my parents hid...and I needed to find it.

CHAPTER 28

DAVYNA

I pushed the covers back and slowly sat up in bed, hoping not to wake Kadeyan. Looking out the window, I took in the gloomy morning still gracing us with darkness like a heavy blanket.

Before joining him last night, I stood in the separate bedroom down the hall until Kade fell asleep in the one we shared. He stirred when I laid down, pulling me into him as he let out a deep breath. Almost like he was relieved and could finally rest. There was something about being in his arms that made me feel safe, but it was just that...a feeling.

I wanted to breathe without shuddering. Wanted to scan over the lands and take in its beauty without paranoia, and to fall into the warmth of my power without it fearing the chilling depths of what housed my demon. Safety was an illusion, and it didn't matter how much you wanted it to become your reality.

Abandoning the thought, I leaned back and interlaced my fingers through his, basking in the comfort. He let out a long breath, his lips pulling up to one side as if we weren't at odds since I returned.

Slowly pulling my hand away, I rose and placed my feet on the marble floor. Stunned, I jumped back, lifting my legs up onto the mattress. Ravyn was sprawled out next to the bed, with her belly rising and falling with each breath.

After steadying my breathing, I remembered putting her in another cell last night after I came inside. How was she getting out?

Her head perked up and her eyes were glowing in delight as she stared me down.

"Stay here," I whispered and looked over my shoulder to Kade, who was still sleeping, before glancing back at her. "Listen to him until I get back."

Stretching out her legs, she lazily stood up before jumping onto the bed and laying her head on my pillow. I looked to Kade, then her again, and I knew that if he woke to see her, he would probably break her neck. And yet, she looked so peaceful as her red eyes began closing again. I didn't want to take that from her.

"Don't let him see you, okay?" I said in a hushed tone. Black shadows sprung from her fur before turning clear, making her invisible. My eyes widened for a moment, taking in the empty spot. The only evidence that she was still there was the bend in the mattress.

I was in awe that she obeyed me. Whatever happened that night when our eyes connected...she saw something in me. Now, if I could only figure that out for myself, maybe it would help with rectifying the situations I plunged this world into.

Smiling at her, I used my magic to change myself into leathers, with a thick, red cloak hanging over my shoulders. Pulling up the hood, I looked over to Kadeyan one last time, his chest rising and falling in steady rhythms.

Taking light steps towards him, I reached my hand out, lightly grazing his cheek. The stubble scratched at my fingertips and he smiled, letting out another deep breath. That smile alone lit up my world, melting away everything else...and I wanted to see that more.

Pulling back, I focused on what I needed to do. I'd be back before he woke...or at least I hoped so. He wouldn't find me where I was going, and I was slightly glad. I needed to do this alone.

Because you belong alone... Always alone.

Shaking my head and ignoring the voice, I let my smoked ashes surround me, and landed downstairs in the weapons room. Blades varying in different lengths and designs sat on blackened shelves like fine art, telling their silent stories of battle and violence.

Walking over to a row, I grabbed two daggers with gleaming

silver steel with swirls etched down the blade. I strapped one to my waist before placing the other around my thigh, but I stopped dead in my tracks as the door behind me opened.

Turning slowly, I took in Evren standing in the doorframe. She looked at me through tired eyes still plagued with sleep.

"What are you doing?" she asked, rubbing her face.

"Why are you up?"

She took a moment to focus, and then looked me over before answering, "I get up every day at this time to go run with the Crescents. Why are you dressed like that? Where are you going, Dy?"

"Don't worry about it, okay?" I said, trying to move forward, but Evren shifted to the side, blocking the exit. Her brow lifted and I could feel her waiting for the explanation.

A minute passed while both of our stubborn natures battled it out, revealing I was in a lose-lose situation. I could either vanish and make her feel like I didn't trust her or push her away. And I didn't want to do either.

"I'm going to the Mortal Realm..."

"Why?"

I looked up at the soft glow of the candles from the chandelier before letting out a long breath. "Because I think my father left something there. Or my mother...one of them."

Her eyes lit up as she stepped back. "I'm coming with you," she protested. Walking over to the wall, she grabbed two daggers similar to mine. I took in the steel in her hands before looking at her blue pools.

"Evren..."

"No, I don't want to hear it. Remember...by your side."

My heart ached with her support, and I abandoned the fight. If anyone should go with me today...it should be her.

No...you should be alone. You don't want to hurt your sister, do you?

I forced a smile, but my stomach sank at the intrusive thoughts crawling out of the darkest parts of me. I would never hurt her...

"Change my clothes, and let's go back to our first home."

Hesitating for a moment, I twisted my hand out to change her into the same outfit I was in, but with a dark orange cloak. Unease formed in my gut as I looked her over.

They are going to kill us for this before we can have our fun, the voice blared in my mind.

Would they be watching me there too? Was there no escape from them?

Pushing everything down, I focused on what I needed to do today. If I needed to, I'd open a portal and throw my sister through it… Whatever those beings out there were, they forgot the most important thing about me: I would fight until the death for the people I loved. And I would have no mercy on them if they touched my family.

You being in their lives is hurting them. They are all going to die, and I hope it's by our hand. Growing louder and harder to ignore, the laughter made my skull ache.

I glanced down at my hand. The scars were changing shades, darkening by the second. Pulling it behind my back, I looked up at my sister, thanking the gods she didn't catch sight of it.

I tried to hide my nerves as smoke surrounded us, pulling us away from Valyner. But the voice in my head kept repeating, *Let me in… Let me kill.*

Sucking in a sharp breath, I looked around, sensing mortals nearby. I was struggling to catch my breath and leaned against the closest tree as my head pounded.

Evren rushed over to me, placing her hand around my arm. "Are you okay?"

I waited for the voice and that power within to surge, but it was calming down, washing back out to sea as if the waves finally took it away. Glancing down at the scars, they were normal again, unblemished by the gleaming onyx hue. I took a few more cleansing breaths. My head cleared, and for the first time in so long, I felt like myself again.

"Yeah…I think so." Pushing myself up, I realized we were off the main path going into town. It looked like we were immersed in the full bloom of spring. Vivid greens carried on for miles and the scent of honeysuckle and wild flowers captivated the air.

As we began walking towards the trail that would lead up to the square, my heart raced. Some women began sauntering our way, and I pulled for my fae magic on how to cloak my ears. When it came to me, I silently chanted it, and the sensation ran over my body, obeying my wishes.

I looked over at Ev, realizing she was doing the same thing, and she winked at me. She turned forward, nodding at the passing humans, and I followed suit.

"Doesn't it feel weird sometimes?" she asked, and I looked towards her as we approached the town. "Having this magic..."

"Yeah, but these days...I'd say mine is way more unpredictable."

"Maybe it's because you fear it." She shrugged her shoulders.

I wanted to protest her statement, but I was at a loss for words as it sank into the marrow of my bones. I did...

"It's as easy as breathing, Dy. Maybe you need to remember that when you are struggling with all this."

I gave her a slight smile before we both turned our eyes on the road and walked in silence. After a few minutes, the town square was in view, and I couldn't help but stop and overlook it all, soaking in the nostalgia that laid here.

It was where it all began.

I expected to see some buildings had changed—where businesses replaced others—and people getting older. However, that was not what I saw. When I left to go to Valyner, it was about five years that passed here. I tried to do the math in my head, remembering it had been six months since I left, plus the time I'd been back in Valyner... They should have been about fifteen years ahead here, and yet, it looked almost the same. Maybe a few years older.

My jaw fell slightly as I turned and walked backwards. I took everything in before turning to Evren.

"Shouldn't it be winter here?" she asked, stopping in the middle of the street.

"What do you mean?"

She paused, a weak grin gracing her face. "I came here six months ago, during Christmas. It was about three weeks after you left. It felt strange being here, and now I wonder if it was me feeling something else." She paused for a long moment. "But I was just more focused on finding you. I thought you would be here so we could celebrate…" Her voice trailed off before she cleared her throat. "With the time change though, it shouldn't be spring…"

My heart sank in my chest. The only thing I relished about that time of year was the tradition Evren and I formed at Christmas, since Hera refused to let me be a part of theirs… And I missed it. I wanted to apologize for not being here for it, and for missing everything in-between, but Evren smiled and moved forward.

I looked over my shoulder, watching the humans pass by. I took in some familiar faces, and they weren't much older. She was right; something was different here.

A man with blonde hair stopped, and my entire body froze in place as I watched him. My body turned to face him fully as my heart beat louder in my ears.

He walked over to a woman, probably around the same age as him—thirty-one, maybe—and kissed her. Their love emulated into the vibrant air. She was holding a baby boy in her arms, and his blonde hair beamed under the warmth of the sun as both parents cooed over him.

My *first* love found love and had a family.

Drystan took the baby into his arms, smiling down at him before looking up. Our eyes collided, and shock filled his.

I instantly sensed his confusion, but mainly delight spilled from him. It wrapped around me, embracing me like no time had passed, and all the good moments from my childhood rushed in. Those were the moments when laughter flowed freely, and I perceived the world through a rosy, enchanted veil.

Our eyes searched each other, getting lost in remembering each moment of a life before, but so much had changed. The world no longer held a hue of innocence, but cold, vivid reality.

He still looked like the man I knew, with stubble grazing his jaw and his hair a little longer now. The most important thing was that he looked happy. That was all I wanted for him when I left this world behind, and I still did.

Curtsying, I let my head fall. Looking back to him, I whispered, "My lord." Even though I knew he couldn't hear me.

I turned and began walking, trying to bite back tears and the urge to run towards him to ask him about his life. Our story ended a long time ago. It took us separate ways, and it needed to stay that way. He deserved peace...and all I would bring him was chaos.

"You okay?" Evren asked as she linked her arm through mine.

"I'm more than okay," I said, looking at her before smiling, and to my own shock, it was a genuine one because I think I needed that. He might have been my first love...but I knew who my last was. And hopefully after all this, Kadeyan would understand why I needed to keep him away.

I hoped the day came when I was ready to let him in and stop believing that loving me was a death sentence, but not until this was over. Which was why we were here.

As we walked farther down, it all came flooding back, and I remembered that we were on the same road as Lana's bar. I picked up my feet, eliminating the distance between me and her. Moving around a crowd of people, Evren and I stopped at the window as I searched the small tavern.

She was still here, standing behind the bar and smiling wide as she got lost in conversation with one of her customers. Her hair was a little greyer now, and her face was decorated with the evidence of the years passed, but she still looked radiant.

"Gods, I've missed her..." I whispered.

"So have I," she said in a hushed tone.

Lana placed down a glass in front of the man and turned to the window, seeing us. Her eyes widened and tears filled them almost instantly. She moved around the bar and my feet picked up, moving to the door.

Swinging it open, I was met with her arms extending wide for an embrace. She pulled me in as a sob ripped from her throat. “Oh my God...Davyna,” she cried. “Evren?”

Pulling back, I felt the tears run down my face as she moved over to my sister and hugged her. After a few moments, she stepped back, wiped her eyes, and looked at us in astonishment.

"I thought I’d never see you two again... How are you both?” she asked, smiling wide.

I went to speak, but the words failed me. I used to tell Lana everything. I used to cry in her arms, but I didn’t want her to see that now. Nor did I want to get her involved with what we were and where we now lived.

It was better this way... Wasn’t it?

“We are good. Living just outside of Qeles now,” Evren said, before looking at me and no doubt seeing the pain I was trying to cover up.

“Did you come to see your mother?” she asked, her expression turning. I felt her unease rise, but not because it was just Hera. There was something else going on.

“No,” I said as she looked to me. “What happened?”

CHAPTER 29
DAVYNA

When Evren and I were far enough into the woods, we used the gap to bring us closer to the house we both grew up in. I couldn't help but envision how I saw it last—smothered in a blaze. I swallowed hard as we came to the opening that looked over the house, expecting it to be in ruins...but it wasn't.

It was all repaired. Just like Lana explained it.

The bricks were white now, with a cherry wood-stained porch that stood out from the lush emerald landscape. I looked over at Evren, sensing her emotions sway. "If you want to go in, I'll stay out here." As I said the words, we both stalled and listened.

Lana told us that Hera had been coming to the market less...and there were rumors of physicians going to the estate, but they stopped a few months ago. No one had seen her, and with not being liked much by the other ladies of court...no one had come by to check on her.

"Do you hear that?" she asked, looking over at me. A heartbeat from within the estate could be heard, but it was slower than it should be for a human...

"Yeah..." Without pause, Ev took off, her boots tracking through the soft grass and flinging up mud. I watched her as she climbed the steps. Pausing at the door, her eyes filled with tears as she looked back at me.

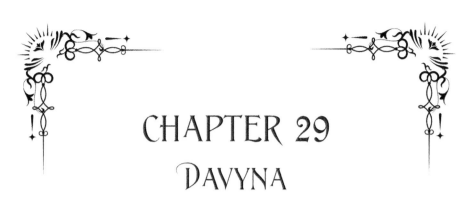

Moving towards the house, my heart began to race at seeing this place again, but I couldn't deny my sister. Not right now, with her eyes begging for me to be by her side. Each beating, degrading conversation, and punishment flashed in my mind, bringing me back to that human girl. And I felt like her these days, even with the power I possessed.

Standing by her side, I came back from the intrusive memories and looked at the door. With a shaking hand, I wrapped my fingers around the doorknob and pushed it open, before looking at Evren's glistening gaze.

"I'll be right here with you."

"Is it really her?" she whispered.

I focused in, sensing the same waves of emotions I knew all too well that emulated from her psyche. It was her without a doubt. I nodded as she took the first step in, making her way into the house. Slowly, I followed behind, taking in the new decor that was similar to what was here before.

The layout was identical too. The dining room was off to my left, housing a long, cherry wood table. Turning my gaze, I took in the parlor to my right, and the fireplace holding ash that sprinkled out onto the wooden floor.

I swallowed hard and my heart skipped a beat as I looked at the staircase leading up to the second floor, remembering the night Hera slapped me. Shaking off the memory, my eyes grazed over the estate. Everything was layered in dust. Even cups of tea were left out everywhere, giving a staleness to the already stuffy air.

Did she not have servants anymore?

I turned in a circle, taking in the place that held good and bad memories within these walls. Elias was my world up until I was sixteen, and all the good somehow fell six feet under with him that day.

I heard Ev's boots climbing the stairs and snapped out of it as I made my way behind her. We stopped in the hall, and after a few silent seconds, Evren ran into her mother's room.

"Mama?" she said softly as I stepped closer, taking in Hera's eyes that were struggling to open.

After a minute, she focused her gaze on Evren, and a broken

smile appeared. "My baby girl? Is that you?" Her voice was hoarse as she tried to fill her lungs with air, and I could hear the fluid in them slosh around.

"Yes, it's me... It's me, Mom."

"Am I in Heaven?" she asked as her eyes scanned the ceiling, before raising her frail hand to Evren's face. I watched her gaze slowly move to me in the doorway, and the spark of hatred returned in her weak body. "What is she doing here?" She coughed, her body succumbing to whatever illness was plaguing her.

"Trust me, this is the last place I want to be today," I said, bluntly, taking in her narrowing blue gaze.

"Mama, what happened?"

Hera struggled to pull her body up, her breathing becoming more labored. Evren looked over her shoulder at me. Her emotions were raging into a cyclone of unease as her eyes lined with tears.

"The physicians say it's incurable. It's been getting worse the last few years." She stopped to cough, taking longer to recover. "I prayed I'd see you one last time. To tell you I'm so sorry...for everything. I should have done better..."

"Mom..." Evren said, grabbing her hands.

"No. I should have done better. I should have been better. For you, my dear, sweet child."

I looked down as a sob broke from my sister, and I couldn't help but feel a sting of pain bloom within. I never got this time with my own mother...only visions shown to me, and a dream of my own.

"I can go now..." she said as she wheezed between each word.

Evren looked back to me, her eyes pleading for me to do something, but there was only one thing I could do for her: stop her suffering. And after a few minutes passed, she knew that. I watched her eyes spill more tears before her head fell between her shoulders.

Moving in, I laid my hand on her shoulder. I was overwhelmed by the emotions in the room coming from the both of them.

"Say goodbye, Ev. And then go outside..."

After a minute, she nodded her head in agreeance, before

building up the courage to lean forward to kiss her mother's forehead.

"Goodbye, Mom..."

I watched as she left the stuffy room, her legs trembling the entire way. I waited until I heard her boots on the stairs. All the terrible things Hera did to me didn't matter right now. At the end of the day, they were bonded by blood. Losing family was never easy, and that hole would never go away.

Hera's eyes opened again, and a tear ran down her face as her gaze met mine. She was struggling with her emotions of anger as she took me in, but she was weakening by the second, barely able to glare at me like she did once upon a time.

"Anything else you'd like to say before..." I looked down at my hands as I sat on the edge of her bed. Her eyes narrowed on me, but she kept her lips sealed. "Okay, but can I ask you something? Why did you hate me so much?"

She coughed, taking a long moment to catch her breath. Those dark blue pools were still cold, piercing into the fragile girl within. "You weren't my child...and Elias loved you. He protected and trained you, more than he ever did with Evren. I believed you were his bastard, and I wanted to hurt you...and him."

Clearing her throat, she let out a raspy breath. "After he passed, I saw you as a constant reminder of the thing that ruined my life."

"I was his brother's child—your niece. Both my parents died protecting me... Does that change anything for you?"

"No...because you brought Hell to my doorstep and took my only family away. You made Elias turn on me, and then did it again with my daughter."

I laughed, looking up to the ceiling as I tried to bite my tongue. Glancing down into her eyes again, I decided to let it out. "Your daughter left because she wanted to. No one forced her. Elias loved us both more than air itself. You did this to yourself, and you deserved everything that came to you."

When I stood, her hand wrapped around my wrist, stopping me

from walking away. "You were always a darkness that ruined lives. I hope you burn in Hell...girl."

Pulling my hand free, I looked over at her as she fell into another coughing fit, her heart slowly starting to fail. I laid my hand on her chest just above her heart and leaned in to keep her gaze on me—and me only. My eyes flickered, the darkness within snaking its way up to my eyes, but it wasn't as intense as I had felt before. Hera's gaze widened as her fear filled the room, and I couldn't help but smile.

"I can't burn...but you will." My power surged through my fingers as I let my shadows out, pushing them through her flesh until they surrounded her heart. Her dark blue pools grew wild with horror as I twisted, hearing the snap of the arteries, before her heart stilled under my hold.

Pulling my shadows back, I stood from the bed and turned away, trying to calm my breathing that was becoming erratic with rage. Tears threatened to build in my eyes, but I pulled them back, refusing to let anymore fall for the pathetic excuse of a *mother* I had.

Deep down, I knew Hera and I would never have a mother-daughter moment, but there was a tiny part of me that hoped for it over the years. Something to erase her evil and her own type of darkness. Maybe in the end, holding onto the darkness was a way of keeping the fighter alive.

Perhaps she needed that. Maybe she wanted the hatred for me to reason with why she was a shitty mother, or wife... Maybe I was doing the same, but I wasn't her. I had reasons for what I was doing.

But you are—

The voice within tried to come through, but it was quickly washed away, making me wonder if I was learning to block it out or if it was weaker here. My power felt as it did before the throne, buzzing within to tell me it was the latter.

Brushing it off, along with the corpse behind me, I walked down the stairs and made my way through the house without looking at another thing. I refused to ever feel anything towards this place again.

It was my past; a life I was never supposed to live.

As the door swung open, my eyes locked on Evren in the distance. She was pacing back and forth, her face stained with tears. She began running towards me and I met her on the front lawn, taking her into an embrace.

"I'm sorry, Ev."

"I'm sorry, too...for what she said to you." Pulling back, I looked her over and realized she heard everything.

"She didn't suffer. It was quick." New tears fell as she looked past me to the house, nodding. "Do you need my help?"

"No, I want to do this myself." I let her go and watched her move slowly towards the porch.

"Bury her where the wildflowers grow... They were her favorite," I said and she stopped, turning to face me with a broken smile.

"I was thinking the same thing," she said, before climbing the stairs and disappearing into the house.

Waiting a few minutes, I heard her sobs as her grief poured out, brushing up against my body. I looked to the woods beyond and pulled myself together for the reason I came here today.

Smoke rushed around me as I grabbed onto my father's stone, imagining the place until the void pulled me far away from here.

My feet slammed into the ground, and my smoked essence evaporated to reveal the world as I pulled my dagger free. The clearing I saw in my dream was the same, and I realized mountains were off in the distance. What part of the Mortal Lands was this in?

In my dream, it felt like it was only miles from the house, but being here now, it was like life around me was silent. And I couldn't sense Evren...or anyone.

Pulling my cloak off, I let it fall into the lush grass as I moved towards the bushes and vines still concealing the cave beyond. My hand rose and I let the flames ignite, consuming the plants that stood between me and the answers my mother wanted me to find.

After a minute, the flames went out, leaving ash and small

embers floating in the warm air. I stopped myself from moving to take in the entrance, and my stomach fluttered.

This was it...

As I went to take a step forward, I heard twigs snap behind me, and I tensed up. Spinning around, I brought my blade up to the intruder's neck, ready to spill their blood, when steel pressed into mine.

"Go ahead, Princess."

CHAPTER 30
DAVYNA

"What are you doing here?" Kadeyan asked as he kept the dagger pressed against my neck. I looked down at his hand, the inked rose doing nothing to hide his veins bulging, along with his anger.

"I...I just wanted to come here."

"To the Cursed Lands? Why?"

I've never actually been here. Many humans didn't even dare stay up here after the attacks got bad. Like...Terry.

"How did you even find me?" I asked, pushing his hand with the dagger away before dropping mine.

"Levanna did a locator spell on Evren since no one could find her, and I figured she was with you."

I wondered if they tried to do it with me but it failed. Looking into his eyes, though, I knew they probably tried that spell every day I was gone.

"I saw you jump into the gap at your old place and followed your scent through the void." He moved in, leaving barely an inch between us as he glared down at me. "So, tell me, why are you here?"

My lips trembled, but I stood taller, narrowing my gaze into him as I remained silent.

"You know, I'm getting sick and tired of all the secrets," Kade stated with venom laced in his harsh tone.

"I don't have--"

My body sped through the air before slamming against ruby stone walls, pulling a groan from my throat. My eyes focused on the cave surrounding us, the same markings from my dream carved into the surface. Cool metal returned to my throat, causing me to freeze as my gaze slowly shifted back to Kadeyan's burning red eyes.

"Let me in, Dearest. Or I'll force my way in."

I swallowed as the steel bit into my flesh. My mind raced with the thought of telling him everything. My gaze shifted around the cave, waiting for the shadow to appear, and to remind me of what it would do if I spoke of them. Focusing on their power, I could tell it was just us, and that the energy looming in the cave was mine alone.

My eyes began to well up and I tried to avert my gaze from him. It only infuriated him more, causing his hand to shift up and draw blood from my neck. The warm liquid started to slide down my flesh as my jaw fell open, the sting of the cut pulsing in waves.

"Now," he growled. His blade traveled down my chest, cutting through my leather top with perfect pressure while avoiding my skin. "Go ahead and try to hide from me. I might not be able to read your mind anymore, but your eyes tell me everything."

Pushing him back, my anger rose. "Leave it be!" I yelled, my hands tingling as they began to heat.

"Fuck that!"

His shadows lashed out, pulling me off the ground, before throwing me across the cave. My back slammed into the wall and small bits of stone crumbled to the floor with me. Before I could recover, he was by my side, picking me up by my throat as his knife burrowed into my stomach. I cried out in agony as he twisted the steel, and my vision blurred.

"I'm sorry, is this causing you pain?" he said before pulling the blade out, and I gasped at the force of it.

Tossing me to the ground, I looked up at him. My eyes narrowed as he looked at the grey blood dripping from the metal.

"I'm trying to fucking protect you!" I spat out.

"Do you need me to torture you like I do my captives? Do I need to make you sing for me like each one of them did, giving me what I wanted?" he yelled, waiting for my response.

I kept my eyes locked on him, biting my tongue as the adrenaline in my body prepared for his retaliation of my silence. He was going to do it, even if he didn't want to...

He moved, pinning me below him as the blade pierced into my shoulder and made contact with the floor below. I screamed, my vision swaying as the pain shot down my arm.

"Giving you space hasn't worked. Sparring with you did nothing... So, I guess now, we are doing it my way." He growled as his gaze took in the blood spilling from the wound before meeting my wide pools.

Yells billowed out of me as I tried to grit my teeth and choke back the emotions within that were floating to the surface.

Stepping away, he brushed the loose strands of hair back from his face and kept his cold eyes on me. I could feel his anger and torment running out of him like the blood flowing from my wounds.

Yet, I could see his wounds ran deeper, harbored internally for too long, and this was his way of letting it out. To make me see I wasn't the only one breaking.

"No!" Pulling myself free, I threw out my hands and laced my fires through my shadows. They wrapped around him, enveloping him in a searing warmth, but I made sure it didn't get too close to his flesh to cause him any harm. His body glided through the air, slamming into the wall. Some loose stones fell and echoed as he stood perfectly silent.

Pulling the dagger free from my flesh, I threw them to the ground as my chest rose and fell. The force of a hundred storms merging together roared within as I glanced up at him.

Something in his gaze wavered, and I no longer saw Kadeyan, but the monster under the surface, turning his irises to the deepest red possible. He pushed against my hold and broke it long enough to soar through the air, grabbing me by my throat. Within a heartbeat, I was back on the ground and his shadows were in my chest.

"I can do this all day, little Ember." I pushed against him as he twisted his phantom hand within my ribs, grabbing onto my heart.

My body went rigid as my lungs protested the pain in my chest, causing me to still and cough violently. "TELL ME!"

"Fuck you!" I cried out, and he squeezed harder.

"NOW!" he yelled, his voice sounding more unhinged.

"You might as well kill me. We both know I deserve it."

He backed up, looking me over with shock, and I began processing what I said. *Fuck...*

He stood silent for a few minutes, keeping me locked to the floor with his shadows gripping the organ in my chest. He pulled another dagger from his leg. The obsidian was showcased in the dull light flowing in from the entrance of the cave.

"Then what do I deserve?" he asked with a soft tone. "Do I deserve death for all the blood on my hands? Do I deserve death because I couldn't save my father... My..." He stopped, his walls within building higher than I ever felt them before. I looked away, pushing him out so I didn't pry into information he wanted to keep to himself. Yet, here he was, prying into mine.

"You need to leave it be. It doesn't matter what happened or what I'm dealing with. You need to stay out of it." I coughed again, glancing back at him.

"Okay...I will." He brought the obsidian dagger to his chest.

"What the fuck are you doing?!" I screamed, still feeling his shadows applying pressure on my heart.

"I'm staying out of it...and that way, they have nothing to hold over your head." He pulled his leather jacket open, exposing his chiseled core with the black swirls inked up his sides and chest. He brought the blade up and pressed the tip into his skin.

Blood began to fall and everything within me broke into a million pieces. His emotions brushed up against me, and I realized he was willing to do it...

No, he was *going* to do it.

I couldn't lose any more people I loved, especially not him! Maybe the bond was still too foreign for me to understand if this was true, or if fate was telling us what to feel. I knew it was there and denying it didn't make it less real.

"STOP!" I yelled, my stomach turning as crimson trailed down his chest.

"Tell me this and I'll stop..." He pushed a little deeper, hissing from the pain. "If your life is worth sacrificing for all of us...then why can't I do the same for you?"

Tears flowed down my cheeks as his shadows loosened their grip on my heart. I pushed myself up slightly, trying to find an explanation to give him.

"I...I..." I sat up more and looked at him with nothing but lost eyes. This was different... This was...

The cold reality slammed into my chest, causing my heart to double over. He was right.

He moved in, dropping to his knees, the blade still at his heart. "You sacrificed yourself to break my curse...to save me, and you died in the process. Davyna...I know why you did it...even if you won't say it, and that's fine. But I love you. I love you with every fiber of my existence."

He pulled the blade back and my eyes followed the open wound still trickling blood before gazing back up at him. "When you aren't near me, I search for you. When I wake in the night, I reach for you... I can breathe when your eyes meet mine, and when you look away, my soul suffocates, longing for just one more glance."

I pulled my legs in as fresh tears fell, heating my cheeks as he continued. "I was made for you, and only you. And would carry your secrets to the grave with me. I would fight and kill anyone who tried touching you. So, I'll ask you one more time... Why did you come here today and what is going on?"

I felt around for the energy haunting me and realized it still wasn't here. Regardless, if it was present right now, I knew there was no turning back from what I was about to do.

We sat in silence for a few minutes. My eyes were locked on the floor where his blood had dripped down, but I could feel him watching me, waiting.

"I had a dream about my mother." I wrapped my arms around my knees, dropping my head as my lip quivered.

"Your mother?" I nodded, letting my head fall lower. "What else?"

"I had a dream—a nightmare—about the throne. I saw myself in there, screaming over a body...but I couldn't see the face. It was blurred." I pinched my eyes closed, shaking my head softly. "But at the end...it was clear. It was me, lifeless..."

We both sat in the quiet for what seemed like an eternity before his arms pulled me into his lap. He brushed my hair back and held me close as his hand slowly traced up and down my arm, bringing me a small comfort in the horrors plaguing me for giving life to my reality.

"Tell me more."

"The person I met in whatever realm I was in wore my face... She was the one who marked me..." I sobbed, causing him to hold me tighter. "She and her mate threatened to kill you all if I didn't fix the throne."

"What else?" he whispered.

My breaths grew shallow as I allowed the tears to stream down my face, crumbling further with each drop that fell. My body started to tremble. I pulled back, looking into his amber pools graced with so much understanding and patience. It made my heart break.

"I was pulled into my father's stone and heard a male talking about the throne. He said the one holding light and darkness would be able to control both, but I'm not that. I can't control it."

"What do you mean?" he asked.

"I know you've seen it—the scars turning dark...my eyes—and the worst part is, I think it wants to take over...because I think I won't feel it all with it. At least, that's what the voice says."

Moving me back, he turned my body to straddle his lap as his thumbs brushed over my cheeks, removing the tears still lingering on my skin. I waited for the voice inside me to laugh, to taunt me, but it stood silent, giving me this moment. Or maybe it was reveling in my weakness, my truths, and biding its time to torment me with it later.

"I don't want anyone else to die...by their hands...or mine."

"We will figure this all out. Together." He leaned in, softly brushing his lips against mine.

Every nerve in my body woke under his touch, pushing out the grief and anxiety. I let my hands travel up into his hair, pulling him deeper into me, and savoring the taste of him as our tongues collided. Our kiss went from romantic to feral within seconds. Greedy with need for more, like it was the first and only time we would be in each other's arms.

Kade's hands came up, ripping the last bit of leathers and pushing them down off my shoulders as a moan escaped my throat. "And remember this, Dearest..." He turned us around, laying me against the large stone. His hand dropped low, pulling at the top of my pants and sliding his hand down to my center.

I arched into him, his fingers dipping into me before moving up to circle over my throbbing clit. "I am your one and only nightmare... I'm the one who will never stop haunting you. You are mine to torture..." I moaned louder as he applied more pressure. "Mine to play with..." His other hand came up, pulling the leathers down over my thighs. "Mine to fuck..."

My stomach tightened as my orgasm climbed, before looking back into his lust-filled eyes swirling with blood.

"You are mine. Today. Tomorrow. And always."

Before sweet ecstasy could take me away, he removed his fingers from my center. I let out a whine from being left on the edge of my release as I watched Kade start undoing his pants. His cock sprung free, and I couldn't help but lick my bottom lip, aching to be filled with every inch.

He pulled me in, dropping to his knees as he hauled me onto his lap, and a gasp ripped from my throat.

Slowly, he guided me down on the length of him, filling me with pure pleasure, and my eyes rolled back. He growled as I pulled my body down fast. Curses fell from both our lips as my skin instantly began to glow, shimmering off the ruby walls of the cave.

We might have been crafted by magic, possessing a high power, but this transcended all forms of enchantments. This—us—was something more. His hands dug into my hips painfully as I moved over him, basking in the power that we created with each thrust.

Every part of my body vibrated as I took him in, my mind wandering to his words. Since I first laid eyes on him, he anchored me in the middle of a storming sea. He made me fight, pulling out who I truly was, all while pulling me ashore. And yet, I still couldn't let him have my heart for the fear of losing him. Or the fear of this turning out to be a cruel trick. Because this kind of intense love wasn't for the real world, only for the fictional ones. *Right?*

Looking down, I watched his hands move to my hips and press down on my lower stomach as he began thrusting into me with more intensity. The tip of his cock hit that spot within, causing my walls to tighten as I moaned louder. I dug my nails into his neck as I chased the only abyss I wanted to bask in and surrender my soul to.

"Fuck... Kade!" I fell over the edge, letting my head fall to his shoulder as he continued to work each wave, making my pleasure linger. My walls tightened around him, and curses spilled from his lips as he came.

His hands wrapped around to my backside, slowly guiding me up and down over his shaft to savor each pulse his body released. Our breathing was heavy as he laid us back against the stone, pulling me close to hear his heart beating in his chest.

We stayed still for a few minutes, lost in some semblance of tranquility of being away from all the problems... It was almost nice, calm, and part of me never wanted to leave this cave in fear of losing it.

I swallowed hard, sitting up to look into his eyes as my heart swelled. I wanted to say the three words that bled from my heart, wanted him to know I felt the same. It was moments like this that I wished he could read my mind. It would be so much easier, but saying it right now with everything that was going on...I couldn't. I just...couldn't.

I wanted to be freed from the burdens I created, freed of the constant reminder that something was inside me, and free to live a life where I could open up and allow someone to love all of me. I hoped that when the time came, I didn't nail the coffin shut on the story of us and what could have been. Even though he said he was here for me...I knew that could change in an instant, and I would once again have to learn how to hold myself up against the horrors of life, alone.

His hand wrapped around my neck, pulling me to his lips and kissing me deeply as his heart sped up to match mine. I wove every emotion I harbored for him into the movements of my lips as they devoured his, praying he could feel it all.

My hands began to buzz, making me pull back and scan the cave. At first, I thought it was them, until I realized the feeling. "Dy, what is it?" He looked around like the soldier he was, ready to attack anything threatening to come for us.

"No...it's..." I stood, using a spell to redress myself in black leathers as I glanced around the dim surroundings. "This feeling...it was the same one I felt when I was learning about my power." I moved deeper into the cave, looking around for any sign to pull me closer.

After walking a few steps, my hands began to heat, making the glow emerge and show off the dark grey wall in the back. The buzzing began piercing my ears, but I stood calm, letting my hands travel up and graze the rough surface.

"Kadeyan?" I yelled out, waiting for him to join me.

"What is it?" he asked, lifting his brow.

"I don't know."

He moved in, pulling my hand away before punching into the stone and causing it to crack open. He repeated it again until the stone crumbled in, exposing a hidden bookshelf. We both looked at one another for a moment before glancing back to see the small shelf lying within.

Kade moved out of the way as I stepped in, picking up the large, black leather journal that was clearly aged. Every worn-out crease and weathered page told a story in itself, whispering a tale that was hidden long ago. Wiping the dust off the front cover, my heart stalled in my chest, before the world slowed around me.

"What the..." he asked, leaning over my shoulder. My entire body refused to move as my gaze stayed locked on the name before me.

Nyna Ember.

I let my fingers trace the engravement as my eyes teared up once again. Was this what she wanted me to find? Was this the answer we all needed? Looking at Kadeyan, I knew the hope in my eyes was evident as he gave me a small grin.

"It's my mother's."

CHAPTER 31
DAVYNA

Darkness whipped past us as we fell through the void, landing outside the Foster estate... Well, it was technically just a home now. One that anyone could claim as their own. Maybe they would have good memories of raising their family here, filled with love and laughter. Or would it be forever cursed with heartache and hatred until it consumed them too?

I believed it was the latter.

Evren slowly walked out from behind the property. She dragged the shovel through the green grass, leaving a trail of dark, earthy soil in its wake. I started making my way towards her but slowed quickly, her grief stealing the air in my lungs. She wasn't in the mood to talk, and I could respect that... When you felt that numb, the last thing you wanted to do was open up.

I would know.

"Let's get back home," Kadeyan said, moving towards us.

Evren stopped a few inches away from me, tears still streaming from her darkened blue pools and onto her bright pink cheeks. I nodded and an orange glow surrounded her body, pulling her away from our old lives. Kadeyan wrapped his hand around my waist, snapping me out of my trance before his cool, black shadows swallowed us whole.

Landing in the hallway of his castle, I tightened my hold on the journal in my arms and pressed it against my chest. I avoided opening it because looking at the cover made me feel overwhelmed.

What would happen when I saw her handwriting? Or hear her voice within her words?

Over the years, I thought about my mother, but I held onto what Elias told me about my father: that I needed to find him. Guilt racked through me in moments when I was hell-bent on finding him, not giving her the time of day.

I figured she was dead, and that was why he didn't bring her up. Now, I couldn't help but wonder if Elias knew they were both gone. My father said he helped them hide me... So, how many more secrets were out there, hiding in the grave? I understood they were trying to protect me from Persephone, but didn't I have a right to know all this? Would her journals reveal that? I prayed it would, and that this family curse of hiding things was finally over.

Maybe I was the one meant to break it.

I walked behind Kadeyan as we made our way down the hall. Looking at him, I waited to feel the relief of sharing what was happening with me, but it wouldn't come. It was moving further away, only leaving me more paranoid than before. Would they know I told someone?

I knew Maeve saw bits of it, and she was still okay, but this was different. The words poured from my lips, exposing their secret. Would they kill him over this?

Kadeyan stalled, and I almost slammed into his solid form as he peered back to look me over. "You ready?"

"Have I ever been ready for any of this?" I asked, clutching the journal harder against my chest.

Silence fell between us for a long minute before he turned and kissed my forehead.

"Just don't tell them..."

"I know," he said before using his shadows to push the doors open.

My gaze shifted up to see all my friends standing, lost in conversation. The energy quickly changed, their voices trailing off as they focused on me and Kadeyan.

"What is going on?" Calix asked, moving towards us.

Sorin straightened up, ready for whatever was to come next.

Kade and I moved in, and I watched their eyes shift down to the journal. Instinctively, I tightened my grip on it. "We found this... I–it was my mother's."

Levanna moved slowly, resting her hand on my shoulder as she led me over to the couch. The room was as hushed as a tomb when my body sank into the plush embrace of the black velvet cushion.

I looked towards the mountains beyond on full display in the glass room, with grey clouds obscuring certain parts. Almost like they were concealing their own secrets; shielding whispered tales behind a foggy curtain.

Slowly, everyone took a seat, and all I could hear was their heartbeats pounding in my head, along with the anxiety building within. Leaning forward, I dropped the journal onto the small table. The echo reverberated, causing more panic to surge through me.

"What is inside it?" Axel asked, leaning forward to look at the cover.

I glanced over, watching Kadeyan move to the glass wall, before leaning against it as his gaze roamed over the lands. His own emotions were heightened, and I knew it was about everything I told him. It was weighing him down as he tried to figure out how he could take the burdens away. Deep down, I knew that was my responsibility alone, and I may have complicated it all by opening up.

I cleared my throat and his head slowly turned to look me over, like he was assessing if I was alright. I think he could tell I was the furthest thing from that.

"I don't know. I figured we could look it over together," I said as Evren entered the room.

Her body slowly dropped to the ground at the end of the couch I was on. Sorin's and Calix's gazes burrowed into her, both laced in concern. Her eyes were bright red, but she tried to push away her grief as she took the book. Flipping to the first page, she glanced at me and gave me a broken smile before reading.

"The Untouched fae held the keys..." Evren looked up at me,

making my heart race. "But there is only one lock." Air refused to fill my lungs as I watched my sister peek up at me, her eyes filled with worry. "The lock contains it all...every line of power. It is able to save or destroy, and in the end...both will occur."

My mouth went dry as my heart stalled in my chest, sending a searing pain through my body. What did that mean? Was I the lock? Or was it the throne? We both contained the power of this realm.

Evren let the book rest in her lap, her heartbeat picking up as her voice broke. "Davyna..."

Kadeyan moved through the hushed room, taking a seat next to me. He pulled me near him, his pine and leather scent a momentary comfort.

Levanna grabbed the journal next and scanned the pages before turning to face me. "The six stones are needed to break the link."

Kadeyan pulled my body closer to him, his grip constricting me as if I would vanish again. What link was she talking about? Our link to the stones, or was it to the other Realms?

"Is your mother talking about you?" Levanna asked as she flipped a few pages before looking at me with her crystal-blue eyes, searching for answers. She handed the book over to Calix as Nesrin, Axel, and Sorin leaned over him, silently reading from it.

I focused on Kadeyan's hand on my side as it gently swayed back and forth over my leathers. My own magic began spinning inside, clashing together within as one side wanted to end this, while the other side laughed. It was a dark and twisted sound, matching my voice once again.

My breathing picked up as the words of the demon within spoke: *Let it all burn and bask in the ashes of death.*

It was back...

I didn't hear it while in the Mortal Realm, except for that short moment it tried to come through. Now, it was deafening, banging against my walls and promising a war within.

I'm always with you. I'm the only one you can count on.

As I was about to jump up, feeling the desire to run away from myself, Axel cleared his throat and looked towards Kadeyan. I paused, turning my head to my right. Reading his expression, I knew whatever it was, it wasn't good.

Nesrin looked at the journal, her body stiffening before looking to me. A shiver ran down my spine as I let my eyes shift down to the book in Calix's hands, like it was a weapon that could kill me.

The deadliest thing in this world was not a sword...but rather the combination of ink and paper intertwined with the words you chose to write. Because those could change your life, change the world, and leave an everlasting imprint on those who held the knowledge. And something told me that my mother knew what was coming.

Kade reached his hand out and Calix rose, handing it to him as he cleared his throat. His hand holding my waist tightened and I closed my eyes, trying to take a cleansing breath. Bringing my gaze to him, he began reading over the page before glancing at me. The tension in the room grew by the second, and my stomach started twisting into knots as my apprehension rose.

"When the flames sit upon the throne...light and darkness will rage war until one stands between, able to control both. But loss will be their friend, betrayal will be their follower, and love will be their fight. The walls will fall, merging something new."

"What does that mean?" Evren asked, her voice shaking a bit.

My blood ran cold as I looked down at my hand. The scars shimmered white before they slowly shifted, showing the darkness looming below the surface. That voice in my father's stone said a part of that to me, but how was I supposed to control it when it clearly controlled me?

"It means, war is coming..." Kadeyan said as he stood taller, his face going cold with the realization. The room fell into an eerie stillness again.

I started to slowly shake my head. "No..."

I looked up, taking in everyone's gaze on me, before I stared beyond at the mountains. They were now covered in storm clouds, as if they were a promise of what the days would be like ahead of us.

"It's already here."

CHAPTER 32
DAVYNA

A few hours passed and rain pelted against the windows as we all scanned the pages of my mother's journal. It was hard not to get lost in her delicate script, imagining her somewhere in the Mortal Lands, writing this all out.

Something felt rushed in her words, like she couldn't get them down fast enough, and it came off as very deranged and fearful. Even her drawings were harsh, the lead pressing into the page harder than needed.

Nesrin and Evren brought food up. Everyone went over to the table on the back wall to grab a plate, but I couldn't think about eating. I flipped a few more pages and realized most of this information she wrote down didn't go together. Each small entry had a few lines about different things in Valyner, the stones, and the greatest evil, but she never named who it was. Was there a reason for that?

Flipping towards the back of the journal, I stopped and looked at the ancient language filling the page. *La etsa beluiva di tus el notaches.* I silently read it over, my hands buzzing more intensely the further I got into it.

Stopping, my eyes widened, realizing it was a spell. I examined it once more, taking in every intricate letter and symbol etched on the side, yet its meaning eluded me.

Not even my seer ability that helped me with knowing other spells could make me understand this. Did she make it? Or find it somewhere? Was it from another realm? What struck me with curiosity was how it ended, like it was missing the final piece.

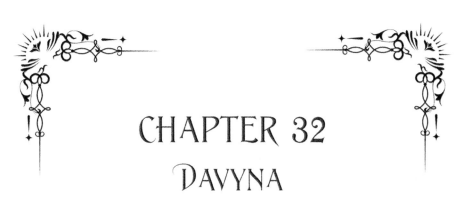

What were you trying to tell me, Mom?

Sorin moved over to the couch, glancing over the page I was on. "How are you doing, Dy?"

"I'm okay..." I said, keeping my eyes on the book, knowing it was the furthest thing from the truth.

After a few minutes of silence, I sensed his gaze on me and slowly shifted my head to the side to look into his hazel eyes.

"Your mother wrote very cryptically... Not uncommon for the older fae," he said, looking back to the journal.

"What do you mean?" I asked, glancing back and flipping through the pages.

Sorin grabbed the book from me and began searching as I glanced over his shoulder, taking in each piece of paper as he skimmed through them.

After a minute passed, he stalled on a page and I read silently.

The three Realms of fae... The veils... The six stones.

History lied to us.

"So, you think my mother kept it all separated for me to decipher? Why not just keep it all together?" I asked as my own annoyance surfaced from the mystery laid out before me.

"Well, fae wanted to—"

"My mother was born into the Cursed. She wasn't ever fae."

"Yes...but she was the only one of her kind with multiple lines of magic. Like you," Sorin stated. "Your mother was something more than the Cursed, just like you are something more than us... and she knew that. The real question now is, will this journal tell us? Or will you still have to figure it out on your own?"

We sat there in silence once more, looking at each other.

My parents clearly had secrets—more than I could have imagined—but why wouldn't my father warn me about this? Or were these my mother's skeletons she kept from him?

Everyone started moving back over to the couches and chairs. Calix reached out his hand, wanting to take another look. Passing it over, I watched his eyes fall to the floor and his whole body stiffened.

Kadeyan moved over to him, looking down as he picked up a letter that slipped free. I stood still as he looked at the side facing him, but my eyes were on the back, where it showcased a seal with an *E* emblem. The same one I'd seen before on the small white chest my father left me. My jaw fell open slightly as I gripped my nails into the cushion, bending the material within.

"Where did that come from?" I asked as Calix flipped through the pages.

"I have no idea..."

Flipping it around, Kadeyan showed me the front of the letter. *Davyna* was written across the front.

"Everyone out," Kadeyan demanded, taking in the shock on my face.

One by one, everyone began to leave the room without question.

Evren stood up, looking me over before glancing towards Kade. "Give her a minute, Ev. You need one too."

After a long moment, she nodded and began walking towards me. She placed her hand on my shoulder, squeezing lightly. I clasped my hand over hers before she turned and left us.

Once the door closed, Kadeyan moved towards me, looking down at the letter before handing it to me. "I can leave...or I can be here for you. What do you want?"

I stood there, lost in a daze for a minute, and Kadeyan took that as his answer. He began walking towards the door, dropping the letter on the couch, but everything within screamed to stop him.

"Please... Don't leave..." The words tumbled from my lips in a desperate plea. Tears trailed down my cheeks as I turned to face him, and anxiety coiled within, pressing down on my chest.

He smiled as he took my hand, moving over to the couch. "Never." He got comfortable, lifting one leg up and patting between his legs for me to lay with him. I didn't hesitate to move into those arms that would forever be a refuge. "Do you want me to read it first, or... out loud?"

I went to speak, but more tears fell, and I knew that if I was to read it myself, it would be inaudible as sobs ripped through me.

Trying to open the letter, I realized there was a force keeping it closed. A spell.

I blinked away the tears, focusing my gaze on the piece of paper. My hand began to tingle as I hovered it over the seal. This magic was strong and matched mine perfectly in a way...but less dark and haunted. My mouth curled up as each thread of her spell came undone, causing the seal to break open.

Laying back onto his chest, I handed him the letter and waited for him to start reading...

"My beautiful daughter,

"I never thought the day would come where I would be writing this, mainly because I never thought that I could conceive after my transformation...and I always wanted children. Your dad did too.

"Yet, here we are, sitting in this old house in the mountains, with you kicking my stomach as we speak...and me knowing that our lives were never destined to be with one another.

"I thought I knew love. And in a way, I know I do. I have that with your father. But a love for your own child is beyond this world. It means you will do whatever needs to be done to make sure your little one is safe.

"How I wish this wasn't the life for you. The burdens you will carry with what you truly are. I know what is coming because I was told. I wish I could tell you who... but I can't. And every day since then, I have spent finding ways to make sure it never happens. But, sweetie, I don't know if that is possible anymore. Can we truly

change our fates?

"There are so many enemies out there, Davyna. Ones that should have never become yours. I asked to take your place, but I don't have what you have. So, I did the next best thing.

"I know I will die the night you are born. I know you will become a true fae as you grow. And I know you will use the power deep inside you to unleash the evil that is now coming.

"The power inside you, my daughter...it is greater than you could imagine and will shatter the wheel so long as you don't lose yourself.

"You know what to do... Look at this journal. Use your father's stone. Connect the pieces. Because you are the only one who can stop them now.

"I'll see you in your dreams.

"With all my love,

"Your mother, Nyna."

Kadeyan dropped the letter in front of me as I looked over the words, and my world began spinning. She knew this was going to happen...all of it.

Everything I thought I knew about being fae was slowly coming unraveled, along with the secrets still lost with the dead. I wrapped my hand around my father's stone, and a nauseating shift in the world made my head spin before it ripped me in.

Coming to an abrupt stop, I stumbled into the small, circular room. It was glowing, with delicate swirls passing through the ruby gemstone walls.

Moving around the edge of the room, I could see many memories of them before she passed. Their bonding ceremony, my father singing to my mother's stomach as she smiled down at him, and them sharing laughter as they walked along a lake. Beautiful and happy memories of two people so in love, but that didn't mean it was without its pain.

My eyes widened by the second as the color changed in the walls to a vivid white, showing my mother in each one. Her writing in her journals and burying something in the ground. The last ones had me stopping dead in my tracks. My mother dying, with my father's death right next to it.

Moving towards it, I brought my hand up to the stone wall as the tears escaped my eyes, not realizing they were there. My hand trembled as I let out a shaky breath, the weight of despair blanketing me.

This shouldn't have happened to them...

Touching the stone wall again, the memories and the scene in front of me dissolved, compelling me to retreat a step. The swirls roared through the crystal as if a storm was opening up, seeking its next landfall to tear up anything in its wake. And I had a deep feeling in the pit of my stomach that it was coming right for me.

Turning around, I watched as another memory took over every inch of the room. My jaw fell open as I watched my mother walk away from my father, her golden eyes beaming with fury.

"Nyna! Don't you dare walk away from me again!"

"Why, Ezekiel? You clearly can't handle the truth."

"No, I can... I just won't accept it! The truth and what will happen are two different things."

I took a step back, bringing my hand to my chest in hopes it would calm my racing heart. What truth?

"No, they are one... Everything I told you will come to fruition."

My father's silver eyes began to melt as his glare burrowed into my mother before he turned away from her. Looking into his eyes, I saw the tears threatening to spill over as he shook his head slowly.

"I don't want this for Davyna...but it will happen. My father told me everything, Ezekiel."

"How the fuck is any of this possible?" he yelled, throwing a crystal vase across the room as my mother's eyes softened and looked down. "Why didn't you tell me sooner? Why didn't you tell me what you were?"

"I didn't know until recently... He told me the day I found out I was pregnant."

"So, you kept this from me for the last two months? If what you are saying is true, then we have...."

They were quiet for a long moment before her eyes softened. "You have one more month with me...and maybe two more months with her..."

It took him a minute to collect his thoughts as the tears fell, matching the ones now falling from my mother's cheeks.

My father rushed over to her, grabbing her by the face and pulling her close. "I love you so much, Nyna. I love you more than the air I breathe, more than life itself, and that will never cease to captivate my world... Even in death." His breathing was heavy, matching my mother's as they gazed into each other's eyes. "So... what do we do next? How do we protect our baby girl?"

"I have it all in place..." She pulled a dagger from her side, forcing my father to glance down at the blade. I couldn't see it clearly, but there was a soft glow of light and darkness radiating off it. "But there is a spell I need to do...and it requires a sacrifice."

Jumping up, I looked around the room as Kadeyan's hands pulled me back. His voice was a soft echo, but I couldn't hear him.

They knew... They knew they were going to die. They knew they were going to leave me. And they still wouldn't even give me the piece I needed to know what the fuck I was!

And that dagger... I'd seen it before...on the castle doors in that land void of color.

"Davyna!" Kadeyan yelled, breaking me from my trance. "What did you see?"

"My parents... They knew... They knew—" I said, falling back into the craze of all of this.

I stood up and began pacing the room, my breaths becoming shorter with each second that passed. Kadeyan rose, moving over and encircling me with his strong arms. He held me taut as I cried. The tears slid down his leathers and my knees buckled, causing him to fall with me.

Everything I thought I knew about being fae was slowly becoming unraveled, along with the secrets rotting in the ground. I didn't need this to prove it when everything else was as clear as day. I was something else.

I didn't want to know anymore.

I wanted this to stop.

Make it stop...

I can fix that.

CHAPTER 33
DAVYNA

Climbing into bed, I felt like life was moving around me in a haze, and I wanted it to stop. I wanted everything to vanish: the voice in my mind that was growing harder to ignore; the creatures haunting me; the guilt; and most of all, finding more to my lineage.

The thought of that alone caused my stomach to turn sour, and my eyes closed. Why give me half-truths and veiled secrets, tainted in mystery that made nothing clearer for what I was now facing?

I was confused, angry, and hurt at the same time, and it was all directed at them. *My* parents.

Kadeyan slid in between the sheets, pulling me to him, and said, "It will be okay, Dearest..."

Not believing it, all words failed me as I stared off in a daze, while the darkness pulled me away and into what I hoped would be a momentary sanctuary from this life I was living.

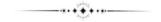

The throne room was in ruins, covered in large stones, and exposed to the sky above painted in a darkened red hue. Rain pelted against my head, the droplets rolling down my face as I brought my gaze to the throne. Standing before it was me, glaring at the shadow figure as tears ran down my face.

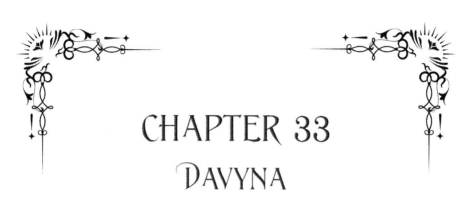

The room began to spin, and I glanced around, watching the images before me blur. I dropped to my knees and dug my fingers into

the stone to hold me in place. Gritting my teeth, I heard the voice of the male but couldn't make out what he was saying before a familiar scream pierced into my ears.

Breathing heavily, I pushed myself up and the room became still, showing this other version of me standing over someone, just as it did the last time I was brought here. Fear rose as I slowly moved in, watching the puddle of blood grow on the ground. I stopped as it met the tips of my boots and glanced up at the blurred faces flashing from the corpse.

Bile rose in my throat as I waited to see if it would tell me who they were—who was dead. But it ended the same, showing me on the ground: lifeless.

Backing away, a hand dropped onto my shoulder, causing me to jump. Before I could turn and see who it was, we began falling through the void until the woods were the only thing surrounding us.

My feet slammed into the ground, forcing a groan from my lips. Turning, my fury rose, thinking this was the shadow, but the face staring back at me forced me to go still. "Mom?"

"Hello, sweetie," *she said, her sweet smile turning up as her eyes glistened through sheer blue mist.*

"How is this even possible?" *I moved back, looking her over.*

"When I died, I used a part of my power to link me to your life force so that I could help you when the time came."

I looked at her, confused. Memories flashed in my mind as I thought about growing up, trying to find my father, and breaking the chains placed on me that kept my power mute. She was with me all along and never made herself known?

"Why are you just now appearing to me then? Why didn't you help me before? You knew I was going to go through all of this, and yet you decided to keep me in the dark?" *I spat out, feeling overwhelmed with anger once again. I should have been basking in the reality that I was talking to her, but it didn't remove the sting of her words.*

"I wanted to...but I couldn't. It could have altered the course of your life if I interfered..."

"How do you know? What if it made my life easier...or better?" *I gritted my teeth together, waiting for her response.*

She dropped her head, shaking it slightly before slowly meeting my gaze again. "I know a lot, Davyna... I think more than I ever wanted to, because carrying this burden breaks me. Even now, in death." *Her eyes shined brighter, showcasing the tears welling up.*

"Then tell me: What are the stones going to do? Who are the creatures I met, and what realm was I in? Who was your father and how did he tell you all this?" *I moved in and she pulled her shoulders back, standing taller as one tear slid down her cheek.* "No, actually, I want to know this first... What am I?"

She was silent as I stared her down, my fury evident in my eyes.

"You need to control this side of you... As for your questions, I can't answer them."

"Why?!" *I screamed, moving back and running my fingers through my hair.* "Then why leave me your journal? Or tell me you knew this was going to happen?" *My eyes locked on my hand as I pulled it down, seeing the scars shimmer into darkness.*

"I am bound by my blood oath to not speak these things unless you figure it out on your own... So, I wrote as much as I could to give you a direction in what you needed. That's all I can give you... I wish I could give you more. I really do."

Her voice was soft—sincere even—but it did little to stop me from turning around, walking right up to her, and saying, "That's no excuse. You and Dad lied to me..."

"We withheld the truth...but we did everything possible to make sure you lived. You would do the same for your child."

I shook my head, slowly stepping back to put distance between us.

"You think this is living? Pushing everyone I love away because a fucking monster threatened to kill them? You think I'm content with having no clue what I am, or how I fucking tore a realm open and...." *I choked on the words as a sob ripped from my throat.*

I turned away from her, remembering all the blood on my hands of the fae who had died since I burned the throne. If I hadn't done what I did, they would all still be alive.

"This isn't living...and a mother would see that."

"I do see it. I see it every day!" *she yelled and her voice broke.* "I see you falling into the darkness. I see every tear fall from your cheeks. I see you carry the world on your shoulders...and I can do nothing but watch and die over and over again inside." *She moved in, but I retreated, shaking my head at her.* "Please, Davyna... I need you to know I never wanted this for you."

The darkness within crept out from its hiding place, moving through my veins until it consumed my vision. Narrowing my gaze on her, she stood still, unfazed by what monster lived inside me. Taking a step forward, the silver in my eyes beamed onto her sheer blue form, showcasing her features.

"I guess it doesn't matter... I am what I am because of you." *My lip rose to one side as I looked her over before meeting her gaze once more.* "Thanks for nothing."

I began to walk away, my nails digging into the flesh of my palm until pain bloomed. This was all a waste, wasn't it? Hoping that she would give me anything to help, when she and my father were the orchestrators of the life I was forced to live. I wanted to understand, but I couldn't because I needed to know what I was up against. I needed to help Valyner, my friends, and myself before I lost it.

I was trying to be strong and carry this weight, but I was fracturing...and she could see it. Yet, that made no difference in giving me what I needed to survive.

"Davyna, you need to be careful with the power you hold. It will—" *I stalled, turning back as she struggled to find the words. After a moment, her head fell.* "You need to control it...or something worse is going to happen."

I looked her over as a sense of hollowness seeped in deeper, before glancing back into her eyes. "Nothing can be worse than this."

CHAPTER 34

KADEYAN

Hours passed by in a blur as I held Davyna to my chest. I was captivated by every little scrunch of her face, and how her chest rose and fell. Plus, I couldn't bear the thought of sleep. After tonight, my heart broke for my mate, tearing it more than I thought possible.

Her parents knew so much more than they chose to share with her, and I couldn't help but try and think back to when our fathers were together. Did they mention any of this?

I wanted to bring her peace, to give her what she needed, and to stand with her in what was coming. Because she deserved it...regardless of what had transpired between us.

I understood now.

And if I was in her shoes...I'd do the same. I would do anything to protect her, my friends, and Valyner. I forgave her the day she came back to me, even if the pain was still ripping me apart. There was nothing that she could do that would keep me from her...from what this was between us.

Were all mating bonds this strong? Or was it just us?

I believed it was the latter because what we had was beyond this realm, beyond this universe... Without even joining as one, I still couldn't deny the love that bled from my veins was for her, and her only.

Glancing down, my lips ticked up as her brows furrowed before nestling closer to me. Her body pressed into mine and I felt my dick twitch within my slacks, bringing on the consuming hunger that always beckoned me in her presence.

Laying her back, I shifted to the side before scooting down the bed. My mind clouded over with need to see her arch in pleasure; to drink down her sweet moans. Pulling the sheets down, I looked down at her nightgown riding up her thighs and groaned under my breath.

Lowering myself, I fixed my eyes on her pussy as my hands brushed the thin material up. I moved in slowly and glanced up at her as my tongue slowly glided up her center. My dick hardened as her breath hitched, and I grinned.

I worked slowly, savoring her taste and the way she began to melt into my touch. Her tense expression fell away as her lips parted, and I dipped my tongue into her cunt. Her eyes fluttered open and looked down at me as I moved up to her clit again, sucking lightly.

"W–what are you doing?" she whispered, her voice plagued with sleep and desire.

"Taking care of you." I brought my mouth back down, licking and sucking. Her moan sent shivers down my spine, causing my balls to tighten.

"Fuck... Kade," she whispered.

As I glanced up, I took in how she arched. My hand went to my cock, stroking it as she rocked her hips, following my rhythm.

This wasn't about *me*...this was about *her*.

Dropping myself, I wrapped my hands around her thighs, pulling her gently until she was pressed into my mouth. Her body shuddered as her small pants grew heavier, and I picked up my pace.

"Kadeyan...I want...you...inside me."

Averting my gaze from her sweet cunt, I watched as she grabbed her breast. Her hypnotizing silver pools were on me, forcing my cock to release precum.

Fuck...me.

"No, Dearest. This is all about you tonight. No matter how much I want to come all over you."

Her lips turned up as I went back to devouring her, pulling more moans from her lips. "Give...me that," she moaned out as I felt her walls tighten around my tongue. "I want my skin dripping with you."

My slacks vanished from my body, and I glanced up to see her nightgown was gone too. Both her hands went to her breasts, and when her fingers pinched her nipples, I growled.

Burying my face into her, I feasted on her, pulling louder moans as she fell into the bliss I was giving her. I brought my hand up and slipped three fingers into her tight pussy before I started moving them.

It didn't take long before her walls pulsed, and her moans echoed into our room cloaked in night. Pulling my fingers back, I licked all over her, cleaning her as she came down, before bringing my fingers to my mouth. I sucked off her essence, my dick throbbing as I sat up before her.

Pressing herself up onto her elbows, she drank in my form, stopping at my cock. "Come on, Dark Lord...give me more."

I shook my head and my smile tipped up. "You asked for it." Crawling up the bed, I straddled her as my shadows lashed back, filling her.

A gasp fell from her lips as they fucked her, and I began stroking my cock. Leaning down, I wiped the precum on her chest. Her body quaked, and the liquid traveled down her skin.

"You are perfect...do you know that?" I asked her as I pumped harder. Her hands came up, pressing her breasts together, and I leaned in, placing my cock between them as I growled.

"Fuck, yes...Kade," she cried, and I moved faster, my balls tightening as my release built. Her own shadows lashed out, holding her perfect peaks together as she brought her hand to her mouth. She bit deep into the flesh of her palm, and the smell of iron drove me wilder as she offered me her grey blood.

I gripped her wrist and brought it closer to my lips. My breathing grew heavier, matching hers. I traveled my tongue up her palm, her blood shooting through my body and making it heat.

Pulling back, I brought my hand to my dick as chills skated down to the base of my spine. I pumped hard as she screamed, her orgasm ripping through her again as my shadows struggled to move in her, and I released my own all over her chest.

Her hands traveled down, rubbing my essence into her skin before coating her breast. I continued to come, my vision spotting with black dots as I doubled over, fisting the sheets.

"Fuck, Davyna..." Every pulse lasted longer than the last, stealing my breath as I glanced up at her. She lifted her hands, and I could see my cum coating them, her desire still evident in her eyes. Bringing her fingers to her lips, she sucked them off, moaning, and I was in awe.

My little Ember...

Leaning down, I gripped her jaw and consumed her mouth. Our tongues got lost in a dance of passion and I wanted more. But I also wanted to go back to holding her, to letting her know I was here. For everything. Whether it was to make her lose herself from her problems, or to fight and hold her when she was breaking.

I wanted this...always and forever.

An hour passed, and Davyna and I took a quick bath before getting back into our clothes. She fell back to sleep fast, and I wanted to believe that holding her helped. I couldn't take away all her problems overnight, but I hoped that tonight helped her in some way.

Pulling her in closer, I laid my head back and started to close my eyes as I heard a soft knock at the door.

Turning, I watched as it cracked open, seeing Axel peek his head in. I pushed into his mind. "*There was an attack.*"

I got out of bed, making sure to not wake Dy, and I walked over to grab my leather jacket. Moving out of the room, I shut the door softly as Axel's brows furrowed. "Are you not going to wake Davyna for this?"

"No...she deserves rest after the day she had. Where did it take place, and why weren't we notified?" I started walking down the hall, seeing Nesrin leaning against the wall with her leg bent and propped up.

"It was the Crystal Court," Axel stated as he walked over to his mate and grabbed her hand.

"Let's go make sure they are good."

Nesrin huffed. "Like they have for us and the other Courts?"

I paused, turning to face her, and smirked. "I didn't say they deserved it." Black mist poured from me as I encased my friends, pulling us through the gap.

Landing on the edge of the Dark Forest, I could hear the cries reverberate from the town as smoke rose from the south side.

Fae were in the forest, burying their dead in the distance. Although, the souls of the dead fae wouldn't feed the forest anymore; Davyna broke that when she came here last, opening her Crystal power.

Jinx's voice filtered through the trees, talking to her Court members as she caught sight of me, Axel, and Nesrin standing on the border. Anger poured from her as she took wide strides, eating up the distance between us. "What the hell do you want?"

"To see what happened and if you need help, of course."

"Shut the fuck up, Kadeyan. You don't care about the Crystals," Jinx said, venom coating her words.

I laughed, looking over to my friends. "Actually, I care for one Crystal... So, that isn't true." I pulled back my smart-ass demeanor a little, knowing it wasn't the time, even if I hated her. "What was it?"

"I have no fucking clue. They had human-like upper bodies, but they looked vile. The rest of them mimicked a snake. They were dowsing the lands in their venom as they went through. We had to use our power to push out the flames and burn most of the town's shops to stop the venom from spreading." Her eyes narrowed on me, her dark blue irises matching the sky above. "This is all your fault."

"Please, tell me how this is the Lord's fault?" Nesrin bit back, taking a step forward.

Axel reached out and wrapped his hand around her arm as he stood by her, waiting for anything to try to touch his mate.

"My sister wouldn't have gotten sick and would still be here if *his mate* didn't fuck everything up. The creatures wouldn't have killed two hundred fae tonight if we would have closed Valyner!" she spat out.

Nodding my head, I bit back my own anger as I glanced up. "You know... Tell me this, Jinx. What would you do for the ones you love?"

She went to speak, but halted before shutting her mouth.

I chuckled. "Exactly. So, the next time you want to put down someone I love...someone who houses a part of *my* soul...you will no longer be attached to yours." Turning around, Axel and Nesrin followed suit. "Let us know if you need any provisions over the next week. We will have the soldiers bring them!" I yelled back.

Axel came up by my side. "Sorry. I got you out of bed for nothing." He laughed.

"No, you didn't. I will take care of it all if it means Davyna can heal—"

"What do you mean, heal?" Axel asked.

Nesrin glanced at me, giving me a look. I studied her for a moment as she turned away from me, knowing they must have chatted at one point. I knew Dy didn't tell anyone anything, but Nesrin must have picked up on her trauma response. Because it was what she did with us, when she first came to the Fallen Court over two-hundred years ago.

"Let's just get home and sleep..." I said, smiling at him and protecting my little Ember's secrets because they were mine to hold now. And I'd gladly take it all if it meant she could breathe easier.

My shadows swallowed me up and dropped me into my room. I smiled, prepared to take her in, but I was met with a hollowed soul.

She was gone.

I was only gone for about an hour... Where did she go?

Looking round, I focused on her scent, trying to find her as I threw the door open. It was happening again. Did she leave? Did *they* come and take her?

Fuck, no. No...

CHAPTER 35
KADEYAN

Night bled into morning, and before I knew it, the entire day was almost gone as I walked the lands with Axel. All our friends split up early this morning, looking for her, but Axel refused to leave my side. With each step, it sent me deeper inward, forgetting he was still near me.

"Kadeyan, I don't know what you are holding inside...but you know I'm here for you, right?" Axel said, breaking me from my trance.

"I know...but it's not my story to tell, Ax."

He nodded, his eyes scanning over the woods of the Ember Court before he slowed. "But *your* story is worth telling."

"And what if my story is just one fuckup after another? I pushed the person I love to accept our bond—to accept me. What if I did this to her?"

Axel let out a breath, his gaze falling to the ground to watch his boot kick up the crimson and copper leaves. "You did. You pushed and expected a lot of someone who had just become what she was always meant to be. But what's happening now...it's not your fault. You have to fight to show her you're here regardless of the bond. Show her love, Kade."

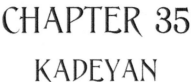

I paused, looking back at him, his storm-grey eyes pinned to me as he continued. "I'm here if you need to talk and share what you are feeling. I always will be. We might not be brothers by blood, but you are my brother." He walked up, placing his hand on my shoulder for a long moment. "Hey, don't the Embers have a lot of caves in their mountains?"

I followed his gaze through the tree line, taking in the rusted stone mountains on display before us. Shit, he was right...they did, but did she know that?

Levanna appeared next to us, out of breath. "We...have a...problem," she got out and my stomach sunk.

"What?" I asked, feeling my world sway.

"Fifteen fae went missing last night from all different Courts. Maeve told me at the Sky temple," she said, looking between us.

I placed my hand against a tree, waiting for the bile in my stomach to wretch. My eyes focused back on the mountains and my wings spread wide before launching me into the air with pure adrenaline coursing through my veins. I needed to find her.

Circling over the caves, I looked at any detail of a struggle, blood... Anything. Turning back around and lowering, I caught sight of Axel trying to meet my pace with Levanna in his arms.

Focusing, I pushed forward, and almost stalled instantly as I noticed something amiss. The gravel outside one of the caves was creating a line, trailing into the stone structure. Dropping down, I walked over to it as my heart slammed against my ribs.

"Kadeyan?" Levanna said as she ran over to me, before Axel looked at what I was taking in.

"Axel...do you smell that?" I said as my body quaked, and my gaze moved to the opening.

"Blood," he said, softly.

I glanced up at the sky, knowing the sun would be setting soon... I needed to go in there. I needed to see it for myself. Yet, every bone in my body fused to the ground, denying me from taking the smallest step, and my lip quivered.

"Let us go in, okay? We will look first," Levanna said, as she began walking in. Her own hesitation was evident in how she approached with Axel by her side.

I stood as still as the mountains surrounding me, trying to breathe as they went in. After a few dreaded minutes, Levanna came out. Her eyes were plagued with horror, and she placed her arm out, gripping the stone.

That's all it took for me to run in, taking in Axel kneeling before the bodies. I looked over each one, taking in their charred remains with their blood. It wasn't fresh...but it had to have happened early this morning.

Within the pools of crimson, I took in the hearts placed throughout before I looked back up. I counted each body, realizing there were only fifteen...

"We know all the Embers... Which one would have reason to do this?" Axel asked, standing up, but I ignored his question as it sunk in...

An Ember who was battling with something dark... An Ember who told me she felt like it wanted to come out.

Looking back to the opening of the cave, I started walking. Axel met my pace, not asking questions, and I was grateful for it. Because I only had one thing on my mind: To find her and make sure that power didn't swallow her whole.

CHAPTER 36
DAVYNA

Sitting up, I took in as much air as my lungs would allow me and scanned my surroundings. I was in the Dead Forest that buds up against the mountains of the Fallen Court. My brows pinched together. When did I come out here? I remembered falling asleep in my bed last night. And based on the sky above, it was nearing twilight.

I took another breath and started to bring my hands to my face before the air was ripped from my lungs. My hands were painted in crimson, the blood dry and flaking from my skin. As panic rushed in, I looked around, searching for an explanation, but none came.

I recounted my memories—seeing the throne room again in the nightmare, and my mother pulling me away and saying she couldn't tell me anymore than what she left me with. I remembered getting angry, feeling the darkness come in and invade the dream. Then, I woke up with Kade, and fell asleep again...

Horror filtered through me. As if the blood on my hands was fresh, it dripped into this madness that was my life. Shaking, I rose, glancing around one last time.

I was alone, but the voice within snickered. *We are the villain in this story... Start acting like one.*

My mouth went dry as I asked the voice within, "What did I do?"

Searing pain shot through my head. I winced as the laughter grew louder and felt as if I was about to be sick.

You let me in...and we had so much fun.

CHAPTER 37
DAVYNA

The chilling breeze caressed my face as I moved through the woods. The deep oranges of the sky were becoming tainted with the dark sapphire of night. My heart raced in my chest as I changed out of my nightgown and into my leathers. I wiped my hands against my slacks, trying to recount my steps from last night and all day.

Where did I go? Whose blood painted my flesh? And why couldn't I remember?

My blood began to boil as the demon within laughed.

"I'm not a bad person! I don't want to be!" I yelled as I came to a stop. My lip started to tremble as my knees gave out, pulling me down and into the damp soil.

When the snickering finally retreated, I released the fury brewing within and screamed. The power that surged from me was enough to force the ground to shake and the trees to bend away from me. Almost like they didn't want to be touched by the torment and pain I was unleashing.

My head fell forward and my fists rose, slamming into the ground. The rage grew, taking root deeper within my soul. My mind was shattering, being put under pressure that made it hard to think straight or to even breathe.

A laugh sounded around me—no, in my mind—but it wasn't the one I've come to know as my own. I shot up, my breathing becoming heavier because it was deep and laced in something so vile that even the gods themselves would shudder.

"You look so good on your knees, little cinder... It's exactly how I like it."

"Leave me alone!" I yelled out, even though I knew his voice was invading my mind. He was near though... I could feel it.

"I can't. Not until you give us what we want."

Looking around, I sensed the cool power wash over me as my lip rose into a snarl. "Fuck you! I'm done!" Growls rose from behind me, making me stand and feel my magic sway within.

Gripping my fingers into my dirt-covered palms, I watched as Ravyn pounced between the trees, her red eyes beaming under the grey clouds. I took a breath and watched her stare at me, tilting her head to the side.

"Go back... I'll be home soon." I smiled but watched her survey the Lands, curiosity making her hair stand on end. She sensed it too.

Looking up, I watched as her eyes turned black. She let out a hiss before running off back towards the castle. My brows furrowed as I took a deep breath and started walking back, too, hoping Kade was home and not out searching for me. Although, if I was gone this long, he probably was.

"You might want to come see what I have for you. I think you'll like it."

Using my sleeve, I wiped my eyes and turned back towards the direction I was walking. I stalled. I didn't want to see him, but something else within me wanted to end this...to end him. And if he was here, then I had an opportunity to rid myself of at least one problem I was facing.

Rolling my shoulders back, I walked slowly as my flames sparked within my hands. My boots crunched down on twigs, sending soft echoes around me as I readied myself to fight.

After about thirty minutes of walking, I noticed the sky changing. The grey clouds vanished almost instantly as I entered No-Man's-Land.

The clearing was filled with lush, red roses budding up against the rich crimson trees in the distance.

The Ember Court.

I stopped, my throat drying up like I drank down sand as my eyes focused on the people lined up. Their fear quickly smothered my skin, choking me and causing my muscles to tighten.

"You disobeyed me, didn't you?" he said, stepping out from behind a male whose face was stained with tears. He was wearing Kadeyan's face again, but the voice coming from him was his own, coated in something abhorrent.

"I would ask you where you went, but I don't have to. I can't feel anything in the Mortal Realm, let alone pass into it...which means you were there. And so was your mate. How did you figure it out?"

"I didn't--"

He laughed, brushing the tears off the male's face as he looked over the other fae. Nodding, he smiled as a female moved out from the crowd, pulling my gaze to her.

Ash.

She stopped in the middle of the field, and I moved in a few feet before stopping. I took in her tear-stained face, ripping my own trepidation to the surface.

He walked towards her, his grin growing more wretched. "Your heart skipped a beat. You're lying." He cocked his head towards me, looking disappointed as he stopped by Ash's side. "I thought we had an agreement, Davyna? You fix the throne, keep our little secret, and I don't kill people you care about."

My simmering anger towards my parents and the mysteries they left dropped and turned feral on the monster standing before me. "Tell me why it has to be me. You have similar power. Why can't you do it?" I yelled, stepping forward as my fires spun up my arms and into the dying day.

"Don't you think I've tried? But this is your curse. Your mess. And it's affecting all realms, even your precious humans."

I stood there, stunned. Was that why the Mortal Realm was not aging as fast? My eyes focused back on all the fae lined up. They were perfectly still as if... *Shit.*

"What are you doing to them?"

He laughed, grabbed Ash by the throat, and pulled her to him. I moved in. Sensing the fae's power deep within trying to fight his hold, I realized who they all were.

"You care about the Embers, don't you? Didn't you search to understand them when you first got here?"

"How do you know that?" I asked, hesitantly.

"I can learn anything by taking another's face and asking questions. Or use one single touch to break into their head and take what I want." He let go of Ash and began moving towards me. "Your story is very interesting. And I want to know more because, clearly, you are something more than these Valyner fae."

"Well, here I am! Fucking making history, then!" I yelled, placing my arms out wide to make a spectacle of myself. "Now, let them go!"

"That you are... That you are." He looked me up and down, smiling as he crossed his arms over his chest, but it made my stomach turn. "Will you go to the throne and try again...please?" His voice was calm now, and I studied him as uncertainty rose from the pit in my stomach.

I looked over the fae again, before slowly pulling my gaze back to meet the monster before me.

"And you'll let them go?"

"You have my word."

My power within began to spin, and everything went on guard. "Fine... I'll go now and stay there all night if I have to."

"Excellent," he said, turning to face the fae. "But first..." A black shadow bloomed from the left and surged through the lands where they all stood, taking their heads clean off. Everything slowed as I looked back to Ash, her eyes wide as she shook her head *no*...like it was a warning I needed to listen to.

Before the shadows hit her, I dove into her mind and heard, "*Don't do it... He's--*"

The world around me transformed into a blur of motion as I unleashed my fury, interlacing it into each flame. They erupted with a ferocity that barreled through me, stained in sorrow and rage. His reaction was swift and his fist collided with my face, sending me reeling back as the pain bloomed in my skull. My body swayed as I willed all my power to surge forth, attempting to drown him in its embrace.

He pressed forward, the torment I was trying to inflict doing nothing more than acting as an inconvenience. Before I could try again, his fingers closed around my throat in a viselike grip, constricting my breath.

"I released them, as you requested."

I gasped, my fingers digging into his flesh and sending my fires through his veins. But it only made him groan in delight as his grin turned into a full-fledged smile. Spots of darkness bled into my vision as I continued to fight, but they felt like shadows promising peace in the midst of so much sorrow and pain.

"If you would have kept your mouth shut, they would all still be here. But you couldn't even do that one simple thing..." His eyes narrowed. "All the Embers are gone because of you. Even the few I left back in the town," he hissed, his voice a chilling reminder of his threats and his control over me.

Drawing me closer, his breath brushed against my ear like a toxic whisper. "This is the price for your disobedience."

With a violent throw, I crashed against the unforgiving ground. A scream of frustration and pain clawed its way up from within me, and I channeled it into a wave of darkness that surged outward. It stretched, extending its inky tendrils across the clearing, and transformed the day into a never-ending night, as if the sun had never touched it with its warmth.

As I pulled it back in, feeling the loss stab me in the chest, I glanced over the clearing. All that remained were dead roses. My breathing halted in my chest as I turned to look at the Ember Lands beyond, and my heart began beating faster.

I rose on shaking legs and tasted the bile coating my throat as I pushed myself forward until I was running.

They couldn't all be dead... They couldn't.

I ran through the streets after I fell out of the gap, fear sticking to my skin as my eyes scanned the horrors. Bodies laid on the red-bricked path, their heads resting next to their still bodies. Tears began blurring my vision and I pushed myself harder, the air refusing me my next breath.

Fae were stunned, some crying as they held onto the corpses. I pushed myself past them, soaking in their grief. It was mixing with my own, and tears slid freely down my cheeks. As I got to the back of the town, I took in the clearing and searched for Kadeyan.

I began moving, feeling my chest ache as I heard the voices whispering around me.

"Do you think she did this?"

And another said, "It's probably her fault; everything else is. I heard fifteen fae went missing last night... No one has seen them."

My stomach bottomed out as flashes of last night came back to me. My eyes closed and I saw myself as if I was standing beyond, the screams of the fae piercing my ears as I laughed at them... I *laughed* at them...before...

A male's hand wrapped around my wrist, pulling me back. As I turned, cool metal sliced through the air, cutting me across my face.

"What the fuck did you do?"

I pulled myself free and brought my hand up to my cheek. The warm liquid quickly coated my flesh. I pulled my hand back and saw the grey of my blood beam against my fingers.

"What the fuck? What is wrong with her?" someone called out as they tried to make sense of what they were seeing.

"She is a carcinoma to our kind! That's what's wrong with her!" yelled the man who cut me. He moved in, and I started to relish in the pain searing in my cheek. As I faced him, all the guilt and pain turned to mist. Darkness celebrated as it stepped forward, extinguishing any trace of light from within.

"You are just like your father," he spat at my feet. "And I'm going to enjoy watching you die."

I laughed, hearing it become more deranged by the second as I basked in his statement. Lashing out, my hand gripped his throat as I pulled him in, noticing we were only a few inches off from each other in height.

"You're right. I am his daughter...but I am far worse."

Flames extended out towards the fae running in with their weapons held high, while others used their powers to push back. I watched as the smart few ran, then gazed back into the eyes of the male I held in my hand. I tightened my grip, and I could feel the darkness invade my eyes, fully captivating me. It felt good... I *felt* good.

"Davyna!" Kade's voice sounded from nearby.

I slowly turned to see him push through the wall of flames at his inhuman speed. His shadows lashed out, taking the man and dragging him back as his hands gripped my shoulders.

"Davyna, snap out of it!" he yelled again, and I slowly came back down, sensing the pain building once again.

The loss.

The fear.

It was all back.

"It's okay, Dy... Look at me!" he said, moving his hands to my face to keep me from looking at the fae beyond, but I could feel it. Their anger, their anxiety...

"Kadeyan?" I said as my voice shook, but by the look on his face, he already knew what happened.

"Go back to the castle, please. Let me deal with this." Numbness slowly seeped in as I processed his words. "Go!" he yelled and I stumbled out of his hold, turning away as the hatred and disdain from the fae showered me.

"Fuck you, Kadeyan! She is the––" yelled the man who I was about to kill. At the sound of his voice, I turned, only to see black mist swallow them both.

I fell into the void, but only made it to the forest up the hill before I dropped out and emptied my stomach next to a large oak. I stood there for a few minutes, trying to catch my breath, but the images of the fae I killed, Ash, and all the other Embers who were gone made my stomach turn.

My body dry heaved over and over again.

I hadn't yet lost control like that. I had been able to control it. Or, at least, to some extent, but now... A sob rose from my throat as I moved over to another tree, resting my back against the rough surface. I was here to help fix the problem I created, not add to it.

You did good, Davyna... said the twisted voice within, praising me. *You didn't feel pain...guilt... You didn't feel anything. We could have been unstoppable if he didn't pull you back.*

"Davyna?" said a male's voice, breaking my intrusive thoughts and stunning me. But fury quickly rushed in.

I rushed through the air and pinned Alastair to a tree by his throat, glaring at him. I didn't stop, only tightened my fingers around his skin.

"What the hell do you want? Why do you keep showing up?" I yelled as he brought his hands up in surrender. After a moment, I let him go and watched his body slide down as he coughed. "What do you want from me?"

After a few moments of collecting himself, he stood, looking me up and down with worry and fear. "What is happening to you? This isn't you, Davyna."

"Oh, really? Because you know me so well!" I screamed as a tear fell down my cheek.

"I know you don't want this. I want to help you!" he yelled, stepping towards me.

"You are the last person I want helping me," I commanded as I took a step back, watching his next move. "And why are you here?"

"I was checking in on the Crescents and extending my apologies for keeping them out. They are free to return home if they choose." He raked his fingers through his hair, stepping away from me. "I have fucked up. I made mistakes. I'm trying to mend them by helping you through this. I want you safe, Dy..."

I laughed, looking up at the night sky. "And why the fuck would I trust you?"

"You have no reason to...but let me prove it. Let me help... please." His voice was remorseful, but in what world or realm could I trust him after everything he did? "I can dig into Persephone's books at the Crystal Court. Ask around. Just please, let me do this for you. I owe you my life at this point..."

A figure gripped him from behind, choking him, and I jumped back. Alastair quickly began to fight against it, but his attempts slowly began to fail. His arms dropped as he passed out, and his body hit the ground with a loud thud.

I could hear his beating heart as I looked up, taking in the face that I should love seeing... Yet, on this creature, those handsome features were twisted into hate.

"Did you think we were done for the night, little cinder?"

CHAPTER 38
KADEYAN

The body gently swayed back and forth in the obsidian chains I suspended from the ceiling, with a grinding screech between each link. The male—Jaspin—had passed out several times from my various torture techniques.

As soon as I got him into the cell below the Fallen Court, I strung him upside down and removed each fingernail with my dagger, which received broken screams for each digit. Then, I switched over to slowly bleeding him out, waiting until he was close to death to heal him with my blood.

I didn't sleep last night with everything that went on. And after seeing Davyna in the Ember Court, pulling for that dark power so freely... I knew without a shadow of a doubt that those fifteen souls were claimed by her hands.

Did she know she did that? Was it eating her alive?

If I was being honest, I could care less about the bodies, or how Davyna was involved. Because the second I saw her blood dripping down her face in the square... That was all it took for me to see red... and make the person pay for touching her.

My skin still slightly burned from pushing through her wall of flames. Looking at the tops of my hands, I realized they weren't healing. But at the moment, I was more worried about this fucker here...and who else was out there plotting to take her away from me.

Leaning back in the small, metal chair, I breathed in as the obsidian burned into the lining of my lungs. Ignoring it, I slowly flipped my dagger between my fingers.

"Wake up, sleeping beauty," I taunted, watching Jaspin's purple eyes flutter open in serenity. Well, that was, until he saw me. Then, the fear laced with anger returned.

"Let me go!" he screamed, jerking his body back and forth while the chains rocked him side to side. Letting out a frustrated yell, he dropped his head and burrowed his gaze into me. "Lady Jinx will retaliate for killing one of her kind."

I laughed harder than I expected to, my body moving forward in my chair until I rested my arms on my knees. After collecting myself, I glanced up at him, studying his face. "Are you sure about that?"

He was taken aback because we both knew Jinx didn't give a shit about the Crystal Court members on Ember Lands. They left to help fight against the creatures flooding into our realm. Therefore, they weren't able to go home. All thanks to the leaders of their Courts. I may be cruel, even evil at times, but at least I didn't banish my kind for helping other Courts when there was a real problem at hand.

"Who is behind the attacks on Davyna Ember?"

"She is going to destroy this realm. Can't you see that?" he yelled out, grabbing my attention once again.

Taking a deep breath, I sat back and tried to keep a neutral face.

"She needs to die before we all do!"

"Who is behind it?" I growled as I stood, grabbing his head between my hands. I pushed into his mind, sensing his protection spells still in place, but my shadows beat against them. He shook under my hold as I began to feel them crack and saw fragments of what he held.

A room came into view, filled with males and females who all held the same parchment. The script wasn't something I recognized; however, the message was clear.

If you want Valyner back to the way it was, kill Davyna Ember.

Drawing back, I tried to think of who could be behind it as I sat back down. Most of the Crystal Court was angry with her for killing Persephone. It must be one of them. But it could be anyone, from any Court, and this fucker didn't know who was running it.

"Tell me, Jaspin... Did any one of you stop to think that what she did to the throne can't be fixed with her death?" I asked, watching his face turn from confused to grim.

"I didn't need to. I know what happens with the Ember line in charge. She shouldn't be here!"

I laughed. "So, were you blind when Persephone ruled?"

"Fuck you, Kadeyan! You are part of the problem too."

I stood up and quickly moved over to his side, burying my dagger into his ribs. A shattered cry rang out as the smell of iron filled the small cell.

I knelt down, bringing my face next to his ear. "You're right... I've always been a problem. And I highly doubt that will ever change." Gripping him by his throat, I pulled him closer. His body tensed as he tried to breathe through the pain of the wound that wasn't healing. "And Davyna is the furthest thing from a lost cause... Unlike you *Crystals,* who spill innocent blood just because they are bonded to one of your kind! He didn't deserve that!"

Images of Silas invaded my mind, and maybe it was everything going on with Davyna, but the sting of loss was stabbing into every nerve. Reminding me that I could be thrown back into the pits of despair if they took her from me. And I couldn't survive it. I wouldn't.

"You a–are mad!" he choked out. "She is going to kill us all."

"And if that day comes, I'll be by her side, helping her do so." Reaching back, I pulled my obsidian dagger from the back of my slacks and drove it forward, submerging it into Jaspin's heart. Letting go of his throat, I kneeled down, taking in his shock as a gurgled breath escaped his lips. "No one insults her...and lives," I whispered as his eyes slowly began to close before I pulled my dagger free.

Wiping the blade on my leathers, I put it back in my sheath when I heard footsteps approaching behind me. "You know he's right...about me." Turning slowly, I looked over and saw Davyna was leaning against the wall. Her eyes were down as she fidgeted with her hands.

"Not even close," I said. Confusion washed over me as I rose from the ground and moved towards the bars of the cell.

She shook her head as a tear fell. "Everyone, including you, will die if I don't do what needs to be done."

"Davyna, I told you; we are going to fix this. You're not doing this alone," I said, moving out of the cell to be closer to her. Pulling her into my arms, I noticed something wasn't right. She tensed...and her scent was off.

Jerking back, I looked into her silver eyes, studying them when she slowly began to smirk.

This wasn't right...

"Oh, come now, Lord Kadeyan... Did you figure it out yet, or do you need another minute?"

Moving at high speed, I pinned this look-alike of my mate to the wall by her throat as the blood rushed into my eyes. "It's you... You're the one who hurt her... Who's been tormenting her!" She stood completely still but showed little emotion, almost as if this was boring her. "Who are you?" I growled as I pressed her body into the stone wall.

Her flesh began to glow an iridescent white, illuminating the dark tunnel with the six shades of color glistening off the walls. And then, I felt it: the pain. She pushed back, pinning me to the ground as my head slammed into the stone. My eyes spotted with black as she straddled me, brushing a piece of my hair back from my face.

"The more important question isn't who I am, but who your mate truly is. Or should I say, what she is. And that's why I'm here." She smiled again, bringing her hand down my chest.

Slamming my head into hers, she leaned back at the same time I jolted up. Moving quickly, the air rushed by us until her back crashed into stone. I pulled the obsidian dagger from my sheath and placed the blade right over her heart.

Looking down, she let out a giggle. "Do you mean to use that on me, Kadeyan? I wear the face of the only thing you love."

"You do...but you aren't her."

"No, I'm not. I'm so much better," she teased with lust wrapped around each word as she smiled wider.

Fury coursed through my veins as I pressed the blade into her skin, pinning her below my hold. "What is happening to Davyna? What did you do to her when you marked her?"

"Nothing. I only gave her a reminder of what I was capable of so she would listen." She smiled. "But that's not why I'm here. My mate wants you dead... Such a pity. You are delectable to look at." Her hand lifted up and her light entered me, searing my veins as it passed through.

I gritted my teeth, trying to hold back the scream begging to be released, but it was too much. It felt like someone was melting my insides.

Not giving it a second thought, I plunged the dagger into her chest. If this monster was gone, it would solve one problem my little Ember was facing...and stop the torment she was inflicting on me. I let out a scream as my hand fell from the dagger and my knees hit the ground. Her spell lifted from me, yet I still sensed it lingering around, enveloping me like a persistent shroud.

Glancing up, I expected to see her eyes void of life, but was quickly stunned. "What the fuck?"

"Oh, you don't get it. You can't kill us with that." She laughed before looking down at the grey blood flowing out of her wound, matching Davyna's perfectly.

When I tried to stand, she moved in and grabbed my head, slamming it into the stone wall. My vision swayed as I fell back down, and chunks of rock fell on top of me.

"Now, where were we?" she asked, but quickly paused, her body going tense. Her eyes stared off in the distance as I tried standing again, but her power within made it impossible. She huffed, rolling her eyes. "Seriously?"

Leaning down, she touched my arm, and the light within pulsed again. Tears threatened to spill as I tried to pull away, but it was no use.

"It looks like he wants to do something else now."

"What are you doing to me?" I asked as she pushed off my limp form.

"Nothing permanent, but let's see how your mate handles what comes next." The light surged through me, taking me deeper into a slumber that I wanted to run from.

Calling on my own shadows, I begged them to cover the light. They denied me, running away to safety from the blinding blaze she released.

She leaned down, whispering in my ear as my vision went black. "We will see each other again, Kadeyan... Unless *she* kills you first."

CHAPTER 39
DAVYNA

The darkness surrounding me in the void was all I saw, until strings of color came into view. Each one reminded me of what I once saw within, dancing to their own ethereal melody. It made me feel safe, protected. I wanted to join in, to revel in the peace and serenity it was offering, and to never leave.

Closing my eyes, I basked in the smell of the growing smoke. The remains of burning wood reminded me of being with my father before he passed on. Or life before...all this.

And yet... Something wasn't right.

Like a lightning bolt crashing down, I knew this wasn't real. Opening my eyes, I looked around and noticed the void was gone, along with the strings I held within. Now, it was black shadows, creeping closer to me in the throne room.

I was just in the woods with Alastair... So, where was he? Taking a step forward, I tried to look around when my foot slipped on something below. I fell forward, catching myself with my hands when I felt what was below me.

Bones...

Glancing down, I saw the skeletons all around me, blanketing the ground as bile got caught in my throat. The smell of death grew, suffocating me as horror flooded my mind and forced my body to quake.

"You're a tricky little fae, aren't you?"

Turning, I expected to be met with the false face of the man I loved, but was stunned as I took in his shadow form. It was darker than any night I'd seen, forcing more chills to brush down my spine.

"Where are we?" I asked, pushing myself off the ground and swallowing down the contents of my stomach.

"In your head...and somewhere off Valyner's plane. I wanted to talk privately and give you a preview of your future."

"I'm going to fucking rip your throat out!" I screamed as I ran towards him, remembering everything he did to my people—the looks on their faces. They were my only connection left to my father on this Earth, and they were all gone.

He laughed, vanishing as I reached him. I turned, sending my flames roaring through the room. Bones in the blazing wake turned to ash. My breathing became more labored with each passing second, waiting for him to reappear.

"Now, if you are done being a brat..." I narrowed my eyes on him as his shadows reached out, grazing the flames sitting upon the throne. "Who was your mother?"

"That's none of your godsdamn business!" He chuckled, moving down the stairs as his shadows billowed up and rushed back to him. "Why do you need the stones?" I asked, stepping closer and burying down any remaining fear.

"Well, now, I could give you the same response: none of your business."

"How did I curse the throne?" I asked, hanging on his next words.

He moved in and his shadows brushed up against me, reminding me of what death felt like. "I'm still asking myself that... but I have some theories."

"I'm sick and tired of people keeping shit from me. Tell me!" I spat out, watching him move around me.

"I think I like it better with you in the dark... Some fun things might come of it. And then I'll get to see your true colors."

"Is that why you haven't killed me yet?"

He stood quiet. Hovering so close, it was as if I could feel his hand brush my arm, and everything in my body stilled.

"Maybe I like you. Maybe I need something from you. Or maybe...I like to keep my enemies close and torment them until they snap."

"I'm not going to snap. I'm going to fix what I need to and lock you back in the Hell you crawled out of," I stated, my voice shaking as his invisible hand gripped my arm.

"Oh, my sweet, little cinder... You were made for the darkness. I can feel it."

Taking a deep breath, I pulled my arm free and looked into the black mist. "Fuck. You!"

A deep laugh broke from within the shadows, shaking the world around us so much that I needed to steady my feet to not fall again into the bones below.

"Mmm, I do love a fae with some fire in her." He began moving away and my breathing picked up. "Enjoy what is to come... I'll see you soon."

"What the fuck are you talking about?" I shouted, watching the shadows stall. "Show me your face. I think I have a right to know by now who is stalking my every move."

Moving back towards me, his shadows began to shift. Swallowing hard, I took a step back, almost slipping again as beaming red eyes narrowed on me.

"I will promise you this, Davyna Ember." An invisible hand wrapped around my neck, ripping the air from my lungs, and my eyes widened. "I will show you my true form...the day I kill you." He threw me back, and my body sank into the bones. The pain pulled a yell from my lips...and everything went dark.

CHAPTER 40
DAVYNA

My stomach rose as I plummeted downward, my heavy breathing being my only company. Valyner's presence wrapped around me through the dizzying descent as the air pelted against my skin.

I tried to focus my gaze on the sky above to make sense of where I just was. It was close to Valyner, that was for certain...but just outside our realm. Were the other fae realms this close to us? And what magic made me see the throne room? The bones?

Pulling my wings out, I dove down headfirst. I was trying to see through the foggy night, when the smell of the salt invaded my nostrils. Through the misty air, a few things blurred past me as the ground finally came into view.

I fully extended my grey wings, slowing myself down before my feet dug into the dense sands by the shoreline. The cool water brushed against my legs, seeping into my boots as I looked out at the dark sea.

Breathing heavily, I pulled my gaze back and glanced around as the sound of roaring waves continued to crash over one another. My body fell forward, and I let my lungs expand as I gasped for more air, bearing the rush of emotions slamming into my chest.

All the lies.

All the secrets.

All the loss.

And I was no closer to the truth. Only closer to losing more people...because of them. Because of me.

"Davyna?"

Turning, I saw three people walking in the distance, all holding shimmering swords. I knew that voice, and it settled my erratic heart.

"Sahar?" Pushing up, I sprinted to her.

She threw her sword down, and it pierced the sand as she moved towards me. Her arms stretched wide, and I grasped onto her, seeking refuge within her embrace. She enveloped me with her own arms, and I could feel the rapid rise and fall of my breath once more. Her loving aura washed over me, and tears lined my eyes as the waves crashed into our legs.

"What...what are you doing here?" She pulled away after a few moments, looking me over. "Are you okay?" My eyes must have shown her the pain, because hers softened even more before reaching for my hands.

"Mama, we should get back inside now. Just in case..."

Moving over to look behind Sahar, I saw a young fae who looked to be about the same age as me. But there was a youthful, innocent glow about her. She was built like Sahar with straight hair that was dark at the top and faded down to a silvery blue...like Eryx.

"I agree, my Lady," said the other woman, turning as she gripped her hand tighter around her sword. She was dressed in armor engraved with waves on each shoulder as her short black hair swayed in the wind. "We can train again tomorrow when the sun rises."

"Yes," Sahar said, turning and giving me a soft grin. "Let's get you inside, Dy."

We stayed quiet as we made our way down the beach, following after the fae who agreed with the younger one. A screeching sound from within the water made me turn to look over the darkened ocean, and I remembered the last time I was in there with the true siren...

A quake skated down my body as I turned back, seeing the castle come into view. There was a jagged staircase off in the distance, but everyone kept moving towards the large stone before us, which I noticed had an opening. The Salt soldier and the younger fae moved in first, securing their weapons to their hips.

Looking back to Sahar, she waved her hand towards the opening, and it vanished as the sound of water sloshing filled my ears. Turning back, I watched as the soldier dove in after Sahar's daughter, and I took a few steps forward.

Sahar placed her hand on my shoulder, smiling. "It's okay. It's a tunnel into the castle. Go on, I'll be right behind you."

Moving forward, I looked at the small pool of water and hesitated for a moment before diving in after the other fae. Looking around, I took in the sea beyond, realizing we were encased in a tunnel of sea glass.

I moved my hands and feet, pushing through the still water, and breathed normally. I took in the plants adorned in hues of lush greens and sunny yellows dancing with each sway of the current. Fish dressed in vivid colors darted through them, gliding through the foliage with grace. When I looked out at the darker parts beyond, it only mirrored a void, holding a mystery in the depths of what else laid within.

Coming up through the tunnel, I took in the small, circular pool before glancing out to the room, and my jaw fell open. We were still emerged under the sea. I pushed my body up, climbed out of the water, and scanned the room again.

It was made of crystal clear glass, creating a dome to reveal the murky water and sea life beyond. Books rested on glass shelves in front of me, and soft white orbs floated above to bathe the room in their warmth.

Turning my head, I saw there was a desk off to the side, along with a few plush chairs and a couch dressed in turquoise that made the space feel inviting. And the view could take anyone's breath away. I used a spell to change my leathers into a fresh pair and moved deeper into the room, looking it over in amazement.

"That would make things easier," said the young fae as she rung out her hair and moved towards me with water gushing from her boots. "It's Davyna, right? My mama and papa have told me so much about you. I'm Priya." Her eyes matched her father's, with specks of white in the deep blue, creating its own waves within.

Sahar surfaced, pulling herself out of the small pool. The soldier leaned down, offering her a hand.

"That's Alexandrea," Priya said, smiling.

"It's nice to meet you. Both of you," I said, and Priya's smile widened as she looked to Alexandrea.

The soldier closed her eyes, tilting her head down before slowly looking back to me.

"I'm going to make sure Papa got back!" Priya shouted as she moved through the room. Sahar nodded her head, eyes gleaming as her daughter got to the stone stairs on the other side of the large room.

"Would you, Alex?" she asked, and the woman nodded. She bowed slightly to us both before moving towards the stairs, her hand gripping the top of her sword. "Priya is a blessing from the gods. I don't even remember what life was like before having her."

"When did you have her?" I asked, stunned. I hadn't known any fae to have children since arriving here.

Sahar laughed. "I was in my early days of pregnancy when you came here last. We never thought it would happen. It's rare for pregnancy to take place outside a mated bond, but even with one like ours, it can take many years..."

Sahar smirked before continuing. "Fae are typically only pregnant for three months or so. And as you know, we age rapidly before staying frozen in our adulthood. You were held in the Mortal Lands, but here, it goes by even faster."

Shock crossed over my face. I was amazed that it went by even quicker here, but it shouldn't stun me. In two months, I was already five years old before my father locked it all away.

"Dy...why are you here?"

"I–I didn't mean to. I'm sorry if I'm intruding. I can head back home." The words tumbled out, and the paranoia rose as I remembered everything that occurred on that plane he took me to.

"No, don't be silly. You are always welcome here. You are family." The words pierced my heart, melting a small amount of pain that only grew thicker these days.

Silence fell between us as I averted my eyes to the sea beyond.

"Are you okay, Dy?" Her voice—like a siren call—soothed the disarray within, breaking open the flood gates.

"No, I'm not..." I got out between sobs as tears fell down my cheeks. Bringing my hands to my eyes, I tried to brush the tears away. Sahar took ahold of my hands, making me look up into her hazel-blue eyes.

"No, don't hide this. Not from me or anyone. There is strength found in pain, Davyna. And you have had more pain than some who have lived for hundreds of years. You are allowed to feel it. You are allowed to break into a million pieces, and it doesn't take away from the fighter you've become."

"What if I can't pick all the pieces up?" I asked, another tear sliding down my face as her thumbs stroked over the tops of my hands.

"Then you leave some behind, and only take what you need." We sat there in silence for a few minutes, hearing the gentle hum of the ocean around us as it swayed back and forth. "Come, sit. I'll pour you a drink."

Sahar motioned me towards the long, turquoise couch as she moved to the glass wall where a cart of different liquors graced the top. Glancing back, she smiled as she picked up the whiskey bottle and proceeded to walk back, disregarding the glasses.

She sat down and took a long sip from the bottle before handing it over to me. As I took the bottle, I looked at her palm, seeing the grey skin.

"Sahar..."

She looked down at it, before balling her hand into a fist. "I'll be okay," she said, giving me a smile that showed no fear, and her emotions matched it.

"When did it start?" I asked, my stomach turning as I tried to hide my panic.

"Right after the meeting with the Lords and Ladies." Water

dripped down from her braid, causing her eyes to follow the droplet as it lazily ran down her arm. "I feel my magic getting weaker...but it's nothing that I can't handle."

"I'm so sorry..." I said as more guilt slammed into me.

She will die...just like your parents, Elias, Terry, Marta, Akari, and all the Embers. Loving you is the true curse. The laughs within my psyche made my head throb as another tear ran down my face.

"Why is that?" she asked, her eyes softening on me.

"Because this is my fault. If I didn't... If I just—"

"Fate is something we can't avoid, sweetheart. I think this all was fated long ago...for a bigger reason than any of us can understand. And that doesn't make it your fault," she said.

My eyes scanned over her features as she gave me a reassuring grin.

"But what if—"

"No. No ifs. Sometimes it's not for us to understand, but to be who we are meant to be and walk through the trials that come our way."

"Davyna!" Eryx yelled in a joyous tone from the stairwell, and I turned in my seat to see him walking our way. His expression shifted quickly and his worry surfaced after catching sight of both our body language. "Is everything okay?"

"Everything is alright, my love. Davyna came to visit," Sahar said as she stood and made her way around the couch to greet him.

I turned away and a small smile crept in as I took in the sea beyond. I got up to move closer to the glass. It was dark out there, but small, illuminating flashes of light sped past in a blur, reminding me of the life those depths held.

You are weak like this. This isn't who you truly are. You are death incarnate... Embrace it.

"Well, I'm glad you came, Dy. If you'd like to stay the night, you are always welcome here... It's your home, too."

Turning, I forced a smile and tried to let his statement pull me out of the hole I was digging myself into. Before I could even take in the sea beyond again, the air in my lungs became void, and I gasped as I grabbed onto a nearby chair.

"Davyna? What is it?" Sahar called out.

But the world around me shifted on its axis. The bond with Kadeyan snapped, leaving me in a deep, never-ending void that made my body feel lifeless. I couldn't feel him... He was just...gone. It was like something inside me was decaying, breaking apart, and promising me that I would never be whole again.

It felt like death... It felt empty.

And my soul cried out for his.

"K–Kade?" My knees buckled as Sahar and Eryx dropped to the ground with me. Looking at each other, their expressions matched of pain and worry before they glanced back at me.

I couldn't feel him anymore...

Do you believe me now?

Eryx looked out beyond the crystal dome we were in, his eyes slowly going from curiosity to panic. Turning, I looked out at the dark water, barely registering the faces because... Their eyes. They were shining, vivid hues that casted a glow into the glass room. Sucking in a sharp breath, I watched as they sent out their power...

And the glass dome shattered.

CHAPTER 41
DAVYNA

It was almost nice, floating in the cold sea. I didn't bother pulling my fires forth because the cold reminded me of him. Like he was near, and his embrace was holding me through the shattering pain.

He was gone, but I still pushed through the bond that would let me sense him, hoping it wasn't true. Except, I was met with an unending void of nothingness. It seeped into the center of my bones, crippling me beyond repair as I willed my body to drown—to suffocate with the water surrounding me. I didn't want to feel this... I wanted to feel nothing.

Maybe I deserved this after leaving him and pushing him away, only to let him in, before the shadow made good on his promise. What if Kade was still out there, though? Did I have reason to believe *he* wouldn't take him from me? I knew that answer because he took all the Embers.

And this black pit within that was growing by the second told me everything I needed to know—he *was* gone. My lips quivered as I sucked in the chilled water, wishing it would—just this once—drown me.

I deserved this.

I deserved all of this...

My tears mixed with the salty water as a hand wrapped around my arm, pulling me into the gap. Eryx shook me as he looked around, his eyes growing wilder.

"DAVYNA!" he yelled, and I came back, the ache growing

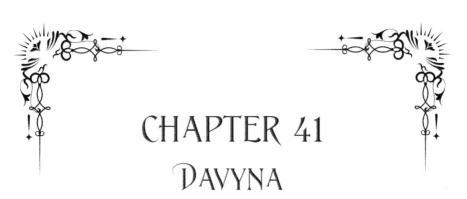

stronger than before. I took in the sea glass chandelier hanging above us, knowing we were now in a higher level of the castle.

Screams from beyond made me look into his raging blue eyes. "We have to go!" He pulled me up and we moved to the window, where I could see the town beyond, going up in flames as screams traveled all the way to us. Waves of their pain and suffering drifted to me, only adding to my own as the daze threatened to take me back under.

Sahar and Alexandrea appeared next to us with Priya holding onto her mother's hand. "It's an attack, my Lord, but it looks like our people are under the influence of the creatures. We are still trying to locate them to break their hold," Alexandrea stated, walking towards Eryx.

"Call for the Fallen Court and whoever else will come," he commanded. She disappeared and Eryx took hold of my arm pulling me through the castle. "Sahar, get Priya out of the Salt Court. Now!"

As he said the words, the castle wall exploded, raining down water and stone. We all fell to the ground, and my head spun as I looked at the fae using their power to ride waves right into the hall we were in. Their eyes beamed bright blues, pinks, oranges, and greens. I could tell they were under an influence—like Alexandrea stated—lost in the lust for blood as they glanced at us. They wasted no time as they rushed in, weapons held high.

Dark obsidian.

I threw my own power out, pushing some back. "Get out of here now!" I yelled to Sahar and Priya.

Eryx sent out water-like chains and threw a handful back out of the gaping hole in the castle, but they came back in almost instantly.

"How do they all have dark obsidian?" I called out to Eryx as I repeatedly tossed the fae back out.

"Most of us own one...but there is a weapons cave for my soldiers. They must have raided it."

I tossed someone, and they slammed into the wall. Their blood painted the light grey-blue stone from the impact as they fell limp to the ground.

"I don't want to hurt them! They aren't in their right minds!" he yelled, and I followed his lead.

Pushing the fae of these lands back out, I felt relief, but it was short-lived. They were coming right back in, growing in numbers, and faster than we could deal with them. They were lost in a craze, snapping their jaws and laughing as they darted for us. Many were dressed in normal clothes, but even more of them were dressed in armor.

The Salt Court army...

Looking to my side, I saw Sahar and Priya still on the ground, unmoving. My stomach sank as I pushed out my shadows with more rage, and a boom of energy spilled from my veins. The castle shook violently before the floor we were on began to crumble. *Shit...* What did I do? Eryx and I ran to Sahar and Priya, grabbing onto them as we fell into the gap and landed outside.

Turning back to the castle, I watched as it began to crumble, falling over into the sea. Water shot up and the mist blew through the air, sticking to our skin. I held my breath as it settled into the sea, knowing the fae within would perish if they didn't get out. Especially if they couldn't breathe underwater.

My attention was pulled back to the growing screams piercing into the dark sky. My skin rose at the sound. My heartbeat traveled into my ears as I looked at the war taking place on the ground. Fae were fighting fae, and bodies began falling, slamming with bone-crunching thuds.

Everything was happening so fast, and more adrenaline pumped through my veins. The smell of death and iron consumed me as I took off, looking for any fae with beaming eyes. I threw some into the sea and warded off others with flames. I choked a few with my shadows until they laid still on the ground in a temporary slumber.

Sweat coated my brow as I glanced around, trying to find the creatures doing this. It had to be them controlling the fae's minds. If I could stop them...then no one else would die.

Focusing through the fight, I sensed it off in the distance; it was a large number of creatures...chanting. A blade cut into my arm, and I yelled as I sent shadows out, throwing the male back through the chaos of battle.

Turning around, I looked to Eryx as he fell to his knees. His hands ran into his hair, gripping at the silver-blue strands as his cries overpowered the fight around us. Was he injured? Sahar held onto Priya as she ran towards her mate, screaming his name.

It was tainted in such love, such horror.

I pushed everyone out of the way with my shadows, encircling them in a spelled barrier to protect them. Fae ran back towards it, clawing to get inside and get to them.

My heartbeat slammed against my eardrums, washing out the cries and metal clashing together. I glanced around, my breath shortening as I watched fae fall victim to this battle. We were outnumbered, and if we kept this up without killing...

Exactly, you need to kill.

"No!" I screamed as I pushed the fae back, sending their bodies flying through the air. The ground rumbled with my power, sending more fear into the air from the fae who weren't consumed with the influence.

Turning, I stopped a blade from barreling through the air that was on course for splitting my skull in two. I threw the female back with a spell and began placing barriers around the hypnotized fae. If I could find the creatures, maybe I could stop them like before... But I needed to get to them.

As I turned, I saw Eryx on his feet within the barrier. Priya was laying still on the ground, her neck cut.

My stomach dropped as I moved in, the world becoming a blur as the crimson puddle grew beneath her mother's boots. I dropped the shield keeping them locked within and screamed, "Sahar!"

I pushed my body into a run, dodging the fae still free to kill their own Court members. Sahar's face was stunned, tears running down her cheeks, before her broken gaze connected with mine.

"Run!" I screamed again but gasped as pain bloomed over me. A sword rammed through my back, piercing through my stomach, and the air in my lungs vanished.

I looked down, seeing it wasn't dark obsidian. I winced and turned, throwing out my shadows at the female approaching me as laughter fell from her lips. My grey shadows launched out, taking her hostage before I threw her in the air. For a moment, her crazed laugh rang out, reaching back to haunt me. A loud crash against the surface of the sea silenced her.

Reaching back, I wrapped my fingers around the hilt and began to pull. Screaming, I summoned my shadows to help pull it free, and the warm liquid pooled beneath my leathers.

I needed to get to my friends.

My entire body tensed as I took ahold of the weapon submerged in me and glanced back to Sahar. A dagger made of pure darkness slashed across her neck and she began gasping for air, her eyes wide in horror.

"NO!"

Did I lock one of the crazed fae in there with them? No, I know I didn't...which meant...

As Eryx's hand dropped, the crimson dripped down and mixed with the dirt already stained with his daughter's blood. I gripped my stomach and pushed forward, each step forcing the trepidation to grow.

Dropping the weapon in shock, I looked at my friend... Her body went still as her blood created a pool of sorrow, merging with her daughter's. I closed the distance, pulling Eryx around with shaking hands, and knew what I was about to be met with.

His once deep blue eyes were now illuminating the night in a vivid orange. He smiled, taking in the battle behind me, and everything surrounding us faded away.

"No..." I whispered as my lip quivered.

He whipped the blade at my neck, and I leaned back, hissing as it nicked my chin. I dropped and kicked my foot out, taking him down to the ground as fury and grief billowed out.

He killed them... He *killed* them...

He jumped onto me and brought the knife down towards my heart, but my hand darted out, grabbing it. "Eryx!" I screamed as the burning in my hand intensified, and I let out a hiss. "This isn't you!"

"We are all *this* in the end!" He laughed as he pulled the blade back, slicing deep into my flesh and causing my blood to fly through the air.

He attempted to drive the dagger back down. The instinct within to fight took over, merging with the grief still coursing through my body. I grabbed his wrist and heard the bones break as I pushed up. We moved through the air in a haze as I settled on top of him, anticipating his next move, but something was wrong.

His body stilled as I looked down at my hand, and my breathing forced my chest to rise and fall in erratic patterns. The scars were completely opaque and the voice within my mind laughed.

I didn't even need to tell you to kill him.

My gaze shifted over, seeing my fingers wrapped around the dagger buried in his chest. "No... NO!" I screamed and pulled it back out, placing my hand over his wound. Crimson soaked through my fingers as I hyperventilated and looked beyond at the fae growing exhausted with their fight. "Eryx! PLEASE!" I screamed as I willed his heart to beat again.

Time slowed and the tears fell from my eyes as I lowered my head on his chest. The sobs ripped from my throat, making it raw. My eyes landed on Sahar and Priya, and the pain grew, consuming everything that I was.

"I'm so sorry," I said over and over again, hoping it meant something to them, or that they could still hear me.

Abomination.

Everything was going to be okay... I was strong. I would not break.

This is your fault.

Everything was going to be okay... I was strong. I would not break.

Give up and let me help you now.

Everything was going to be okay... I was strong. I would not break.

You are death incarnate... Embrace it.

Everything was going to be okay... I was strong. I would not break.

I'll break you... You'll see our way is so much better...

I stared off in a haze, feeling a cyclone of thoughts run through my mind about what my parents thought I was to them: a blessing.

What my friends and sister thought I was: strong.

Even what Kade thought: a light in his dark world.

But they were all wrong because I was a curse and incapable of not leaving death in my wake. I was the embodiment of darkness, and I was done fighting it. I was done trying to find a version of myself out there that wouldn't bring pain and despair. I was this... I was the monster.

And I was done running from it.

Leaning up, I looked at my blood-stained hand as the sounds of battle rang out behind me.

The surge of power within celebrated the call to erase it all. *I knew you would see it our way.*

The pain was burning every fiber of my being as the darkness consumed it, dulling the aching reality of this life. And little by little, it drifted away, as if it was healing me in some way.

The world slowed as I rose, and the guilt and shame turned to mist. My lips tugged up as I took one last cleansing breath, exhaling the loss of all my family, friends, and *him.*

They were gone and I was free...

I was *finally* free.

CHAPTER 42
DAVYNA

Everything shifted and it was like my old life was gone, taking my pain and worries with it. I could remember them—the people in my life—but any feelings I had before were muted, giving me solace that I basked in.

I walked through the battle, smiling. The fae around me struggled to keep their ground as more began to fall under the influence of the creatures beyond.

One ran towards me, his sword held high. I continued to walk with ease as my shadows poured out, ripping his heart from his chest. I pulled it into my hand, squeezing the organ until it crushed in my palm. Blood flowed between my fingers and dripped to the ground as I chuckled.

Tossing it to the ground, I rolled my shoulders back, taking in the sweet crimson painting my flesh. Sucking the blood off one of my fingers, I turned around and reveled in the smell of death as every fiber of my being awakened.

Such a beautiful sight...

A small laugh ripped from my throat as I pulled myself into the void, landing in a forest beyond the fight. I relished in the screams and the melody they produced, but voices pulled my attention to the trees beyond. I tilted my head, curious as to who was out here.

Stalking closer, I saw little, ravenous faeries with wings like dragonflies, consumed in an onyx hue. Their eyes were tiny orbs, resembling a cold and dark abyss, and they had veins to match running down their cheeks. Even their little, sharp teeth were cute rather than scary as they shot through the sky, fighting...something.

The voices grabbed my attention. I moved forward to investigate because I knew them.

Tilting my head again, I leaned against a tree as I watched a group of fae try to fight them off. They threw out their powers and brought down a few, and I laughed at the energy they were exerting to do so little.

"Pathetic."

One turned to face me...and I knew his face, but I didn't feel anything. Not even shock or joy. Just...nothing.

"Dearest?" he called out towards me, and I noticed the group turn, along with the little Faeries they were fighting. The creatures darted out towards me, and I sent out fire with a flick of my wrist, soaring through the air to consume them.

The ones that tried to run were chased down by my flames and turned to ash on impact. It felt good to watch it rain down onto the fae still standing in shock.

"Such a shame. They were pretty cool." I let out a breath and moved forward.

"Davyna?" Evren asked.

I looked to the girl I used to call *sister* and laughed. "Can I help you?"

"What is wrong with you?" she asked as the others moved in, their fear only fueling my power.

I walked up to her, taking her head between my hands, and smiled. "Nothing...anymore." Pushing her back, I laughed as she fell, but Calix rushed in, catching her before she hit the ground.

Sorin moved in, looking her over to make sure she was okay, before glancing at me. Although, it wasn't with anger, only concern.

"Guys, get out of here," Kadeyan demanded as he looked over his shoulder. He placed himself between me and them, his fingers lingering near the dagger at his thigh.

"Aww, are you scared I'll kill them like I killed Eryx?" His eyes faltered, and I could see the blow hit him as his body went tense. "I mean...it sounds kind of fun... Who wants to be first?"

"Davyna...this isn't you. What are you saying?" Levanna asked as she moved forward.

Looking down at her, I dropped the smile. Shadows ripped through me and wrapped around her throat, lifting her in the air. "I guess you're first then."

Kadeyan's body slammed into me, forcing me to drop Levanna as she coughed. My back slammed into the rough bark of a tree. He grabbed my jaw to look at him as a cool blade pressed into my neck. "SNAP OUT OF IT!" he yelled.

I began laughing again. It grew, sounding more deranged to my ears as I leaned into his blade. The freezing blood flowed down my chest as I raised my hands to his face, running my thumbs over his cheeks and into his short beard.

"Oh, honey... Is that supposed to work because you're my mate?" Tossing him back, I let out a wild inferno as he glanced up. "You are nothing." I watched in excitement as I laced more power into each flame.

Axel and Calix jumped forward, using their shadows long enough to pull him out of the way before my flames broke their dark mist.

"Really?" I called out, my annoyance tainting the words.

A small Faerie came down, staring at me in amazement, and everyone stalled. She moved closer to me, her eyes no longer consumed with onyx veins and the darkness staining her form vanished.

She was a pretty, little thing, dressed in vibrant hues of pink from her hair, her eyes, and her small dress. Lowering herself, she kept her eyes on me. I felt that connection once again...and I knew she did, too.

"What are you?" she asked with the sweetest little voice, but it only irritated me.

"I think that's a question we should all stop asking, unless you want to join the dead." I moved away and began walking, feeling them all hesitant to move.

Except Kadeyan. He ran towards me, stalling as I glanced over my shoulder.

"Let go, Kadeyan... It feels good to not care about a damn thing. Especially *you*." I smiled, welcoming the void as it consumed me, taking me away to do whatever the fuck I wanted.

CHAPTER 43
KADEYAN

My mind was spinning as we landed back in the Fallen castle, but I didn't want to be here. I wanted to be with her, and to help her through this.

I needed to.

Everything was spinning, creating a cyclone of loss and confusion as to what happened. I had woken up on the terrace when the beacon alerted us of an attack, and Davyna's look-alike was gone. We took out as many creatures in the woods as we could, before Davyna came, wiping them out as if they were nothing.

Before we left the Salt Court, I found Eryx's guard, Alexandrea. She had been with them since Priya was born. Eyewitnesses said that Eryx was possessed and killed his child before turning on Sahar... Then, he tried to kill Davyna. And she won. That was when they saw her walk through all the chaos, with her eyes dark. She let it in...

She was hurting...and she let it in...

My mind was still trying to process the loss of not only two amazing people I got to call friends but their daughter... Every time I saw her, she was trying to make me smile through the gut-wrenching emotions that swayed like a storming sea. When I came by, she gave me seashells that she got at the bottom of the ocean with her father. She inherited his ability to breathe underwater...like Davyna. I still had each one in my office, lining the bookshelf.

Dropping my head, the grief slammed into me, and my lungs constricted as the tears threatened to spill. She was such a kind soul, like her mother, her father… It was no surprise that they birthed an amazing being who only added warmth to this world, but now…

I swallowed hard, the lump in my throat aching as it grew. Eryx would have never been able to live with himself. As strong as he was, he would have taken his life. And I would have done the same because the thought of ripping the life from another who carried part of your soul… It was something no one could return from. But now, he wouldn't need to feel that pain, and that alone made what she did a mercy.

I hissed as Levanna grabbed my arm. "These aren't healing. Why aren't they healing?" she spat out.

I glanced down at my arm where my leathers were burned away, and bright, red skin marked me, burning with a searing heat. This also happened after she tried to kill Jaspin in the Ember Court, when the dark power was seeping out of her. Whatever magic she possessed was causing my own to deny me in healing like I normally would.

I pushed the pain aside and looked at my friends, but I didn't have words. I just felt angry. That fucking creature and her mate were playing a game with Davyna, and they used me as the bait. They wanted to see what she would do, and she played right into it.

"What is going on with my sister?" Evren asked as she moved in. "I don't give a fuck anymore if she made you promise not to tell us!"

Calix moved and grazed her arm, but she pulled it away, never breaking her gaze with me. I looked at them all, torn on whether to speak the words, but they deserved the truth.

Especially now.

"I'm not sure what is going on inside her right now, but she told me about it. Feeling drawn to let go of pain…like she was losing her mind. And I think that's what we saw. She let it consume her."

"What else?" Evren pushed, her eyes flashing into her wolf's yellow haze.

"She told me about seeing someone who looked like her… It was the same person who scarred her, but she isn't working alone; she has a mate. She showed up tonight and used me to send a message. I think it had something to do with them wanting to see what Davyna would do. They are involved in all of this, and if I had to guess, they are probably from Gelmyra or Anawyn."

"Then, why are they going after Davyna?" Nesrin asked, slowly sinking down into a chair as Axel rested his hand on his mate's shoulder.

"I think they are all connected in some way. At least magically." My arm pulsed from the pain, and I gritted my teeth. Levanna walked over, pulled a salve out of thin air, and started applying it.

"Listen…I'm not going to ask any of you to help me get her back."

"Shut the fuck up, Kadeyan. Davyna is family. She is the Queen, and I will always serve her…whether she sits on a throne of fire or bones. And I won't stand by without doing everything I can to help," Calix said, moving in and standing an inch taller.

"Same here," Axel agreed, looking to Nesrin as she nodded.

"She's family," Nes said, leaning into Axel as he placed an arm around her shoulder.

Evren looked around, her eyes welling up with tears. "Deep down, she always wanted this—a family who would fight for her… And you already know, I'll do whatever I can to bring my sister back."

Sorin nodded his head in agreement as he shifted his gaze to me, taking a strong stance that signaled he was ready for anything I deemed.

Levanna finished applying the salve and looked up at me, clearing her throat. "Like it or not, she is stuck with us." She smiled.

My heart was as fragile as glass right now, and seeing my friends stand around—willing to put themselves in harm's way to get her back—shattered it. I buried down my emotions and slowly nodded.

"I think I can help?" a voice sounded.

I looked up to see the little creature from the woods sitting on the top of my bookshelf. Her wings began beating as she lowered herself, looking at everyone. She was so tiny, and her entire body gave off a shimmering pink hue. From her hair to her wings, and even her eyes.

"What are you?" I asked.

"I'm a pixie...and my name is Dalia." She sat down on the edge of my desk, playing with the small hem of her blush-pink dress. "I'm from Gelmyra. This is Valyner, right?"

"What did you do to our people?" Calix said, moving in as anger radiated from him.

"My clan was scared, and that's how we fight. We possess the minds of others and make them kill until they are forced to kill themselves. Do you think we could fight anything your size and win without it?" she said, laughing a little.

"You little, fucking—" Calix started.

Quickly, her features transformed to black, matching the fairies of the forest and looking like a thing of nightmares, even at her size. "I'd be careful how you speak to me while my master isn't here."

"Are you threatening us?" I asked, turning to fully face her. "And what do you mean, your master?"

Dalia quickly turned back, her body once again emulating its pink aura. "Sorry. I have a bit of a temper..." She smiled, cocking her head to look me over. "There is something about her... When our eyes connected, my entire being knew I needed to follow her and that my power was hers to be commanded as she saw fit."

Was this what Ravyn felt? She really could control these creatures from beyond. Although, the question still remained: What was in her that made them obey, or was it the fact that she was stronger than us all?

"How did you get here?" I asked, puzzled that this was the first creature to come onto our Lands and speak.

"I don't know... I was in our Court—"

"What do you mean by Court?" Levanna asked, stepping forward to meet her gaze.

"I'm from the Pixi Court... We are fae." We all looked at each other, stunned that she wasn't a creature at all...but like us. "We were told about some black holes forming on the outskirts of our

Lands, pulling our own creatures out... But then, one appeared in our village. It was...cold in there."

Her little form shuddered, taking a moment to recover as she continued. "When we landed here, I felt a power... It was dark, and it wanted us to fight. It wasn't my master's...it was something else. Hers felt like life and death mixed into one...but the other one was pure evil."

We all sat there, taking in her words as I remembered the feeling of Davyna's blood in my veins: life and death. And the power she was speaking of must have been from the shadow haunting my little Ember. But who the fuck was he? Was he even fae?

Faelynn and Maeve fell into the room, and I instantly sensed Maeve's anxiety growing until it filled the space and choked me.

Dalia flew up, her eyes widening as she said, "Faelynn?"

Everyone stiffened in the room, and my own confusion added to theirs. "Dalia?" The little fairy flew through the air and stood on Faelynn's shoulder, hugging her face. "How are you here?"

"Beats me." Dalia laughed, excitement radiating from her tone. "How are *you* here?"

"I've been here since the veils went up from the wars between our Realms," Faelynn retorted, tilting her head to stare at her.

Dalia chuckled. "No...that wasn't it. Aren't you supposed to know everything?"

Faelynn was taken aback, her eyes glistening as she recounted the past.

I moved forward, asking the question burning on everyone's tongue. "What do you mean?"

"Dalia, no. It was written down in my realm as such, and the information I have collected all matched the history," Faelynn explained.

"Then your history is a lie," Dalia stated. "There were no wars between our Realms. It was all rumors. My line was one of the first to start the Pixi Court, and the stories passed down said it was a war between the gods. *Your* gods, actually...Tanith and Obsidian."

She took a moment, looking us over, and was puzzled by our reactions that were clearly lost. The gods?

"I don't know why or what they were trying to do...but it was them who separated the Realms for something greater they had planned."

Maeve looked to me, her eyes glassing over.

"Maeve?" I asked as a wave of nausea hit me like a brick wall. She looked at my wounds, before seeing the dagger with Davyna's blood on the edge of the table.

"Kade, drink her blood..." My mind was spinning as I looked between the blade and her. "Please."

I walked over to it and picked it up. Hesitating, I looked at the shimmering grey liquid coating the metal and swallowed hard. Bringing it to my lips, I tasted the bitterness from the darkness that seeped in, causing me to cough. Glancing down, the wounds on my body began to heal. My brows pulled down at the sight.

"What the fuck?" I whispered and brought my gaze back to Maeve. "How did you—"

"I didn't know. It was a guess based on...her powers and why—" she choked on her words, glancing down as her head shook softly. "I couldn't see it before... I couldn't tell until tonight." Her hands trembled as my heart slowed in my chest.

"My connection with Davyna and her family has always been strong since she is blood. I couldn't see anything after she left, and then a few bits and pieces after she returned to us. Nothing made sense and I couldn't see the whole picture." She paused, fidgeting with her hands. "But whatever she did tonight, it opened the door to my visions. And I saw it... I saw *them*."

My stomach sank as I put the pieces together. "No... No fucking way!" I yelled, turning around.

"Kadeyan..."

"Don't say it, Maeve... Please, don't say it." Every nerve in my body fired off, sending a blazing fear through my veins. "Don't tell me it's them... Please, anything but that." We were wrong. This wasn't anyone from Anawyn or Gelmyra, but something greater. More powerful...and they wanted her.

She glanced down as I turned back to face her. A single tear streamed down her cheek. Slowly, she met my gaze with the same silver eyes that I longed for right now.

She cleared her throat, shuddering as she said, "It's Tanith and Obsidian." Stepping closer to me, she took my hand. "I think they wanted Davyna's power fully opened. And with what I felt tonight, something tells me that they are one step closer to whatever they have planned."

CHAPTER 44
DAVYNA

There was something about letting go that freed your soul from the chains of life. And this past week was the liberation I needed from all the guilt and agony I held. I couldn't say that was the case for the males and females on their knees in front of me.

They were in chains.

They were in agony.

"Let us go!" yelled one of the males as he pulled at the shadows keeping him in place.

Flicking my wrist, his heart crushed in his chest and the song was like music to my ears—sweet and an alluring invitation to make the melody continue. His body went limp, falling forward in a loud thud.

"Anyone else want to talk?" They looked at me in anger laced with distress, but they asked for this. I was content in the bar the other night until those fuckers came in and tried to kill me. I laughed the entire time—which only took a minute—as I killed the lot of them. I dove into their minds and found out there were more like them—all determined to rid me from this realm.

But I wasn't going anywhere.

Smiling, I leaned back in my chair and grabbed the glass of blood off the table. I moaned as I took a sip, making all their eyes snap up to me. I knew I didn't need to be drinking this much blood lately, but damn, did it feel good. It threw me further into the ecstasy of the lust for more, and it was mine for the taking. So, why not?

"So, tell me, who is your leader? I'd love to have a chat with them." They all stared at me, and I rolled my eyes. "You can speak now."

One of the fae females at the end looked up. "We don't know. No one does." Her eyes narrowed. "All we know is, if we kill you, all this shit will stop." I looked down at her arms. They were decaying, taking on that sheen of death, and I felt it. She didn't want to die.

I gave her a sympathetic smile as I rose from the chair, slowly sauntering over to her before kneeling down. "How about you try one last time, but if you fail..." I began chuckling, looking down the line at the fae avoiding my gaze. "Oh, let's face it. You will, then I'll put all your friends out of their misery before I kill you, too."

I dropped my shadows from her and stood tall, but she didn't move, her body trembling slightly. Fire extended from my hand, consuming all ten of the fae before me. Screams rung off the stone walls, piercing the air with their horror as I took in the beauty of their melting flesh.

Glancing around the abandoned tunnels that once housed the Embers and other fae who hid here, I smiled. I figured that being in Hell was the best place to torture my captives because it was deep underground. Which meant that their screams wouldn't travel, and *they* wouldn't find me.

I could feel Kadeyan getting too close the last few days, and I was starting to think that idiot had a death wish, along with his found family. I might have to take care of that soon, and it sounded like fun.

I wondered what their terror tasted like. How their blood would feel dripping from my fingers... I chuckled, basking in the thought so much that I almost forgot I still had one more kill before me.

Bringing my eyes back down to the female, her gaze was fixated on her lifeless friends who were nothing but a pile of ash now. "You are a monster," she whispered, unable to tear her eyes away from the flames dying out.

"Aren't we all?" I placed my hand on her cheek, forcing her to look at me. Her eyes narrowed, trying to hide her terror, but it was no use. It wrapped around me, making every nerve light up within. Flames bloomed from my hand and her scream pierced into my skull as the blaze greedily consumed her body.

Stepping back, I picked up my glass. As I drank down the last bit of blood, I realized I was still thirsty. It looked like I was going to need another drink tonight.

Clapping pulled my attention to the hall in the back of the large room, and I turned. Walking towards me was the shadow form, and I let out a loud breath.

"Looks like someone is having fun."

"Mmm, I was." Throwing the glass down, it shattered as I used the gap, pulling me away from him. I landed in what looked like No–Man's–Land, but where? I began walking to find out but stopped abruptly as the shadow appeared before me.

"You don't have a minute to talk with me?" he said, his voice sounding sweeter than ever before.

"Oh, no, I do... I just don't want to." When I tried to push past him, he grabbed my arm and spun me around to face his dark mass of chaos.

"I need something from you." His tone was serious, which made me chuckle as I sized him up. "Your friends figured out something. And I want you to kill them. They are going to be a problem."

"That sounds like a *you* problem. You should deal with it yourself."

"What, are you scared to get your hands dirty?" he teased.

Hearing claws dig into the earth, I smiled. Ahh, that was where we were. Turning my head, I looked over my shoulder as the wolves stood at the tree line of the Crescent Lands.

"I'm not scared of anything...not even you." I turned back, laying my hand over his phantom one still gripping my arm. Shadows poured out like a vicious wave, turning the already dark night into an abyss. Broken cries ripped from the wolves as I listened to their hearts stop, one by one, and groaned. I kept my gaze on him, my lips turning up.

"Aren't you even a little curious as to what they learned?"

"Nope." I popped the *p*, and pulled my arm free, summoning my dark mist back to me.

Looking up, I took in the stars beaming above, along with the full moon, relishing in their souls passing beyond this realm. I turned to see all the wolves were now fae, laying completely still.

"If they get in my way, I'll handle them how I see fit. But other than that, you're on your own."

"Mmm. You intrigue me, Davyna...but I'm looking forward to ridding you from my life."

"The feeling is mutual...prick."

He laughed and moved away, but I could sense his eyes within the tendrils of black smoke, and they were on me. "Have your fun then, but the next time I come here, I'm taking you with me. It's time I got my answers. And I'll either use you...or kill you."

"Well, until then, fuck off!"

He laughed again as his shadows vanished, leaving a mist in the air that smelled of brimstone and smoke.

A few minutes passed, and I could hear the yells grow wild on the Crescent Lands, with one voice above it all. *Alastair.* I turned and began walking, rolling my shoulders back as I thought about the one person in this Court who deserved death. But who really cared as to who deserved it, when death was always stalking closer to each one of us, taking what it wanted?

And I wanted more...

Boots landed behind me, and I didn't need to turn to see who it was. My eyes rolled as I stood still.

"Did you miss me?" Kadeyan asked.

"How can you miss something you never cared about?" I smiled, turning to take in the hurt in his eyes. "How did you find me this time?"

"Alastair sent word that you were out here." My brows furrowed as I looked back. That little bastard. "All the Courts have been informed to report any sightings of you to me. If you didn't want me to find you, then you shouldn't have gone on a killing spree."

"It was just a few. And most deserved it." My tone was flat, uncaring, as I shrugged my shoulders.

He moved in and I stood cool as his hand lightly brushed my face. For a moment, I felt as if another side of me—one buried deep down—was banging on my psyche, but then it was gone. Like the darkness within smothered it, protecting me. *Good.*

"Let me help you, Dearest. Let's go home and talk about what happened."

"Okay..." I said, and he was taken aback. "Maybe that's a good idea." I smiled while taking his hand.

He interlaced his fingers through mine and stepped closer. I ran my hand down his chest, watching his body lean into my touch. His eyes softened and I genuinely wondered if he was always this stupid.

Twisting his hand, I heard the bones break, and he let out a yell laced with pain. Tossing him back with my shadows, I laughed as he regained his composure, before resetting the bones in his wrist.

"Now!" he yelled, and my magic built around me.

Calix and Axel appeared and threw their shadows out, wrapping around my arms. I glanced at each one of them as they let out more onyx mist before diverting my gaze to Kade. Smiling, I pulled my arms in, forcing the males' power to falter. Their shadows fell from me, and I sent my own out, wrapping around them until harsh sounds escaped their lips.

"Did you really think that would work?" I taunted as Kadeyan's eyes narrowed.

"That? No...we are just getting started."

Levanna and Nesrin appeared in front of me. The little witch threw out a dark purple color that poured from her fingertips, while the siren sent out raging water. Both barreled towards me, spiraling through the air with a mighty force that threw my hair off my shoulders.

Nesrin's water wrapped around my body as Levanna's spell embedded into my skin. My lip twitched, sensing the magic crawling through my veins as she tried to subdue me, but it only made me giggle.

Stepping forward, I watched them push harder, and then yell in frustration as growls behind me appeared. Taking a few more steps towards Levanna and Nesrin, I listened to the claws ripping into the grass. I waited until they were close before I moved out of the way.

Evren and Sorin launched through the air in their wolf form, but not at me. I watched as they took Levanna and Nesrin down to the ground.

I laughed harder as strong arms wrapped around me from behind, and my fury returned. My power that was holding Calix and Axel retreated inward as I thrashed against his hold.

Shit... I wasn't watching *him*.

"Faelynn!" Kadeyan yelled as all his friends got up, moving towards us.

Lacing my foot around his leg, I pulled for my shadows, snaking them around his body. He stumbled as they tightened, and I pulled my leg forward, causing him to fall.

Spinning through the air, I straddled him as my arm darted out towards his chest. I relished in what it was about to feel like to take his heart in my hold. I could already hear the arteries snapping, releasing my prize. As my hand reached his body, I stalled and my vision went black.

Reeling back, I gripped the side of my head, gritting my teeth as I saw visions... Visions I knew weren't true.

I was smiling, sitting in Kadeyan's lap as he nestled his face in my neck. I laughed, leaning into him, and the light tone slammed into me. Our friends came into the room, sitting down, and we all fell into conversation, truly enjoying each other's company without a care in the world.

There was something about the setting that just screamed it was untouched by darkness. It was—

No!

This wasn't real. The world would never exist without darkness. And I didn't want it to... Not anymore.

I pushed back on the power filling my mind and severed the link, turning to kill Faelynn. Levanna jumped in, placing obsidian chains on my wrists. My eyes narrowed on the dark material of stone before I glared up at them all, and rage took on new life within me.

"I'll hand it to you guys. That wasn't the worst set up," I said, sarcastically. Kadeyan pulled me off the ground and forced me to stand before them. Evren moved forward, her eyes no doubt taking in the wolves beyond before bringing her gaze back to me. "I would say sorry that I killed your people, but I'm not."

Her fist slammed into my cheek, forcing my head to move with the impact.

Shit, she could throw a punch... Who would have thought? Although, the pain felt good; it felt right. Licking my lip, I tasted the blood and smiled at her.

"This isn't you, Davyna! SNAP OUT OF IT!"

Kadeyan moved over, pulling her back. "Let's just get her back to the Fallen Castle. And in a cell," he demanded, his eyes narrowing on me with a slight grin gracing his beautiful face. Such a pity I'd have to smash it in when we were done with their charades.

"Oh, so, I'm your prisoner now?" I giggled. "Does that mean you're going to eat me?"

"No, we are going to help you before the fucking gods take you from here."

I tilted my head, looking into his eyes. *The gods...* I guess that was why the shadow figure wanted them dead. They found out who he was—who *they* were. Did that change anything? No, I still didn't fucking care. If he came for me, I'd handle it...but whatever came next between this realm and the gods was their problem.

I pulled on the chains, sensing something stir within...something I didn't want to tell them. Because, honestly, in this moment, I wanted to play their game and to show them they were fighting a lost cause. "Can we get on with it? I'm looking forward to this."

CHAPTER 45
EVREN

Four days… Four fucking days of going down into the cells to see my sister and try to get her to talk to me. Yet she would only stare blankly, showing nothing but an ice-cold demeanor that forced me to shudder. She refused to eat or drink anything but blood, which we had to figure out for ourselves because not a single word fell from her lips.

Sitting across from her, I was at a loss. I tried talking about Lana, Elias, Drystan, all of us, and her parents…but nothing. It was like the person I knew was completely gone.

We figured out she was in the tunnels the day before we got her, and seeing the piles of ashes made my stomach turn. She was ruthless; something else entirely that I never would have expected from her. She killed the soldiers in the Crescent Court, and for what?

I bit the inside of my cheek, fighting with the sorrow for my people, but also not being able to avenge them. Even in this state, she was my sister. So, what could I really do? And not only that, but could I even take her?

I knew the answer to that… It wasn't what I wanted anyway, because she was my blood…and I just wanted her back.

"I don't know what to say anymore, Dy." Her eyes met mine, and the darkness invading them sent a shiver down my spine as the silver shined brighter than ever. "How am I supposed to help you when you don't even care to help yourself?" She sat there, not making a sound.

Minutes passed, and my eyes began to fill with tears as I pulled myself off the ground.

"You know…when we were growing up, I wanted to be just like you. And when I found out what you were, I wasn't shocked because I always knew you were extraordinary." I ripped my fingers through my hair before moving over to the bars of the cell keeping us apart. "I wanted to be like my sister… But now, I'm glad I didn't end up like you."

The words burned as they came out because, deep down, I still looked up to her. Aside from Maeve, she was the only family I had left. I stood there, burrowing my gaze into her as she glared at me, but she was unfazed by it all. Giving up my fight, I began walking down the hall when I heard her clear her throat.

"We aren't sisters… We never were." Her voice was hoarse—weak even—but those words alone sent a phantom dagger through my heart.

Pulling for my power, I fell away from her and into my room, where Calix was sitting in a chair. His head popped up from resting on his interlaced hands before he stood and rushed over to me. I didn't realize tears were falling down my cheeks until I went to speak, tasting the mild saltiness.

"Shhh, it's okay…" He pulled me in, his large arms completely encircling me as I gripped onto his black tunic.

"She's gone…" I sobbed into the fabric, molding to his body as my knees buckled.

Calix kneeled, sweeping me off his feet as he moved over to the bed and laid me down. He followed after me, holding me to his chest. "She's not, Ev… We just need to find the thing that makes her want to feel again."

"Nothing works. I brought up everyone she has ever loved…and nothing. I can't do this anymore."

A knock sounded at the door before it opened slightly. Sorin peeked in, his eyes softening as they met mine.

"Sorry, I thought you were alone. I'll come back later," he said, but my body jolted up.

"Sorin, please."

Calix stiffened near me, but as I glanced over at him, his eyes were gentle.

Sorin moved into the room, standing at the end of the bed as he studied my features. "What happened?" he asked, but Calix sat up, shaking his head.

"It's Davyna. She isn't coming out of whatever is holding her," Calix said.

"What do you need?" Sorin asked, keeping his eyes solely on me.

"I want to forget it all for tonight. I want to feel something other than rage, or this..." *Pain of losing her.* I looked over at the two males, their eyes already darkening and pleading with me to choose. But I wanted them both...

"I'll leave," Calix said as he got up from the bed. As he took a few steps forward, I reached out, grabbing the sleeve of his tunic. He slowly turned, looking me over with eyes that longed for more.

"No... I want you both here." Both males looked at each other as I rose onto my knees, undoing the buttons on my blouse. I didn't want to choose anymore. We weren't mates, but I loved them...and I knew we would all part one day. And maybe that wasn't until next week or a hundred years from now. But I knew I wanted them. "Stay... Watch..."

I let the fabric fall and pool around me, watching their eyes drink me in. My hands lowered to my leather pants as I pulled at the string, the fabric loosening around my hips. They glanced at each other, and something appeared to pass between them, before Sorin moved in.

Keeping his eyes on me, Calix walked back, sat down, and brought his hand to his jaw. I leaned back, shivering as Sorin's lips brushed the shell of my ear. "Then take off your pants...and let's give him a show."

I paced back and forth in Levanna's office as she and Nesrin sat in their seats. Kadeyan went down to talk to Davyna over four hours ago, which I only knew because Calix stirred out of a dead sleep, waking me and Sorin along with him. Kade got into his head and told him to come stand watch in case anything happened.

I got dressed and saw Sorin off to check on the wolves in the Ember Lands before coming right here, waiting to see what happened. "Do you think he is getting through to her?" Nesrin asked as her leg bounced up and down.

We all stood quiet in his absence, silently hoping he would succeed. Another half hour passed by before Kadeyan pushed open the doors and I took in his arm, dripping with blood.

"What happened?" Levanna jumped up and moved over to him, inspecting the wound.

"I was close... I could see it in her eyes," Levanna offered him her wrist, but he looked at her with a brow raised. "I'm not going to feed off of you. Plus, it was dark obsidian; it will take a few days."

"What? You had no problem doing it to me," I said as a grin pulled up on my face, and he laughed. There was a time when I really hated him for what he did. I didn't trust him, but I couldn't deny everything he did was for my sister, and I forgave him long ago. Although, I wasn't telling him that.

Levanna turned and leaned against his desk. "Tell us what happened."

"She must have been picking at the obsidian walls, but there was a moment when I looked up at her that I saw her eyes flicker from the darkness to what they used to be. It was almost like she was worried, and then it vanished."

Turning, I crossed my arms over my chest and walked away from them. My mind began to spin as I looked up.

Nesrin walked over and placed her hand on my shoulder, drawing my attention back to see her worried gaze. "What is it? What are you thinking?"

"My sister doesn't need memories to break her out of it...she needs fear... Fear of losing the one thing worth living for." The room fell silent as I turned around. "Levanna, can you do a spell that makes it look like someone is dying?"

"An illusion spell? Yeah, it will require her blood, though."

Kadeyan smirked, pulling the blade out of his sheath. It was coated in grey.

My eyes widened. "You—"

"Calm down, Ev," Kadeyan stated before smirking. "Your sister kind of likes it, anyway."

Levanna took the blade and brought it over to a bowl. Her purple mist shot forth, pulling the blood down before she moved over to grab a grimoire from one of the shelves. "Who is going to fake-die then?"

I went to speak but bit my tongue as I realized...it wasn't me anymore. I knew she loved me—would fight for me—but there was only one thing that could completely destroy her now...

"It has to be you," I said, moving over to him. Processing my words, he didn't speak.

I continued. "Kadeyan...you have been the one to help her through this all... And the bond you guys share...it goes beyond blood. My sister loves you with everything she is."

"I agree," Nesrin said. "Kadeyan, it needs to be you."

A broken smile rose on his face before he finally nodded.

I looked all of them over, balling my hands into fists. "Then, when do we do it?"

CHAPTER 46
EVREN

Everything was in place. Axel, Nesrin, Calix, Sorin, and I stood on the terrace, waiting in the frigid air. My heart drummed against my ribs as I looked over the two males by my side.

Sorin slowly grabbed my hand, giving it a gentle squeeze, before Calix did the same. This was going to work... It had to. And then, we would find a way to help her and get the gods out of here. Even if I had to figure out a way to do it for Davyna.

That was the thing about people you loved. You would take on their darkness, their pain, and make it yours if it meant they could breathe again. In the last twelve days since she shut off everything, I replayed everything Kadeyan told us. About what she was facing, where she went, and how she was trying to protect us all while shattering inside.

I was wrong to lash out at her, and to say she wasn't strong. She was the strongest person I knew, and I needed her to hold onto that strength to break this... To come back to us all. Then, we could show her this battle was not hers alone anymore.

She had us. She would always have us.

My body stiffened and I dropped Calix's and Sorin's hands as I saw Kadeyan and Levanna walking Davyna to us. Levanna moved over, standing by Nesrin's side as Kadeyan threw Davyna down to her knees. A jolt of lightning ripped through me as she placed her hands out, holding herself up.

I wanted to run to her, to help her, but then...

She laughed. "Well...did all of you come out here to see little, old me?" Her voice was raw, distorted even. I looked to Kadeyan and he nodded ever so softly. The spell would keep him immobilized for at least three minutes, and the fake-dagger in my sheath was a part of the spell to activate it.

"No... I wanted you to watch me do this." He rushed over to me, grabbing me by my throat before slamming me down on the ground. The air ripped from my lungs as I glanced over at Calix, his eyes turning red, and Sorin's were flashing yellow.

Kadeyan walked over to Davyna, using his shadows to drag me across the ground. "Would you like me to kill her this time?"

"What?" I asked, pushing more effort into my words to sell the performance we rehearsed. Davyna glanced over at me, before tilting her head and sizing up Kadeyan.

"Seriously? This is your plan?" She laughed, coughing slightly. "You are not going to kill her."

"Kadeyan, what the fuck are you doing?" Axel yelled, but Kadeyan's shadows lashed out, holding them all in place.

"I'm trying to get the real Davyna to decide if her sister is worth saving." My body flew through the air, slamming into the stone arch, and I coughed violently as I gasped for air to fill my lungs. His shadows left my body as he kept his eyes locked on Davyna.

Standing up, I pulled the dagger free and moved over to him. Davyna's pitch-black eyes landed on the dagger, her gaze instantly turning to show she was concerned.

It was working...

Kadeyan turned and gripped my wrist until I heard a bone snap. I cried out, hearing my screams echo over the Lands.

Okay, that was *not* planned.

The dagger fell and Kadeyan tossed me to the ground as he picked it up. "She's nothing anyway. Right, Dy?"

His voice entered my mind. *"Kick my feet out and finish it."*

He stalked over to me, placing the blade's tip against my forehead. "Maybe I should have drained her dry at the ball... It would have been a kinder end."

Looking over at Davyna, her mouth parted, and if I wasn't

mistaken…it looked like she was scared. Pulling my gaze back to Kadeyan, I shifted and let out a growl as our friends began screaming. I bit his leg, and he yelled as I ripped him down. Shadows darted out towards me, and I shifted back as the dagger fell between us.

Grabbing it, I plunged it down into his chest, hearing the air rip from his lungs…and Davyna's. My breathing was labored as I pushed back, looking at his still body, and if I didn't know any better, I'd say he was really dead.

His shadows fell from everyone as they all rushed over, dropping to the ground to look at him. Even Levanna's eyes were lined with tears, and it looked genuine.

My gaze moved over to Davyna, and my stomach dropped. She was…smiling. She slowly stood up, watching me as a demonic laugh passed her lips. "I'm sorry, was I supposed to believe that was real?"

Everyone turned, looking at her with shock.

"Davyna…he is—"

"Shut the fuck up, Levanna. You might be a powerful witch, but I can feel the spell on him."

"How can you feel it when…" I said, glancing down at her hands, where the chains were rubbing her skin raw.

"Want to know a secret?" Shadows poured from her, holding us all in place. Pain coursed through my body as its constricting hold squeezed, stealing my next breath. I looked down and saw the onyx vapor swirling with subtle hues of magic.

Davyna pulled at the chains, breaking them from her wrists, and sighed in relief. "Those were getting annoying." Shock was plastered on all our faces. It didn't work on her…which meant that she was biding her time.

Throwing us all back, our bodies slammed into the stone. "Now, listen. I know he wants you all dead. And, honestly, I kind of do, too, right now…but I'll let him deal with you. You're his problem now."

"Davyna! Obsidian is going—" Levanna yelled, pushing herself up as she winced.

"Let me stop you there, my little witch," she said, turning to face her. "He can do whatever he damn well pleases, but killing me or using me isn't going to be one of them."

She looked down at Kadeyan's still body and stalled, but nothing showed in her eyes.

"What if Obsidian and Tanith go after him?" I called out.

"Then he will probably deserve it." She began walking away and rage built deep within. I ran after her, not caring anymore of what she could do. I needed to keep her here; to make her see this wasn't the way. Her shadows wrapped around me, pulling me into the air.

"Listen to me because I won't give you all a second chance." She glared at everyone before looking up at me. "Leave me alone...or I will burn this realm to the ground." She pulled my body down, slowly smiling at me. "Let's see if one of your lovers makes it in time..."

Her shadows launched me through the air and I gasped. Pain exploded in my head and my vision swayed as sleep called for me. I tried to fight it, but it was no use.

The last thing I saw was the valley below, and I knew she threw me over the cliff... There was no fighting, no calling out for help. Everything faded, and I was lost in total darkness.

CHAPTER 47
KADEYAN

When I woke from the spell the other night, I prayed my amber eyes would be met with silver ones...but that wasn't the case. Calix held Evren in his arms as she cried, her wails of grief making my own soul break. It didn't work. Then, after hearing what she said to them, and how she threw Evren over the cliff...

Calix made it just in time before her body slammed into the jagged rocks below, but she still hit her head on the way down, causing it to bleed. Calix gave her his blood to help her heal but wouldn't let her go, and I didn't blame him. I could see the love he held for her... Even if they weren't bonded, it was strong.

I noticed they were all on edge today when I left; they worried she would make good on her threat. I held no regard for her pathetic attempt to scare me off, though.

I was going to get her back.

Flying over the Lands, I kept my eyes peeled on the streets below and the people walking by. Many wore blades across their backs or sheaths strapped to their legs, and I knew the blades were obsidian. Fear was rising more each day with the chaos unfolding in our realm.

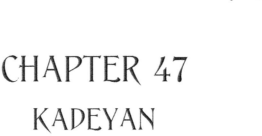

More people had been getting sick, and it seemed to be progressing at a faster rate within the last two weeks. Fae were attacking their friends and family or anyone near them. Was it a coincidence that it was two weeks today that Davyna turned off her humanity? It wasn't just that, though. The fae were more fearful of the attacks, like they were waiting in the eye of a storm; waiting for the cyclone of chaos to unfold.

And then, there was Davyna...

Rumors of her kept spreading. Tonight, alone, I had to kill several people gathering to hunt her down. I mean, I could have let her kill them, but I wanted their blood on my hands for even thinking about hurting her. Those deaths hadn't bothered me, but it was the innocent blood she was spilling that worried me most. I knew that when—not if, but *when*—I got her back, this would affect her.

Picking up on screams, I turned my head to the left and noticed I was back on Fallen soil, right on the outskirts of the forest. Lowering, I watched as a door to the bar flung open and many ran out.

Shadows wrapped around their bodies and their screams became lost to the wind as they fell to the ground like solid weights. Blood roses and ash filtered up to me and I dropped down, pulling my wings in and ignoring the corpses to my left. I walked to the door, taking a calming breath as I pulled the cold persona forth before hauling the door open.

A small dagger flew past me, piercing into a male's eye. His scream pierced my ears, and I noticed Davyna's black shadows immobilizing him. Turning to my left, I saw Davyna was sitting at a table. Her feet were up, and she was smiling at the male still crying out in pain on the far wall.

Blood coated her lips, staining them darker as she smiled at the man across from me. The expression quickly faded as she narrowed her dark eyes on me. "That was a nice stunt the other night... Too bad it wasn't real."

"Would you like to finish it then?" I asked as her body slowly leaned back, sizing me up for a minute.

"What do you want, Kadeyan?"

Getting up, she walked over to where the males and females were lining the wall, immobilized by her power. Pulling a dagger and a cup off the table near her, she ran the blade down one of the male's forearms and he whimpered. Blood began pouring almost instantly, making my own rush to my eyes. Standing there, she let it collect in the cup, while she waited for me to respond.

"Tomorrow is Saawyn. It's a ritual to honor the dead," I said, studying her cold features that were growing more annoyed by the second in my presence.

She laughed, pulling the cup to her lips. With her eyes on me, she drank every drop. Pulling the cup away when she was done, she tossed it to the ground. A drop ran down her chin, and I resisted the urge to move in, cleaning it up with my tongue.

Her darkness didn't scare me; it made me want to challenge her with my own.

Stepping over to a chair, I sat down and cleared my throat before I continued. "The veil between the living and the dead will be at its thinnest, and the Sky Court will pull them to our plane so we can talk with the ones we lost."

"I'll pass," she said, walking to the door. It took everything in me not to turn around and grab her.

"Even if you get a chance to see your father? Your mother? Or Elias?" I called out, keeping my eyes on the fae of my Court and others lining the wall.

"I would rather eat glass, cut off my wings, or shove a dagger in my own heart before seeing their faces again." Her boots scuffed against the wooden planks of the bar, before placing her cool hands on me. Leaning down, she brought her lips to my ear. "You might be a good fuck, Kadeyan...but do not test me again. The girl you knew is gone. Deal with it."

"I see you, Davyna..." I smiled, glancing up to look into her soulless eyes as she pulled back. "You're still in there. And the fear you inflict on others doesn't work on me."

"Is that so?" Bodies began to drop around us, and I kept myself still as her gaze searched mine. "Stop showing up. I didn't want you before, and I sure as hell don't want you now."

My heart twisted in my chest as she backed away, her shadows devouring her.

The day passed in a blur as I sat in Levanna's spell room. I switched between looking over the mountains in a daze and trying to read more of Nyna's journal.

But my mind kept returning to the pain that was embedded in me long ago. Loss was something I was never good at. And even though she was still here, I was beginning to doubt she would ever come back from this. Why would she? I didn't care if she fixed this realm or burned it. I just wanted her to feel loved, protected, and know that she wasn't alone...

Scanning through a few more pages of the journal, my eyes caught on a spell with the stone on it. Something about it felt like it was for me. It wasn't the Ember stone; it was the Fallen one. Looking over the small text lining the side of the page, I noticed a phrase my father used to say.

'Val tes brutalia, Le vas et viau.' *Even in death, I am with you.* But it was what was after the phrase that made my heart speed up: *Come see me. We need to talk.*

Looking up, I felt my eyes widen as Levanna turned. "Look what I found," I said as I moved in and placed the journal in her hands.

She read it over several times, before looking at me with shock. "Kadeyan, this spell allows you to see your father." She shook her head, almost laughing.

"Can you do it?" I asked, impatience taking over.

I could see him...

"Yeah, I don't see why not. This spell was made for someone like me... Well..."

"What?" I asked as my heartbeat quickened.

"It was like it was made for me. The dialogue is exactly how I speak in spells. How did Nyna—"

Pulling the stone to me, it appeared in my hand, and I placed it down on the journal. "Please...send me in there."

About ten minutes passed while Levanna set up a circle of black salt, imbued with my blood, before handing me the onyx stone. "I don't know what you are going to feel when I send you in. It could be nothing, or...painful."

I laughed. "I don't care." The tears built in my eyes, and I blinked them away. There was no need for them, not when I was getting something I longed for and never thought was possible. To see the man who raised me and molded me into who I became, even just one more time...it was everything in this moment.

That ceremony that the Sky Court would perform, Saawyn, gave me so much hope. Everyone in attendance would cut their palms with dark obsidian, letting their blood fall into a bowl. Then, an elder of the Acolytes would cast the enchantment needed to pull the dead to us. A sheer dome would appear in the clearing in the woods of the Fallen Lands, and if you had a connection with someone in the afterlife...there was a chance they would come to you.

He never came, but now...

"When you are ready, Lev," I said. She nodded while I prepared myself, taking a firm stance with the stone gripped tightly in my palm.

Levanna began chanting, her magic creating a cyclone of wind around the circle, and my hair got pulled into the building disarray. Pain radiated through my body, and I gritted my teeth as it coursed through me.

I looked down and saw that my veins were turning grey, like it was stopping the blood from rushing through them. They reminded me of Davyna's scars in a way, but they weren't taking on an onyx hue.

It was like sand replaced my blood, making everything burn with an intensity I didn't want to feel. Yet, there was no way I was going to ask her to stop. I could endure this.

Falling to my knees, I let out a yell before looking into Levanna's eyes. "Keep going!"

She nodded as she continued to chant louder, forcing the spell to move fast, until it took me over. The breath was ripped from my lungs, causing me to gasp for air, but there was none to satisfy the need. It felt like meeting death as each organ shut down, and my heartbeat slowed.

Panic rushed in for a moment as I fell forward into utter darkness, and I was swallowed alive by its promise of ripping my soul away from the living.

Throwing my hands out, I touched what felt like ground, but when my eyes focused on it...I couldn't see anything. Where the hell was this? There was...nothing. Like the void I saw so many times in the past that swallowed Dy whole.

"Well, took you long enough, Kade."

Turning to look over my shoulder, I saw the face that matched my own. There were slight differences in his nose and jawline, but the amber beaming bright in the dark had me searching for air all over again.

"Dad..." I jumped up as fast as I could and rushed through the utter darkness until I slammed into his body, wrapping my arms around his shoulders. "I've missed you so much," I blurted out as a sob worked up my throat.

"I've missed you, too," he said, holding me tighter. "But we don't have much time."

My heart felt like it was shattering as I pulled back and looked at his gentle expression.

I glanced around. "Where is Silas? Is he here?"

"There is no time for that, Son. Listen. Nyna made sure you'd have this one chance...to ask me what you need to help Davyna."

Taking a step back, I felt lost for a moment.

"You knew Ezekiel's daughter was my mate?"

"Yes...just like I knew she was going to struggle with what was to come. She needs you, Kade. She needs you to help her with picking the light over the darkness."

"What is she?" I asked.

He looked over his shoulder as if he felt pulled back to the world his soul resided in. Turning slowly, he looked deep into my eyes.

"You will know soon, but there are two endings to this all. You need to keep her from falling. You need to protect the Queen."

"I will. But, Dad...how do I stop them?"

"It's not your place yet."

"What do you mean?" I asked, but I noticed my father's form becoming more sheer, matching one of a ghost. "Dad, please. What does that mean?"

"Keep her safe. And get the stones...all of them. You need them to save Valyner."

He was fading quickly, making my heart race faster. "Dad, please don't go!"

A sorrowful smile graced his face as a tear fell, trailing down his cheek. "Kadeyan, I'm already gone... But please, don't forget who she is to you." Confusion ran through me as I went to step forward. "I'll see you again one day, Kade. Until then...give them hell, Son."

Sucking in a sharp breath, the spell room came back into view. I frantically sought him out, praying he was still here, but he was gone.

"Are you okay? Kade, you were completely grey. I thought the magic— I thought..." Levanna said as I sat up.

"I'll be okay."

"Did you see him?"

Turning I looked into her eyes and knew mine were glassed over. Nodding, I looked down at the stone in my hand and smiled.

"I did."

CHAPTER 48
KADEYAN

The world around me was cast in a swirling blur as I tried to blink and focus on my surroundings. I could feel the slight breeze whip past me, and I turned as my heart rate began to climb. Slowly, I started to see the woods surrounding me, painted in a blue sheen. I blinked a few times to clear my vision.

What was going on? Was this a dream?

"It will pass in a moment."

Turning around, I focused on the blue form, seeing right through her before her face came into view.

"Who are you? Where are we?"

"My name is Nyna. I think you've heard of me. It's a pleasure to finally meet one of Osiris' sons."

My breathing became labored as I stepped closer to her.

"And we are in the Mortal Lands. Sorry for the haze. It took a lot more power than expected to pull you here. My connection is with Davyna. So, I had to push through her state to get to you."

Her eyes softened on me as she gestured with her hand to follow. Pushing off the balls of my feet, I ran until I was by her side.

"If she doesn't break through soon, I won't be able to see her ever again," *she said. The ground beneath our feet shook, making me still, but Nyna continued to walk.*

"What are you?" *I asked as I caught up, walking by her side.* "What is Davyna?"

She kept her gaze forward.

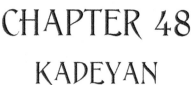

After a few minutes of walking, she cleared her throat. "Something more. Something that shouldn't have been made, but was... I can't tell you the rest."

Weaving through some trees, we came to a clearing surrounded by mountains with the tips painted in white. Glancing up, I watched as snow brewed in the clouds before the chilling breeze pierced my leathers.

"Did you know it was the gods all along?"

"Yes, but you have to know this, Kadeyan. I wanted to give her everything. Every answer...but I couldn't. Her searching for the truth is what's going to get her..." *Her lips pressed together, before her eyes showed the frustration tainting them.* "I can tell you about them now."

Taking a step closer, I watched her gaze take in the grass and trees before looking up to the sky. "The gods were never supposed to create their own race. They took the stones from their makers to do so."

"Makers?"

"Yes... Two brothers cast out of their home created the six gods of this world." *We moved on into the clearing. When I slowed, she turned to face me.*

"So, what, is one God, and the other the Devil?" *I asked, thinking of the humans and how I taunted Davyna when I first met her with the tale of their beliefs in the Mortal Realm.*

"No." *She turned.* "They are technically gods, but more powerful than the ones who rule over the fae realms. Obsidian was close to one of the brothers." *She dropped her head, her shoulder falling an inch.* "And it's the reason Obsidian has done everything he has, up to now."

"What do you mean? What did he do?" *I asked as the chill grew deeper into my bones.*

"He and Tanith have been siphoning every fae's power to emulate their own with the goal of being untouchable by one of their makers. They locked the fae inside Valyner to keep your power feeding them. But also, Obsidian wanted you all to have access to the Mortal Realm to kill the humans. He looked at them as an abomination to the fae—unworthy to be in the same world.

Although, everything he tried to do wasn't enough for him to get what he truly wants."

"What does he want?" I asked, my chest tightening.

"That is something I can't tell you..." *Hurt flashed in her eyes, and I truly believed she wanted to tell me, but couldn't.* "We come from something very different, Kade—Davyna and I. Something that defies balance. Without our lineage, this wouldn't be possible."

I went to speak, but she cut me off.

"Promise me this: you will help her destroy them...Obsidian can't get what he wants... Neither can..." *She paused, biting her tongue. Again, I could tell she wanted to say it, but couldn't.* "Just promise me you will help my daughter."

"I will..." *I abandoned the questions still floating around in my mind, because I knew she wasn't going to give them. But this alone showed more to who the enemy was.* "How do I kill them?"

She smiled, looking around at the clearing. "Make sure you don't lose it. You're going to need it." *Confusion rushed in as she disappeared before me and the world fell into oblivion.*

Coughing, I sat up and looked around. The sun was peeking over the mountains around me, and I instantly felt the change in power here.

The Mortal Realm.

Pushing myself up, I brushed the dirt off my face. Lifting my other hand, I stalled. Gripped between my fingers was a dagger.

As I examined the blade, I noticed its striking contrast. On one side, it gleamed with a pristine, white stone, while the other side exuded a darkness even deeper than dark obsidian. The gold handle elegantly spiraled from the grip down to the hilt, ending in sharp points that seemed capable of piercing a person's heart with ease.

She brought me here to give me this...to kill them.

Turning it over, I noticed it was empty at the top, as if it was missing a stone. Or was that why her journals pointed towards the stones...and my father said to get them all? But how were we supposed to fit all the stones in this? It was designed to hold one by the looks of it. So, did we need to combine them all?

Standing up, I looked over the clearing once more. She said there was a reason she couldn't tell us these things…and I trusted her. I didn't need all the answers when I knew there were only three things to end this all.

Get Davyna back.

Get the stones.

And kill those fuckers once and for all.

But first, I needed to get back to Valyner for Saawyn, and see if my little Ember would take the bait.

CHAPTER 49
DAVYNA

My eyes darted open, looking around to see if I was in the room. The anxiety was quickly masked, taking away the fear and worry if someone I knew was behind those blurred faces before seeing my own.

Even now, that godsdamn nightmare was haunting me. Anxiety rose when all I wanted was to stay lost in the numbness that had become my rescue.

But there was something else... A feeling deep down. It was a familiar power...and something I felt in the dream with her... Was she trying to get to me? I laughed it off, sitting up and brushing the forest's debris from my leathers.

"Sorry to disappoint, Mom..." I said to that place deep within that tied us together. Smiling, I stood. My eyes locked on the sky above, seeing it was dark out—even darker than normal for the Fallen Lands—but it was definitely morning...

As I began to walk, I felt my head sway as something—or should I say, someone—pounded against my skull. It was as if hands were trying to beat their way out from within. I noticed it in the cell when Kadeyan touched me, or when I threw Evren, and again now.

Let me out!

I tilted my head, recognizing the voice. Maybe there was a true fighter in me after all... Too bad she wasn't getting out.

Letting out a breath, I listened into the Lands beyond and realized everything was silent. My eyes rolled, irritation pricking every nerve.

They must all be at that ritual.

Thinking about Kadeyan's invitation annoyed me. Why bother with the dead when you couldn't have any fun with a spirit? Standing in the silence of the forest, my lips tugged up to one side as I thought about how maybe I could have my own kind of *fun* at this ritual.

Silently laughing, my magic spun around me, powered by its sheer excitement to cause mischief. After all, didn't they deserve it?

Dropping into the foyer of the Fallen Court castle, I glanced both ways before listening in. Everything was soundless, casting an almost sorrowful atmosphere.

"Davyna?" Turning, I looked at Faelynn, her snowy white skin and hair beaming bright against her black gown. "Are you—"

"Here for the ritual...absolutely. I wouldn't miss seeing all the people I sent to the afterlife."

Her face stood neutral, unamused by my comment.

Turning, she looked up the stairs before glancing over her shoulder. "Would you like me to help you get ready?" she asked.

"Why not? Lead the way."

Moving up the stairs, we climbed four flights before finally working towards the fifth floor. I'd never been up here, and as I took in the cobwebs lining the stone, I figured most probably hadn't either.

Faelynn led me down the narrow hallway that was exposed to the world beyond, and the nip in the air hit my cheeks. Although, I didn't want to ward off the chill anymore because it fed something within, fueling the darkness. Glancing over the Lands, I slowed down, enchanted by the sky cloaked in night.

After a minute, Faelynn cleared her throat, pulling my attention back to her dark pools. "The sun won't shine over any of the Lands until tomorrow. Today isn't for the living...it's for the dead."

"Well then, let's not keep the dead waiting..."

At the end of the hall, Faelynn stood in front of a door that was painted in a dark red hue. The design in it was enough to make me pause.

Flames...

Let me out! Let me out!

Shaking my head, I watched as she used her hand and sent out a wave of white mist that pushed the door open. I moved forward, taking in the room that resembled a small office, but there was a bed off to the side to overlook the mountains.

The large table in the center caught my attention, and I noticed it was made of solid stone that had clearly aged. Stepping closer to it, I saw it wasn't just a simple table... A map of Valyner was carved across the top.

"Whose room was this?" I asked as my hand grazed over the Ember Court on the map...feeling something.

"Your father's." The sting sat in my chest for a moment before the darkness swallowed it and I turned to face her. "This level was his when he needed to get away from the Ember Court. Or wanted to strategize with Osiris."

"Did little to help, don't you think?"

"Mmm. Well, I think he would have liked you to have this." Moving over to the armoire, she opened the door, and dust billowed into the air. After pushing some clothes aside, she pulled out a gown, and I narrowed my gaze.

"It was your mother's... Well, it was supposed to be," Kadeyan said from within the doorframe, where he leaned with his arms crossed over his chest. Vexation pricked over my skin as I took him in, with that fucking cocky grin plastered to his face. "I'll take over from here, Faelynn." Kadeyan moved in and she laid the dress over his outstretched arms. "And can you please get Dalia to stop siphoning Ravyn's magic and using it against her?"

She let out a small laugh before shaking her head. "Enjoy your ritual," she said, closing the door behind her, and I glanced at Kade with one brow arched.

"You care about the cat now?"

"No...but I think you did. So, I'll keep it around a little longer."

Kadeyan moved over to the table and laid the dress out, allowing me to see the detail of it. Half of the material was white silk, while the other half faded down into a pitch-black. Armor was attached to the shoulders, connecting with delicate chains across the chest. The corset caught my eye. It was hollowed out in between the gold metal, crossing over to create an intricate design that held the top and bottom of the gown together.

"So, were you ever going to tell me my father used to come here?" I asked, unease stretching up around me.

"I was going to bring you here before your coronation...so you could see it and wear your mother's gown." He fell silent, watching me, and I felt another question on my tongue as to why my father had this dress made for my mother.

Glancing up, I saw Kadeyan waiting, and I smiled. Undoing my leathers, I let the top fall first before pushing down my pants. His eyes drank me in, and I couldn't help but laugh.

Males...

"It was supposed to be Nyna's coronation gown..."

"Did I ask?" I spat out as he moved in, picking it up.

"No...but the way your eyes took it in made me think you wanted to know something about it." Kadeyan ran his fingers up my arm, causing heat to surface for the first time in two weeks. "I still got it," he whispered.

"What? Being an ass? Yeah...I'd have to agree." I pulled the dress out of his hands and used the spell to place it on my body. "So, tell me, what do we do at this ritual?" I asked with a sarcastic tone as I took a seat in the chair behind me.

"Everyone will use a dark obsidian dagger to cut their hand and bleed into a bowl. Then, the Sky Court will perform the magic that's needed to call the dead to us."

"Sounds like fun." I smiled, running my tongue over my fang as it dropped down.

"Listen...today isn't for your games, Davyna. So, don't start shit that I'll have to finish."

"Ooh, is that a threat?" I laughed, standing back up and taking a few steps closer to him. Something deep within called me to close the distance between us, but I ignored it. "You shouldn't tempt me with a good time."

"And you shouldn't underestimate me." He turned to face me, walking my way, and it forced me to back up until my body was pressed against the wall. "I'm just getting started with you." His hand ran down my chest, pulling the heat within to the surface again.

"Is that right?" I said, my breathing picking up.

Fuck... What the hell?

Focusing, I moved in and forced a sweet smile. "Then do your worst... I can't wait to be painted in your blood."

Smiling, he grabbed me. "As long as I'm painted in yours, too." Grinning, his onyx shadows circled us, and everything fell into sweet, blissful darkness.

CHAPTER 50

DAVYNA

Dropping into the clearing, I noticed we were next to the base of the mountains in the Fallen Court. It was bursting with fae from every Court, dressed in black suits and gowns. Some held flowers in their hands, moving towards the stone altar that was set up at the base of the mountains, and there wasn't much talking going on among them.

"This place is a bummer," I spat out, forcing heads to turn my way. At first, they were angry, but when they saw who I was, they moved away. It made me giggle.

"Knock that shit off and show some respect."

"Coming from the guy who completely disregards respecting anyone." A laugh got caught in my throat as I began moving.

Somber music echoed through the land, setting the tone for today, and everyone else seemed to feel it. Like it was a plague, burrowing into the very marrow of their bones. But for me, it felt like home.

"Davyna?" Turning, I looked at Levanna, with Nesrin standing by her side. "Kade, why is she here?" They were both dressed in black gowns, similar but different. Levanna's had black crystals molding to her torso while Nesrin's was covered in what looked like sea glass painted black.

"I invited her, and she promised to be on her best behavior. Didn't you, Dearest?"

"Not one bit." I gave them a gentle smile. Looking beyond at the altar, I saw where everyone was cutting their palms, their blood falling into the large bowl. The scent of iron made my blood pulse in my veins, longing for it to fill me, but not yet. I wanted to play with my prey first.

"Where's Maeve?" Kadeyan asked.

"I just saw her, but she must be at the altar. Make sure you go offer the sacrifice soon," Nesrin said, and I tilted my head.

"A sacrifice? Really?" I teased, crossing my arms over my chest.

"The blood that runs in our veins is living, but as the dark obsidian blade draws it out, it dies. If anyone on the other side with ties to our blood is there, they will come forward. Well, most of the time," Levanna said, her eyes beaming with more hope than I'd ever seen before.

"Oh, you're hoping your mate shows." I laughed, finding all of this funnier by the second. Her eyes locked on something behind me, and any ounce of hope faded away, being replaced with raw fury.

Kadeyan must have seen it, too, because he moved in, grabbing her arm to redirect her attention. "Breathe. Today isn't the day to let them get to you. Today is about you and Silas."

Looking over my shoulder, I took in the male and female who were about six and a half yards away. The disgust on their faces was directed towards Levanna, but slowly, it shifted to me.

"Can I help you? Would you like me to remove your heads from your necks?" I yelled, causing people to turn. The two fae moved off, not giving me a second glance.

"Davyna!" Kadeyan growled and I glanced back at him, smiling.

"Right. I'm supposed to be on my *best* behavior," I said as I began walking away from them.

Getting into a smaller line to the side, I watched as Axel, Calix, Sorin, and Evren came down off the altar. Each one was wrapping their hands in black cloth to contain their still-bleeding palms as they walked.

I studied Evren's face, seeing the tears build in her eyes, but it quickly faded as she caught sight of me. Calix was quick by her side as he placed his hand around her waist, causing her to slow.

"What the fuck are you doing here?"

"I wanted to see my dads. Think they will come?" I turned away from her as I felt her anger grow stronger.

"Knowing my father...he wouldn't want to see you like this," Evren spat out, her tone painted in truth but also anger.

Smirking, I took in the silk gown she was wearing. A simple onyx gown molded to her body with a matching fur shawl draped around her arms.

My gaze connected with hers and I said, "Knowing your father... I think he preferred me over you."

"Evren, let it go." Calix pulled her back, and she started walking away from me. I couldn't help but take in her eyes one last time as she glared back at me. They flashed a bright yellow hue, showcasing the wolf that lived within.

Taking a deep breath, I sighed as the line began to move. I tried to ignore the soft cries of the fae around me because, if I didn't...I was going to force them to stop.

"Do you mind?" I yelled out, and heads turned to look at me. "Some of us don't want to hear that shit."

I took another breath, willing every nerve in my body to go numb. It wasn't time yet. I needed to wait for the perfect opportunity to show them all what I was made of. And I'd know when it was time to rain my own fun on this gathering.

"Davyna..." Turning, I saw Alastair approach me with caution. He was with Alta and Katarina, who stood a few paces behind him. They seemed off...and something told me it didn't have to do with being in my presence.

"Princess, it's an honor to see you again," Katarina said as she curtsied, before Alta followed.

"How sweet. Did you come to see your dead mate, and your father who killed my mom?" All of their bodies stiffened, and a snicker passed my lips.

Alta shook her head. "I'm not."

Katarina hushed her daughter as Alastair looked back at them, but I could see something below the surface there.

Boredom washed over, and I turned away, but Alastair touched my arm. Rolling my eyes, I lashed out and twisted his wrist until he fell to his knees.

"Don't ever lay a hand on me again, or you won't have a hand."

"I was just trying to tell you..." he choked out as I released him. He took a moment before standing and cleared his throat. "I have those books I think would help in your search if you're still interested, but you'll have to come to the Crescent Court for a visit."

"And why is that?" Kadeyan asked as he walked up behind me.

Oh, here we go. The males were going to argue to prove who had the bigger dick. I mean, I'd seen both. So, I already know who would win.

Alastair laughed, moving out of the way of some fae trying to get back to their spots before the ritual began. "Because anything that's in my Court can't leave. Jinx spelled it so that if someone takes it off my Lands, it will turn to dust."

"She isn't your puppet, Alastair."

I sat there, looking between both males, and becoming more uninterested by the second.

"And clearly...she isn't yours either." Moving forward, he stood by Kade's side and leaned in, whispering, "I hope you're the next one she kills."

Kade lashed out, his shadows tightening around Alastair's throat. His face instantly turned blue. "You want to say that louder, little Lord?"

"Gods... Shut the fuck up!" I demanded, feeling like today would have been better spent anywhere else and with daggers pierced into my ears. Kadeyan released him, and Alastair burrowed his eyes into him as he stepped back.

"Sorry," Alastair said, straightening his black jacket.

"No, I mean, you two can kill each other. Just get it over with already."

Kadeyan laughed and I glanced over at him, taking in his audacity to think I was joking.

"I apologize, anyway... And remember, Davyna, my offer still stands. The Crescent Lands just aren't the same without you."

"Aw, I know. That's what happens when you lie. You lose people. You should really try to accept that," I spat out as I left the two males standing in the line that was almost nonexistent now. I came here for my own entertainment today, and I was sick and tired of dealing with everyone's emotions.

As I moved up the small platform, Kade appeared next to me, but I ignored him as I watched Maeve. She brought the small knife to a cloth, swiping it clean and staining the fabric. It vanished almost instantly, the material beaming like freshly laid snow, and I knew she was using magic to do it.

She looked at me with worry before glancing at Kadeyan. "I told you she can't do it."

"And why is that? I'm fae, so why can't I see my dead family?" I asked as the smile fell from my face.

Kadeyan took the knife from her and cut his palm quickly, letting his blood fall into the bowl. I glanced down at it and grinned, craving everyone's life force to fill my veins.

"Davyna... It's just... I don't think it would be a good idea with the power you hold. I think it would do something to the spell we have to perform."

My brows furrowed as Kadeyan gave her back the dark blade. He turned to face me, his own vile grin growing as his gaze locked on mine. "I wanted you to come so you had to watch others connect with their loved ones. I didn't mean you would get to see any of yours." The smile on my face quickly fell as his grew. "How's that feel? Are you hurt? Sad? Angry?"

Turning, he began to walk away, and I pulled the dagger from his sheath, slicing into my hand. I glanced down at the blade, furrowing my brows as I took in one side that was completely black, while the other side shimmered a bright white. Placing my palm over the bowl, I watched him turn, his eyes darkening.

"Davyna, don't!" Maeve yelled as I glanced back, watching the red blood slide down my hand and into the bowl.

Why was it red?

Pulling myself back from the thought, I let out a breathy laugh and smiled at him, because I knew this was my moment. "Oh, Kade... You shouldn't have pissed me off... Now, I'm going to have to kill everyone here."

CHAPTER 51

KADEYAN

Confusion was all I felt. That was, until the ground began to shake beneath our feet. Davyna looked at me with glee possessing her eyes as she threw the dagger straight at my chest. The one her mother told me not to lose; the one I knew I needed to keep safe on me because I didn't trust it falling into anyone else's hands. I grabbed it with my shadows before her own power knocked me back.

She bled and it wasn't grey...it was red. Why? Was it because of the dagger her mother gave me?

"Maeve, what is happening?" I yelled as I sat up, watching Davyna glance out at all the fae cowering in fear as the winds grew louder.

Maeve ripped off her veil, and it got swept up in the vicious cyclone as she placed her fingers into the blood of all the fae. Her chants were barely audible as thunder cracked and rolled across the sky.

Turning, I saw the fae looking at the growing black smoke with worry engraved in their expressions. It crawled up from the ground, slithering and twisting to block out the world beyond as it spread like wildfire around the dome.

What the hell was happening?

Did Davyna's blood do this? Turning, I watched her painting the perfect picture of ease.

I got up and moved through the air as fast as I could, gripping her by her throat. "What did you do?!"

"Honestly? Nothing, but this is pretty cool." She looked around, taking in the chaos as if it was a peaceful day in summer that brought ease and serenity.

"The spell is underway! Her blood must have started it!" Maeve yelled as she looked at both of us with wide eyes. That was impossible without the Sky Court... This couldn't happen.

Fuck. But Davyna was a part of the Sky Court, and something much more, because this wasn't normal for Saawyn.

The black smoke began settling over us, creating a dome. Fae began to beat against it, but it was no use...we were trapped. The roaring sky subsided along with the worrying cries of some fae, leaving a dead silence over the Lands.

Davyna ripped my hand from her neck, and tendrils of glistening onyx smoke rose behind her. I stood my ground, refusing to give her the satisfaction of pulling terror from me. She moved in, her eyes darkening as a grin lifted her lips on one side, but then stopped.

Her shadows went back in as she turned, and I followed. A figure came through the smoke, walking towards the dome. Tilting her head, I noticed her shoulders fall an inch before moving towards it.

Slowly I moved closer, and Ezekiel's face came into view.

"Dad?" she whispered, and that voice alone made my heart ache for her. Looking over, I saw her eyes flicker from their possessed state to normal. Lifting her hand to the veil, she watched as her father did the same.

Why was he the only one here? Did her blood overpower the spell and bring him to her?

"Davyna...I'm so sorry I couldn't give you the whole truth," Ezekiel said, his expression going cold as he looked past the both of us. Screams from fae made me turn to see the dead coming to the veil, their faces decayed and vile.

Every time we did this ritual, the dead came to us as they were when they were living...not as this. They began clawing at the dome, wanting to join the land of the living. Whether to come back to life or kill, I didn't know. The cries from the dead fae made the others stumble back, their fear drenching the air we were all breathing, and my spine quaked.

Turning back to our former King, I watched as he flickered between his true face and one of death. At the sight, Davyna staggered back into my arms.

"Davyna!" her father screamed as I heard someone take in a shuddered breath. "You need to stop him!"

Turning, I looked at the bodies falling to the ground, their hearts lying next to their corpses. Chaos bloomed over the assembly, and fae tried to use the gap to leave, but were unsuccessful.

We were stuck.

Davyna pushed out of my arms, her eyes returning to the darkness, but she had come through... She was still in there. Fae turned, looking at her. Some even tried to rush in, but my shadows lashed out, holding them still. I truly believed this wasn't her doing... Otherwise, she would have taken the credit for it.

Throwing the fae back, they struggled to stand again, but Davyna laughed. "You should be more concerned with your own life than mine."

More horrific screams sounded off, and fae ran away from those falling beside them. I looked around, trying to make sense of what was happening, but all I was met with was the cold reality that the fae on the ground were now dead.

Their spirits crossed over just beyond the dome, where I could see them reappear, fear still consuming their features.

Looking for my friends, I ran into the crowd and prayed I didn't see them on the ground. Bodies shoved me back and forth, their cries piercing my ears as I turned.

Nesrin stood there, looking at me with wide eyes, and the blood in my veins turned to ice. "Kad—" The air was ripped from her lungs and everyone's screams became distant, almost obsolete, as I fell into my friends' green pools.

Her body went rigid, not moving an inch as blood began to fall from her lips. My stomach turned, the world around me spinning as I prayed this wasn't happening. That I wasn't going to lose one of my best friends.

Running, I pushed fae out of my way to get to her, to stop all of this! Her eyes widened, bulging with fear as I yelled her name. I jumped into the gap, appearing before her as her body fell in my arms, and I dropped to my knees.

"Nes! NES! COME ON!" I yelled, shaking her as I felt her warm blood coat my arm.

Looking up, the pounding in my ears intensified, because standing behind my friend's corpse was *me*... My shadow self.

If Nyna was right, then this had to be the gods—Tanith and Obsidian. They were doing all this. It wasn't Davyna.

A scream to my right overpowered the craze of the assembly, and my stomach sank because I knew the voice well. Axel's gaze was on Nesrin in my arms, and his eyes filled with tears that painted the story of the agony within. He sucked in a breath as he fisted his leather jacket over his heart, letting out a deafening scream.

He slowly shifted, taking in my shadow self, and his fury quickly consumed him. Roaring, he ran towards him with tears sliding down his face, and threw out his shadows.

"Axel! NO!" I screamed, throwing out my hand and willing my own power to stop him. I couldn't lose him, too.

But it wasn't enough. The rage and grief pouring from him was stronger than anything in this world. It washed over me, giving me another glimpse into how it felt to lose your mate. I had sensed it with Levanna...and now him. It was pure torture, and it rolled off of him in thick, suffocating waves.

I pushed more shadows out to stop him, but his pursuit of vengeance was more powerful than my will to save him.

Tanith appeared next to Obsidian, wearing Davyna's face and a smile as she took in Axel. She sent out a bolt of white light, and it ripped through the air as I screamed and placed Nesrin on the ground to stop this.

Standing, I readied my power to bloom over the Lands, when I watched the light sear through Axel's chest, tearing his heart out. He fell to the ground, rolling a few times before his body stopped. I stumbled back, falling to my knees.

The blood in my veins stopped moving, along with my heart, refusing to take its next beat. The world closed in, feeling so small as the sound of death rang in my ears, and I was reminded that this wasn't over.

Glancing back towards the platform, I looked at my Davyna. Her eyes were locked on their bodies, before turning to look at the veil where Axel appeared next to Nesrin. He grabbed her and held onto her for dear life, tears evident even from this far away.

This *wasn't* happening...

The loss began to take root, multiplying with the brokenness that still hadn't passed from losing Eryx and his family. And now, this?

Who was next?

My eyes darted back to Davyna and a sick feeling in my gut rose, coating my throat with bile. Davyna shrugged and moved in towards Tanith and Obsidian, smiling wide and without a care in the world that they wanted her power.

"Silence!" yelled my shadow self, and all fae obeyed his word.

My eyes glanced over the crowd, who were confused by what this was. Some even stared at me before averting their eyes to Obsidian wearing my face. They didn't know who *they* were, but I did.

My hand moved to the dagger at my side, and I was tempted to throw it... At least to knock one of them down for taking two of my best friends. I settled the roaring within because I didn't know if it would work. Did I need everything else first to actually kill them?

Or what if I lost it? I wanted them gone and away from Davyna before they used her to do their bidding with the throne *they* created. I wanted to protect her power from them and whatever else they had planned for Valyner. But I couldn't risk exposing the only weapon to eradicate them from this world.

"Now... Davyna, you're coming with us."

She laughed, her eyes locking on my shadow self. "No, I don't think I am."

"I'm sorry..." Obsidian said, using my own voice, and it made my skin crawl. "Did you think you had a choice?"

"She isn't going anywhere with you!" I yelled, pulling myself up to stand before them.

They looked at each other before turning to size me up. Smiling, they both dropped their illusion and took on shadow forms. One was of iridescent mist, with the Courts colors shimmering within, while the other was similar but coated in onyx. Many fae turned away from them, but I refused.

"You must be the one they call the Dark Lord," Obsidian said in his own voice. It cut deep into my soul, making even my shadows within want to bow and obey. "But that power you bear comes from me...and I have no problem taking it back." I looked away as his power circled me, but Davyna moved in, unfazed by their power.

"And what of my power? Have you come to take it back? If so... I'd like to see you try." Her voice was like nothing I had ever heard come out of her; something booming with authority and influence, making me unable to look at her.

Why did she pull their attention back to her? Was she trying to protect me, even in this state? Or was I thinking too much into it?

Obsidian laughed, and Tanith fell in with him as they moved forward. "Oh, my little cinder. I thought you'd never ask."

Pushing past their power and the apprehension within, I looked up to see them moving in on Davyna.

"Davyna! NO!" I yelled, stepping forward.

A flash of light and darkness consumed them...and they vanished from the clearing. In their absence, the fae around me let broken sobs pass their lips.

Looking around for my friends, they came through the crowd. Levanna, Evren, Sorin, and Calix ran over to Nesrin's and Axel's bodies, and I took a step back. I glanced back to the veil between us and the dead, hoping I could see their souls one last time...but they were gone, along with the black smoke that covered the Lands moments ago.

Fae were using the gap to leave the clearing.

Dropping to my knees, my stomach sank as the sun began to shine behind the grey clouds.

The spell was gone, and the dead along with it.

CHAPTER 52

DAVYNA

Blinding light surrounded me, swirling with black, while two shadowed hands gripped tightly around my arms. I tried my best to push down the weak version of myself within, but she was challenging me. She wanted me to feel fear, she wanted me to grieve the loss of her friends.

I'd much rather cling to this part, where I could focus and assess my next move. Emotions made you weak and messed with your judgment in all areas of your life. That was how you ultimately lost everything, and I wasn't going to let that happen.

My feet made contact with solid ground, bringing me back to the present problem I was facing. *These assholes.* My gaze scanned over what looked like a dining room. The table was filled with every food imaginable and surrounded by three chairs made of pure gold.

My eyes wandered over the room, realizing this wasn't a room per se, but more of a holding place. And it wasn't in Valyner; it felt like it was just outside it, like we were on another plane. The ceiling was a vast, bleached void, while the floor was a never-ending abyss.

Before I could even get one word out, the two shadow figures began dragging me to the table. I hissed under my breath as their invisible hands dug into my skin before tossing me to the ground. I played the part, allowing my body to crumble, and then turned back to gaze at them as they moved over to their chairs.

"Take a seat...before I get angry," Obsidian demanded.

"I think you're always angry." I used the chair to lift myself off the floor to stand before them. "Does she not suck your dick enough?" Sitting down, I looked between them as a smile crept in.

"Watch your tongue, little fae. Or I will rip it from your mouth and feed it to you," Tanith said, but I laughed. "Your little stunts lately have caused us major issues."

"Okay... And you want me to do, what? Ah, that's right. Fix it for you." I leaned back in my chair, letting out a silent laugh. "Well, since it looks like you two are gearing up for a long chat, everyone in Valyner will probably die from the creatures attacking them or the sickness before I can do my *job*."

"You little cunt. Do you think you can speak to me that way?" Tanith hissed.

"Yes...I do. Because, if we are keeping score, you were a cunt first."

She went to speak, but the dark tendrils of smoke darted out, holding her back. Smiling, I waited.

"When you burned the throne, you broke our power on it and brought every realm onto the same plane. Time is moving at the same pace for all fae now. Even for those degenerate humans. And if it's not stopped, all Realms will collide, and we can't have that happen. Not yet," Obsidian retorted.

Looking around, I took in my surroundings again. I was growing jaded with this conversation already.

"Now, listen to your master...and if you roll your eyes again..." Tanith pierced the table with an obsidian dagger, making me slowly look up to her and smile. It didn't neutralize my power in the chains, but it was still a weapon that took my life once before...and maybe it could do it again.

"Of course. I'll be good."

Her white mist began to vanish, along with the glamour of magic surrounding her. As it faded away, I realized she was revealing her true form that hid beneath. My eyes widened in shock. For someone so vile, I wasn't expecting this. She was beautiful. Her pale blonde hair beamed as it cascaded down her chest in perfect waves, only complementing her fair complexion. Cracking her neck, she smiled before her pastel, icy blue eyes narrowed on me in disgust. She was intimidating, I'd give her that, but it did little to deter me or my gaze.

"So, tell me..." His voice matched the tone of boredom. Obsidian leaned back, his shadows wrapping around the solid metal chair and flickering off into tiny onyx embers. "How did it feel to watch your friends from the Salt Court die?" he asked, and my lips turned up.

"I didn't lose any sleep over it, if that's what you are wondering." I chuckled, my head throbbing for a moment from the girl I kept locked away. Rolling my shoulders back, I looked back at his swirling shadows.

He leaned forward, his murky vapor crawling across the table. "I've realized lately that once the creatures are in our realm, I can control them. I made them go to the Salt Court when they passed through, to teach you a lesson...but it seems that they also listen to you. Isn't that something..."

Tanith looked over at her mate, her eyes narrowing in confusion at his tone, which was smooth as velvet and held wonder within it.

He continued. "It was fun watching you let go of your humanity so freely..."

"Listen. I don't really give a shit about walking down memory lane. So, why don't you tell me what you really want with me? Because, clearly, the throne isn't the only thing," I stated, lifting my elbows onto the table and leaning in.

Obsidian let out more of his shadows, pushing them over the food that divided us, until they poured over the edge. The cool tendrils brushed against my legs before vanishing. For some reason, the urge to shudder at that contact was unbearable.

"I want to know how you were made."

I gave him a sweet smile, raising a brow. "Well...when two people have sex—"

"Do not play this game with me, little cinder." He growled, making the table shake.

"I didn't do anything to get this...other than being born with it," I retorted.

"Your father didn't contain more than one Court power. We made sure of that when making the fae." He paused, his shadows growing more chaotic. "He could only access limited amounts from each Court because he was their King, but that wouldn't have made *you* what you are. So, who was your mother?"

A sick feeling turned in my gut as the girl within banged against my walls, wanting me to let her out. She was scared right now, but didn't she know that fear was going to get us both killed? Pushing into my psyche, I let the darkness within blanket her protests and suppress her so I could focus.

"You probably know more than I do." My response made Tanith place the dagger down before gritting her teeth.

"We are gods. That doesn't mean we are all-knowing... Not even our makers know," she said as she sat back in her chair.

"Makers? You all were made?" I asked and leaned back, looking between the both of them.

Tanith glanced at her mate, and I knew he was looking at her through the mist of darkness shrouding him. They stood quiet, no doubt talking through their bond.

I cleared my throat.

Her eyes snapped back to mine, and after a few more moments, she spoke. "His name is Zaryk." Tanith visibly shuddered at the use of his name, before glaring at me. "He and his brother made us all..." I watched her eyes dart over to Obsidian as she said, '*us,*' but something about it told me that wasn't the entire truth.

Obsidian laughed, and the sound forced flames to skate down my spine. Why was that funny? Did he not see it that way or respect the gods who gave him life?

"So, this Zaryk and his brother made the six of you?" I thought back to the books I read when I first arrived in Valyner, knowing that there were six gods all together. Obsidian and Tanith created Valyner. So, the other four must have split off and created Anawyn and Gelmyra.

A question billowed up, wanting to be answered by the old version of myself: Where did their makers come from?

"Someone has been trying to brush up on us." He stood, onyx smoke still billowing around him. "But this story, Davyna, is not one you will find in your history books."

I kept my mouth shut, watching his form move behind Tanith.

"Zaryk was cast out of his world along with his brother. They were sent to earth as a punishment, where they used their power to create a plane and...us. Oh, how he regretted that..." Stopping at the head of the table, he laughed again as he leaned over. "And, so, the humans that occupied the Lands below us became his pride and joy."

"Let me guess...you're the jealous type?" I spat out, forcing his shadowed form to straighten.

"Mmm. More like the vengeful type." He stepped closer to me. "Zaryk wanted to keep us in-line after he banished his brother to a lifetime of torment."

"This all sounds similar to the stories I grew up with in the Mortal Realm. Are you telling me one is in Heaven and the other in Hell?" I laughed.

"Call it what you want...but Zaryk and his brother created a realm for all of us to live in. It was called the Oasis... That was, until the Abyss was created." His voice was cold, unwavering as the shadows slithered through the air, filling it with their deathly chill.

"Like a dark void?" I arched my brow, thinking about— *No.* I wouldn't think about my father...

"Yes, my little pet... I think you've been in one before if I heard correctly. But the Abyss is something more... Somewhere no one would wish to go because there is no escape..."

I went to ask him how he knew that, but he continued. "Zaryk became a shell after that and asked the six of us to stay in the Oasis with him. I think he was afraid of us being alone." A chuckle filtered through the mass of shadows. "It didn't take much for me to get everyone to turn on him, or to combine our magic to create Solyus."

"What is that?" I asked.

"The realm for gods just beyond the veils—the one you entered when no fae or humans should be allowed..."

"Is that where we are now?" I asked, cocking my head to one side as I glanced around the room again.

"No, this is simply a plane between our realms, showing you whatever I deem. Do you remember the throne room filled with bones? It was in here." He chuckled deeply.

I made a small humming noise as I pondered his explanation of the world I was in, before moving on. "And what happened to his brother? What was his name?" I smiled, tilting my head in his direction.

"That is none of your business," he growled. "All you need to know is we broke free from our remaining maker and started the races of the fae with one goal in mind."

"To kill the humans?" I grabbed an apple off the table and leaned back, biting into it. "Or were you raising an army for when the time came to kill your maker?"

Turning, his glowing, bright red eyes peered through the smoke. Good, he was angry. Which meant I was onto something and closer to getting my opportunity to gut them both.

He laughed and unease rose to the surface at his raw tone. It made me feel...worried.

Why was he telling me so much now?

"See, even in this state, you can't help yourself," he taunted. "And, of course, we wanted the humans dead. There have only been three times we have been able to pass over into the Mortal Realm. Before Zaryk's brother was banished, when we created our fae, and then there was a surge of power once that allowed me back in to get what I needed. That's how I knew you went there because we can't go or feel our fae when they pass over."

Obsidian took in a long breath, sighing as he released it before he went on. "With everything we did, *he* tried to stop us at every turn. He didn't get far, but he did enough to weaken us. That was, until I found his weakness and took something from him."

He looked over at Tanith and she smiled wide at him, eyes filled with love...if you could call it that for these two. I couldn't help but wonder if the thing he took was Tanith. Did that mean she wasn't always Obsidian's mate... Was she Zaryk's?

"Ever since then, I have been just as strong...if not stronger. And I will not lose what I have gained over the last thousand years. Not when I am this close."

"Am I ruining it all for you? Aww, that sucks."

He took a few more steps towards the chair and his shadow form bent down, his red eyes burrowing into me. "You are." He growled. "I've worked too hard on this all to not get what I want."

His shadows lashed out, pushing my chair away from the table to face him. Moving in, he leaned down. My eyes widened as the onyx vapor thinned out, exposing his true form. His skin was blackened and charred with cracks running throughout—much like how my scars branched over my arm. Fire laid below the surface, and no hair graced his head, making him look like a thing of nightmares...

If you were afraid of things that looked like that.

I wasn't, but I was curious as to why he looked this way. Tanith was a beauty, and he was a beast.

Smiling at me, Obsidian looked me up and down. "So, tell me, Davyna. What do you know about your mother's powers?"

I closed my eyes for a moment before staring down at the monster in front of me. "Only what my aunt told me. She showed signs of being a wolf and a witch, and then died at the hands of a siren and a vampire that transformed her... But, clearly, she was something more, and she didn't think it was important to make sure that information was passed down to her own daughter before she died."

Fuck, what was wrong with me? Why was I feeling? It was anger...yes, but why was it making me sad? Leaning forward, I forced a grin, burying the emotions down and letting the darkness swallow it back up.

"But she knew of a prophecy," I stated.

Obsidian straightened himself up before glancing over to

Tanith, who was now standing, her hands balled into fists. "What prophecy?" she demanded.

"The one where I apparently stop you." I smiled. My power within swirled to challenge them and make my move to have two fewer beings to deal with.

Obsidian's hand wrapped around my throat as he ripped me out of the chair to stand before him. He was around the same height as Kadeyan—maybe a little taller—which made it a struggle to keep my feet on the ground. As Tanith moved over, he tightened his hold, and small sounds passed my lips.

She gripped my cheeks with her fingers, turning my gaze to her. "Take the throne and give up the magic in your veins to us, or I'll kill you right here and now," she spat out and dropped her hand from my face.

"You...want to...c–curse me...like...my father..." I got out, forcing Obsidian to lessen his hold on me.

"It's only fitting. Like daughter, like father," Obsidian said with a sweet, alluring tenor, smirking at me.

"Go ahead..." I hissed and Obsidian let go, moving back a few paces. "You can't kill what's already dead. And judging by how much you told me today...you weren't going to let me live, anyway." I smiled, taunting her. I wasn't going to let the weaker version of myself come through because she would kill me before they could.

Tanith growled as she used her power to pull the dagger from the table. It hurled through the air, until it buried itself into my chest. "You're right...you weren't getting out of here alive."

CHAPTER 53
DAVYNA

It happened so fast that I didn't have time to react, nor bring my power to the surface to stop it. And a rush of panic took over every fiber of my being.

Sucking in a sharp breath, I glanced down at the dark obsidian dagger submerged in my chest. I could feel the cool steel imbue its purpose into the beating organ, wanting to kill me, and I remembered the same pain I felt when Persephone did it. The way it bloomed over me, turning my body cold, but this felt different now...

Stepping back, I fell into the chair, breathing heavily. Everything within me—including the dark power—realized in this moment that I didn't want to die. I wanted to live...to have a life outside this chaos I was born into...

I *wanted* to live...

My breathing picked up and I glanced into Obsidian's beaming red eyes. He was smiling, but it began to fall, his shoulders doing the same. He was shocked. And so was I... I was back, and the darkness slithered away, almost like it didn't want to feel the death I was about to face.

I waited for my heart to stop... For the world to fade away, and for my soul to enter Hell—the Abyss, the afterlife...anywhere but here.

That was where I belonged after...after I...

But I was still breathing.

I was still alive.

"Why isn't she dying?" Tanith blurted out as she turned to look at her mate, but my eyes locked on the dagger around her thigh, exposed by the slit in her opal silk gown. It matched the black and white dagger I saw on the castle doors in Solyus...and the one Kadeyan had at Saawyn.

Breathing heavily, I brought my hand up to the dark obsidian hilt, and used all the power within me to rip it free. A hiss escaped my lips and I shifted my gaze down. Grey blood flowed down my chest and the wound began to heal as I glanced up through wide eyes.

"I'll be damned..." Obsidian muttered, but my power surged and all I could sense was darkness again as I lunged forward.

Throwing the dagger, it buried itself into his gut as I used my power to pull the other one from Tanith's sheath. The hilt slammed into my palm, and I curled my fingers around it. I threw my free hand towards her, sending out a roaring blaze.

Tanith threw up a shimmering, iridescent shield and cried out in anger. "You little bitch! You will not touch my mate!" Water poured from her, eating each of my flames and creating a smoke screen.

Looking over at Obsidian, he pulled the knife out of his stomach and dropped it, but he wasn't charging towards me... Why?

Tanith's glowing body emerged from the mist in a blur as she yelled, "What are you?!" Her power pulled me to her and her hand wrapped around my throat.

Her influence invaded my mind, and both our eyes widened at the intrusion. Beating against my psyche, she tried to search for what she wanted, and the same pain returned in my skull. Although, this time, it was intensified, and I faltered.

She got through and I was pulled back into the cave with my mother during my dream. Pulled to when I read her journal, and the memories I took from the stone.

Letting my magic build, I pushed back and grabbed her arm. All the visions shifted away, and I fell into her mind, seeing a cabin. The same one I saw last time with the baby crying inside. But I was in the cabin this time. There was a baby with light blonde hair...and another with black. They both were deep in slumber, letting out soft hums that barely filled the cabin.

A blur of darkness moved in, picking up the baby with blonde hair and causing her to stir. A hand reached out, sending out a dark mist that consumed the baby with black hair. My stomach turned and I watched in shock as the little baby's skin began to grow grey and sink in, decaying until it was nothing but ash. I stepped away until my back slammed into the uneven wood wall.

This wasn't my start at all... It was *Tanith's.*

So, who was the other baby?

Tightening my hold on the two-toned dagger, I drove it up, burying it into her side before glancing at her face. Shock filled it as she began to cry out in suffering, her hand going to the deep wound.

Pulling the dagger free, I backed away from her and stopped. My heart was pounding louder than I'd ever heard before. Glancing down at the knife, I saw it was dripping with crimson, and I looked back at Tanith. Her pristine, opal gown was stained red, and my mouth fell open.

She was bleeding red, which meant this could kill them... and me?

The dagger was ripped from my hand, flying through the air, until it was in Obsidian's grasp. I turned, looking at him and he smiled wide.

"*Alyahiia,*" Obsidian purred as he narrowed his eyes on me, stalking forward.

It wasn't possible... It couldn't be. I'd never heard that word before, but my seer ability brought it forth, and it somehow made sense...like an old tale being brought back to life generations later.

I swallowed hard and my stomach dropped as my eyes locked with red ones getting closer to me.

"Goddess," I whispered.

Tanith clutched at her side, still crying out in pain, as Obsidian smiled at me and ignored the cries of his mate.

"Trying to run again, little cinder? Haven't you learned you can't run from yourself...or me?"

"Stay away from me," I said, each word coming out shaky. I could feel my old self piecing back together, bringing every wavering emotion to the forefront of my mind.

He smiled, nodding his head. "Watch your back when you're home. I've got eyes on you."

My power took over and grey smoke swirled around me, pulling me off this plane.

Before I fell into the void, I heard him as clear as day entering my mind.

"You better pray to something far above that you aren't the one, because if you are...you will be mine."

CHAPTER 54
DAVYNA

My mind was clouded with panic as I fell to my knees in Kadeyan's study, trying to find air willing to fill my lungs. How was this possible? I couldn't be a...

But I was.

I was a god.

The hums from around me grew into loud thuds and cracking glass. The sounds pulled me out of my trance, and I saw Kade. His chest rose and fell fast, and his anger was on full display. The sight caused me to hold my breath. Our eyes locked and a wave of sorrow washed over me, remembering everything I did.

"Dy!" He ran over to me, and I picked myself up off the ground. His arms wrapped around me, and I could feel the sob wanting to escape my lips, but I swallowed it down.

"How much time passed?" I asked him as the salty tears coated my lips, but he didn't answer. Pulling away, I asked again, with fear smeared through each word. "How much time has passed since I left?"

"It's only been an hour... How did you get away? How did you..." He gripped my face, looking deep into my eyes, and I saw his were completely bloodshot and puffy.

Everything I'd done the last two weeks slammed into me, causing the world to blur as visions replayed in my mind.

The darkness beckoned me back, and my blood turned cold once again. I tried to push it away—tried to not see the horrific things I did—but it was all there.

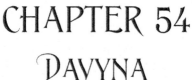

I could feel the fae's pain as I burned them alive. How my nails punctured their hearts before ripping them free from their chest. Their eyes all matched in the end, locked in a horrific stare at the monster before them. And that monster was me...

I did that to them... I killed Eryx. I tortured my friends, tried to hurt my sister, and stood by when Axel and Nesrin...

And then, there was Obsidian, claiming me as his... What did that mean? Were we...bonded?

No...we couldn't be.

Pain shot through my head as I winced, hearing the voice within my psyche laugh, and I tried to stay... I tried to fight it, but the pain was too great, the grief too intense, and the guilt...was suffocating me.

I was weak...

You need to be alone.

My body began to tremble...

You are broken this way.

My fingers dug into Kadeyan's leathers, clinging to him like an anchor to a ship.

You are a monster.

"Dearest?" Kadeyan called out as I pulled away from him. "Damn it, Davyna! Don't you fucking dare turn it off again! Please!" His words became more distant by the second, staying at the surface of the dark ocean that was pulling me back down and refusing to let me win this fight.

I stepped back, digging my fingers into my scalp as I pulled on my hair. A cry bubbled up my throat and I gritted my teeth, trying to bear the pain, but I was failing. The darkness was always going to win, wasn't it? Whether I wanted it to or not. I couldn't fight myself... Couldn't fight this higher power, and win.

"Davyna, I need you..."

You are a god. So, be a god.

Familiar hands wrapped around my arms, and the touch that once filled me with heat and life now felt vile and void. Cracking my neck, I looked down at his hand, and the screams from within of the girl I used to be shattered into pieces.

I pushed through the veil of darkness separating us to deliver the last message I'd ever give her: *You failed; I won't.*

"DY!" he called out, and I slowly looked up at him as a grin pulled at my lips.

Tossing out my glistening, onyx shadows, I made him fly through the study before I used the gap and fell into the woods.

Brushing my leathers down, I smiled and rolled my shoulders. Sighing in relief, I started to walk, but shadows wrapped around my neck and pulled me back.

My body slammed into the ground. Before I could react, Kadeyan was on top of me, his eyes a dark crimson. "Where the hell do you think you are going?"

"Away," I said, bluntly.

He snarled at me in response.

Leaning back, he threw his hand out and released his inky tendrils of smoke. They wrapped around me and ripped me off the ground, before slamming me into a tree. I grunted from the impact and looked down at the shadows, watching them swirl in chaotic movements as they tightened their hold on me.

Looking up, I narrowed my gaze on him while he stalked forward, and my lip twitched with rage.

He was a pain in the ass.

"You think this shit is okay? Do you think your parents, Axel, and Nesrin...or even Sahar and Eryx would want this for you?"

"What does it matter? They are dead, and if you don't remove your power from my body, you'll join them."

"Yeah, you keep saying that. Yet, here I am," he yelled, looking around and letting his arms go wide.

Silence fell over us and the darkness surged within, wanting to be freed. I let out a boom of power that broke his hold, sending him hurling through the air. I took a few steps forward, and with each thud of my boots against the ground, my fury seeped from every pour of magic, begging to inflict mayhem.

I stretched out my hands and watched as the black flames stained with their iridescent sheen encircled his body. His eyes narrowed on me as he sat up, trying to assess his next move.

Walking in a circle around him, I smiled. "Maybe I don't want you dead yet. Maybe I think that's too generous for you."

I placed my hand out, running my fingers through the blaze, and the flames grew taller. They wrapped up, creating a dome fused with a barrier spell so he couldn't escape.

"I think this is what I want for now—to make you watch me live this life, knowing you can't do a damn thing to stop me."

"And why's that?" he asked.

I stopped at his question and pushed the flames away to create an opening.

I drank in his anger, sensing it fuel my veins, and smirked. "Because I am just like them. And you can't kill a god."

His expression softened into confusion, his lips parting as he looked me over. "You are one of them?" He moved closer to the flames. Our bond washed over me, forcing my body to quake and my power to falter. The flames and the barrier spell fell, and I tilted my head, glaring at him. "Your mother must have been—"

I placed my hand out, rolling my eyes. "Okay, well, you can mull that over," I seethed. "I don't give a shit about the mother who brought me into this world."

"Even if she told me in a dream how to stop all of this?"

I paused, looking down and shaking my head slightly.

Tilting my head up, I glanced into his amber pools. "It looks like you have some work to do then. Along with burying your friends."

"You're not even going to come to their funeral?"

Turning, I began walking and placed a barrier around me for good measure. If he tried to touch me again, I'd kill him just to shut him up.

"I would miss it for anything else in this world," I said as his shadows banged against the barrier. I paused, keeping my eyes forward, and balled my hands into fists.

"You know...the Davyna I love wouldn't be such a fucking coward. Or this soulless."

Turning my head, I peered over my shoulder. "And what did you ever really know about her, Kadeyan?"

"I KNEW EVERYTHING!" he yelled, his voice breaking.

The wind brushed by, creating a hum that filled the silence.

"I watched you for years, Dy. I read your thoughts. I knew when you found happiness in the arms of your best friend...and I felt your pain when you were breaking under Hera." His breathing grew heavier, and I turned to face him. "I was there, every step of the way after you lost Elias...watching and planning to set you free."

Silently laughing, I looked up at the dark sky above before glancing back at him. I realized he never anticipated me becoming something more than he thought I was, and that wasn't my problem.

"And all I know about you is that you try to be this big, bad vampire fae...but in reality, you are just as afraid of being alone as I was. And if that's the reason you need to hold onto this—to me—I feel sorry for you."

"Fuck. You," he spat out, holding his ground to not come any closer. His wrath wrapped around me. I expected it to make me feel my power stir in joy, but it did the opposite. The bond circled me again, and it was pulling back the darkness, forcing me to feel... regret. "Do you know how much I want to die right now just to prove a fucking point? That this," he gestured between us, "is something that neither one of us could hide from. That the pain would forever be there. And not even *you* in this state...could run from it."

He stepped forward and a lump formed in my throat as he continued. "You think you're better off alone because *you* fear it! I've lived it for 1,500 years. And I'm living it right now, while you hide behind a wall of darkness that you think will protect you. But it won't!" he yelled, taking a moment to collect himself before looking me over.

"There will come a day that you are forced to let it all in and it will shatter you more than you ever thought possible. And guess who will be there to hold you through it all...*me*. Because I don't scare easily, Davyna. I don't run. I don't hide. I don't give up! Especially when I love someone as much as I love you.

"So, go... Live with that reminder in the back of your head, until you give me back my mate." He turned and walked away, and I stood still. Watching him.

I wanted to feel rage, to laugh at his words and pity him, but all I felt was numb. It bloomed over me, thinning the veil of darkness within and showcasing what laid beneath. And it was fear...

Fear that he was right.

CHAPTER 55
DAVYNA

For two days, the Fallen Court was silent, still. Even with the grounds filled today with soldiers and fae from town, it remained so. I was propped in a tree yards away, behind the assembly for the funeral. So far, no one had spotted me.

I still didn't understand why I came... But after the other night with Kade, I stood alone in the tunnels below the Fallen and Ember Courts. I didn't kill... I didn't feel the desire to, and for some reason, every time I closed my eyes, I saw him. This fucking bond was bullshit. Every word that spilled from his lips was on repeat and I was doing everything to not let them into my psyche.

The darkness was faltering, bringing in waves of emotions that I was having to bury each time. Because this connection wasn't real; no one was connected to another by fate.

Fate was a deceiver, and I needed to figure out how to break whatever was between us.

Crossing my arms over my chest, I leaned back and rested against the bark of the tree before glancing over the grounds. Fae were still moving towards weathered, stone benches embedded into the forest floor and climbing up the hill.

"Lev!" Evren yelled and my eyes immediately snapped to her from across the clearing. She gestured with her hand to a bench in the front where she, Sorin, and Calix were already sitting. Levanna moved through the crowd in a long, black dress, taking her seat.

My eyes continued to scan, looking for him.

Black mist began to swirl, revealing him standing tall in his fighting leathers before them all. Everyone's voices trailed off, and the forest fell into a hushed state as he looked them over with a darkened gaze.

His sorrow was dense, traveling through the assembly and slithering up to meet me. The intensity of it made my stomach turn.

"Calix, join me." Calix nodded and got up, walking with Kadeyan until they both stood before the tomb. "Val tes dul et vësa al fallen," Kade projected, grabbing everyone's attention entirely. "You can't kill what has already fallen." His voice was softer, but it still traveled, and it was like everything stopped moving at his words.

I looked at all the fae as still as the trees surrounding them. Glancing back to Kadeyan, I stalled.

His eyes were on me.

His gaze burrowed into me. It was as if I was exposed, and the unease I'd been feeling doubled. Before I could even react with a vile smile or flipping him off, he returned his gaze to the assembly, as if I wasn't here.

"This is where I would normally tell you all the great things these people achieved...talk about their character, and how much I'm going to..." He paused, looking up and burying down his pain. "How much I'm going to miss them, but I won't. I don't need to. We all loved and respected Axel and Nesrin. And their void will never be filled...but we can honor them..."

Moving over to the side of the clearing, he grabbed a chair and the nature of the fae turned. I looked at the Fallen and saw their demeanor wasn't corrupted by grief anymore...but something more —something darker and vengeful. Turning back to Kadeyan, I watched him take a seat as Calix pulled his blade from his hip.

Kadeyan's hand moved up, removing the leather tie from his hair and each strand tumbled down his shoulders. He looked at me again, forcing me to ball my hands into fists until my nails pierced into my flesh.

What was he doing?

Calix flipped the blade between his fingers before raising it to the sky, his face tilting to follow. My eyes narrowed, seeing his lip quiver as a tear streamed down his cheek before his emotions of grief and wrath billowed up and encased me. Bringing his head back down, he glanced over at his Lord and waited.

Kadeyan dropped his head almost as if he was praying, but to what? Not to the gods... Not anymore. He nodded slightly and brought his gaze up to meet the Fallen members before him.

After a moment, Calix parted the side of Kade's hair. He brought the blade flush to his scalp and pulled fast, cutting the long, dark brown hair off.

Kadeyan kept his gaze straight, his eyes going hard. "The other side too," he demanded, and the energy around me grew, making my own power stir within. Calix moved over to the other side and Kadeyan parted his hair. "But I will do it..." He glanced up, his eyes cold, and it made me feel like ice pierced into my chest.

Calix handed over the dagger and then bowed, before stepping off to the side. Kadeyan looked over the assembly and cleared his voice. "When the Fallen shave the side of their heads, it's symbolic of a personal war path they must take. To avenge their family or friends. We all grew up with this custom." He looked up at me for a second before averting his gaze to his Court. "But when the Lord cuts both sides...it's a call for war."

Looking down at the blade in his hand, I threw my legs over the branch and watched him intently.

"Will you answer the call today? Will you fight for your Lord to avenge not only Axel, Nesrin, Eryx, Sahar, and Priya...but all we have lost in these past eight months? Will you fight for the ones who are next? Will you answer the call to war, until we are free of the gods and their torment?" he shouted before receiving battle cries from fellow members.

I felt for all their emotions, noticing their shock at his statement about the gods, and yet, they were going to follow their Lord. I chuckled, knowing how that was going to end. With all of them joining the dead. Kadeyan was really that stupid, wasn't he? He was putting a target on his back, and for what?

They already wanted him and his friends dead for figuring out who they were. And even though they appeared at the ritual, I knew that the people in attendance didn't have a clue who they were. This was going to spread like wildfire, and he would have no one to blame but himself for the blood spilled.

He parted his hair, pressing the blade to his scalp as his eyes traveled back to me. He pulled the blade slowly at first, and I watched each strand fall from his head.

Sahar's words from...just before all this happened filtered into my mind: *Fate is something we can't avoid, sweetheart.*

She was wrong. You could avoid it if you were wise enough to stay far away.

While he pulled the blade through the rest of his hair, I watched as it fell to the ground. Glancing up, I saw Calix was cutting his hair in the same way. More Fallen fae followed Kadeyan's command and began cutting the hair from each side of their heads.

Chants and yells filled the forest, creating an echo that went on for miles. My bones vibrated from within, and the power circled me. I glanced over them all. I could feel those damn eyes on me, pinning me down.

Rage built up under my skin as I looked to him, seeing a grin slowly pull up on his face. And through all the chanting and cries of war, I picked up on his voice alone, whispering out loud, "I'm coming for you, Dearest."

Shadows crept out of me, circling my body as my lip twitched. Shaking my head, I whispered back, "Then you better use that two-toned blade to take me down."

"Maybe I will... I'll see you soon," he murmured, before turning back to the crowd. "It's time. Let us honor our dead!" he called out and they all began to move forward towards the tomb.

I jumped into the gap but stood close, hearing some talk about Nesrin being buried in the Salt Court. It seemed both Courts had very different burial rituals.

The Fallen members were laid to rest in that very forest, with a feather from the Court members in attendance. They would lay one over the corpse with a drop of blood. The feather was symbolic of flying again and making it to the afterlife, while the blood was to represent a part of the Court members falling with them. Which felt like a waste if you asked me.

With the Salt Court, they were wrapped in seaweed at the shore before being carried to the bottom of the ocean, becoming one with the power that once coursed through their veins. However, since she and Axel were mates, Nesrin was to be buried here with him.

"I will avenge you both. I promise," Kadeyan said from beyond, and I tilted my head to listen in.

"I wish Nesrin could have the peace she deserves..." Levanna said, sniffling at the end.

My eyes fell, and emotions pricked through the thick wall within before I pushed them back. She was growing stronger, more determined to break through...and I blamed *him*... I was doing fine before he slithered his way in.

We wanted this—deep down—and I gave it to *her.*

The forest went silent, and I waited another ten minutes or so before dropping down outside the tomb. It was spelled shut, but I could see their bodies within, lying on the slab of stone. I stood still, not being able to turn away or even decipher what was going on inside my mind.

Tilting my head, I observed their corpses through the metal gates. "You didn't deserve this...but good people never get what they deserve." My eyes dropped to the forest floor, and before I could think about it, I lifted my hand, creating a barrier on one side of the tomb before allowing the water to spring forth.

Looking up, I watched it rush in and fill only Nesrin's side, the salt mist spraying back and coating my skin. The water swirled, creating small waves until it filled her side. After a minute or so passed, the water became still.

You happy now? I did something you wanted, I spoke to the girl within, before slamming the door shut on her.

I turned and saw him in the distance, leaning against a tree with his arms crossed over his chest. Kadeyan's eyes were hard, watching my every move.

"For someone who doesn't care about anything, sure does make me wonder..." he said, not moving from his spot.

The power within pulled me under and forced me to drown in its furious depths, and I wasn't going to resist it... Not when this was exactly what I wanted to feel right now. It was the clarity I needed after the last few days and what I wanted moving forward.

"I take back what I said before. I am going to kill you. And I'm going to enjoy every minute of it."

"I bet you will...then you can hold yourself when it's over." He laughed...

He fucking *laughed*.

Taking a step forward, my hands burned as the blaze snaked up my arms.

"Your temper is cute...even now." He turned and began walking. "Come find me when you're ready to end this."

Shadows veiled him like a blanket of death, taking him away, and I found it fitting. Because soon, death would blanket him, and he would be nothing but a shadow, lost in the darkness I could only bring.

CHAPTER 56
KADEYAN

"Kadeyan...this isn't a good idea. You know them. They're not going to help you or me," Levanna said. I turned away from her, staring at my father's stone. Five days had passed since the funeral, and I was fixated on this plan to get all the stones. We needed them.

Davyna still had hers around her neck. Honestly, I was shocked she hadn't tried to destroy it or toss it aside like it was nothing but trash. If we couldn't get the old version of her back, then the battle to rip it from her neck was going to be the death of many.

Maeve said she would start undoing the wards on the Sky Court one, but it could take time. Her mother protected it since the beginning, warding it almost daily with other powerful Sky members. It made me wonder if she saw all this coming.

The Salt Court's stone was a little trickier to find.

Alexandrea and I talked when I went to my friends' funeral, and I asked her if she could help me. She knew how close we were and said that Eryx would have moved the ocean to get it to me. So, that was what they were doing—searching the ruined castle in the sea with the fae who could breathe underwater.

She was still angry with Davyna for killing her Lord and I understood her anger, but even she could understand that Eryx wouldn't have been able to live with himself. I wouldn't be able to either... I would have wanted that same fate, lost in a haze, while unaware of what I inflicted on the person I loved. Alex also knew the love they had for Dy, and it made her emotions sway even more.

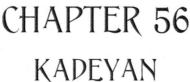

The real problem seemed to be finding the Crescent stone. Alastair claimed he'd never seen it, and that it was never on their Lands. If Elias had it with him in the Mortal Realm when he was Cursed... then it could be anywhere. I asked Evren if she ever saw an orange stone similar to her sisters, but she hadn't and had no clue as to where it could be.

"I think I broke Ravyn..." Turning, I glanced in the doorway to see Ravyn on the ground, dragging her body around in a circle. Dalia giggled, staring down at her before looking at me. "She was fine, but then—"

Slamming my hands down on the desk, I let out a long breath. "I'm going to need you two to stop so I can fucking focus."

Levanna moved towards the cat and used her magic to put it into a deep sleep, its body going limp almost instantly. Dalia fluttered in, her little wings patting against each other as she lightly dropped onto my desk.

"What's wrong? Is it my master?" Worry tainted her voice and little pink pools searched my amber ones with so much hope.

She had asked almost every day when Davyna would be back. I asked why she wasn't out searching for her if they were connected in this way, and the only response was because she didn't want to be found. They must have sensed her magic—her wishes, maybe—making them stay put.

I hadn't told anyone what she shared with me, about what she was... I was still trying to make sense of it myself, all while grieving my friends.

It did make sense. Nyna said her lineage was something more. Something that shouldn't have been made...but was.

She'd said, "*Her searching the truth is what's going to get her—*"

Get her what? Killed? Used? Wasn't it better to know so you could prepare in a fight, than to go in blind?

"We need to get all the stones...and we are meeting with people today to ask, but I know they will say no," I said to Dalia, glancing up at her. Her gaze was still searching mine, wanting the next part of her question. "And Davyna is...still out there."

"Do you think you can bring her back?" Dalia asked.

"I won't stop until I do..."

Levanna's eyes peered over at me, her own fear billowing into the air. She was worried about me, and I loved her for that. Although, whatever happened from this point on, I wouldn't have regrets on how it ended. I was exactly where I needed to be.

"Something tells me that you have a part to play in all that is to come. So, don't die," she said.

I huffed, keeping in the laugh working its way up my throat. "Thanks, Dalia."

"Ready to go?" Levanna asked, moving in.

I nodded, but before I could move, Dalia sat on my shoulder. "You know, I could come and mess with their minds. And if you want them to kill each other, I can make that happen, too."

Levanna laughed, shaking her head as she glanced over at me.

"Thanks, but we've been waiting a long time to kill these fuckers. And I don't think today is the day. Plus, I don't want them more on edge because we have an outsider there...no offense. We need that Crystal stone."

"Okay, suit yourself." Moving over to the cat, she paused before turning to face me and Levanna. "I never apologized for my part in you all losing your friends... I am so sorry...and despite it...you have all shown me kindness I didn't deserve. It will always mean something to me...and the Pixies if I ever return home."

I nodded my head, feeling the sting of their loss all over again as she dropped down in front of Ravyn. Placing her hand on her snout, she shot up, eyes beaming a deep red as a growl ripped from her throat.

"Come catch me, kitty!" Dalia teased, taking off down the hall.

Shaking my head, I tuned out the growls and laughter filtering back towards us as they both ran off.

Taking Levanna's hand, I looked into her eyes that were possessed with fear and fury, but I kept my mouth shut. Purple mist shot out from her as she narrowed her gaze, pulling us away from the Fallen Lands and into No-Man's-Land.

I looked around, taking in the same lush yellows of the brush before turning to face the Dark Forest. My mind flashed, showing me and Davyna standing off in the distance.

This was the same forest we took Davyna to unlock her Crystal magic. It seemed like forever ago that I looked into those silver eyes with blood dripping down from her face, while her scent mixed with mine. And the fight that led to her grinding over my lap in the kitchen later that night.

My heart ached before I pushed it aside. We needed to stay focused...and we weren't leaving until we got what we needed.

We paced for ten minutes, lost to our thoughts as we waited for Jax and Verena—Levanna's parents—to arrive. Every fiber within begged to kill them the second I saw them. I wanted— No, needed to avenge my brother, who they killed in cold blood, and my father because I knew their crimson-stained hands were involved in Persephone coming to power. They idolized her...

Levanna looked up at me, her eyes darkened with each passing moment. "They aren't going to give it to us. This is a waste of time. Persephone made them the keepers of the stone...and from what I heard, Jinx told them to hold onto it. And we can't even get into the Court to steal it without starting a war," she said, crossing her hands over her chest as she turned and stared out at the Dark Forest.

"Then we'll go to war... I'm not leaving without it."

"We are talking about my parents, right? Nothing will ever change their minds."

Jax and his mate appeared through a purple mist and began walking towards the edge of their lands. "Now, if you could tell us why we were summoned?" Jax didn't acknowledge my presence and barely his own daughter's before he straightened his lavender jacket.

"We need the Crystal stone. The gods are trying to destroy Valyner, and we need to combine all the stones to block them out."

Verena glared at her daughter for a split second, and my shadows came up to the surface. I took a deep breath, pushing that aside, and waited until her eyes met mine.

"You mean sever the link," Jax stated.

Levanna glanced at me before taking a step forward, her anger radiating. "What link?" she asked.

"Those stones are what link us to them. They can't be broken alone, so you need to combine them and use the new power source it creates. Which would break our link with our makers," Verena said, her tone matching the vile expression on her face.

Levanna rolled her shoulders before taking a step closer to them. "How do you know this?" she asked her mother, who only gave a silent chuckle in return before staring her down.

It had to be Persephone...but how did *she* know that?

"Then hand it over so we can stop them," Levanna commanded.

"No," her father stated without hesitation.

"What do you mean, no?" Levanna's voice was harsh, tainted in ferocity that was seeping from her pores and circling the air around us. "They need to be dealt with."

"Oh, honey... If anyone needs to be dealt with, it's you two and your friend Davyna." Verena laughed. "We would never give away what is sacred to our kind to the half-breed who killed our Queen."

"You are partially responsible for the horror that has been inflicted on this realm. You have a duty to uphold, do you not?" Levanna spat out.

"Oh, my sweet daughter. Still speaking when you have no right to," Verena said, smiling at her daughter with cruelty sitting below the surface. "That's what got your mate killed."

"Don't. You. Fucking. Dare!" Levanna's hands began glowing purple, shifting into a dark plum. She stared her mother down, her chest rising and falling unevenly, and I slowly shifted my weight to look at them straight on. My shadows danced around, begging to be set free, and it took everything in me to deny them.

"None of you have authority over the Crystal Court. And even if you did, we would fight to the death to keep any of you from getting your hands on that stone."

"No...but I am one of you." Davyna appeared, standing between the Lands and smiling at us all. "I do have the same power that courses through your veins and a little more... So, maybe you should hand it over."

What was she doing?

Jax looked at his mate before his eyes scanned over Davyna's form. He was nervous to be near her, getting lost in her cold, black eyes with her silver irises glowing brighter. "Listen, Davyna. There is no way we are going to work with you. So, instead of wasting our time, maybe you should leave this Land before you completely destroy us all."

She nodded her head, kneeled to the ground, and ran her hand between the lush grass. Her power shook the ground, creating a trail of dirt that shot up and withered the green petals until they were charred remains. The path led right to Jax and Verena.

"You know what? You are right. I should leave. But destroying you all...now that sounds kind of fun." Darkness poured out of her, shimmering in the midday rays, and the ground began to shake violently.

"Levanna, go now!" I yelled. She stood there for a long moment as the ground beneath our feet began to crack open. We both glanced at Davyna and she smiled, raising her brow as if it was a call to challenge her. She was gearing up for something and I wouldn't have Levanna fall into it.

Over my dead body.

Finally, Levanna did as I asked, even though I could feel her hesitation to leave me alone with her. Ease washed over me as her power spiraled out and consumed her, leaving me with Davyna and Levanna's parents.

Dy stood unnaturally still, narrowing her gaze on me like she was amused with my attempt to save my friend.

She was up to something...

"That's the child I birthed...always running. What a disgrace...

Just like you, Davyna. No wonder why you're friends," Verena taunted.

Davyna's hands burned a deep onyx as she stepped forward and onto their Lands. Jax and Verena's faces faltered. "Well, I'm not running...but you might want to."

Fuck... Here we go.

The flames in her hands turned out, and before I could reach her, she sent out a blaze. Jax and Verena jumped into the gap, but a scream sounded off within. She must have got one of them with the fire, and honestly, good enough. They both deserved agonizing pain...but not by her hands or anyone else's but mine and Levanna's.

And if they were the ones entrusted to carry the stone—like Levanna's inside witch told us—then I needed them alive long enough to get it. Or it could fall into someone else's hands.

A cruel, distorted laugh fell from her lips as she turned and looked at me. "You wanted to come and ruin this, didn't you?" I asked, taking a step back.

"No," she said in a sweet tone, and my heart began to ache as I stepped back again. "I wanted to come and kill you." She grinned, pulling more flames to her hands, and they spiraled up her arms.

Fury pumped through my veins as I slowly looked up at her, not seeing the woman I knew anymore. She was lost. She was fading away with each second that passed.

My father's words came back to me, *"Don't forget who she is to you."* Every fiber in my body burned, firing off a blaze of pain and sorrow, and I stood my ground. I wasn't going to give up... I couldn't, because I knew that deep down, she wouldn't. She didn't when she saved me from my curse...when she sacrificed her life to give us all a chance to fight another day against Persephone.

"You won't do it... You can't kill someone you love."

"Do you know how pathetic that sounds? Have I ever said those words to you, Kadeyan?" Her eyes were cold, and it felt like a dagger was buried into my chest, twisting over and over again. "I can kill you...and I will," she teased as she threw out her flames, forcing me to move out of the way, but the intensity still made my skin heat in pain.

Her laugh was wild as another set of flames darted out, barely missing me while I rolled out of the way. Glancing back up, I saw another wave coming straight for me and pushed my wings out before launching myself into the sky.

If she wanted to play...so be it.

Flames followed after me as I darted back down to the ground, landing behind her. I moved fast, pushing my shadows out and taking her into my hold, before ripping her back into my arms. I sunk my teeth into her, taking her essence into me, and began coughing again. It was bitter, just like when I licked it off the dagger after she first entered this state. It tasted like acid as it flowed down my throat.

"Aww, what, Dark Lord? Do I not taste sweet anymore?" She turned as I fell to the ground, choking on the blood as it came back up. It was like, in this state, she was turning her blood into venom to protect herself and weaken her prey.

"So, where would you like it to happen? Here, or in the throne room, where your father was killed? I think that could be poetic. I can throw you into the flames after I have my fun with you," she taunted.

Anger took over every nerve, every bone, and I pushed myself up, glaring at her. She smiled wide, tilting her head and waiting for my response, but I was done doing this.

I. Was. Done.

Jumping up, my hand wrapped around her throat as a growl passed my lips, pulling her up until her face was an inch away from mine.

"What can you really do to me, Kadeyan?" She laughed and I tightened my hold, my hand shaking from the force.

I was not one to deny the darkest parts of myself, but not without control of that power—of my humanity. And I wouldn't allow her to suppress the woman she had been for the last twenty-five years. Not anymore.

Because that person had fervor, dedication, strength, and resilience, and I admired every bit of her. She was strong as a human, as a fae, and of course, as a god. Which meant, she could overcome this.

And I knew this was the only way now… I needed to force her to stop playing this game and truly fight, without a way to run… It would be a risk; it was each time I stepped into that death ring, but I was willing to take it.

"You should stop underestimating me, Dearest. Because, by tonight, I'll have you begging for the life I can only give you." I dug my nails deeper into the flesh of her neck and pulled her into the pitch-black void…praying to whatever higher power was above our gods that this would work.

CHAPTER 57
DAVYNA

Landing on the ground, Kadeyan ripped his hand down, releasing my throat. Smiling at him, I tilted my head. "So, what is your feeble attempt to stall me now?"

"If we are going to fight...we might as well have an audience. Follow me, Your Highness."

I scoffed at his sarcastic tone before following after him through the Dead Forest. I sensed my power within build, begging me to end this.

And yet, I was now genuinely curious of what he had planned. And if people were going to watch the Lord they feared be killed in less than a minute... That sounded sweeter than what I had planned for him.

After a few minutes, the mountains came into view, spreading across the Lands in a perfect line. Kadeyan continued on, not looking back as he approached the sharp stone. Lifting his hand to a carved circle embedded in the mountain, he sent out his shadows and a loud grinding of stone began to echo beyond. Slowly, an opening appeared, and he looked back at me with a vile smile.

"What is this?" I asked, frustration rising to the surface and tainting my voice.

"What, is the big, bad goddess...scared?"

My lip twitched and he laughed, moving into the tunnel.

Looking back at the forest, I steeled my spine and moved in after him. Assessing my surroundings, I waited for another ambush he could have up his sleeve.

We walked in silence through the long tunnel, our boots being the only thing creating sound against the gravel below. I watched as he moved, searching for any weakness in his form. But it didn't look like he had one, unless you counted his heart. And in this case, I would use it to my advantage tonight.

You couldn't trust your heart, only your mind. That was what kept you alive, while your heart would kill you over and over again.

Coming to the opening, I noticed yells roared from within. It was like sweet music to my ears, and I picked up my feet to be closer to it. The mountains surrounded us in a circle, creating an arena, but no one was in the stands. Rather, they were surrounding what looked like a glowing sphere. The screams grew and I followed the beautiful melody, pushing past people until I saw it for myself.

Two males covered in blood were in the ring, using their power and fists to attack the other.

"It's beautiful," I said, falling deeper into the glory of the fight as the energy of bloodlust pulsed around us.

"It's a death ring," Kadeyan said as he came up to my side, keeping his eyes on the males before us. "It's outlawed in all other Courts, but here… Alastair took you to one of the old arenas in the Crescent Lands to do the binding spell."

I glanced over at him, remembering the pain, the run through the woods, and all the blood that forced its way up my throat. Yet, it was only a reminder that when I let my guard down, I fall…and I wouldn't do that again. Not with anyone…and most certainly not with him.

"People come from all over now to show their strength…but also to die."

"To die?" I laughed, looking around at the fae surrounding us. Some were graced with the discolored skin on their arms, crawling up to their chests. It made sense why they were here, but the others who were healthy clearly held no regard for their immortality. What a waste.

Turning, I looked at Kadeyan, and his face turned cold as he glanced over at me. "Not all fae want to live forever…"

Something within me flickered, reminding me of the girl within. I suppressed it again, knowing that, by the end of day...she would be gone because *he* would be dead.

I looked back to the fighters, watching one use his shadows to pull the other to the ground, before he dropped down on top of him. The male began beating his face in with zero remorse, the sound of cracking bone joining in with the chants. Smiling, I watched as his skull began to break open like an egg and I leaned in, touching the barrier.

My hands burned at the contact, and I looked at the sheer barrier. It was old magic; I could feel it in my bones. Somehow, it was laced with something familiar, like my own. Kadeyan looked at me, his eyes darkening.

"So, what is the point of this?" I asked, pulling my hands down and turning to face him.

The crowd cheered and I stole a side-glance at the victor yelling within the arena. A part of the dead male's brain was in his hand.

"You are going in there, Dearest." Smiling, I looked back. "But you should know this: once you're in there with your opponent, you can't leave until one of you is dead. And since you can't die without a special weapon, you'll keep killing. Are you okay with that?"

"Sounds perfect." I ripped off my leather jacket, revealing the skintight shirt that stopped just below my breasts. The sight had Kadeyan looking me over. His heart raced as I threw the jacket at him and walked towards the barrier.

"It is spelled to make you use all the power you contain, that way the real victor steps out alive. Remember that when you are in there...you can't hold back the darkness. It will only grow stronger."

"What makes you think I'm holding back?" I laughed as I stepped through the shield, relishing in the pins and needles pricking at my skin. "Just because I haven't killed you yet? Please... don't flatter yourself. That is happening today."

Turning around, I looked over the stunned fae and the chants fell, becoming nonexistent. Crossing my arms over my chest, I yelled, "What? Are you all afraid to die now?"

The demeanor of the crowd beyond shifted. Whispers stretched around me, causing me to turn. My gaze narrowed on the male as he stepped up into the ring, rolling his shoulders.

"I'm not."

CHAPTER 58
DAVYNA

"Bring the real Davyna out for this fight. I want her to decide if I live or die...not you. Or are you scared she will want to keep me around?" Kadeyan taunted, smirking to one side as he slowly stepped towards me.

Don't do this... Please, don't! the voice within my psyche rang out and I seethed.

"We are one... We want the same thing." I glanced over at him, my wrath seeping out as I take a step forward. "I hate you," I murmured.

"You sure about that, Dy?" The nickname made my skin crawl, and images of my father, Elias, and Evren filtered in. "I came here every day for the six months you were gone...wanting nothing but death to touch me, to rid me of the pain you caused."

My eyes widened as the war within began to brew.

Because his words...they did something... They kept doing something, and I needed it to stop. "Well, I wish someone would have finished you off!"

"So do I...but I think I like this better. It's more poetic. You'll kill me...but I can take you with me." He pulled a dagger from his sheath and I froze, my skin rising in response. He had the two-toned dagger in the barrier. The one that made Tanith bleed red...that made *me* bleed red. If he used it on me...

Fear slithered its way into my core, twisting tightly until nausea rose. *Fuck.*

"Maybe this was always supposed to be our happily ever after, little Ember. Let's make the best of it."

"Where did you get that?" I asked, hearing the unease taint my voice.

The spell settled over us and his primal side shredded through his once-amber eyes that I used to love, replacing them with beaming crimson. His demeanor changed and a vile creature stood before me with no remorse for what he was about to do. Although, something in me began to shift, pulling everything I possessed to the surface...including the light.

Shit... The spell wasn't only intensifying my dark side...but the light power as well.

He held up the dagger, taking in the craftsmanship, and chuckled before looking at me. "Your mother." Shadows poured from his hands, putting up a wall of darkness that surrounded me.

Standing still, my breathing intensified as I thought about my mother. She gave him the dagger that could kill me... The betrayal stung deep, ripping through me, and the doors within my mind cracked open.

Images of the past flew in, and I was furious because I couldn't stop them. I could see the people from my past and felt the effects of their love wash over me. Lana, Marta, Lizbeth, Terry, Evren, Drystan...before it switched and showed me the family I made here in Valyner...

A fist slammed into my jaw, knocking me to the ground as I let out a growl. I tasted blood and turned, seeing him coming at me again with the dagger gleaming in the rays of the dying sun.

Yelling, I grabbed his wrist and twisted it until I heard a bone crack, before pressing my feet into his chest and kicking him back. His body slammed into the barrier before he fell to one knee. He gritted his teeth as he rolled his hand, ignoring the pain. That hand still gripped the one thing that could hurt me...that could kill me.

You can stop this... You can break through. Love needs to be your fight now.

Wrath pulsed through me as my flames ignited in my hands, and

I sent it out towards him. He smiled as he dodged each blow, looking entertained with my state.

"You ruined my life!" I screamed as I walked towards him. He threw his fist again, but I ducked, punching him in his gut instead. Spinning to the side, I wrapped my arm around his throat and pulled, flipping him over. "I never wanted this!"

"I don't give a fuck!" he yelled, elbowing me before stabbing the dagger into my leg. I cried out as his shadows threw me across the ring, rolling to the ground and feeling...pain. "You deserved the truth!"

Needles pierced into my brain, and I gritted my teeth as the spell pushed my body to fight. "What? About a bond that I didn't ask for?" I yelled, venom coating each syllable.

Shimmering onyx flames curled up my arms as I wrapped my hand around the dagger and glanced up, seeing he was in front of me. Grabbing me by my throat, he lifted me into the air before he twisted the dagger with his other hand. I cried out but his voice rose above my own.

"Fuck the bond, Davyna!" he yelled, his eyes wild with pain from fighting the spell, but there was something else... Grief. "You deserved to know who you truly were!"

I kicked him back, and his hands left my body, allowing me to suck in a sharp breath. The dagger was now on the ground and I gripped at the wound, noticing it wasn't healing at all. The warm crimson slid down my leather slacks and the pain made me feel like I was human again.

My breathing went rigid and I glanced at him. Those crimson pools drew me in, reminding me of too much of our time together. *Shit*... No... No...

"With or without it...I would've chosen you!" His voice broke, and my heart did the same. "I would choose you again and again. In this life and all the ones that come next."

And now, I knew the truth... The bond wasn't controlling his love for me.

It was real.

Fire licked beneath my skin as I moved towards him. All our memories flashed in my mind, breaking through my walls like it was mere mist. I didn't want to feel this. I didn't want to think about us...because if I did, I'd fall back into his arms, into a love that was all-consuming.

I couldn't. I was...scared.

Throwing out my flames, I burned his arm. Curses spilled from his lips before he charged me again.

"I'm always going to be alone!" I said, feeling the pain invade my heart as I punched him over and over again.

Flipping me, he pinned me to the ground. Blood ran down his nose as he filled my senses with his pine and leather scent. "You were never alone, Davyna! You chose it! I've been right here...and I will be here until every star dies and the world turns to ash."

The voices chanting around us faded and I looked up at him.

I saw him through the war raging within, but my soul was still captive to the darkness. It was angry, controlling my movement, and I was falling victim to it.

That's not true. You are in control here. You choose your fate now. So, choose!

Flipping him over, I straddled him and buried my hand into his chest, hearing his ribs crack. My fingers wrapped around his heart that was beating rapidly, and I noticed mine was beating exactly the same. "I–I can't..." I struggled to speak, the tears invading my eyes.

The pain from the spell and the darkness within pushed me to finish what we started, and I could tell Kadeyan was fighting it, too.

"I was dead for ages, Davyna Ember. You brought me back to life... So, it's yours to take." He raised his hand to the back of my neck, pulling me in. "But kiss me one last time...so I can remember the taste of you for eternity." His lips crashed down on mine and my hand gripped his heart tighter, shaking as I battled with what to do.

The spell surrounding us demanded I end him, pushing for all my power to obey its command. Even the dark power coursing through my veins pleaded with me to act, but I was fighting it... I was fighting what felt so instinctual, so right, because I wasn't sure I wanted to do it.

My lip quivered and my eyes blurred with tears.

His voice sounded in my mind, just outside my psyche, and I pulled away. *"I love you for you, Davyna. Darkness and all."*

A tear rolled down my cheek as I glanced down at the scars on my arm, seeing most of them shimmer white, while the others stood dark as the galaxies beyond.

I could make my own fate... I needed to.

"Kade...I love you."

His eyes softened as I turned my hand and pulled back. A sharp breath left his lips as I screamed, shattering the spell that surrounded us. The fae ducked as the magic shot out, leaving a glowing light hovering over the arena.

Trying to catch my breath, I looked down at Kadeyan, his eyes in shock as he sat up, his hand going to his chest.

The darkness retreated within, furious with me that I won, but for the first time in a long time, I felt like me again. The light side of my power dowsed me in its warmth, invading every nerve and illuminating the strength I hid away.

My jaw fell open as his gaze locked on my eyes, and I knew they were back to normal. "Davyna?" Kadeyan asked, pulling me back onto his lap. His hands grabbed my face and he smiled.

Before I could say a word, he pulled me in and our lips locked in a possessive desire. The world around us turned into a haze as we fell into each other, feeling the strings of our bond interlace like never before.

Pulling away, he rested his forehead to mine. "I got you, Dy. I'm right here."

I looked into his amber pools and could only say the three words again: "I love you."

"I love you too." He smiled wider and it was like the pieces of my life that were all shattered began fusing back together. "Try and remember that the next time you want to kill me, though."

I chuckled for a moment before everything that happened since

I was gone crept in on me. Kadeyan used his shadows to pull the dagger my mother gave him from across the ring into his hand before placing it back in its sheath.

Standing up, my arms crossed over my chest, and I held myself tight before I glanced at him again. I knew my expression told him all the pain and suffering I caused was coming for me, preparing to make me feel every small detail of agony I caused.

He moved in, grabbing my face. "Come on, let's go somewhere where you can fall apart. And I'll be right there holding you until it passes."

I nodded, my eyes filling with tears. I turned, taking in the fae around us still lost in shock. It was clear that they weren't sure what to make of the power I unleashed.

Nausea bloomed from deep within my core and my body went rigid as I sensed the last thing I wanted near me right now.

"Kadeyan..." I turned just as an onyx flames shot down like a lightning bolt, landing behind him, and a black shadow appeared.

Obsidian.

"Well, isn't this sweet... Let's change that, shall we?"

CHAPTER 59
OBSIDIAN

"Did you miss me, my little alyahiia?" I asked, stepping closer to her and her *mate*. Kadeyan moved by her side, narrowing his gaze on me. Was he being serious? I could kill him before he could even blink.

Davyna placed her hand up on his chest, taking a step forward as her eyes glistened, but that did little to wipe away the hatred within them. It looked like someone found their way back to the light...What a shame.

Laughing, I looked around the arena and watched the fae quake in response.

"What are you doing here?" she asked.

"I wanted to see if you would accompany me for a stroll around town...so we can chat more."

"Fuck you, Obsidian," she spat out, taking a few steps forward.

I laughed again as I moved in, dropping my shadows to reveal my true form. Gasps sounded from behind me as fear rose into the air. I didn't always look like this—charred and cracked—and I missed my old face, but oh, how good it felt to be feared by my creation. Yet, the two in front of me only steeled their spines, refusing to cower.

"You know, I could just take you away from here, strip you of everything you possess, and make you my plaything for the next millennia."

Kadeyan moved forward, his wrath purging to the surface. "You will not touch her. Or I will kill you myself."

I smiled, moving through the ring and drinking in the panic rising into the air. "Did you forget who the true Dark Lord is?" I turned, looking at Kadeyan with disgust laced into every feature. "Last time I checked, she didn't want you anyway." Kadeyan grinded his teeth, his fists balling up at his side. Davyna stepped forward, glaring at me. "Or maybe my little goddess has changed her mind."

"Why are you here, Obsidian?" she asked again.

"Something isn't adding up, but...answer this for me." I looked her up and down. "How did you break this death ring spell? I created it over a thousand years ago..."

She refused to answer, but I could see the tremble skate down her body. "I want to know what you and Tanith have planned," she demanded. Taking another step closer, she tilted her head up more to look into my eyes.

Grinning at her, I stepped in and lifted my hand, but kept it a few inches from her face. Her power tingled against my skin, and I could feel my own in her, along with Tanith's now that she let out both sides. "You will know...when I want you to know. Or you'll be dead, watching it all unfold from the afterlife." I huffed before dropping my hand and walking behind her.

As I turned, I placed both hands on her face and a searing pain rushed deep within as I broke through her psyche, opening her mind to show me everything. I saw a ghostly figure, but her face wasn't familiar.

I took in the surroundings, knowing it was the Mortal Realm—a place I had already been, when I took Tanith from those same lands before I was locked out again. Looking deeper into her mind, I felt her pain and pushed, until I saw a journal. It contained instructions to break our link. This bitch knew more than she should... How?

I tried to pull back, but her hands clasped around mine, deepening the hold. I gritted my teeth as the images began to change. A beaming light blanketed a small village, opening the veil between my realm and theirs. The cabin came into view, and I walked towards it, opening the front door.

The two newborns laid next to each other in their own bassinets, sound asleep. A gloomy vapor came out from the shadows, picking up the baby with blonde hair, and I knew how this ended. My power danced out, encasing the infant with black hair and taking her life.

Drawing back to the present, I didn't have time to deal with her as Kadeyan charged at me. His shadows held me by my throat as a dagger sliced into me, trying to find my heart. Throwing him back, I looked down at my chest and saw red pool up before glancing at the weapon in his hand. My head shook as my anger rose, burning through my cracked skin to illuminate outwards.

How did he get that?

"Did you really think you could kill me, Kadeyan?" He glanced towards me, smiling, and I averted my gaze back to Davyna. "You'd be happy to know that Tanith is well...after you stabbed her. You missed her heart."

"I didn't think you cared, since you did nothing to stop it," she spat out and I chuckled. "You took her... She was born in the Mortal Realm, wasn't she?"

My eyes burned with fury and my lips pressed together as I took a cleansing breath.

I couldn't kill her...*yet.*

"Not even back an hour and already wanting answers." I chuckled, shaking my head, which only made her fury grow.

"Why did you take her and kill the other child?" she asked.

"Because I could." Shadows corrupted with spiraling flames spilled from me. "And I can do a lot worse...trust me." Her heart sped up and I looked over to Kadeyan, who was pulling himself off the ground. "Stop trying to find a way to beat me at this game and do what you are told."

"I'm not taking the throne. Or telling you anything I learn about my mother," she stated, her own irises melting in perfect silver swirls.

"I don't want you to take the throne, little cinder. I don't even want you cursed... That's Tanith. I only want you to lift *your* curse you placed on it."

"There is more you want... Why won't you tell me?!" she yelled.

A laugh billowed out of my lips as I released my fight. "I do love how furious you get when you don't know what's coming next."

My power sprung forth, stretching out, and all the fae around us let out loud gasps. Their shrieks of pain echoed beyond the mountains as they fell one by one. Blood fell from mouths, eyes, and even ears as Kadeyan and Davyna glanced around in disbelief.

"Let that be a warning to you... I never lose." I grinned.

Black flames shot through the air, charging for them. But Davyna blocked them, pushing them back, and I felt my power falter. My eyes narrowed and I could tell she saw the fury in them. But also...I think she knew it shocked me.

"Watch yourself, alyahiia." I brought my hands down and she did the same.

"You're right... I am a goddess. And you are going to watch me lead your creations into war against you."

Stunned, I looked her over, and something deep within told me she was the one... She was what I needed.

Throwing her hands out, her power slammed into my chest, and it confirmed my suspicion even more.

Sending my power out, I ripped the dagger from Kadeyan's hand and pulled it into my grasp. Opening the gap behind me, I fell in to return to Solyus with the one thing that she needed to kill me. I pushed into her mind, giving her one last thing...

"Even goddesses bow to me. You have until the full moon, and then...I'm coming for you."

Back in my castle, my anger grew more intense by the second. I paced back and forth in front of my mirror, clutching the dagger between my fingers until the metal painfully dug into the flesh of my palm. I was waiting for him to show up, and each second that passed made my own nerves spiral up and twist around my lungs.

Tanith walked in, her eyes scanning me as I tried to ignore her existence.

At first, I thought she was what I needed, but maybe I took the wrong child because she didn't have *it*.

So, how did Davyna?

"Obsidian, you need to kill her," Tanith said, and my eyes rolled. "There can only be two gods in a realm... We know now that she is the unbalance. There can't be three gods in a realm, which is why we keep losing our fae to that toxic sickness."

I'd suspected it for a while. Really, since she ended up here. But how did a goddess go undetected her whole life? Someone hid her powers, which I knew, and Ezekiel couldn't have done it all alone with only the throne's power.

It had to be her mother... Because she also hid Davyna's goddess power below it all. My little cinder unleashed it on the throne and unexpectedly cursed it. But the problem still remained: I couldn't fucking kill her because what if she was from the bloodline I needed?

Tanith stepped closer. "We need the fae's power to—"

"Is that why you are fighting so hard? For our King? Or are you scared she will replace you?" I grinned, pulling her unease to the surface. Moving towards her, I threw the dagger to my desk before I placed both hands on her face, kissing her deeply. "Nothing can replace you, my love. I will get her out of the picture as soon as I can channel her power, okay?"

She nodded, giving me another peck before glancing over to the mirror.

It was so easy to make her believe every lie pouring off my tongue. I didn't want to channel Davyna's power, I wanted it to start the war.

"Does *he* want the stones yet?" she asked.

"I'm sure he does, but I'm going to let the fae collect them for us. It will keep them busy until they try and take the dagger back. And we can get ready for what comes next."

She smiled, glancing up into my eyes. "We are going to make things right...and rid this world of *his* touch," she said, taking my hand and running her thumb over my charred flesh. "And then I can finally see the man below this curse."

I chuckled, smiling as I looked up at the chandelier burning with black flames. "Yes...but go. I want to speak to him alone."

She squeezed my hand before heading towards the door, and I let out a frustrated breath. As the latch clicked into place, I placed a shield over the room and shook my head. Tanith was just a pawn... and how she let me play her this long without seeing it was beyond me.

She was dedicated, I'd give her that.

The mirror began to swirl and I straightened. "What have you learned?" his voice boomed with authority.

"I think you were right...but as to where she came from, I still don't know."

"Do you think she will find out?"

I laughed, looking into the dark Abyss. "That girl won't stop searching...it's not in her nature," I said, pulling the seat out and sitting down before him.

"She needs to kill Tanith," he commanded.

"Why? I mean, not that I'm opposed...but what are you thinking?" I asked. My heartbeat grew faster because I knew better than to question him.

Although, he began to chuckle, the vibration of it forcing the swirls within the mirror to move faster as his piercing green eyes shined through. "Call it a hunch. My brother is a sneaky bastard after all. And if it doesn't work...she'll be your new replacement to keep that realm intact."

A smile crept onto my face and I silently agreed. "Should I make arrangements now?"

"No... Give Davyna some time to get the stones and learn more, but make sure *your* people on the ground are there, interfering with her. I want her on edge until the time comes."

"Yes, Your Grace." I bowed my head.

"And Obsidian... If she won't do it, you will have to," he stated, and I smirked.

"Not a problem."

"Also, do not kill the mate. We might need him as leverage in what's to come if you are right."

Smiling, I looked up. "As you wish. And as the Fallen say..." I silently laughed, thinking how that Court had it wrong, but still... close enough. "To raising *Hell*."

CHAPTER 60
DAVYNA

Kadeyan wrapped his arms around me and pulled me into the dark void, but my mind was already lost to everything filtering back in. Along with the reality that we lost the only thing that could kill them.

When we fell into the forest, I instantly recognized the area. We were just a few miles from where I grew up. As I turned, I took in Kadeyan's black cabin.

"Are you okay?" I asked as I moved in and looked him over, trying to push away the emotions clawing at me.

"I'm more than okay..." He brushed the hair back from my face, giving me a sweet smile as he took my hand and led me towards the front door. Picking me up off my feet, Kade used his shadows to open the door and carried me over the threshold, before placing me down within the small space.

I remembered it from the last time I was here. The fire pit outside was on full display in the large window behind the bed dressed in black. A few feet away, the small couch sat directly in front of the fireplace, where the wood popped and sizzled from the spell that kept it burning.

Crossing my arms over my body, I glanced at the table that we joined around when Kadeyan was dying from his curse. Weapons still adorned the walls, matching the ones we used on the Cursed that night that now felt like ages ago. I turned back around and was met with his gaze locked on me, assessing my state.

"Are you okay?" he asked softly, and the tears flooded my eyes.

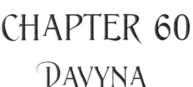

I gripped onto my leathers, my nails digging into them until a slight sting grew under the material. "I–I'm...so sorry..." I got out before my legs began to shake, but Kadeyan was already moving towards me. He took me into his arms, holding me up with each step, until we were in front of the couch. "I didn't mean to kill Eryx... I–I didn't."

"I know..." he said as he pulled me down with him onto the couch and laid my head against his chest. "Let it out."

"I could have saved Nesrin...and Axel..." Another sob broke through my lips and his hand came up to my head, holding me to him.

But then, I heard something over my cries... Sniffling. Pulling away, I watched him as he stared into the fire, his eyes glassed over.

"Maybe...but they could have still died." A tear ran down his face and he slowly turned to look at me. "What you did at the funeral, giving her that small gift of laying her to rest in water... You gave her that when none of us could."

"I was a monster..."

His smile looked broken as another tear streamed down his cheek. I lifted both my hands to his face, brushing the lingering droplets away.

"I don't hold it against you, Dy. I don't think any of us do...and I don't think you can hold this against yourself for eternity or it will come back and keep you as a prisoner."

"I don't want that... I want to feel..." I waited for the voice within to tell me that feeling was what got me into all this, but it was silent.

"You want to feel alive...and *this* is what makes you alive—feeling deeply and passionately. That's who you are." He pulled me back to his chest and ran his hand up and down my back as I stared off into the flames.

I replayed every kill, each loss, and all the harsh things I said to the people I loved. It felt as if my heart cracked like a window, each memory chipping away at it and forcing the pieces to fall around me. But I didn't want to run from it anymore because he was right. I felt alive...even in the pain.

I *felt* alive.

"I want to tell you about something..." he said, and I glanced up, feeling his emotions shift. "When I said you were never alone, I meant that in more ways than just me being here for you... I know your pain. I'm no stranger to misery."

I sat up more, looking into his eyes filled with sorrow. Taking a deep breath, I calmed my racing heart and waited for him to go on.

"I lost my mother in the war when Ezekiel's father killed her. That was my first real loss...and it broke me at such a young age. But there was more..."

"I know...your father too."

"Not just him, but Silas...my little brother." My eyes widened and my heart ached even more. "He was my half-brother. His mother died when he was still a baby. He looked like me, but with pure icy blue eyes and hair that was as black as night... He was Levanna's mate."

My jaw fell open and his pain transferred to me, forcing my body to ache with sorrow. "Kadeyan, I'm sorry..."

"Every time I see Jax and Verena...I want to kill them. But I hold back because my father made me promise a long time ago that I would let it go...that he needed me to be the leader of the Fallen. And the time will come when they will suffer for what they did."

Looking down, I grabbed his hand, interlacing my fingers through his.

"I never wanted to be a Lord, Davyna. And, honestly, I think Silas would have done it better, even though he was younger. But after Silas was gone, I vowed I would take it and be as vile as everyone believed our Court to be. I wanted them all afraid." I leaned in and rested my head on his chest, savoring my heat molding into his cold body. "I was lost in the darkness... I let it drive me for years. And when my father passed, it got worse... Until I saw you."

"Why are you just telling me this now?" I asked softly.

"Because you always resort back to thinking you are going to be alone, not only physically but with the pain you bear. And you're not. I know it better than anyone else."

Placing his other hand on my face, he tilted it up so that I looked into his holy amber eyes that were still glistening. "I slowly saw a light growing around me when I let my friends in... But you, Davyna... You were the reason my world was engulfed. You were the reason I fought. The reason I wanted to keep breathing. And why I want to live every day like it is my last with you by my side."

"Never back down from the darkness that comes for us all," I whispered as a tear rolled down my cheek and onto his leathers. "Elias told me that..."

"We get one life, Dearest... Let's make it count for all the ones who aren't here with us."

I nodded my head as I pulled him in, kissing him deeply. Our souls weren't only bonded, but our lives were like a mirror image of one another. We carried the pain alone through different times, only to now bear it with another who could see you clearly and understand. Maybe fate was still a mystery in all this, but this—us—we were no mistake.

This was real.

Pulling away from me, he smiled with his eyes closed. "Say it again."

"Say what?" I asked, but I already knew what he wanted to hear.

"I can make you scream it if you prefer..."

I laughed, and he joined in. "You're such an ass sometimes...but I love you anyway."

"I love you too...goddess."

I shook my head.

We sat still, listening to the wood pop and the embers stream out into the air around the fire. I could see the broken pieces of my life around me, but it was different now because I knew which ones I wanted to take moving forward in what was to come next. I needed to accept that I did terrible things... It would take time to forgive myself...time to control what lived within, but I was going to do it for her. I was going to do it for that young girl I hid away so long ago, thinking she was the epitome of weak.

She wasn't... She was scared of letting people see she had a heart...and that she longed for passion, love, acceptance, and people who would fight with her... Another tear ran down my face and I remembered what I used to say to myself after Elias died: *Everything was going to be okay... I was strong. I would not break.*

But I knew it needed to change.

Even when things weren't okay, and I was breaking...I was still strong.

I said it over and over inside my head, willing my mind to accept that strong people break...and that was okay. It needed to be okay, because I wasn't done. There was too much at stake now...and I wouldn't run from what I was born to be.

I needed that girl deep within with a shattered past... I needed my friends—no, my family—Kadeyan, and all of Valyner to take them down.

CHAPTER 61
DAVYNA

We talked for hours about everything that had been going on and what they all learned about me while I was enthralled in my darkness. We talked about how everyone was doing, and the guilt sliced into me, but I forced myself to listen. Kadeyan also told me about seeing his father and my mother and it made my heart yearn to see her right now.

"What are we going to do about the dagger?" I asked.

"We will get it back, Dy... We will." His head dropped for a moment before he gazed into the fireplace, his demeanor shifting into the soldier I knew him to be.

He had a plan, which required the stones and the dagger. My mother's journal pointed to that. If it was truly the way to sever the link...then we needed to do it, along with closing the veil and lifting the curse I put on the throne.

"Davyna, I'll be right there, helping you however I can."

"I know..." My eyes blankly stared out the large window over the bed. I worried that the dark side within could come back, pulling me away and keeping me captive once again.

Kadeyan handed me a drink and I slowly brought it to my lips, taking a sip.

"You fought that part of you and won today, Dy... But you need to do it again."

"What do you mean?" I placed the drink down and stood up, sensing the panic rushing in at the thought.

"Light and darkness will rage war until one stands between, able to control both." The prophecy... "That is you, Davyna. And I want you to let it in again... I want you to embrace every dark corner of your mind and make it obey you." I let out a breath as he leaned in, his lips brushing my ear. "I want to watch you break them to your will."

"What if I lose control?" I asked, looking at him as I pulled away.

"Then I'll lose control with you." His hands grabbed my ass, leading me back towards the bed. We both fell and he tilted his hips, pressing against my center with his cock. Shivers ran down my spine as his length pressed into me, hard and begging to be freed. And my own desire surged within. "I don't want to be in control right now anyway... I want to fuck you until you are begging for mercy."

Our lips brushed as I brought my hands to his chest, breathing heavier. A swirl of purple mist rose from them, removing his clothes, and I continued down until my fingers traced the V on his core. The bond circled us, begging me to take the next step with him, but I still didn't understand it myself.

"What happens when we bond?" I asked, glancing up into his eyes.

"Why? Do you want to do it right now?" He smirked.

"No. I mean...not with all this going on. But what will happen?"

He stepped in, running his fingers down my arm until he picked up my hand. "We will both cut our palms, joining our blood as one, and then say the words that bind our souls together." He pulled my hand forward, running it down his core until my fingers wrapped around his cock. "And then...let's just say, we won't be doing much talking."

My heart doubled over in my chest, and he smiled. "But not until you are ready," he whispered. "Right now, I need you to let go... Let it in."

"Just promise me this..." I closed my eyes, letting out a shaky breath. "You won't let me fall," I pleaded as his eyes searched mine.

A gentle smile rose on his lips because he knew what I meant.

I didn't want to lose myself again.

Rising from the bed, he used his shadows to grab a dagger off the wall and pulled it into his hand.

"We fall together. And we rise...together," he said. He spun the blade once before he threw it at me, burying the blade into my left shoulder. I cried out as I looked back at him in shock. "Let *her* out to play..." Vicious intent beamed in his eyes, and I couldn't help but smile.

I focused on the pain. I focused on the hurt that had been unwavering. And like a siren call, the darkness answered, peering through the light and consuming it. Pulling the blade free, I looked at my grey blood as the power within slithered up, and I knew my eyes were slowly shifting.

I glanced at him, feeling the smirk grace my lips. "No holding back..." I threw the blade back at him, sinking it deep into his thigh, and he growled.

"There's my dark Dearest," he said as he threw his shadows out, wrapping them around my ankles before bringing me to the edge of the bed. I sat up, pulling the blade from his leg and pressing it to his throat.

Dragging down, I cut into the delicate skin enough to draw blood, hearing the sweetest hiss as he broke his hold on me. My power took over, pulling him to his knees before me as I brought the blade to my lips. My tongue slid up the steel, falling deeper into ecstasy, and all I wanted was more. I wanted to be covered in his blood, but even more...I wanted his life in my hands.

Hauling the blades off the wall, I sent them through the air. They pierced his skin and he yelled out in pain as his eyes darkened.

"You look good on your knees."

His shadows lunged out, pulling each blade free before his hands tore at my leathers. I brought my foot up, kicking him in the face, and he stumbled back as a laugh passed my lips.

"You can do better than that," he blurted out, wiping the blood from his nose.

Using my power, I removed my clothes and slowly ran my hand

down my stomach towards my pussy. His eyes followed, getting lost in desire, and I laughed again.

"I know." Sending my shadows out, I wrapped them around his body and threw him through the air.

He crashed into the glass window before tumbling through the wet grass, coating his body in dirt. I stood on the bed, flames igniting in both hands as I smiled at him.

Breathing heavily, he pushed himself up and his eyes fell deeper into a lust-filled crimson haze. "Mm, that's my good fucking girl... Now come take what you want."

A smiled turned up on my face and the battle within started. On one side, I wanted to chase him down, to rip him to shreds. And the other side wanted to embrace him, to fight by his side until we took our last breaths.

My wings opened wide and I darted out of the cabin, the cool night air caressing my bare skin. When I landed next to him, he moved fast, grabbing me by my throat before his wings spread wide. Kade pushed off the ground and I gripped his hand, searing the flesh as we flew into the woods.

We moved at inhuman speeds, the trees flying past us in a blur, and he hissed from the pain at his mangled flesh. As he slammed my back into a tree, the darkness slithered back into its holding place, and I took a shuddered breath. He sank his teeth down into me, and the flames went out, healing his skin almost instantly.

"I'm going to hurt you again...stop."

Dropping to his knees, he threw my legs over his shoulders, causing me to slide down against the rough bark, and I hissed.

"Good. I like pain." His tongue ran up my center and everything within faltered. Heat boiled up from my core, enveloping me into its searing embrace. He moved down again, letting his tongue slip into my cunt before slowly gliding up to my clit and biting hard.

I cried out, pulling on his hair and feeling each stroke more intensely then the last. I might have been the god here, but the way he moved made me want to worship him.

My body was thrown to the ground, and I was caught off guard as he stalked up to me, with his shadows gripping each limb. "Fight back... Or are you going to be its little bitch for eternity?"

Rage from inside me bubbled up as he dropped down, stroking his cock with a vile grin. My mouth watered but the demons within called to me, telling me to end this, that he was nothing.

A black mist shot out of my hands. It was infused with all the Court colors, almost creating its own galaxy, as it tossed him into the air. Crashing onto the ground, he let out a yell before slowly pulling himself up to look at me.

I snickered, shaking my head. "Didn't anyone ever warn you to not tempt a goddess with a good time?"

I walked over to him and placed a barrier around us as I restrained his hands and feet, keeping him pinned to the ground.

He pulled against the onyx vapor, his eyes growing darker as he glanced over my body. "Well then...stop being a tease."

Smiling, I lowered myself to straddle him. Bringing my hand up to his chest, I traced his flesh in a circle where his heart laid beneath. He tilted his hips up, causing me to rock forward, and the friction sent tingles up my spine.

"Fuck..." I breathed out, and he did it again.

"You like that, little Ember? Then take what you want from me."

I began rocking my hips, falling deeper into my pleasure. And with each thrust over his cock, everything within felt like it split down the middle. On one side, I felt the stabbing ice freezing over my veins, while the other side was blooming into an inferno. The light and darkness were raging their own war, and I focused on it.

I watched it move, how it craved different things, and I began to get angry with it. I wasn't their puppet...I was their master. I'd say when or where things happened, who would live or die. I would break them to my authority, and mine alone from this day forward.

Grabbing his cock, I lifted my hips and slowly guided him in, savoring each inch filling me with what I wanted. I moved my hips up and down, grabbing my breasts as I fell into sweet oblivion.

Arching into him, I moaned. "I want you..."

"I'm all yours, Dy... I'll forever be *yours*."

Leaning forward, I dug my nails into the dirt and realized I let the power fall that was holding him in place. His hands slammed into my ass, making me ride him harder, and my body began burning up.

"This cunt is mine to pleasure...your heart is mine to love...and your soul is mine to possess."

I was walking the line of darkness and light, basking in the power that was merging for the first time, and the fear was nonexistent. I let go, throwing my head back as Kadeyan sat up. He lifted us off the ground, his dick pulsing within my pussy as he pressed my body against the closest tree.

His fangs punctured my neck as he thrusted into me, and I cried out from the pain he was inflicting. He drank deep, and I reveled in it, feeling the haze from the blood loss.

Pulling back, he looked into my eyes as he continued to drive into me with no remorse. "Keep those pretty eyes on me." My breathing picked up as my core tightened and I wrapped my arms around his neck, digging my nails into his flesh.

My body succumbed to my release and I cried out, keeping my gaze on the male who was my other half, *my* god. He growled as he poured himself into me, and I savored each sound and each pulse my body gave as a genuine smile graced my face.

Catching my breath, I looked at him and couldn't help but feel lighter...*stronger*.

"How do you feel now?" he asked.

I laughed, looking up at the dark sky peeking through the pine needles above us. "Better...I think I figured it out," I whispered as the weight lifted off my shoulders.

Smiling, he leaned in and kissed me softly. "Good...but that was just the warm-up, Dearest." He threw me to the ground, and I sucked in a sharp breath. "You need to give it more of you. You need to embrace the demon within like it's the only version of you alive."

I furrowed my brows as he stepped back, his face going cold.

"If the Mortal Realm helps you with control, you need to give it everything you've got. And let's face it...you didn't."

Turning, I watched his shadows whip past me and pulled two blades into his hands. He tossed one down at my feet and said, "Now...should I run, or should you?"

CHAPTER 62

DAVYNA

The next morning, we returned from the Mortal Lands after Kadeyan forced me to bring the dark power forth so many times that I lost count. Each time, I learned more control, breaking different areas within my power to obey.

He also helped with the voice inside my head, building new walls around my psyche until they were impenetrable. I pulled for each line of power, submerging the small fortress until it was locked away and there was no key to open it again. I was beyond exhausted each time I gave it more, but I pushed until my body trembled under the weight of it all, refusing to stop.

It was easier over there, but the real test was going to be being back here... And it made me nervous.

Although, after doing that all night, I felt more like myself—like the version of me who once didn't possess power and was unstoppable to get what she wanted. I didn't realize how much I missed that side of me...until now.

Kadeyan was sitting across the table, glancing at a book as I was trying to read from my mother's journal, but I could barely focus. We fucked more times last night than we ever had before, and I still wanted more. And from how his eyes kept stealing a glance of me, eating me up...I knew he was feeling the same.

"Godsdamn it, Dearest. I'm going to fuck you over this table if you don't stop looking at me like that."

"Like what?" I said, innocently, and gave him a smirk.

Both of our heads turned towards the doors as they opened,

revealing Levanna and Calix. I swallowed hard as I looked at them. Their bodies were tense until they saw my eyes. My gaze jumped to Ravyn, her red eyes beaming so bright before she ran towards me.

She jumped on the table and licked my face, purring so loud that it made the table vibrate. I laughed, whispering, "I missed you too." After a minute, she jumped down, curling up by my feet. I looked back to Kadeyan with eyes that begged him to talk to them. My stomach twisted as the shame returned...

I didn't know what to say.

"It's all right. I broke her in last night... She won't kill anyone, right?"

I tilted my head, stunned by what he said. *Seriously*? That was what he chose to say. Calix began to laugh, and I rolled my eyes playfully at Kade before glancing over the page I was on.

"So...what have you two..." he asked as I turned back around, his eyebrow rising. "You know what, never mind. I can smell it on both of you. Get a fucking room!" He laughed again and he made his way over to the cart, drinking straight from the bottle.

"Really? And judging by my sister's scent all over you...I'd say you were with her last night as well," I retorted.

Calix's eyes widened and Kadeyan chuckled.

"I told you she would find out," Kade said.

I shook my head, glancing back down at the book as the unease lingered. "Where is Evren?" I asked, flipping to the next page and thinking about the last time I saw her... What I did.

Levanna moved in, looking at the book before clearing her throat. "She is with Sorin and Dalia in the Ember Lands..."

Kadeyan told me about Dalia last night...and how she was from Gelmyra. She knew that our gods were involved the night I...left. He also talked about how she felt when she came here with the power that was directing her to fight, and I explained that Obsidian was behind that. He could control them on our Lands, but so could I. Which was why when our eyes connected, it was like my power left an imprint on them, wiping away any previous influence.

I couldn't help but wish that I got to the pixies before Eryx...

They would have stopped causing the fae to harm each other. And they would all still be here...

Sahar's words flooded back into my mind, pulling my lips down. "*No ifs. Sometimes it's not for us to understand...*"

I missed her so much... I missed all of them.

I nodded and waited for her eyes to meet mine. "Levanna, I'm so sorry... For what I said, and—" I choked, feeling Eryx, Sahar, Axel, and Nesrin's names lodged in my throat as the guilt washed over me again.

Her eyes softened as she said, "I know... I'm just glad you're back and we didn't lose you too."

"Same here! Dark Davyna is kind of a bitch... No offense, Your Grace," Calix blurted out and it broke the tension surrounding us. "So...find anything new?"

Kadeyan glanced up, and I stood still as his emotions encircled me with opening up to our friends. I swallowed hard, slightly nodding.

He leaned back in his chair before saying, "Well...we know what Davyna is."

Both Levanna's and Calix's eyes darted between us. The tense silence rose, thickening the air until it felt as if I could cut into it.

"What?" Levanna asked after a long minute passed.

"She's a goddess...which means Nyna was too."

The room fell silent again for what felt like an eternity and my mouth went dry as I looked back to Kade.

But then, Calix began laughing. "Get the fuck out of here! You're a god?"

"Yeah, so you might want to stop banging her sister," Kadeyan said, humor tainting his tone. Calix straightened, his whole body going rigid, and I couldn't help but laugh before Levanna joined in.

"Don't worry... I won't hurt you, unless you hurt her, but I would be saying that regardless of what I am." I smiled.

"So, what's the plan?" Calix asked, but I shrugged, looking back to Kadeyan. His eyes were drinking me in, lust filling his gaze.

Stop, I mouthed, and he smiled as he grabbed my mother's journal, flipping to the next page. "Obsidian took the dagger. So, until we can come up with a solid plan to get it back, we need to get all the stones."

"My parents aren't going to just hand it over," Levanna said, crossing her arms over her chest.

"I'm not asking them. They will give it to me the easy way or the hard way. It's their choice."

And I hoped it was the latter because after hearing about them and what they did to her mate—to Kadeyan's brother… They wouldn't be breathing when this was all said and done. Although, I knew it couldn't be by anyone else's hands but theirs because they deserved to get justice for Silas.

Kadeyan's confusion lifted into the air, and I glanced over at him, noticing his eyes were locked on a page in the journal. His demeanor changed almost instantly as his shoulders dropped. "What did you say you saw with Tanith?"

"That she was born in the Mortal Lands and Obsidian took her."

Turning the journal towards me, he pointed to a phrase saying: *the child taken and the one forgotten.*

My brows furrowed. "The child in the vision I saw was dead… not forgotten."

The deafening quiet was clinging to us as we all sat there.

Calix cleared his throat. "Or maybe someone made sure she was forgotten…to them."

I stood up and started pacing the room as my mind spun. About a minute passed before my foot halted mid-step and my eyes widened. Walking over to Calix, I took the bottle from his hand and brought it to my lips.

"Davyna, what is it?" Levanna asked, concern smeared in her tone.

"The child forgotten…another goddess," I said. Kadeyan stood up, his eyes widening as his jaw fell open. "What if that child was my mother?"

CHAPTER 63
DAVYNA

The upper room in the Sky Court temple was as silent as a crypt as everyone stood in place, their eyes scanning over me. The smooth, wooden door pressed against my back as my gaze steadily fell lower with each passing second.

Kadeyan called them all here after we found that portion in my mother's journal, but he also told them about me. It made me nervous, wondering if they would look at me differently now. Or think that I would turn and take the gods' side, since I was one.

I wouldn't; I was never going to side with those monsters.

Evren took a few steps closer to me, her breathing growing heavier, but words failed her.

"It makes sense..." I looked up at the sound of Maeve's voice, taking in her gentle eyes locked on me. "But what doesn't make sense are your ties to Tanith. She was one of the six gods made... And they didn't procreate in the beginning to form us fae, they created us." Confusion marked her face as she tried to understand it.

There was more to this...and something told me deep down that mine and Tanith's paths were more intertwined than I wanted them to be. Was she family? Was she my aunt?

If that baby in the cabin did live, then it explained how I was born because no one else had ever shown this type of power, except my mother... But who were their parents? Who started this line?

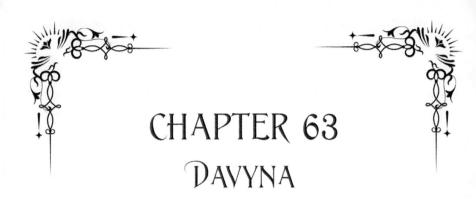

My gaze moved back to Evren, replaying what I did to her the night on the terrace. I remembered every second, while I screamed at the cold demeanor that was choking me out, silencing me back into the corner to watch and convince me that this was the better version of myself. I cried and yelled at myself to stop, but it was pointless, proving how weak I was to fight and control the darkness in that moment. And from the way she was looking at me, I knew she was remembering it too.

"Are you really back?" she asked with a cool tone, her eyes hardening as she stood taller.

"I am..." I took a step closer to her, but she held her ground, the anger in her facial expression not flinching. "Ev—"

She put her hand up, stopping me from apologizing, and the act caused me to recoil. My gaze fell to the floor and a feeling of hollowness filled me.

I deserved that.

"So, how do we figure out if that child was Davyna's mother?" Evren asked.

"From what Nyna implied, I don't think we should be digging any deeper into this," Kadeyan protested, rising from the chair and moving over to my side. His hand slid to the middle of my back, gently swaying his fingers, and it brought a warmth to my chest that I needed right now. "We need to stay on course with what she gave us." Kadeyan looked to Levanna and nodded. "Summon the Court leaders to come here now."

Levanna walked behind the desk and pulled out a paper, silently chanting as the paper began to glow. Black ink appeared on the page, writing her message to the Court leaders, before it vanished into thin air.

"I'll go set up the meeting room with a protection barrier for when they arrive," Maeve said, moving towards me, but she stopped, resting her hand on my arm. I gazed into her eyes, watching them turn a foggy white for a split second. I was pulled into her head and saw flashes of me somewhere, speaking to a crowd.

Smiling, she looked at me with a tender gaze as her eyes returned back to normal. "I'm glad you're back... We are going to need her soon."

She walked away and I watched her, feeling curious as to what that meant... The woman was me, so what was I doing that they needed?

Kadeyan kissed my forehead as everyone began to leave the room, but Evren stood still, her arms crossed tightly over her chest. "I'll give you two a minute," Kadeyan said as he went to the door.

Everything went silent as the door clicked. Evren began pacing as she spat out, "You threw me over a cliff... We lost four of our friends and more fae than I can count right now. Along with wolves you killed for sport." I stood quiet, averting my gaze back at the floor as disgrace coated my flesh. "Why did you do it?"

"Have you ever seen me actually break down before, Ev?" I asked as I slowly lifted my eyes, daring her to look at me.

She remained quiet, with her hands clenched tightly at her sides. She blinked, trying to push away the tears invading them. And my own began to build.

"Have you ever seen me give up before?" My voice broke and her gaze found mine. "I was trying my best to do this alone, to protect everyone...and I was failing. I was angry and I couldn't be the person you knew—the one who held it together while I failed over and over again to fix my mess. Or to hold the weight of the world on my shoulders because I was tired... I was so fucking tired."

Her lip quivered and I took a deep breath before I continued. "It doesn't excuse what I did and—"

"No, it doesn't excuse what you did...to anyone." Her gaze hardened.

We sat there for a long moment as I tried to collect my thoughts, with tears burning my eyes.

"I know it will take time to undo the pain I caused, but I promise I won't become that again...because I realized it was all a lie. You still feel deep within even when you give up. And no dark corner of your mind is safe from the agony life throws at you."

"How can you be so sure you won't shut it off again and do

worse? How am I supposed to watch you become everything Dad taught you not to be?" Her voice cracked, and I wiped my eyes as I nodded.

I walked closer to her, taking her hand. "I am so sorry, Ev." Her lips pressed together, her fury still strong, but faltering slightly. "But I also think I needed to give up. I needed to break so that I could come back and realize I had everything I needed...right here. I had a family who was by my side, ready to fight with me. And I needed to remember exactly what our father taught me: to fight for love."

Her head dropped and several tense minutes passed between us before she met my gaze again. "Are you okay now?" she asked, looking into my eyes.

"No...but I'm okay with that." I started to move towards the door. Stopping, I glanced over my shoulder. "I'll use it to keep me going. To fight with you, and everyone else...if you'll have me."

"I need time, Dy... I need to see it for myself now. But I can promise you this because we are sisters." She paused, her features staying cool. "I'll be by your side fighting those bastards, and if you switch it off again...I'll fight you. This realm means too much to me to see it go up in flames."

I nodded, my gaze falling to the ground as I pulled open the door. Before I could step out of the room, Evren's hand darted out, pulling me back until her arms encased me. I grabbed onto her, tears springing from my eyes as she gripped me tighter.

Pulling back, she wiped the tears from my face. "I love you, Ev. I will do whatever it takes. I'm not going anywhere." I would never forget the things I did, and would hold onto them to drive me away from ever thinking that turning it off was a choice again. I wanted this—a future with everyone in my life—and I wouldn't let that go.

Evren gave me a small smile before heading down to the room, where they were waiting for the other Court leaders to arrive. Instead of following, I decided to walk through the temple.

Getting to the main level, I moved over to the railing and looked down at the floors below, switching between light and darkness.

After a few minutes, a familiar sensation ran through my fingertips, consuming my hands.

Turning, I spotted Faelynn walking up with a small fairy on her shoulder. "Faelynn...hey." The little fairy jumped off her shoulder and smiled at me, the vivid pinks creating a glow around her. "Dalia, right?"

"It's nice to finally meet you, Your Grace," she said. I went to correct her, but Faelynn grabbed my attention by tilting her head, her black eyes widening.

"Davyna...your aura is back to a shimmering white. I'm glad. Come with me." She smiled and Dalia's small wings took off, heading down the staircase. "I wanted to show you something that I meant to give you last time you were here."

With each level we descended, my hands began to burn. The call to whatever was done here pulled me closer with each step.

The staircase continued to turn in on itself, leading further down into the mountain we were on, but we only stopped about seventeen levels down. The floor that was before us was shrouded in darkness and I used my hand to bring flames forth, guiding me to still follow the buzzing in my hands. The small blaze illuminated the books lined against the wall.

"What are we looking for?" I asked.

Turning, her lips tipped up. "Akari was the one who told me about it. She was the one who met you here last time." Stunned, I glanced around before looking into her obscure pools.

"How do you know about that?"

"After meeting you in the Fallen Court, I couldn't shake the feeling that you were so much like your mother.

"Akari knew I was looking into you, and the day you came to the temple, looking at these books, she refused to see Kadeyan because she needed to speak to you in private." She moved a few steps forward to run her hands along the spines.

"Did my mother ever tell you anything else?"

"About being a god? No. But she was pregnant the last time I was with her in the Mortal Realm, and the energy she gave off...

That feeling... I will never forget it, because I feel it right now, only much stronger. Your mother's was muted, and so was yours before you accessed it. I believe that your mother's powers were never fully opened."

"But she was a goddess... How is that possible?"

"Fae can hide magic. Where do you think we got it from? The gods. And I don't think you truly unlocked that side until you burned the throne."

I remembered what I felt in that moment of burning the throne. The anger and fury that unleashed from a deep depth within me as I watched the flames tie around and up above the throne. Then, something within me broke open, pouring out what I thought was more fury... But what if that thing that broke was the remnants of the spell placed on me?

Faelynn cleared her throat. "I think your mother's power was always locked away, and maybe she chose not to unleash it. But I think she had to at some point...and if I had to guess, it was when she was dying; to protect you," she said as Dalia sat down on her shoulder.

My eyes watered, and I blinked them away. "We know Obsidian is the God of Darkness and Tanith is the Goddess of Light, but who are the others?"

Dalia looked up to Faelynn before redirecting her gaze to me. "In Gelmyra, it's Slate, the God of Night, and Amara, the Goddess of Day," Dalia said, brushing her small hands down her pink dress.

"And in Anawyn, it's Bion, the God of Life, and Onyx, the Goddess of Death," Faelynn said. "They were the six that created all the realms."

"Not all of them. There were two who created the gods." Faelynn and Dalia exchanged a puzzled look before glancing back at me. "At least, that's what Obsidian said."

"Hmm. That's strange... Why is that not documented?" Faelynn pondered her thoughts. "Actually, even conceiving a child as a god is unknown to us fae..."

"Maybe the gods wanted us to believe they were the highest

beings," I stated before shaking my head. "And, well, I'm proof they can. So, does that mean that one of your gods could be my..." I stopped myself.

"Yes, I suppose it's possible that they could be your family. But you do favor the Court magic of Valyner... So, what's not to say that your grandparents aren't Obsidian and Tanith?"

My stomach turned at that thought, and I shook my head. It wasn't that. Tanith and I were connected somehow, but not Obsidian and me.

"I think this might help you in finding those answers." Faelynn's hand directed me to the shelf, and I moved closer, reading the titles on the spines.

The Six Gods.

The Realms Beyond.

The New World.

I thought back to that day Akari pulled me out of here... These were the books I touched. Was it a coincidence that I stopped on this floor the last time I was here, looking at the same books? Because being here again, feeling the power in my veins swirl and hum...I knew it was leading me to these three books for some reason.

My jaw fell open slightly and I slowly looked back at them. "Do you know what's in these?"

"No. No one knew they existed but me and Akari," she said. "Your aunt used her power and blood to hide them from others. And only you could see them." I pulled them down as my stomach tightened. Was she in on this too? Did my parents tell her to do this?

"Faelynn..."

"I can sense your heart, Davyna. Even in that state you were locked in. The energy you give off is illuminating, and it will obliterate the darkness. You need only to remember who you are." She moved in, hugging me. My eyes stung as she whispered in my ear, "You are a god. So, let yourself be one."

Pulling away, I readjusted my books and smiled.

Dalia's wings flickered as she flew over to me. "I am at your service whenever you need me, Your Grace. And I do apologize for my part in the loss of your friends."

I looked down, feeling the sting return, but slowly looked up and nodded.

They both began walking up the stairs, and I used the void to pull me back to the main level. My heart was pounding as I looked down at the books, and then I felt it... That looming energy just beyond, and I knew *he* was watching.

When I turned to go upstairs, I was stopped dead in my tracks as I took in Alastair.

"You're back?" he asked.

"Yeah..." I went to move, but his arm grazed mine, sending pure heat through my veins, and I sucked in a breath before dropping the books.

What the hell was that?

We both kneeled, and I picked up two before glancing up to see he was holding the other. "Is there anything I can do to help you?" His smile was soft...sincere. And for the life of me, I couldn't muster the hatred I felt for him right now. Or maybe I just didn't want to let the darkest parts of me have a leg to stand on. Not today. Not after the things I did to his people who were innocent.

"No, I think I can handle it from here on out." We both rose from the ground, and I took the book from him, his skin warm against mine as our fingers touched.

Our eyes locked for a moment, and my power stirred within, sending off a heat that never happened in his presence. I couldn't tell if it was a warning...or a sign from my power that he was truly trying to help me, with no lies veiled behind his honey-brown pools.

Alastair tilted his head up the stairs and smiled. "Kadeyan...it's been too long."

"Forever would be too short," he said back before looking at me. "Everyone's here. Let's go."

CHAPTER 64
DAVYNA

The tension that radiated off Kadeyan was suffocating. Trying to push it aside, I focused on the soft hum of echoes we left behind with each step. My mind was still trying to wrap around what Akari left me, and how Alastair's touch made me feel heat instead of a frigid cold...

I glanced over at Alastair, thinking back to when Obsidian wore Kade's face, and what it felt like when he touched me... This wasn't that. This was the Alastair I knew, but I couldn't get past the looming power I still felt nearby.

Reaching the second highest level, Kadeyan led me and Alastair down the short hall before opening the door. I stood still, watching Alastair move ahead as I peered up at Kade, his eyes narrowing on me as if he was searching for the thoughts still lingering in my mind.

He stepped in, his shadows concealing us, and looked me up and down. "What the fuck was that about? And what are those?" He pointed to the books.

"I don't know. He was being nice, and I figured I didn't need to test my dark power in Valyner yet."

He smiled, shaking his head. "If there is anyone to test it on, it's that dog."

Rolling my eyes, I glanced back at him as he pulled one of the books from my hand as his shadows disintegrated around us.

"It's something Akari left for me, but I can feel the wards she placed on them, and it's hiding the text... So, I'm going to need to undo them after this."

"And what would that be?" Jinx came up behind me, pulling a book from my arms and skimming the pages before I could react. I wanted to lunge at her, to break her nose. Instead, I stilled myself, taking deep breaths to calm the beast within.

"It's none of your concern, Jinx," I spat out.

"Since it's your fault we are in this mess, I think it is." She kept skimming the pages before her face pinched in annoyance. Purple mist began to swirl in her hand, and I yanked the book back, slamming it shut. "What? Don't want to let us in on your secrets now?"

Taking a step forward, I stared into her dark blue eyes, before sizing her up. "I don't have secrets...I have enemies. And if you want to keep this up, you'll be added to the list."

"Are you threatening me?" she asked as Kadeyan moved in, wrapping his hand around my arm.

I laughed softly, moving forward until our noses almost touched. The darkness within swirled up from its depths of my soul. "No. I'm warning you. A threat would be: touch what isn't yours again, and I'll rip your arms from your body."

Jinx swallowed hard and I smirked, feeling the power within sway to death's melody. I pulled it back, willing it to obey my command with a promise that, if the day came, I'd let it help me with her.

"Come on, wouldn't want to get blood all over the books anyway," Kadeyan said as he pulled me to the door, a smile evident on his face. I sensed a privacy barrier encircle us both before he leaned down and whispered in my ear, "Don't you dare kill her without me there. I want to watch."

Glancing up, I took in his roguish grin. I couldn't help but smile as I shook my head, feeling the spell fall away from us.

He moved into the room, and I looked at everyone, realizing we were missing a Court. My heart sank, remembering Eryx's warm blood on my hands, and my heart began to beat against my ribs. I silently chanted a spell on top of Maeve's privacy one, trying to protect this conversation more from listening ears beyond. I could still feel Obsidian nearby, lingering and waiting for his next move.

"I have talked to Alexandrea, and she has declined to take her position as Lady of the Salt Court. She said that whatever is agreed in this room, will be passed along to the people and they will follow our lead," Kadeyan spoke as he took a seat. I moved in, placing the books down on the table. "And now, this is to talk about who attacked Valyner at Saawyn."

"It was her. That's what I was told," Jinx said, leaning back in her chair as she carelessly pointed her finger at me.

"No...it was Obsidian and Tanith," Kadeyan corrected her, and she stood utterly still. Her emotions felt off. Not so much surprised...just off.

"The gods?" Alastair's eyes widened in shock as confusion swirled around him. "Why?"

"They thought I stole the power from them...but I didn't," I said, glancing down.

"What does that mean?" Jinx asked.

Looking to Kade, I hesitated because I didn't know how much information I truly trusted in their hands. "That doesn't matter. What does is that they want something. Maybe my power or more."

"Then why aren't you giving it to them?" she asked, disdain drenching her tone.

"I don't know, Jinx. Would you offer up your power without knowing what exactly they would do with it?" My anger flared up again and I narrowed my eyes. "They have something planned. Something more for not only Valyner but the Realms beyond us, and I won't allow them to do it—whatever it is."

"What do you need from us?" Alastair asked, awaiting his orders. He turned to Kadeyan, shocking even him.

"Davyna's mother left behind a journal and it all points to the stones. We need them all together to stop them," Kadeyan stated, leaning back in his chair.

"That's why you asked if I knew where the Crescent stone was..." Alastair said, leaning forward and placing his elbows on the table.

"You already know where I stand with this," Jinx retorted.

"Even if it can save this realm?" I asked, burrowing my gaze into her.

"I'm sorry. We are supposed to give up a powerful relic of each of our Courts to give to you...so you can fuck up another thing?" She stood, and without warning, my shadows slashed out, circling around me and awaiting their orders.

"Davyna, I think I have an idea," Alastair stated.

I looked at him. "What?" I asked with a harsher tone than what was probably necessary.

"What if we use all the stones as a channel to block them from coming here, and then repair the tear in the realm?" He looked over at Maeve and she sat forward. "Would that work? It would keep them out, and then Davyna could have the time to work on it without them trying to do whatever it is that they have planned."

Kadeyan looked to Maeve, who cleared her throat. She averted her gaze to me as she said, "Yes, I don't see why not. They gave the stones to the Untouched fae, so they're linked to them in some way... And with Davyna's blood, I think it could amplify the spell enough to keep them out, among other things. It just depends on the spell trying to be performed with that magnitude of power."

"How did you come up with that?" Kadeyan asked Alastair, his eyes coated in suspicion.

"My dad had an old Crystal Court book that belonged to Persephone. I told you about it many times, but no one seemed to give a shit. She wanted to do something similar with the stones, but not to help anyone... It was only to make her stronger." He turned and looked at me. "I could show you."

"No!" Kade stood up. "You always have to make this about her going back to you. To that fucking Court."

"It's not about that, Kadeyan. I'm trying to help her! I want to help!"

"Helping her would be searching for the stone from your Court! That's it!" Kadeyan yelled.

They both got lost in a yelling match as I looked over at Maeve. Her eyes spoke truth that I didn't want, but I knew it too. I needed that book; I needed to see what Persephone was up to. She studied the gods more than most and wanted to be like them. And whatever I didn't get from the books that Akari left me...I could get from Persephone.

"I'll do it. I'll come before the next full moon happens," I said over their shouting.

"Davyna!" Kade turned, his anger shooting out towards me.

"No. We are all here for the good of the realm, right? Then we need everyone on board," I commanded, the authority tying into each word. "Jinx?"

She huffed before looking at me. "No. Do it without ours."

"What is your problem?" I asked, but then I sensed her wrath bubble to the surface, and she slowly narrowed her eyes.

"Everything you touch turns to ash...and you know it. What would make this time any different?" She disappeared and it was like a bolt of lightning shot through my body, bringing the demons back out to play in the storm brewing within.

"I'll see you soon then, Davyna," Alastair said as he rose from the chair and I took a deep breath, pressing them back down into the darkest depths of myself. I nodded, watching him vanish before our eyes, and I could tell Kadeyan was pissed.

"I'll take these books back to my office," Maeve said and picked up Akari's books before walking towards the door. "And, Davyna, Persephone's book holds something. I don't know what...but I know you need it." As she spoke, her eyes were cloudy before returning to normal.

I nodded. "I'll get it, but first, let's deal with those," I stated, but before I could even make it a foot away from Kadeyan, his shadows lunged out.

The door slammed shut and my body was pushed through the air, slamming into the solid stone wall. "What the— What are you doing?"

"I've been hard since you threatened Jinx...but I also noticed you pushing closer to that edge, Dearest... Do you need another lesson?"

I smiled and glanced away from him, but his hand gripped my face, turning me back. His lips brushed mine, making my center throb as his teeth sunk into my bottom lip, drawing blood.

Pulling my head back, I licked my lip and felt the power within swirl together. "You have ten minutes."

He laughed as he moved his hands to my leather jacket, ripping it open. "Then let's not waste another second."

Air was barely filling my lungs as I chanted over the three books before me. We had been in this room for hours as I carefully undid spells upon spells that were placed on these books. Akari left nothing to chance, and no one could help because the magic was stronger… I had a feeling my mother gave her something to ward them past the abilities of any Sky or Crystal fae.

As I got to the last line of the spell, a beaming white light seared from all three books. Everyone else shielded their eyes at the sight, but I couldn't turn away, getting lost in the beauty as it danced across my skin.

It caused my scars to reflect the shades of the Court more vibrantly. For the first time, I didn't view them as a horrid reminder of what Tanith left me with, but as a story of strength. We were all scared in some way. Whether internal or external, they told our stories. Our battles… And if we were still breathing, then it showed we didn't let it consume us. They were a reminder of strength. A reminder that we were healing.

As the light began to fade, I pulled one closer to me and read the spine. *The Realms Beyond.* I flipped to the front page and began reading.

The three fae realms were created by the gods on the same day, using the

My brows furrowed. Why was that one sentence cut short? It was like the person who wrote this didn't want to write it down or forgot to. I flipped through a few pages that explained each Court in our realm before landing on Gelmyra.

Gelmyra was created by Slate, the God of Night, and Amara, the Goddess of Day. Their fae possessed different abilities from the

The Court names are as follows: Glint; Alter; Soyl; Pixi; Frost; and Rayn.

I flipped the page, seeing their different abilities. But again, I was confused as to why it was missing a piece in the text.

Anawyn was created by Bion, the God of Life, and Onyx, the Goddess of Death. Their fae also held different abilities from the

The Court names are as follows: Hollow; Scaled; Soul; Sage; Vine; and Phantom.

"This is weird," I stated, turning the pages again before glancing up at my friends. "Some information is missing in this one."

Kadeyan moved in, taking the book. "What do you mean?" His brows furrowed and I grabbed the next book: *The Six Gods.*

The ______ created them all, giving them the certain power that was origin to

"This one is doing the same thing," I stated.

Levanna pulled it towards her, taking in the missing words. "It's like portions have been erased."

The truth was, Tanith and Obsidian wanted the other Realms divided. Because their equals didn't all agree with their plans to

The page went blank, and I stared at it, willing it to tell me what they were going to do. But it wasn't there.

Shaking my head, I couldn't understand why Akari would want me to only have part of the story? If she hid these books for only me to find, then it had to be in there, right? What should have been a victory turned into a defeat, causing anger to bubble up. We needed to know their plans, and the information was in here... So, what happened?

My palms began to sweat and anxiety bloomed in my core. "What the fuck is happening?" I spat out, looking at Maeve.

Levanna grabbed the last book about *The New World* and slowly looked at me after fanning through the pages.

"What?" I asked.

"It's all empty… Except for the last page," she said softly.

I walked over and she handed it to me.

There are two paths. Which one unfolds is in the hands of the gods now.

"No… This was supposed to help us!" The tears filled my eyes. "Who did this?"

"Davyna, those books have been here for over twenty years. Someone could have removed things," Levanna said.

"No, Akari hid them. I was the only one who could see them on the shelf." I tossed it across the room, before running my fingers through my hair. Turning back, I caught a glimpse of myself in a small mirror on the shelf. Seeing my eyes lined with tears, I turned away.

"Who took you to them?" Kadeyan asked.

"Faelynn and Dalia." Just as I spoke their names, they appeared next to me. "What the hell is this?" I asked her, picking up a book and handing it over to her.

"What's wrong?" Faelynn asked, concern laced into her sweet voice.

"It's missing everything that was supposed to help us…to stop all this."

She ran her hand over the page, and a tear ran down my cheek. I turned my gaze away from everyone, but Kadeyan was there. His eyes softened and he moved in, pulling me to him before averting his gaze to Faelynn.

"Davyna, the books were altered… There is a stain of magic on them… Much like yours."

I pulled back, looking at her before moving forward to take it. Focusing on it, I realized she was right. How the hell did I miss that?

"What does that mean?" Evren asked, sitting down in a chair as Sorin and Calix watched her intently.

Faelynn thought for a long moment, while Dalia flew over, landing on the book.

"You said your gods could take yours and Kade's faces… That is a power from one of the Courts of my realm. We call it Mïl veserii... Skin walking," Faelynn said, her voice growing softer. "How are they able to do it? Unless the gods are all connected in some way," she spoke to herself, but I hung on every word before she moved her gloomy pools to me. "It's possible they took another's to fool you."

"No, I would have..." The realization dawned on me, stealing my voice. I did feel something downstairs and in the meeting with the Lords and Ladies. It felt far away...not that close to me. "No..." I shook my head, before walking over to the other chair to sit down. A sob broke through, and I knew their eyes were on me, but no one dared to speak... Just waited to see what I would do.

I wanted to scream; I wanted blood...

The power within twisted together, boiling the blood in my veins with one thing in mind: revenge. I took a few long breaths, but the feeling remained. I was sick and tired of their games, and I wasn't going to stop until they both were in that fucking Abyss.

I ran through every conversation Obsidian and I had... And then, it hit me. He had people here helping them, watching us—watching me.

"So, how do we fix it?" Evren asked, standing up and looking us over.

"It could take time, and it's possible that only Davyna's magic can reverse it... But there is a good chance they made sure it was erased entirely," Maeve stated.

"And if they were in the room with us today, they know we need the stones," Kadeyan said, making my stomach drop.

"No, they already knew that. And it wasn't them, only *someone* who is working with them..." I stood up, balling my hands into fists at my side. "It was Jinx."

CHAPTER 65
KADEYAN

My eyes slowly opened, seeing the early morning sky still painted in darkness. I needed to get up and find Calix. We were going to visit Alexandrea today to help her find the Salt stone, while Maeve got more members for the Sky Court to help break her mother's wards. Davyna offered to help yesterday when we were there, but her cousin didn't want to add to her stress.

At the sound of pages flipping, I rolled over and saw Davyna sitting in the chair, wearing nothing but my black tunic. Her eyes slowly scanned over the words from her mother's journal. I couldn't help but smile at how determined she looked to solve the puzzle laid out before her.

I laughed softly and she looked up, sitting forward. "Did I wake you?"

"No." I smiled as I sat up, patting the space next to me. "Come here. Tell me what's on your mind."

She slowly pushed herself up from the seat, exposing her bare legs, and my eyes drank her in. Climbing over me, she laid down and rested her head against my chest with the book in her hand.

"I think Jinx is working with them," she stated.

"I wouldn't put it past her, but why are you so sure it isn't Alastair?"

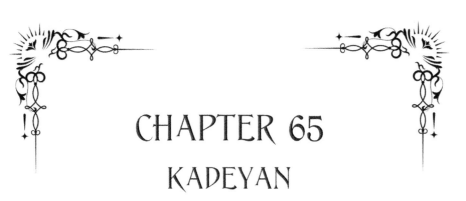

"Call it intuition. I've felt for his emotions every time I've been around him, and I don't think he is lying. I think he regrets what he did to me. I don't trust him...not like I did before all this. But I'm trying to give him a chance to make it right. Don't we all deserve second chances?"

Fuck. This little Ember and her heart... It made me wonder if I had one to show grace to people I hated. I grinned because I already knew that answer.

"And Obsidian said he had eyes on me. I think Levanna's parents could be involved, too, with how close they are to Jinx."

"So, let's kill them. Problem solved," I retorted.

"I know Jax and Verena need to die, but it is up to you and Levanna on the how. Jinx, on the other hand...I'm going to wait and watch what she does next. Then, I'll take care of her myself. I won't spill innocent blood...not anymore. Not even hers if I'm wrong."

She stood silent for a long moment before opening the book again and studying the page she was on. "Look at this."

Taking the journal from her, I brought it closer and read it out loud. "La etsa beluiva di tus el notaches." I arched a brow and tried to place the language, but it wasn't our ancient one. Which led me to believe that this was higher magic—beyond us. Glancing at her eyes, I took in her gaze burning into each letter. "What is it?"

"That's the thing, I have no idea. I think it has to do with binding the stones, but it's incomplete and nothing else ties to it in this journal."

"Why don't you take a break and come with me to the Salt Court?"

She looked up at me, her silver pools growing heavy. "I...I think I want to stay here today. Work on this and come up with a plan."

"Dy, I think it would be good for you to come..."

She shook her head, and I pulled her in, kissing the top of her head. My grief rose from within, and I did my best to push it down, but the reality of walking their Lands and not seeing them...

It was haunting.

"What if they all hate me?" she asked, sitting up.

"Correct me if I'm wrong, but you did call yourself a goddess recently—embracing who you are. And not everyone loves them. But you, Davyna, are something that is truly impossible to hate. I tried in the beginning, and look how that turned out." Bringing my hand up to her face, I brushed my thumb over her cheek before letting it trail down to her bottom lip.

A knock at the door broke our gazes from one another, and I already knew who it was. "Hey, you ready?" Calix called through the door.

I looked over to Davyna as she wiped her eyes. "Are you?"

Using her power, she changed us into black leathers and swallowed hard. "No...but let's go anyway."

Walking the Lands felt eerie. Listening beyond, I could barely pick up on the voices in town. The Court was still in mourning, not only for the friends and loved ones they lost but for losing their Lord and Lady. That would be a void no one in this land could fill.

Calix walked ahead of me and Davyna as we slowly approached where the castle used to stand. Her eyes stood fixated on the ground, where the battle took place, almost as if she was replaying it in her mind.

Grabbing her hand, I pulled her closer as we stopped along the rocky cliff overlooking the sea beyond with a part of the castle still peeking through the surface. The waves crashed against it and Davyna slowly pulled away, walking in a trance as she moved along the cliff.

Calix pulled me aside and whispered, "So, you two seem to be in a better place."

"Yeah, we are, but I hope this doesn't push her away from me."

"No. I think she needed it," he said, but his smile faltered. "Can you still not feel her?"

"No...but I don't care about that anymore."

Calix smiled as he looked at me. "So, how are we supposed to find this stone?"

Boots scraped against the ground, and both of us turned to see

Alexandrea walking towards us. "I am sorry for my delay. Hello, Lord Kadeyan, General." Calix bowed his head and I followed. "If you wouldn't mind, Calix, I'd like to speak to Kadeyan alone."

Calix looked at me before giving her a gentle smile. "Of course. I'll go check on Dy." He used the gap, appearing next to Davyna, who was walking down by the rocks near where she unlocked her Salt Court power.

"She's here?"

"Alex..." I said but paused. She took a deep breath, her short black hair getting caught in the breeze as her blue eyes pierced into the sea beyond. "She never—"

"I know. But I served them, and they were my family too."

"I know they were...but she is the only one who can stop what's coming. Obsidian isn't going to rest until he gets what he wants."

"And you think he wants her?" she asked.

"I do. I just don't know why yet."

Her eyes scanned over to Calix and Davyna and mine followed, watching them fall into a conversation.

"Eryx and Sahar loved you, Kadeyan. Respected you. And I will honor them in their death to help in any way I can..." She tilted her head towards Davyna, watching her intently. "Did you know they weren't training Priya to rule this Court? They were teaching her how to fight..."

"Why?"

"I asked, too, but all he said was that his Grandmother Orla said that things were going to change...and we needed to be ready. I think he was talking about all this... About Davyna."

Orla was the Untouched fae of this Court. She died a few years before Davyna was born. And Eryx's father, Alaric, passed when Persephone took over. Did they know Nyna? Did she share something with them?

"I will honor his wish and fight... Even by her side, as our Queen."

Smiling, I looked back at my little Ember. "So will I."

Moving to the rocks where Calix and Davyna were, Alex kept

pace as we came up behind them. Davyna stood on the small platform with her legs submerged in the chilled water, no doubt soaking through her leathers.

When Alex cleared her throat, Davyna turned and my heart broke. Scales shimmered down her cheeks and her eyes were a brighter silver, the slits evident even with the tears invading them.

"Your Grace, we only have a few fae here who can breathe underwater. They have been searching the castle, but it's been unsuccessful," Alex said. Based on her tone, she was doing her best to bury down her emotions and take on the role of the soldier she was.

"Then, maybe I could help," Dy said as I moved forward, stepping into the water. "I'll go now, and please tell the other fae to rest and recover. I won't stop until I find it."

Alex nodded her head before using the gap to fall away.

I lifted my arm to pull Davyna near me. "I don't want you going down there alone," I said.

Davyna gave me a broken smile. "Get in the water and let me try something."

I looked at her with a puzzled expression and she reached her hand out. I couldn't go down there with her. So, what was she trying to do?

Taking her hand, I walked to the edge of the platform where Eryx showed her the power Salt members possessed. The small waves slammed into my shins and I took a deep breath before jumping in. The cool water soaked through my leathers and my feet kicked below in the vast sea as I watched her move to the edge of the platform.

Davyna changed her clothes into a similar suit she wore that day, and the memories came flooding back. When the true siren attacked her, and then sitting by her bed... Gods, I knew I loved her with every fiber of my being that day. But if I was being honest, I loved her from the moment I chose to bring her out of the life she was living under Hera.

She took a deep breath, preparing herself, and then she dove in.

Her body disappeared below the murky water before reemerging a few feet away. I swam over to her, the waves crashing into my face.

She pulled me under, and my eyes shot open to see her in front of me. Her lips touched mine quickly and tingles fell over my body like a waterfall before she pushed away.

"It's okay. You can breathe now."

Taking in a deep breath, I looked around me and noticed a barrier formed in a sphere protecting us and pushing the water away. "How are you doing this?"

"I just merged the two powers of Crystal and Salt together..." She gave me a half smile that didn't make it to her eyes as the barrier began to lower towards the sunken castle.

The stone structure was broken in pieces, sitting on the ground below us. Fish swam by, entering the windows and gaping holes of what used to be my friends' home. And now it belonged to the sea.

It felt like hours passed while being down here. We searched every spot within the castle and the surrounding area, but there was nothing. "Maybe it's gone. Or maybe it was never here, Davyna."

"No, because I can feel it... It's like heat traveling through my body, telling me it's out here."

I smiled as she turned around, continuing to search.

I knew what she meant. I felt it in close proximity to my father's stone and the one she wore around her neck, but it never happened when I wasn't near them. This extraordinary being was something else, and she constantly kept me in awe of who she was.

I pulled her into me, kissing her deeply. "Have I ever told you just how much you amaze me?" The sweetest smile graced her face and I longed to make that permanent. To give her a life where that was her constant state, and I'd make it happen for her if it was the last thing I did.

Turning from me, I felt her body tense in my arms and all my defenses went up. My eyes narrowed on the creature swimming towards us at the same time my heart sank.

A Waar Sairini. *True siren.*

It swam closer to us, its beaming white eyes illuminating the sea around its body. Its mouth opened, letting out a strange sound, and I instinctively pulled Davyna back into me. In all honesty, though, I was in more danger than she was now. And yet, the love I had for her and the bond that I couldn't feel—but knew was there—compelled me to protect her.

"What is it doing?" she asked and I shook my head.

Within a minute, more began to swim up, lining behind the one who stayed unmoving.

Davyna moved forward and I held onto her. "You are not doing what I think you are."

She turned to face me, but her eyes remained glancing to the side. "Kadeyan, it's here," she said and I began to feel it—that power of being near one of the stones. "If I can control the creatures coming into our realm, then maybe I can control the ones that live here too. And if not, I can kill them all. I'm not the same girl who went into the water eight months ago. Well, two months for me... but still. I can do this." She gave me a half smile and rested her hand on mine.

"Fuck, Davyna. Go...and then I'm going to need those lips back on mine."

She pulled away, and my body went frigid, the ice in my veins only growing with the distance as she stepped through the barrier. My shadows within shot around, feeling helpless and angry, but I willed myself to stay still and watch. She swam closer to them, and the first true siren's face tilted, looking her over.

It wasn't attacking her. None of them were.

The one standing before them all swam up to her. It slowly reached out its hand, the bone-like claws concealing something it held within its palm. I moved to the edge of the barrier, and my heartbeat quickened as the creature lowered itself and brought its hand up.

Glancing behind them, I watched the other true sirens bow before turning my gaze back to Davyna. My heart slammed against my ribs as the dark green creature reached out and opened its hand. My eyes locked on the stone within its palm, glistening regardless of the murky water we were submerged in. The beauty of the turquoise shined upon Davyna's face, showcasing a smile laced with shock as she looked back up into its white pools.

She reached out, taking it slowly, and the true siren began to lift its head. Another noise sounded from it, and the others joined in the melody.

They were...chanting.

One by one, they began to leave, and Davyna watched them go before turning to look at me. She pulled the barrier to her, encasing her wet body in the air bubble she created, and I just looked at her.

"See, Dearest, I'm always so fucking amazed by you." As the barrier began its ascent, I pulled her by her waist and crashed my lips down on hers.

CHAPTER 66
DAVYNA

I was back in the throne room as a guttural scream pulled my attention to the shadow looming over a body casted in a blur. Moving in, I tried to steady my breathing as I glanced down at the faces, but they were obscured once again. It was flashing, and I wondered if it would be anyone I knew. My heart tore with each image, feeling the pain grow with an intensity that made it hard to hold back the tears, until my face appeared. The air left my lungs, and I watched as the red blood pooled out, coating my boots in death.

But something felt different. I straightened and wipe the tears from my cheeks.

Turning, I saw the throne room open, leading into a forest with small cabins placed throughout. The same cabins I saw when I was in Tanith's head.

My mother appeared, her sheer blue mist taking on a form before she looked at me with a soft expression. "Come with me..." *she called out, moving into the woods.*

I pushed off the ground, forcing my legs to move as fast as I could. But it felt like I was submerged in water, holding me back from getting to her.

"Mom!" *I screamed, but she didn't turn back.*

I kept pushing myself forward, determined to break free of this hold and get to her. She entered a cabin, and I heard the soft cries of a baby before she reemerged behind Obsidian. She watched him walk into the forest and a tunnel of darkness appeared, swallowing him and the baby whole. Her eyes were filled with sadness before turning back to look at the cabin.

The blonde-haired baby beamed bright in his arms until the darkness consumed them both.

I pushed harder against the current pulling me back and I cried out again, "Mom, please!" *As my foot connected with the ground, it crumbled beneath me, and I fell into a dark abyss.*

My breathing picked up as I looked around, fear washing over me before everything came to a halt. Voices were muffled for a moment before they cleared, and I turned my head to see Obsidian with the small child in his hands... There was also a woman across from him. She was beautiful, with long silver white hair and eyes that matched. And I could tell something about her was kind, gentle...good.

"Obsidian, you are going to ruin us all... *He* will not stand for this." *Chains made of black and white adorned her wrists as she tried pulling against them, but it was no use. They looked like the dagger my mother gave to Kade...the one we lost. Was it neutralizing her power?*

Taking a step forward, I stilled as his laugh sounded off. It chills down my spine, but also something else—Wrath that wanted to silence him for eternity.

"Oh, Tanith... That's exactly what I want," *he stated, smiling wide.*

Tanith?

My mind began to race as I thought about the Tanith I met, and looking at the baby in his arms, I knew that was her. So, who was this other person with the same name?

His power surged out in pure obscurity, laced with fire that matched. The two-toned dagger appeared through the vapor and flames, and plunged into her heart. She cried out in agony, and I turned away, feeling my own stomach twist.

The screams fell away, and I slowly looked back to see Obsidian smiling. The power from Tanith was filtering into the child, shimmering with all the shades of the Courts as it filled her small form.

My mouth dropped, realizing the Tanith he just killed was his mate—one of the original six gods... She was the one that created Valyner with Obsidian, and he killed her to be replaced with a new one. One that he could mold to do his bidding to do what he wanted for this world. Something that was still unknown to me.

Moving closer, I tried to look at the baby as a hand fell onto my shoulder. I jumped and turned to see I was in the woods again. "Mom?"

"You shouldn't have done that," *she said, looking around in fear.* "You shouldn't be in his mind!"

"Who? Obsidian? That was his memory?"

Her eyes burrowed into me, warning me. "He will punish you for this." *Her voice was laced in panic, and my skin crawled.*

"Mom, who was the other baby in the cabin? Was it you? Is Tanith your sister?" *I went to grab her, but she stepped back, shaking her head.* "Who started our line? Please...tell me."

"I can't give you all those answers, Dy. Because if I do, everything will..." *Her eyes filled with pain and I believed her, but it did little to stop the thing inside me from wanting to understand this all.*

"That truth will seal your fate, sweetie. Especially if they are still alive. But the Tanith you know was his replacement to the original goddess. That child had another name long ago. Obsidian made her take it so history would never reveal what he did...what he took. It all started that day—the prophecies, the change in power... This all started because of him."

"I thought there was only one prophecy?" *I questioned, feeling the pull within to demand more, but judging by her face, I knew she wasn't going to tell me that either.*

She tilted her head up, scanning the sky above before reaching out to grab me. "He needs you...and you need to kill him. Then I can tell you everything. I promise."

"But Mom..." *I was lost for words. Before I could try to speak again, she pulled back and pushed out a ball of light that threw me into the never-ending darkness.*

Jumping up, I gasped and looked over Levanna's spell room. My skin was slick with sweat as I tried to catch my breath. I looked at the journal and the Untouched stones laying out before me. I didn't even remember passing out. I was trying to figure out that damn spell she left me, when everything went black.

Picking up the book, I threw it across the room as curses fell from my lips.

The chaos of their story was like a generational curse that was unbreakable, but also, it was my legacy—my duty. The anger started to fizzle out as I looked out the window, tears lining my eyes.

They sacrificed everything for me. Everyone I loved did...and I needed to be worth it. And if that meant I got half-truths for now, I would take it and trust her reasoning. Because I wanted to get to that day where she told me the whole story. I wanted to break this wheel that clearly has been turning since before I was even conceived.

Evren opened the door, and I wiped my eyes before turning to her. "Are you okay? I heard yelling..."

"Kind of," I said.

She moved in, taking a seat on the ground next to me. "What's going on?" she asked, resting her elbows on her knees.

"My mother," I huffed, glancing up at the ceiling. "I'm starting to think she was behind all of this, and my father followed her."

Silence fell between us, and after a few minutes passed, she shifted to sit before me. "Dy...I think they both loved you with everything they were. And they did it together to protect you for as long as they could. Sometimes people are faced with one option, and they need to take it."

I looked up at my little sister, her eyes tenderly connecting with mine.

"Do you think I'm in their position now?"

She laughed, looking out the window. "I may still be pissed at how you handled everything...but yes, I really do. You were right. You have been carrying so much since our dad died, and I'm at fault, too, for expecting you to always be there for me..."

"Ev..."

"No. It's true. When you were gone for those six months, I had to learn how to become this version of me...and I don't regret it. I needed It. Just like I think you need to be exactly where you are right now to stand tall again." Looking back at me, she smiled. Joy blossomed within her, but I still saw the weight in her eyes.

"What is it?"

She shook her head, her eyes looking up for a long moment before glancing back at me. "I want to be with the Crescents... I want to help them. There are only two handfuls left in the Ember Lands, including the ones who were Cursed. But we've lost so many...and I can't shake this feeling that something bad is about to happen inside the Court. And I want..."

"You want to lead..."

She nodded her head in agreement, giving me a weak smile. "Did you ever imagine this would become our lives back in the Mortal Lands?" She laughed.

"Not even a little bit." I pushed myself up and walked over to my mother's journal, picking it up.

"Davyna..." I turned at the sound of her voice and looked at her as she rose from the ground. "I'm glad this is the life we get to live, and I'm proud of you for coming back to who you are."

My heart skipped a beat and my eyes instantly started burning.

"I'm proud of you, too, Ev."

She rushed into my arms, gripping onto my leathers for dear life, and I did the same to hers.

Kadeyan walked in, stalling as he looked us over, and my eyes caught on a note grasped in his hand. "What is that?" I asked. Breaking my embrace with my sister, I walked over to him and took it from his hands. Unfolding it, I read it over twice before looking at Kade.

Princess,

Please join me at the Crescent Estate today. I think you need to know something about what you're searching for.

Katarina.

"Why is Alastair's mother requesting I come to the Crescent Court today? And what is she talking about? Their stone?"

Kadeyan's eyes darkened as he looked at Evren and back to me. "I don't know, but I know her. She wouldn't have sent this without good reason. And something tells me that Alastair doesn't know about it."

Glancing over at Evren, I saw she was reading the note. When she looked at me, her worry for her people spread over her skin.

Moving back over to the Ember, Salt, and Fallen stones, I picked them up and placed them and my mother's journal in a white and black salt circle on the table.

"Three down...three to go," he said, giving me a small grin.

I nodded before placing a protection barrier interlaced with each line of power.

Finishing the spell, I stepped back and steeled my spine. I looked at Evren and Kadeyan, then took a cleansing breath as images of the Crescent Lands and what happened there played within my mind. And ready or not...I was going back there.

"Let's go."

CHAPTER 67

DAVYNA

"I don't like this plan," Kadeyan murmured as he looked at me, then to Sorin and Evren.

We walked through No-Man's-Land, bordering the Crescent's territory, and I looked back at him, remembering the last time we were here. I ran out here, upset about the power I possessed, when the Sentores arrived. I couldn't use my power without alerting Persephone, not that it wanted to come forth anyway. But then... Kade showed up.

Maybe the creatures they had been dealing with had been far worse, but at that point in my life, I was terrified, and he was there. I hated him then, but he was there...

Smiling, I turned back, taking in his stony expression as he scanned the tree line.

"He won't do shit, Kade. Relax," Evren said as she laughed, glancing to Sorin, who smirked. "And if he does, I'll kill him for you."

Shaking my head, I fell back and walked by Kade's side. "I'll be okay."

"I'm not worried about you, Dearest. You could burn this whole Court down. And if you feel the urge, I say, go for it. I just don't trust that he won't try something."

"I know." Stopping, I grabbed his arm. "But we need to follow every lead. Obsidian said we have until the full moon. That's in a week." Lifting onto my toes, I wrapped my arms around his neck and pulled him down until his lips crashed down on mine.

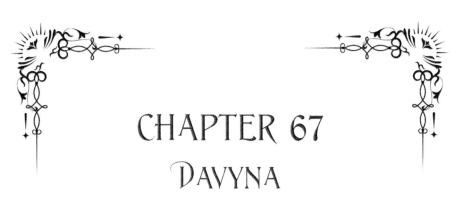

"Come on, lovebirds!" Sorin called out, and I pulled back.

"Any chance you are good with letting this world burn to run away with me?" Kadeyan whispered in my ear.

"No more running, remember?" I glanced up into his amber pools and my heart burned with an intensity that only he could make me feel.

"I know." He looked me up and down, his amber pools shifting into their crimson state.

Pushing him slightly, I walked backwards and gave him a devilish grin. "How about tonight, I make you feel like it's only me and you left in this world?"

He growled under his breath before chuckling and I laughed.

The lighthearted moment quickly ceased as I turned and saw Alastair at the tree line, crossing his arms over his chest with a darkening gaze. Swallowing, I straightened and moved next to Sorin and Evren.

"Why are you all here?" he asked, his voice laced with contempt.

"Your mother invited me."

His honey-brown eyes softened, landing on me. "Well, you are always welcome here, Davyna. But they aren't."

"What? Is the little Lord scared to have me as a guest?" Kadeyan teased.

Alastair's lips twitched as he looked to Kadeyan. "No. I just don't trust *you* with my people," he said before turning his gaze to Sorin. "And you have some balls to show up here, thinking I would allow you back on these Lands."

"Listen. Kadeyan isn't coming. I know he isn't welcome here, but you are going to let Sorin and Evren through," I stated, moving closer to the border. "They are with me, and these are their Lands just as much as they are mine."

He was taken aback by my words, and I sensed him battle with his emotions before running his hands through his red hair.

"Fine, but they stay within the estate at all times under the watch of my guards."

"Deal." I walked over the line and heard Kadeyan clear his throat.

"I'll see you back home, Dearest. Remember, if the urge presents itself, I know a dog deserving of your anger."

Turning, I glanced at him, his wicked grin growing as he winked. Black vapor swallowed him whole, and I could feel Alastair's subtle rage as I passed him. I forced myself forward, but I could still sense Kadeyan's trepidation reach out through the gap, clinging to me.

It would be okay... I'd get what I needed and leave.

We all walked in silence for a few minutes before the back of the estate came into view through the dense forest covering the grounds. Keeping my eyes forward, I focused on the patio until I was climbing the stone stairs. Alastair moved ahead of me, and my gaze shifted over to the greenhouse. I fell into the memories of the last time I was here, how I was willing to give up everything and fall into his words.

Alastair opened the door to the patio, and my stomach turned as I pulled my eyes back to the parlor laid out before me. I steeled my spine and stepped into the estate. It was just as it was the last time I stepped in here, with rich woods laced in soft paints and art adorning the walls. I paused, taking it all in again as he walked up, standing by my side.

"Princess!" Katarina called out as she entered the small living room. "It's a pleasure to see you again."

Sorin and Evren moved through the room and two guards followed after them. Alastair called them over as we got to the back of the property and told them to stay by their sides.

"You didn't tell me you called for Davyna, Mother," he said.

"Well, you told me she was well again, and that she planned on coming anyway. So, I figured it would be nice to go over what you found in your father's books." She waved her hand, beckoning me and Alastair as she began walking. "Come, Princess."

Looking at Alastair, he smiled at me and placed his arm out. "Ladies first."

Something felt off as I began walking, and I sensed it was coming from Katarina. Thinking back to Saawyn, I didn't care that she was acting peculiar, but now, it made me wonder what was going on. Burying it down, I moved forward, following after her as Alastair stayed a few steps behind me, with Evren and Sorin in his wake.

With my eyes straight, I made my way down the hall, feeling my chest rise and fall to accommodate for my racing heart. "You don't need to be nervous here, Davyna. You never had to be nervous."

"You sure about that?" I looked at him, feeling the sting of the lies surge, but I tried to push them aside. "Why did you want me here so badly?"

"Like I told you, I found something that I thought you should see. I'm not the bad guy here...just a guy who did some bad things and is trying to make you see I'm sorry. Please, at least consider that when you look at me. I don't think I can live an eternity knowing you hate me." His voice was broken, and his emotions matched it once again.

Was I in any position to be the judge here after the things I did?

Katarina turned around, almost as if she was listening in, and I couldn't help but notice the look on her face. She was nervous about something...

We moved into the study and Alastair stopped at the door. "Dansel, would you show the other guests to the dining room? They can wait there." I turned, catching a glimpse of my sister's face before the door closed and everything good and evil shot to the surface.

"If they touch them..." I growled.

"Nonsense. Alastair will not allow your friends to be harmed, Princess. I promise you that." She smiled, and Alastair bowed his head. As I turned around, my rage amplified when I saw Jinx sat behind the desk, grinning at me.

"What is she doing here?" I spat out.

"Helping my friend." She looked towards Alastair before standing up from her chair.

"Would you two mind giving me the room with Davyna for a moment? Alastair, you can collect the things you need and bring them to the library. It's such a lovely day, and the light in there will be better for reading," Katarina said as she stood tall, her green eyes beaming.

"Of course, Mother," Alastair said.

Jinx walked through the office, slamming her shoulder into mine as she walked by, and a rush of power rose up within. Like the stain of magic on the books from Akari, I felt it all over her.

Turning, I watched her walk out as Alastair picked up the books on a table nearby before smiling at me. The door slowly clicked shut and I took a step forward, digging my nails into my palms.

It was *her.* She was working with them...and that just signed her death warrant.

Darkness within urged me to go after her, but Katarina turned me around and waved her hand to place a protection barrier over us. She grabbed my arms, her eyes locked on mine. "Please, Davyna. We don't have much time."

I took a few deep breaths, studying her distressed expression. "What is going on?"

"Your parents did everything to hide you... There is nothing like a parent's love to protect their child."

I pulled back and sensed her fear circling me. "Why did you want me to come today?"

"I found this in Keres' safe. I am the only one who knew where it was. I tried to help your father to make that fucker pay for all he did to me... And what he did to our daughter..." Her voice trailed off, her eyes holding such horror, it made my stomach turn.

"What did he do to you?" I asked with hesitation.

"Keres was a vile creature and creative with how to torture me. He knew I was trying to bring him down with Persephone. I could take the beatings...but watching it happen to your daughter and being helpless to stop it... Our time in Hell with the other fae hiding from Persephone was paradise. But I never stopped thinking about this." She pulled a small paper out of her pocket and handed it over.

Keres,

The gods are growing impatient. You need to bring what we talked about. And please try not to disappoint me again, my love. Our makers are counting on us to make this world right.

Persephone

My eyes slowly looked up. "What is this?" I asked, feeling my voice shake.

"Persephone was on their side, and your father knew it," she said in a hushed tone.

"What did they have planned?"

"I'm not sure, but I'd say it had to be horrid enough for them to never write it down."

"How is that supposed to help me though? Persephone is dead. I locked her away in an endless void when I killed her." I shook my head, looking into her beaming green eyes that were glancing towards the door.

"They had a close circle of people in the Crystal Court—Jax and Verena, and I believe Jinx is now involved, too—to carry out what she started. I just don't know how they got to Jinx. She was never like this in all the years I knew her. She hated Persephone for taking her little sister, Nyx."

Or maybe it was all an act?

"Davyna, the fae here working with the gods won't give you what you need to stop what they have planned. But if you locked Persephone away…isn't there a way with your power that you could––"

The doorknob turned, and I sent flames to devour the paper in my hand as I looked back. I broke through Katarina's privacy spell, feeling it evaporate around us as I took in Alastair standing in the doorway.

He looked at the both of us over and tried to assess the obvious tension in the room. "Are you ready?"

I nodded. Moving forward, I felt Katarina's eyes burning into me, but I didn't turn back. Walking down the hall, my skin prickled as I neared the library with Alastair, wondering if there were more fae on their side. Were the people set out to kill me under Obsidian's orders? But why would they be when he could do it himself? There was something else—something that would make sense of all of this.

Was Persephone the key to figuring all this out?

He opened the door and I moved in. My mind was so fogged over with everything rushing through it that I barely noticed the three levels of books around me.

What was I missing here? Obsidian hated Zaryk for turning his back on his own brother and favoring humans over the gods they made. He killed his mate and took a child, making her into what he wanted. But it all had to be for a reason... What did this new Tanith possess that helped him in his fight against Zaryk? Or was he fighting for the brother who was locked in the Abyss? I felt like I was falling into my own personal Hell right now, still wondering why I was at the center of it.

"Davyna?" Alastair asked with concern laced into his tone. I turned around, looking at him as he opened an old book on the table. "Are you okay? Did my mother—"

"No. We were talking about my father, and it just brought a lot back. I'm fine." His eyes softened and he sat down, gesturing for me to join him. "Do you know where the Crescent stone is?" I asked, stepping closer to him and crossing my arms over my chest.

"I've never seen it. My father tried searching for it when he started his rule over our Lands, but he never found it. Elias must have hid it, but I promise I'll help you find it."

Looking over the books, I sat down and studied the entries.

"What do you know about Elias' death?" My heart raced, unsure why I was asking the question, but something within me pushed, like it was another factor in this crazy world I fell into. Elias must have known all this, too, or why hide the stone?

"Nothing really. I just know he was killed. Why?"

"Did you know wolves did it? I was there...and killed one who turned back into a human," I said, watching it unfold in my mind as if it was yesterday. It still scarred me with the horrors I'd carry until my dying day.

"I'm so sorry, Dav—"

"The one I killed was Cursed because a normal blade killed him. But were the Crescents in on it?" I asked, feeling my darkness creep up within, flowing into my veins. "Did Persephone give the orders? Or did you?"

"Davyna, I swear to you, I knew nothing about his death. But knowing Persephone...I wouldn't doubt it." His head fell, and I could see the shame he was carrying, but it did little to sway my emotions. "I know my father wanted him dead... He viewed him as a threat to his rule over the Crescents.

"I looked up to my father for so long, wanting to be just like him. But now...I hate him for what he did to our family. For betraying our people. He was a monster."

"He was," I spat out, feeling the sting from my words hit him like a dagger to the heart. I took a deep breath and rested back in my seat. Waiting for my power to calm down, I glanced at him. "I'm sorry... That wasn't fair."

"No, you have every right to say that. He broke your family and mine."

We fell into silence, and I pulled the book forward, reading Persephone's notes on the gods. Obsidian and Tanith were listed first, but after that, only a few other names were written. Ones I already knew from talking to Dalia and Faelynn, along with the book Akari left for me.

Skipping down the page, I stopped.

Together, the brothers created the six gods with the stones. And if it wasn't for what Obsidian did—convincing the gods to leave Zaryk's realm—the fae would have never come to be. Being human was a vile experience, but being fae...now that is extraordinary. But becoming a god...that's what I want. And if I get all the stones, maybe Obsidian will change me, let me rule by his side.

The stones created the six gods...because of the brothers. That was missing from the books Akari left... I thought back to a journal entry from my mother where she said: *History lied to us.*

The stones weren't made for the fae of Valyner...they were taken. So, were the fae made with the stones? Was that why we needed all of them to break the links?

It made sense.

Flipping through the pages, I scanned over her words, which felt more like a journal entry of rants and drama in the Courts. Then, I saw something about my father.

Ezekiel has something powerful—more powerful than the both of us put together—and she took him from me. She took my King...my mate. And I hate her for it. I deserve the power, the glory. I've been serving the gods since he met her, and he doesn't know what I'm capable of now. And I won't stop until I take everything from him. Until I put his own child in the ground and draw on her power to bring the gods here. Then, I'll give them back the stones so we can change this world. He can either join me or die.

Looking up, I glanced at Alastair and my brows furrowed. "Did she know what I was?" I asked.

"What do you mean?" There was a confused look on his face, and I bit the inside of my cheek. He didn't know what I truly was, and I needed to keep it that way. "That you contained all Court magic? I mean, it seemed that way."

What are you? She asked me that before I took her life. Maybe she figured it out at the end...

Alastair flipped the page of his book, before meeting my gaze and continuing. "All I know is that Persephone studied higher power for over a thousand years. She wanted it to be hers."

"Do you think the gods drove her mad?"

"No, I think she did that to herself and got lost in her own power. The gods wouldn't have let her keep your magic even if she was successful. They would have killed her."

"Then why haven't they killed me?" I inquired.

His face fell to the book. "That's what worries me. Not only for you...but what will become of Valyner if they get what they want in whatever comes next."

A small smile pulled at my lips and his gaze slowly turned up, meeting my own. "Then we don't give them the chance."

CHAPTER 68
DAVYNA

Over the next two hours, Alastair and I talked through different theories and read through more of Persephone's outrageous entries, which made my head hurt. He started walking around the library, gazing up at the dome as I skimmed through the last book. It contained spells, but one was unlike anything in this realm. It called out in my blood, and I remembered how it felt to be near someone using it.

It was the spell for skin walking.

Did she figure out how they did it? Was she trying to achieve this magic? I read it over a few times, memorizing the dialogue, when the doors swung open, revealing my sister.

"Your guard touched me, so I broke his fucking nose," Evren spat out as Sorin laughed, placing his hand on the small of her back.

"That's my girl," he whispered low enough to not be heard, but it was crystal clear to me.

"Excuse me?" Alistair said as he moved towards them.

I did my best to hide my smile. *Good job, Ev.* As I turned to the back of the book, their voices carried off, transforming into hums as I looked at what it said.

The child born to light and darkness will fail them. It will fall on the lost child to restore the rightful power to whom it belongs to. For if not, the one who holds light and darkness will rain fire and turn the Realms to ash.

"I don't give a fuck who you are!" Evren shouted, pulling me out of my trance.

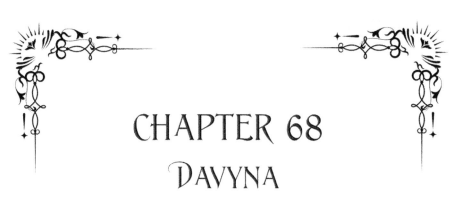

I stood up and started walking towards the door, ignoring them all as I made my way down the hall of the estate. Ringing blared in my ears, drowning out anything and anyone around me like I was under water.

Two paths...two prophecies, and I would either rise above it or fall. The nightmare flashed in my mind, showing the throne room with the bodies cast in a blur, and my face void of life at the end. It was going to happen. I kept seeing it play out and my seer ability was trying to tell me something. I wanted nothing more than to protect my friends and this realm, but was this inevitable?

I couldn't guarantee there wouldn't be more casualties in this war with the gods, and it shredded my heart to pieces...

Pushing the glass doors open to the back of the property, I walked aimlessly towards the greenhouse and barely felt the cool breeze whip past me. Everything within was blazing, making my own skin feel sticky and irritated.

"Davyna? What's wrong?" Alastair called out and I pulled the greenhouse door open, taking in the overgrown plants lining the walls. The sound of Alastair's boots on the stone neared, before he pulled open the door, but I didn't turn.

"What prophecy was that in Persephone's book?" I asked, feeling the fear coat each word. "Who is the lost child?"

"Growing up, my dad used to tell me and Alta about it. I never thought anything of it until...all of this started happening."

"My mother left me with another one." I turned around.

"What was it?" he asked, moving towards me as I took a deep breath.

"When the flames sit upon the throne...light and darkness will rage war until one stands between, able to control both." I took another breath, shorter this time as I looked into his eyes. "But loss will be their friend, betrayal will be their follower, and love will be their fight. The walls will fall, merging something new."

My mind got stuck on the second part, realizing loss was my friend in all of this. How many people were gone because of what I was, what I did? Betrayal was my follower because I felt betrayed by my parents, by my power, and people in this realm... And love being my fight was why I was here today, fighting to make sure I wouldn't lose anyone else, and that this world could be free and live in peace.

What did the prophecy mean with creating something new? How was I capable of doing that? And how could I make sure that happened over the other path laid out before me—the one where I failed them...and this world burned.

He smiled. "Davyna, why does it matter if two crazy people came up with some prophecy?"

"Because it's real. Alastair, I burned the throne. I have both sides."

"How did she know?" he asked as one of his brows arched.

"Someone told her..." I ran my fingers through my hair. Alastair's hands gently touched both my arms, and a tingling heat passed through my veins.

"Look at me. I might be the biggest fuckup around here, and you have done things with your power that you regret, but you, Davyna Ember...you are good. And you know what you need to do."

"No, I don't. I'm taking a chance here with half the story and hoping I'm right."

He dropped his hands and I pulled back, breathing heavier now.

"Look at me. You know what you have to do." Narrowing my eyes, I looked at him, feeling the craze in my head pounding harder. "I've had a bad habit of underestimating you and what you hold within...but that stops today. We are going to get the stones and finish this. Even if I have to steal the Crystal one. I will do whatever it takes."

"Jinx is working with them."

"I think you're right... I saw her a few weeks ago with someone who looked just like her. At first, I thought it was Nyx, but she passed away a while ago... If I didn't know any better, I'd say it was her twin." He shook his head, and I could sense his own emotions surge. Anger, betrayal, and sorrow. For whatever reason, they were close, and I think he hoped that one of his closest friends wasn't capable of this. "And if that's how they appeared to you..."

"Why didn't you tell me this?"

"You were...not really here."

I dropped my head and my blood began to boil as Alastair pulled a white flower that looked like a rose from one of the beds, twisting it between his fingers, before looking at me.

"I'm going to stop her. I have a plan to get the stone. She will trust me, Davyna. And I promise this to you..." He took a deep breath and looked down at the flower before glancing up to meet my face again. "I will follow you as a friend, as the protector I should have been, and your loyal subject for as long as you'll have me." Kneeling down, he dropped his head. "My Court is yours and your enemies are mine. I choose you, Your Grace."

"I'm not the Queen..."

Offering me the flower, he smiled. "You've always been the Queen. And I'm sorry it took me this long to see it."

I saw the person I once knew, before the lies and deception stripped that version of him from me. And the lingering anger towards him faded, being replaced with...forgiveness?

We all did horrific things, but it didn't make us horrific people.

Lifting my hand, I went to grab the flower when the smell of something familiar invaded my nostrils... It reminded me of the tea he gave me before the binding spell. Was this the plant he used? I thought he only grew poisonous plants.

My hand grazed the stem and ice shot through my veins as a massive shadow flew over us, obscuring the light beaming through the forest surrounding us. When I looked up, the world slowed and my stomach dropped.

I ran out of the greenhouse just in time to see its jaws open wide...

And fire began to rain down.

CHAPTER 69
DAVYNA

Part of the estate crumbled like it was nothing but sand as fire continued to rain down from the beast's mouth above. Alastair jumped up, his fear coating my own skin as we took in the destruction unfolding before our eyes.

Evren... Sorin.

I took off towards the estate as other fae began running outside, their cries of horror traveling into the air. Looking off to the left, I saw fae drop to the ground. Some of them were burned, bleeding, and completely disoriented.

Alastair grabbed me, pulling me back.

"I need to get my sister!"

Another beast covered in scales flew over us, its wings spread wide as it let out an ear-piercing roar. It soared through the sky, blazing a trail towards the town beyond the woods, and more screams lifted into the air.

Pulling my arm free, I started running towards it and heard Alastair keep pace behind me. These creatures were huge, even larger with wings spread out, and the fire pouring from their mouths... The Crescents couldn't fight this; they weren't equipped to.

Getting to the front of the estate, where the trees were nonexistent, I took in the beast hovered in the air. Its large mouth opened and showed off its sharp teeth as the back of its throat began to glow.

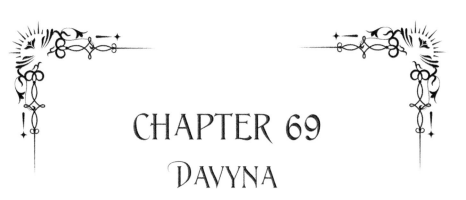

Throwing my hands up, I sent out everything within as fire spewed from its jaws. A shield of light infused with the shimmering hues of the Courts took the force of its blow, and I let out a yell. Its blaze was strong, pushing me back, with my boots ripping up the grass as I did my best to hold my ground.

"Get them all out of here! NOW!" I screamed at Alastair, and he began yelling to his guards, who were running in a daze. The other winged creature landed next to me, its growl shaking the ground as it released fire across the lawn and the north side of the estate. Fire blazed around me, making my skin raise, and I turned to see fae engulfed in flames before they fell to the ground.

The beast looked at me, digging its large claws into the grass as it opened its jaw wide. Flames shot out again, barreling towards me, and I felt my heart pause in my chest. Rolling to the ground, I yelled, placed my hands out, and hit it on its side with black flames.

You are both, Davyna, but hold onto who you *are,* Kadeyan told me that over and over when he was helping me control the darkness... And I needed to hold onto not only my power, but who I wanted to be using it.

I pulled for everything good and evil within, and then pushed myself off the ground. I sent more onyx flames out, flying through the air with vengeance as it hit the beast in the chest, and it cried out. Turning, it looked at me, the slits in its eyes beaming a bright orange.

Smiling, I faced it as it lunged forward, its jaws just barely missing me. Its skin around its jaws lifted, showing me its sharp teeth as a growl worked its way up its throat.

"You will obey!" I yelled, standing my ground as the darkness spread through me. Turning its head again, its eyes locked with mine and it stopped, pulling its wings in.

It slowly lowered itself and my breathing picked up, the adrenaline spiking in my veins.

A roar to the east caused me to turn and see the other one was coming closer, hell-bent on destroying more. Raising my hand, I sent out a blazing light and turned. It shot through the air like a lightning bolt, entering its chest and letting out a shrieking scream. Its wings tucked in, curling in on itself as it fell out of the air.

Its large body shook the ground as it collided with it and went limp, sliding until it stopped just before me. I looked into its icy blue eyes as they glassed over, while it let out its final breath.

Turning back to the other one, I said, "You will stay here and not harm anyone else."

It bowed its head again, lowering its body as I took a deep breath and pulled the surging energy within back to its hiding place. The cries overtook the land, and I looked over the ruins before me. The estate was cut in half by their fire, completely exposed to the elements with the roof caving in on both ends. And then, it hit: the panic because I needed to find my sister and Sorin.

Running, I got to where the front door used to be and screamed, "Evren!" Sorin!" I looked around, feeling my heart beating against my ribcage. Distant cries fell from people around me, and the screams of the injured made my stomach turn. Was she one of them?

Running through the halls, I noticed the stones blocking my path. Turning, I ran my fingers through my hair as I listened for her voice.

"Da–Davyna," someone said, but it wasn't Evren.

Running towards the study, I stopped before the doors that were blocked by large stones. I used my shadows to move them aside, before burning the remainder of the wood doors.

Scrambling through the debris, I fell to my knees next to Katarina. Looking down at her chest, I saw the gaping hole where her flesh should be, exposing her beating heart that was slowing with each second.

Glancing around us, I noticed the ground was charred and the sky was on display above. She was hit by their flames...

"Help... Help Alta," she said before coughing up blood.

"Mom?" Alastair cried out from behind me as he ran into the

room and slid to his knees. Tears streamed down his face, with his eyes filled to the brim. "Davyna can help you, Mom. Davyna..." He looked at me. "Please."

Moving forward, Katarina shook her head. "Alastair...where's... Alta?" He turned away, showing me his pained expression, and I sank down lower. Alta was gone... "No...my baby," she cried out as her eyes looked up at the sky.

"Katarina, let me help you," I said, but she shook her head.

"I'm here, Mom... I'm right here. Don't leave me again," Alastair cried out, his tears falling to the ground below.

"Alastair..." She coughed again and raised her arm that was void of flesh and muscle, exposing her bones. He leaned in and she whispered. My eyes slowly widened as she spoke and my jaw fell open, while his face was frozen in shock.

"Davyna!" Evren screamed from the hall, and I jumped up.

"I'm right here!" I watched as she ran towards me with Sorin close behind her. My heart settled in my chest as I ran into her arms, sobbing for a moment. "Are you hurt? Are you guys okay?"

"Yeah. We jumped into the gap when we heard the stone crumbling. And we ran back in to get fae out as they were turning around. What were those?"

"I have no idea. Have you guys seen anything like them before?"

"No..." Sorin stated. "Some creatures with wings, yes, but they looked more fae-like. But nothing like that and with fire." Sorin looked outside, seeing the beast sitting there on the front lawn, before looking back at me. "Many are wounded and need help. You're the only one with the power to do it... Some can't wait for us to send word to the Fallens or Crystals to use their power."

I nodded my head before I turned back, realizing there was now only one heartbeat in the study.

Alastair pulled himself off the ground and barely looked at us as he started walking towards the trees beyond. My heart hurt for him right now. Not only because he just lost the last of the family...but because...

Evren gripped my arm, pulling my gaze back to her. "Davyna, come on."

Over an hour passed as I ran from fae to fae, using all the power I had to help heal them, but even after everything, we still lost over a hundred people in the area. Some fae witches showed up to help the people in town, while I focused on the fae here at the estate.

While I healed the burns on the male before me, tears fell from his eyes as the magic coursed through him. He would always have the scars, but he still had his life. After I finished, I stood up, feeling the exhaustion all over from expelling so much. Watching him close his eyes, I focused on his breathing and sighed in relief. It was normal. Sorin gave me a weak smile and I nodded my head, backing away as he took a seat next to him.

Evren moved through the lands where everyone was laid out, offering them water and checking in with smaller children that were clinging to fae next to them. My stomach turned because some of those children just became like me: orphans. And I hoped— No, I'd make sure they had an Elias there... They wouldn't be void of someone to raise and love them, even if their childhood was short. They deserved that.

Walking through the property, I looked at the beast still resting in the grass as its head popped up. "Stay here," I said in a hushed tone and it brought its head back down.

I moved towards the walk path, knowing he was over here. After a few minutes, I made it to the bridge that overlooked the lake below. And Alastair was staring down at it.

"Hey..." I called out, walking a bit slower until I was by his side. The lake shimmered with each Court's color in its iridescent white water. He told me last time we were here that it resembled the gods' powers as a reminder of what it gave them. And now, I knew that was true.

"How many people..." He kept his eyes on the still water, his emotions lost in a haze.

"One hundred ten...but I think they are still counting."

"Thanks for helping them..."

I nodded my head as I looked out. "Alastair..."

"I don't want to talk about it..."

"But you need to..."

He slowly turned his head to look at me, his eyes red from the tears that were still falling. "They lied to me my whole life... And took away my right to know who my mother was."

"I know how that feels." I rested my hand on his forearm. "But you still had good memories with them. Filled with love. Just like I did with Elias."

"I had a right to know." His voice broke as a tear slid down his cheek.

My heart hurt for him. Because the emotions that went through me after learning about my parents...it was unbearable. I was angry and felt rejected...like I wasn't good enough for the people who brought me into this world. I knew exactly what he would go through learning this, and I wouldn't wish it on anyone... Not even him.

"We all have a right to the truths of our lives...and I'm sorry it took over five hundred years for you to get yours." Standing up, I offered my hand to him, and he took it.

Rising, he looked in the direction of his old estate. "I'm going to find her...eventually...and ask why she let Keres take me away." Anger surged in him, and I knew that all too well because it was what led me here to Valyner.

"When this is all said and done, I'll help you." The words falling from my mouth shocked me, but after everything, I knew I meant it.

"Really?" He looked at me with a puzzled expression.

"Yeah... But right now, let's go help our people."

We walked in silence as we approached the ruined estate, but I felt an ease slowly blooming over him. He had hope and that was all we could ever ask for as we went through the journey of life. Hope kept us focused on a better tomorrow. And while it could still be a bitch, it was something I never wanted to lose again.

My skin pebbled, feeling like a thousand needles pricked into me, and I looked around. Every line of power within came alive, and I already knew who was nearby. Stopping, Alastair looked at me with confusion, but I pulled my gaze away from him to see the beast I connected with still laying on the ground.

It wasn't asleep... It was dead.

A laugh sounded off, making my bones feel like they were splintering as Obsidian appeared next to the creature. His true form was on display—the chard skin with fire beaming through the cracks, matching his eyes.

"Such a pity... Dragons were some of my favorite creatures born to the fae in Anawyn...until today. They were obeying the wrong god."

"God?" Alastair asked, but I kept my eyes on Obsidian.

"You said I had until the next full moon."

"Yes, and you still do... But I wanted to motivate you. And you do love to try to save people when you are in this *state*." He walked around me, and my eyes took in Evren who walked towards us but slowed when she noticed who was here.

Leaning down, he whispered in my ear, "And I wanted to punish you..." His deep voice made chills run down my spine. "Did you think you could enter my mind without consequences?" His gaze took in Sorin running up to join Evren before glancing to Alastair by my side.

"Then take it out on me..."

"Mm. So noble... I think I liked you better when you'd laugh at their deaths."

His shadows tainted with black flames crawled out towards Evren, and I grabbed him. Throwing my hand out, I pushed my friends into the gap as his power turned on me. He threw me back, knocking the wind from my lungs, and I rolled through the seared grass, groaning from the pain.

Sitting up, I looked at him as Alastair bent down to help me.

Laughing, Obsidian took in the both of us, shaking his head. "Why aren't you running, wolf? Do you want to die?" Obsidian's power roared to life as I heard the growls from beside me from Alastair shifting into his wolf form to guard my body.

"Alastair, leave!" I yelled, but he glanced back, his yellow eyes beaming just like that night in the woods when he almost took my life, but they were different now. They held a determination to protect me at all costs, and I could sense his emotions coming through before I heard his thoughts: *"I won't let her die... I won't."*

Glancing up, I watched as Obsidian's power shot towards us, and I used my shadows to throw Alastair out of the way.

His power slammed into me again, but I let it in, feeling my hatred for him only grow more. It stung inside me, burning my veins, and I could tell something about it felt unhinged—soulless even. And yet, it was like it was fueling the power I expelled.

Pushing myself up to my knees, I watched his expression change as I slowly began to smile. Pressing my hands forward, I sent everything back towards him. But, with his teeth bared, Alastair jumped into the air towards Obsidian. Shadows consumed them both and I dropped my hands.

"NO!" I screamed as darkened flames imploded from Obsidian through his onyx vapor. The force threw me back down to the ground, and everything slowed. Coughing, I scrambled to get back on my feet, feeling my head sway.

"Let's be honest...you didn't want him here anyway," Obsidian taunted as he reappeared though his mist of shadows, but my eyes stayed locked on the pile of ash surrounding him. "The full moon will be here before you know it. And you will finally give me what I want to know."

He vanished and my heart sank as I let my body go limp. Kadeyan appeared across from me, his eyes beaming a dark crimson before locking on me.

He ran over, dropping to his knees and looking me over. "What the fuck happened?" he asked, taking my face between his hands before looking me over to see if I was hurt.

My eyes glanced over his shoulder to the pile of ash. The male I knew... The male who hurt me by lying, doubting me, but was doing everything to redeem himself... He was gone...

"Alastair's dead."

CHAPTER 70
DAVYNA

Landing in the dining room of the Fallen Court, I looked around, my breathing coming in rapidly. Everyone was in here talking about the attack, the creatures that came in, and Obsidian, but their voices began to trail off as they took in me and Kadeyan.

"What happened?" Evren asked as she moved towards us, but I didn't have words.

Sorin took a few steps forward, his eyes searching mine. I shook my head, causing him to drop his gaze. They grew up and worked side by side for half a millennium. They weren't as close as before, but even a distant friend's loss could still inflict a sting that made one reflect on all the good shared with them.

Kadeyan turned, glancing over his friends. "Alastair died, protecting Davyna... Obsidian was angry with her and pulled the creatures from Anawyn to attack the Court."

"Did you learn anything in Persephone's journal, Dy?" Levanna asked, tilting her head to draw my gaze to her.

"The stones made the gods...and more than likely the fae." I glanced at Kade, knowing he was thinking of the second prophecy I told him about before we came back.

I wanted to believe it was nothing. That since I learned how to balance the darkness within, the first prophecy was the path I was walking down... But what if I veered off course? What if I did rain fire on the Realms?

"We need to figure out what he has planned and get these

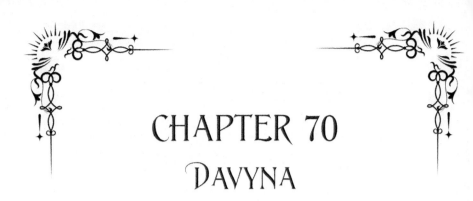

fucking stones," Calix stated, running his fingers through his hair still on the top of his head before turning to walk a few paces.

My mind was processing everything from today, everything I learned, and anger swelled up within. Katarina's word slammed into me: *But if you locked Persephone away...isn't there a way with your power that you could...* That was what she meant. With my power, the stones... I could see her like Kadeyan saw his dad.

Pulling back, I looked towards Levanna. "I want to see Persephone," I stated.

"Davyna, how would that even be possible? You killed her," Evren said, her brows pulling down, and I sensed her confusion on why I would even want to see her.

I didn't, but she had what we needed. I could feel it in my bones, with my own power surging to agree with me.

"With everything I possess, it has to be. I saw my dead father. I've been seeing my dead mother. And I placed her in a void... I can access it." I ran my fingers through my hair, catching sight of the blonde strands as I pulled them forward. "She has what we need."

Levanna and Kadeyan looked at each other and I could feel their emotions waver. "I can do it," Levanna stated as she moved towards me. "But I think we would need her stone to perform it."

"Then I'll get it." I started walking away.

"Davyna! How?"

I turned back, looking at my friends with worry struck in their eyes. I wanted those looks to leave them. I wanted to see them smile again, to have their lives back...and to start living the one *I* wanted.

"I'm a god. And if they can take on another's face, then so can I." I grinned. "I'm going into the Crystal Court and taking it."

"Are you sure this is going to work?" Levanna asked as we stood on the edge of the Crystal Court.

After I told them what I had planned, she asked me to wait a few hours to get some witches on the inside to help us. We had been waiting in silence for about twenty minutes, and I could feel her worry. But me, on the other hand...all I wanted was to get this over with. Whether the witches showed up or not, I wasn't going to leave without the stone.

"Yeah...it will work." I took her in for a moment, noticing something was off with her emotions and she was trying to hide them. I went to ask her if everything was okay, but two fae began walking towards us. One, I recognized, her tight curl still laying at her shoulders and hypnotizing caramel eyes. "Nova?" I asked.

"Hey, Davyna..." She gave me a weak smile, stopping at the border of the Dark Forest, where the sun beamed on No-Man's-Land. The light caught her face, her bronze complexion shimmering as she cleared her throat. "I just want to say...I was trying to help you back then. I knew nothing about Marta's plans...or that Jinx was..." Her head dropped and her friend next to her grabbed her hand.

"Nova, it's okay." I cut her off, not wanting her to feel guilt for what happened. "The past is the past, and you are here now helping... That means more than you know."

A smile tugged her lips up as her gaze met mine, but the fae next to her drew my attention in. Her icy blonde hair swayed in the wind and her blue eyes scanned over me before glancing over to Levanna.

"Jinx is in the Crystal Court Castle, and Jax and Verena are at their home. This is your window." She threw a small vile of blood towards me and smiled as I caught it. "It's their blood. Drink it and it will keep their locator spell active for longer."

"How did you get my parents'... You know what, I don't want to know," Levanna said, shaking her head.

"I'm Thea, by the way."

"Thank you for helping us," I spoke. "Both of you..."

"It's the least we can do. But get moving. Jinx is having a meeting soon with Jax and Verena," Nova explained.

They both started walking away, but Levanna called out, "Hey, Thea! Nova!" They paused, looking over their shoulders. "I wouldn't go back in there if I were you. If any of the witches catch wind of you both helping me, they will kill you."

Thea smiled, a glint of wickedness tainting her gaze as she glanced to Nova. "Then we will have a fun fight on our hands. We will all be with you guys soon." Purple mist consumed them, and Levanna and I glanced at each other.

"All?" I asked.

"Not important right now. So, are you ready?" I looked down at the vile of blood and took a cleansing breath. "Just act like the cunt Jinx is and they will hand it over." She laughed, and I joined in. "But be careful. There is no guarantee that Tanith or Obsidian won't show up to fuck with you."

"I know. I've got this." I thought back to the spell I saw in Persephone's book about skin walking, and began reciting it in my mind. It washed over me, and my skin began tingling and molding my form to who I focused on. It flowed over my head, down my torso, and stopped at my feet.

Levanna's eyes widened, taking a step back. "Holy shit!"

"I'm guessing it worked?" I asked, looking down at my purple gown before seeing my hands with longer nails painted in the same shade.

"If I didn't know any better, I'd say that Jinx had an identical twin," she said, her eyes still looking me over in shock.

Breaking open the crystal vile, I drank the blood of Levanna's parents. Silently chanting the locator spell, I felt their essence guiding me to where I needed to go. "I'll be back."

Falling into the gap, I closed my eyes for a moment before seeing I was standing before a crystal estate. The path before me was made of pure amethyst, while the building was a beautiful shimmering quartz. A rainbow reflected through the crystals as the sun beamed down.

I rolled my shoulders back, knocking on the solid tanzanite door.

As it swung open, Verena stood there, taken aback. "You're early."

I took a moment to collect myself and narrowed my eyes on her, gesturing inside the estate. "Well?"

She moved aside, her arm going out wide to welcome me in. I held myself high and walked in, glancing around. Crystals were in everything, their energy pulsating into the air, but it didn't feel pure... Not in this house. Not with these people. Both of them were just as evil as Persephone in my eyes.

They took Kadeyan's brother... Levanna's mate. And they were helping the gods. I wanted to kill them for it right here and now. I wanted to burn this place to the ground. Power rose within and it took everything in me to calm my emotions.

"Where is it?" I asked, turning to face her. Chills ran down my spine from hearing Jinx's voice fall from my lips.

"This way, My Lady." She moved through the estate, leading me down a flight of stairs until we entered a tunnel. "What did Tanith say about Davyna? Are they going to take care of that problem for us, or do we need to do it ourselves?"

My fury bloomed again, and I smiled, knowing that when this was said and done, I was going to enjoy watching Kadeyan and Levanna tear them apart. "They will be taking care of her soon, but Obsidian requested the stone in his possession since she is hell-bent on getting her hands on it."

Un-spelling a door, she walked into a room filled with vials on the wall and spell books laid out. But my eyes caught on the small table in the center with black sand and three hearts surrounding the stone. The magic was sacrificial, coated in death as it hid the stone from anyone searching for it. Even I could barely feel its power surging from it.

After a minute of preparing herself, she chanted over it. I felt the power of the spell slowly fall, and with it, the energy of the stone amplified, making its presence known. As the spell fell, I realized it was tainted with something...like it was a higher power. Not quite mine...but close to it. What did that mean?

She reached down and picked it up. "What about Alastair?"

"What about him?" I asked, making her look at me like I had three heads. "Right...he is—"

"Jinx, are we finally moving forward?" Jax asked from the door. I turned and smiled, burying down the unease of what they had planned for Alastair. I was guessing the news of his death hadn't traveled here yet.

"Finally. We are one step closer."

"It will be an honor to meet our true King." Verena walked towards me and handed the stone over before moving towards her husband.

King?

"I need to go meet them. I expect you both at the castle later tonight to discuss the next move." I glared at Verena and she bowed her head.

Using the gap, I fell in the Dark Forest and felt my breathing pick up. Who the hell was the King? Were they talking about Obsidian? That didn't seem right...

And what was Jinx going to do to Alastair? Did she know he was dead yet? Did she plan that with Obsidian?

I began walking towards No-Man's-Land, when I heard a crack behind me. Looking up, I saw Levanna in the distance, pacing back and forth. She stopped dead in her tracks as she caught sight of me before glancing over my shoulder, her eyes wide.

Turning, I saw the *real* Jinx, coming towards me. Her confusion only grew as she looked to Levanna and back to me.

"Tanith? What's going on?" she asked before looking over at Levanna again. "Why is she here?"

Standing taller, I smirked. "I got her to strike a deal with me. She is getting the other stones I need. Since you failed to bring me this one," I spat out, making her move closer in.

"You told me to keep it safe..." Her mind started to spiral, and I knew I only had seconds.

Throwing the stone through the air, I used my shadows to carry it across the border into Levanna's hands.

"Go!" I yelled before turning back to Jinx.

"You little bitch."

Dropping the spell from my body, I glared at her. "You're one to talk. You call me the abomination, but you turned on your own kind."

"With good reason: to get you out of here so this world could finally be what it was always meant to be."

"And what's that? Ruled by two power hungry gods hell-bent on destroying us all? What about Nyx? What would she say about you doing this?"

"Does it matter? She's dead. Because of you." Hissing sounded from beyond and I looked over, seeing the Sentores stalking towards us on their hind legs. "Remember them? They used to follow Persephone...but now they listen to me."

I felt a second of fear before it passed because I knew something about the creatures of all Realms at this point that she failed to pick up from Ravyn. They would listen to me.

"I tried to get rid of you back then by summoning them with her spell, but fucking Kadeyan..."

It was her? I mean, it made sense. Persephone didn't suspect I was there until after Lunavas...

"Not surprising. You were a bitch back then too."

She laughed as they moved closer, but I chose to look them in their eyes, willing my power to grow over them. One by one, I saw their shift, but Jinx was oblivious.

"It's going to feel great. You know, to get you out of the picture so Alastair and I can finally be together...and prepare the Realms for the last war."

Last war? The Realms? The gods were wanting a war...but with who? Zaryk...or was it for something more? I pushed into her mind, passing her spells undetected, and realized that was all she knew, along with the promise of their "true King" ruling over them.

"Careful now...you sound like Persephone. And look where her lust for one man brought her...at the end of my blade." I laughed, feeling the darkness seep into my eyes. "And Alastair is dead."

She paused, like air refused to fill her lungs, before her expression turned feral. I looked to the Sentores when she moved in, yelling as a dark purple mist poured from her hands. I let out a breath, showing no amusement in her attempt, nor did I use my own power because...I had *them.*

"Venetee," *Kill,* I commanded as she closed in, watching the Sentores pounce into their attack.

She threw up a barrier, yelling in frustration as I stepped back. They clawed to get to her, and our eyes locked. Her anger was penetrating her own spell, filling the forest, and I smirked, relishing in it.

I lifted my hand, sending out my power that swirled with the hues of these lands, and began breaking her spell.

"You fuckin—" Her voice was cut off and screams replaced it as I turned around and began walking away with a smile on my face. As I got to No-Man's-Land, I turned around and saw the Sentores starting to back away, purring and clicking their tongues. Bones laid on the forest floor.

I threw my hand out, and flames darted through the trees until they consumed the last trace of her remains, making her what she was always destined to become...

Nothing.

CHAPTER 71
KADEYAN

I paced back and forth through the dead grass in front of my castle, balling my hands into fists as I waited for Dy to come back. Not long ago, Levanna fell into my study, the stone clutched in her hands, telling me Jinx found them. Davyna was adamant on me staying here no matter what…and it took everything in me to respect her choice.

But fuck, if I wasn't ready to cast this entire realm in my power if she didn't come back in the next ten seconds.

The smell of ashes and blood roses pulled my attention, and I turned around, seeing her appear. Her eyes were closed, but she smiled wide, tilting her head up slightly.

"What the fuck happened? Are you okay?"

Her gaze slowly met mine and it was like the stars above refused me my next breath, forever promising to keep me breathless in her presence.

"I'm fine, Kade. Jinx, on the other hand…" She smirked. "She won't be around anymore to help them."

Fuck me…that smile.

I moved in, grabbing her face and possessing her lips in a bruising kiss. She met my intensity by wrapping her hands around my neck and pulling me deeper in, welcoming my tongue to taste every inch of her mouth. Her fingers slid back, grazing the shaved sides of my head, before moving up and gripping my hair tied in a bun. Sweet chills ran down my spine, causing my dick to swell.

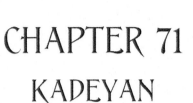

The front door opened, and I groaned, pulling back to see Calix in the doorway. He lifted his brows twice and I dove into his head. *"Cockblock."* Which only made him laugh.

"Both of you, get your asses in here," Calix demanded, laughter spilling out with each word.

"We need to use the stone to see—"

"No...not tonight, Your Grace. That can wait until the morning. Come on." Calix turned around, walking back into the castle, and Dy's brows furrowed.

"What was that about?" she asked.

I shrugged and moved in after her, watching her hips sway as she walked down the hall. She peered back, catching me, and shook her head with a smile.

I picked up my pace, smacking her on the ass. "Don't tease me, little Ember. I will fuck you in this hall. Right here...right now," I whispered before glancing up at the parlor filled with our friends.

Davyna paused and her jaw fell open. "What is this?" she asked as she stepped in. Food was laid out on the table in the center of the room, and my friends all had a drink in their hands, smiling wide.

"We are celebrating tonight!" Calix said, throwing his arm up in the air, which caused his drink to spill out.

Evren stepped in, giving her sister a gentle smile. "There haven't been many wins the last few months, and with the loss we all..." She swallowed hard before shaking it away. "We figured getting the fourth stone was worth celebrating...together." She handed Davyna a drink before glancing at me. "We all deserve tonight."

"What if I didn't bring it back?" Davyna asked.

"That thought didn't even cross our minds, Dy," Sorin said as he took a seat and picked up his glass. "Jinx will be a problem for tomorrow."

I laughed, moving farther into the room and picking up a bottle. "Yeah, no, she won't. Davyna killed her."

Everyone exchanged glances before Calix began laughing. "See, look! Another thing to celebrate! The witch bitch is dead!"

Davyna moved in, shaking her head before a small laugh passed her lips. Sitting down, I reached out to her, and she took my hand, turning to sit in my lap. Mist swirled next to us as Faelynn, Dalia, and Maeve appeared.

Picking at the food, we all fell into conversation, talking about what happened in the Crystal Court. Slowly, we moved away from the day's events and started sharing stories of the past, and Davyna relaxed into me. The laughs falling from her lips and everyone else's —including mine—brought a life to this room that I think we all desperately needed.

I couldn't remember the last time we did something like this, but it had to be before losing Silas... I glanced over to Levanna and noticed her eyes heavy regardless of the lightness of the room. Kissing Davyna on the cheek, I slid her off my lap, and she continued with her story about when she first got her horse, Lexi.

"I'm telling you, she was so stubborn at first. I called her a bitch...and she headbutted me!" she said as Dalia sat down on her shoulder, lost in her words.

"Bullshit!" Calix yelled, which made Evren laugh.

"No, I saw the blood," Evren chimed in.

Shaking my head, I looked down to see Ravyn jumped up in my spot and was blinking at me. Reaching out, I pet her head and received a deep purr before I moved over to Levanna. "Everything okay?"

She nodded with a genuine smile, but tears began to fill her eyes and I pulled her to the balcony doors. Opening it, I ushered her out before closing them behind me. Sobs broke from her lips, and as I turned, she wrapped her arms around me.

Fuck...

"It's okay, Lev... It's okay," I said, placing my hand on her head and holding her tighter.

There were moments over the years where she would break down like this, her ties to my brother hitting her harder from the absence of his presence. The mating bond was a blessing from the stars above, but it also felt like a curse...especially when you had to live on without your other half.

"I was just thinking how I... How I wish he could..." She sucked in a sharp breath, trembling in my arms.

"I know... I wish he was here too." Pulling her back, I wiped the tears from her face. "But, Levanna, I believe he is still here in a way, watching over us. Probably telling me to stop being an ass and to use my words." She laughed and I continued. "I know he is so fucking proud of you...for continuing to live and fight through the pain. He wouldn't want you doing anything else."

"I know...I just miss him so much." Her lip trembled and I pulled her back in.

"I do too. And one day, we will all be together again."

A long minute passed, and she pulled back, glancing over the Lands. "Kadeyan...if I don't make it through all this..."

"What are you talking about? We are not losing anyone else," I stated, feeling my heart speed up.

"Just promise me that you will live a full life." She smiled, crossing her arms over her chest.

"I will...with my *sister* by my side."

"I love you too." She smiled.

The doors opened, and Faelynn peeked her head out. "Kadeyan, Calix started a drinking game with Davyna." Laughs filtered out of the room and I shook my head before glancing at Lev.

"Do we stop him...or laugh at him?" I asked.

She chuckled and wiped the tears from her cheeks. "Laugh... hands down. He has always been determined to beat an Ember. There is no convincing him otherwise." She moved into the room, and I turned, taking a few steps to lean in the doorframe.

Levanna sat down next to Davyna and she turned to her. Dy's eyes softened on her before pulling her in, holding her. I smiled as the love of my life's eyes locked with me.

Calix yelled, "Come on! Hit me with another, Your Grace!"

"Calix, I swear, you will sleep in the woods if you start puking!" I yelled. He flipped me off, and I shook my head.

I took a full breath and felt relief wash over me, realizing I hadn't really taken one in the last eight months. It was strange because we weren't done with the gods...but this... This was everything in this moment.

Faelynn leaned in. "Remember when I used to show you visions of a happy evening like this, surrounded by people you loved? You thought that was a nightmare."

I turned my gaze to her, her onyx pools on me. "I thought you were torturing me with something I'd never have again..."

"No, Kadeyan..." She smiled as another set of yells and laughter filled the room. "I wanted you to know it was possible...and here it is."

It was well past one in the morning. Everyone had ventured to bed, tears still staining their faces from how hard they laughed after Calix finally admitted defeat and ran outside to empty the alcohol in his stomach.

Somehow, he missed Davyna's skin beaming with an orange hue every time she took a drink, burning away the alcohol in her system. Everyone, including Calix, knew Embers could do this. All they had to do was bring their fires forth and they would burn the alcohol from their system. But he never could back down from challenging one.

Stubborn fucker.

I walked down the halls, the echo of my boots being my only company as I followed her scent. She had walked Evren to her room, laughing, and it was nice to see her and her sister overcoming what had passed between them. As I moved towards the stairs to go up to her, I noticed her scent was coming from down the hall...where the ballroom was.

Picking up my feet, I moved down the hall and slowly pushed open the large metal door etched with swirls. Davyna was looking up at the chandeliers before she sent her fires out to light them, illuminating the room in a warm glow.

"Do you remember what my thoughts were before Persephone took my life?" she asked, and I moved in, closing the door behind me.

"If I'm being honest, all I felt was pain that I couldn't stop what was about to happen to you..."

"Was that when you realized we were bonded?" she asked, turning to face me.

"No, that was when—"

"When we were in Hell...the first night we..." she said, smiling, and I couldn't help but grin as I took a few steps into the room.

"Yes, that confirmed it...but I knew long before that." I grinned. "What's going through your head, Dearest?" I tilted my head, following her gaze to the chair where the dress she wore the night of the Fallen Ball laid. The one I had custom-made for her with black crusted diamonds that faded down in to a fiery red and apricot sheer material. And next to it sat a black suit with red swirls on the lapels that came to a point, creating a drop of blood.

"When I looked at you with that spell coursing through my veins, all I thought about was how I wanted to dance with you one last time...to be in your arms." Her heartbeat picked up as she lifted her hand, sending out a purple mist that replaced both our clothes into the items she had on the chair. "I don't want to go to sleep tonight without that dance..."

My heart swelled in my chest and I walked towards her, taking in her silver eyes locked on my amber ones. I stopped before her, bowing slightly as I sent my shadows out to turn on the spelled orb that stored the music of that night. It slowly began to fill the room and Davyna looked over at it as I glanced up.

"Then give me your hand, Princess." I stood up, placing my hand out and she slowly raised hers.

As our skin touched, sparks rose from her hand and I spun her around, pulling her in until our bodies were flush. My other hand slowly trailed down her back, her skin pebbling at my touch, as I began to move us into the waltz.

Our eyes didn't leave each other as the music pulled us deeper into its melody, our bodies gliding through each move as if we had done this our whole lives. I tightened my hold on her waist, pulled her closer, and leaned down to rest my forehead on hers. And everything going on in our world faded away...

It was only us.

The music began to fade and I pulled back. Lifting our hands that were joined as one, I spun her around, her gown flowing through the air. She was breathtaking...

She was my everything.

Pulling her back in, I leaned down, kissing her softly, and the heat of her lips ignited my body. "I love you," I whispered.

Her hands came up, pulling my gaze to hers. "I love you too. And, Kadeyan..."

Picking her up, I wrapped my hands under her thighs and carried her over to my throne, decorated with skulls on each side. Sitting down, I adjusted her to straddle me. "Yes, Princess?"

"I'm ready..."

My heart stopped in my chest as I brushed back the blonde and dark brown strands from her face. Listening to her heart beating faster, mine did the same.

Davyna grew up human, and I still wanted to give her the fantasy she probably imagined she'd have some day. Even if it delayed the bonding ceremony for a few more days... I could wait another 1,500 years to bond with her... So long as she wanted me, I'd be here, giving her everything I could to make her smile like this for eternity.

She smiled wide at me and I furrowed my brows, biting my bottom lip. "You can read my mind through my walls, can't you?" She nodded, and I shook my head, pulling her closer to me. "Would you want me to do that?"

"Yes. The fact that you even think about what I imagined as a human... Kadeyan, it means everything. *You* are my everything."

"Then I guess I should come up with an extraordinary way of proposing, huh?"

CHAPTER 72
DAVYNA

I paced back and forth in the white and black circular room of the Sky Court while Maeve and Levanna looked over the spell. Kadeyan watched me intently as I fidgeted with my hands, but all I could focus on was my heart slamming against my ribs. Anxiety was all that I felt this morning when my eyes opened, waiting for Obsidian to come and ruin this plan, and nervous that Persephone wouldn't talk to me...

Everything was hanging on this last chance to know their true plans. Then, we still needed two stones and to get the dagger back. I had no clue how we were going to do that.

He walked over to me as I turned, stopping me from taking another step. Picking up the pale blonde strands, he wrapped them around his finger. My eyes locked on the colorless reminder Tanith gave me, along with the scars.

"You okay?"

I took a deep breath before glancing into his amber pools. "I will be," I said, pulling my power to the surface and chanting softly. It consumed every fiber of my being, and heat washed over me. I wanted to change what I saw in the mirror, to use it as my own call to war, like Kadeyan did at the funeral by shaving the sides of his head.

After a minute, I opened my eyes and saw the blonde strands were now a fiery apricot, shimmering as the ray of the sun bounced off of it. Kadeyan dropped the piece of hair, and I smiled.

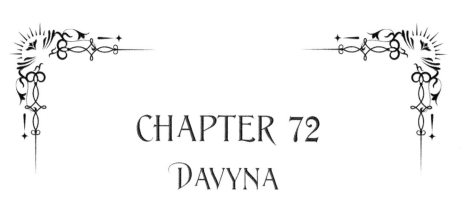

"Mm. I love it. It's very...you." He pulled back and his eyes narrowed on my chest, pulling my leathers aside. "I'll be damned..."

I looked down, widening my eyes as I took in the skin on my chest decorated in a tattoo. It was a delicate design of flames flowing from one shoulder to the other and down to my sternum. They rose up, blooming like a flower, burning bright below my skin.

"Embers would mark themselves in times of war, drawing their fires to just below their skin to create a tattoo... How did you know?" he asked.

"I didn't... I just thought about fighting...about you." Smiling, I looked up at him and saw pride laced with undying love in his eyes.

Evren walked over, crossing her arms over her chest. "I don't think this is a good idea. She is going to lie to you."

"I won't let her," I retorted.

"What can you do to a dead woman, Davyna?" she asked, making me look into her sky-blue eyes as Sorin walked up to her.

"I've been making her feel things worse than death. She will give me what I need."

Calix smiled. "Damn straight!"

Kadeyan shook his head and placed his arm around me. "Are you ready for this? It's going to hurt," Kadeyan said in a hushed tone.

"I was born ready." I looked up, smiling.

He told me before we fell asleep last night that being pulled into the afterlife felt like death itself. He said he could feel the blood stopping in his veins, as each organ shut down, forcing him to feel nothing but pain. But that didn't scare me. What did, was the fact that we were running out of time.

With some trusted Sky members, Maeve finally undid the wards protecting her mother's stone early this morning, and it sat on the desk next to Persephone's. The stone was pure white, smooth, and completely contrasting against the hard cut of the Crystal one, which was deep in various shades of purple.

Looking up at Kade, I said, "After this is over, I want a month where it's just me and you. No Courts, no magic..."

Leaning down, he whispered in my ear, "If we do that, I'm fucking you until we have to come back." My stomach tightened as I looked into his eyes, swirling with blood, and I knew I wouldn't want it any other way.

"Okay, we're ready," Levanna said, standing up from the circle she created on the floor.

As I started walking forward, Kadeyan moved with me, stepping into the circle first, and I paused. "I'm going with you, Dearest."

"What?"

"Where you go, I go." Leaning forward, he grabbed my hand and pulled me in, kissing me briefly. "Even if it is to see this psychotic bitch..." Smirking, he hugged me tightly.

Pulling back, I looked at Levanna holding the Crystal stone in her palm. I took it in my hand and grabbed Kade's so we both were touching it. "Send us in."

"This is going to hurt a bit. And I'm not sure how long you'll be able to stay in there. So, get her talking," she said.

I nodded my head, glancing up into the eyes that called my soul by name.

Kadeyan smirked as Levanna began chanting. The pain started flowing through us, but I noticed it was affecting him more than me. Our veins quickly started turning grey, and I could feel it racing up towards my head, causing the room to blur around us. The sound of this world faded as I sucked in a breath and everything fell into obscurity.

Looking around, I saw Kadeyan sit up and gasp for air as he took in our surroundings. "Fuck, that hurts like a bitch."

"Don't be a baby. It wasn't that bad," I taunted. Standing, I offered my hand and helped him up. We both scanned over the dark void, listening beyond at the utter silence.

"How do you know she will be here?" Kadeyan asked as we started walking.

"I used a spell that kept her from passing on to peace, creating this."

"How did you even know how to do that?"

"I just thought about it...and willed my power to create it." I gave him a devilish grin and he bit his lip, holding back a laugh.

"Well, when it's my time, make sure I don't end up in a place like this."

My stomach turned at his words, feeling everything within fear that more than anything else we were facing. I couldn't lose him. I didn't think I'd ever be able to come back from it. "No one else is dying."

Except maybe me...

We moved through the darkness, and when I heard a groan to my left, I turned. Persephone was on the ground, her hair disheveled and bags tattooed under her eyes as she looked up towards us.

"Hello, Persephone..." I said, forcing a smile on my face as I pushed the unease about my nightmare out of my mind.

Her eyes narrowed on me as she smiled, before looking over to Kadeyan. "Hello, *my love,*" Persephone teased as she pulled herself off the ground and wiped her hands on her torn, white dress, still coated in dirt and blood. "What do you want?" She turned, looking at me with disdain.

"I need answers about the gods."

She laughed, rolling her eyes. "I'm not giving you shit," she spat out, shaking her head. After a few moments she glanced up through her lashes, her dark blue eyes swirling with purple. "Unless...you set me free from this torment."

"Deal," I said, quickly, causing her to step back and look me over. Kadeyan stiffened next to me, confused by my statement, but I ignored him. "Start talking."

"What do you want to know, child?"

"Did you know I was one of the gods? Or that my mother was?"

"I've had nothing but time to think about your dear, old mommy." She stared off and her rage surfaced, drenching her skin.

"What about her?"

"When you came back after that spell was done, I figured it out. The spell your father used to save you was done by your mother. It was a spell beyond our fae realms, and his death must have activated it. It was sacrificial magic after all. And yet, I'm curious as to how she died with dark obsidian...or how you went down with it too."

My mind snapped back to my mother talking to him. It made my heart hurt more, because they knew they needed to die...for me to live.

Pushing the thought away, I looked back into her eyes. "Why would the dark obsidian stop working on me?"

Her voice was coated in venom as she narrowed her gaze. "I'm assuming Nyna didn't want that side coming out of you. And when you sent me here, it probably started to open. Because only gods can recreate voids like this to lock people in. Maybe her power was suppressed too."

"Why is Obsidian obsessed with finding out who Davyna's mother was? What does he need?" Kadeyan stepped forward, crossing his arms over his broad chest.

"He needs the right goddess. He thought Tanith would be it, but she isn't. I tried bargaining with him once to make me his equal, but he just laughed...saying it came down to bloodlines and that I didn't have it." Persephone glanced over at me, her eyes sparkling before her lips turned up into a smirk. "I did tell you *he* would come for you..."

My mind flashed back to when I killed her...her threat. I just assumed at the time she was trying to scare me, but she wasn't. She was telling the truth.

"What bloodline?" Kadeyan asked.

She turned back to Kade, her smiling falling. "The bloodline to a very powerful god. One of their makers, actually." I stepped back, looking at Kade. "Oh...so, you don't know that part yet?" She hummed, smiling wickedly. "When the two original gods were doing a spell long ago, they combined their blood, which in turn cursed Zaryk as he was banishing his brother to the Abyss. That blood flowed in Zaryk's veins, but it denied him any rights to the power his brother held.

"The Tanith you have met is the daughter of Zaryk. Obsidian trusted me with the truth, since I served him for so long." She beamed, no doubt relishing in the memories she spent with him. "Zaryk had two children—twin girls with one of the Cursed witches." She looked disgusted and moved through the darkness in a circle around us.

"And the other child died," I said, but I knew deep in my bones that she didn't. She was concealed...just like me. And my life matching up with this child wasn't a coincidence.

"Yes, Obsidian killed her and took the other in hopes she would have what it took to raise Arcadyus."

"Who is that?" Kade asked, but my stomach dropped.

"The humans would probably call him the Devil, but he is a powerful god, my sweet Lord. How ironic that your Court pledged *to raising Hell*...because that's what Obsidian wants—to free our true King from that personal hell his brother locked him in."

"So, Arcadyus is in a void like this?" I asked.

"Somewhat like this. You placed me here. So, only you can free me from it. But in his case...he needs blood of his line and the stone." She looked down at her broken nails and chuckled. "Arcadyus can kill Zaryk, and after that...the last war can take place."

My mind began to spin, remembering Jinx mentioning the last war. It included the brother. "Why am I mixed up in this?"

"Because...you are a god. And a realm can't have three. It creates an imbalance of power. Tell me, have people been getting sick?" I didn't say anything, and she started laughing. "Oh, Davyna... How does it feel to be the reason they are all dying?"

"You will not speak to her that way," Kadeyan growled.

"Or you'll do what to me?" She walked up to him, looking him up and down before giving him an evil smirk. "Kill me?"

"Persephone. Am I from that bloodline?" She tilted her head, smiling at me in a way that made my blood boil. Moving towards her, I wrapped my hand around her throat and pulled her in. "Am I?"

"If you—" She choked on her words, and I loosened my grip. "If you are still alive, then he probably thinks you are his loophole.

Or he would have forcibly taken your power by now." I threw her body back and she fell to the ground, giggling.

Kadeyan moved over to me, his eyes lost in the same chaos as mine.

"We just need to get the last stone, Dy. Then we can break the link. He won't take you from me."

"The stones..." Persephone laughed before she looked up at me. "You won't find the Crescent one."

"Yes, we will," Kadeyan growled.

She rolled her eyes before pulling the smile back to her lips, and her eyes beamed with secrets she was still holding onto.

"What do you know?" I asked, stepping forward.

"I won't tell you unless he leaves."

Kadeyan moved forward, his anger filling the darkness. "I'm not leaving her here with you," Kadeyan spat out.

"Then it looks like you'll never get that stone..." she said, looking off into the distance, and my body froze.

"Where is it?" I asked softly. Kadeyan looked over at me, but I kept my eyes fixated on her. She refused to speak another word, and I asked again, "Persephone. Where. Is. It?"

We sat in silence for a minute and my own rage grew. I turned towards Kadeyan. I didn't know how much time we had left in here, and I needed to know what she was holding back. I knew he would be angry about this later...but this was my last chance.

Stepping up on my toes, I pulled his head down and kissed him, lacing it with an apology for what I was about to do.

Pulling away, he looked at me, concern tattooed across his face. "I'll see you soon."

"Davyna, don't!" I placed my hand on his chest and pushed his soul out of the darkness, leaving us alone.

Closing my eyes, I took a deep breath to calm my emotions before turning to face her. "Start talking."

CHAPTER 73
DAVYNA

"There is a prophecy—" Persephone began, but I cut her off.

"I know. There are actually two. I read about the second in your book," I seethed and balled my hands into fists at my side. "Where is the stone?"

"Obsidian only knew of one." Furrowing her brows, she looked puzzled as she ignored my question. "What was the other?"

"The first one was about burning the throne and holding both powers. I burned the throne, Persephone. I never took it." Her eyes perked up, and she looked astonished, and I moved towards her. "What do you know about the lost child prophecy?"

"This is very...interesting." She stood up, giggling as she looked at the scar on my arm and my hair. "The prophecy was never explained to me, only shared. I spent a long time trying to decipher it. There was even a ruby stone cave in the Mortal Realm with etchings on the walls about it. But now...I think I understand."

I swallowed hard, remembering that place, because that was where my mother brought me. "Tell me."

"If I'm right...you'll find out soon enough." She smirked. "But I will tell you about the Crescent stone."

"Where is it?" I demanded, but she hesitated, almost like she was trying to find the words. "Persephone." My heart raced in my chest and nausea bloomed from my core.

"He made a deal with the gods, just like I did. He killed your precious Elias and took the stone from him. Although, he brokered a deal so that's why I had to help him hide it. Little bastard knew I wanted it."

My stomach turned as I looked into her wicked pools, turning a lighter shade to expose the purple. "Who. Has. It?"

"My son, of course. Obsidian gave me a spell and told me to hide it in his heart, cloaking its magic. I don't know what deal they struck, but it pissed me off because, clearly, he got the better end of the bargain."

"Who is your son?" I asked, pulling my brows down as I studied her face.

"You Embers...forgetting everyone who isn't your mate." She grinned. "How is my little temperamental wolf these days?"

My jaw dropped and I shook my head in disbelief as an image of his face flashed through my mind. He lied....and I fell for it, again. He killed Elias... He was working with the gods...

"No, that isn't possible."

"It is. Alastair was mine and Keres' son," she huffed, letting out a half laugh as she took pleasure in the shock evident on my face.

"Well, he's dead. So, he can't help them anymore," I snapped, but then I thought back to the pile of ashes...the stone wasn't there. Fuck, Obsidian must have it.

She laughed. "Ah...what a pity. I'm surprised he made it that long, honestly." Her head fell back and she looked up into the darkness. "But who is going to help you, Davyna? Because when Obsidian finds out you are the key to bringing his King back and to starting the last war...he will never let you go."

"I'm not."

"I'm going to go out on a limb here... The child Obsidian killed must have not died, but was hidden. Your mother was the only fae —even if Cursed—to possess more than one line of power...and so do you."

"But my—"

"I'm not finished," she stated, placing her finger up. My stomach turned as I looked away from her, and she chuckled. "You're a goddess...which means so was she. And the six gods have never been able to procreate... Maybe that was their own curse for stealing the stones to make us. But your grandfather was able to because he was one of their makers. He wasn't from this world.

"Zaryk was Cursed with Arcadyus' blood in his veins. He could have passed that on to his daughter...or maybe *their* daughter."

"Get to the fucking point!" I growled, feeling the darkness creep into my eyes.

She laughed, enjoying my reaction as I staggered back, pulling the power back in.

"Oh, Davyna," she said, her smile on full display. "You are––"

"I am not Zaryk's granddaughter!" As soon as I said it, everything fell into place, making my lungs tighten and my mind implode with everything I had learned. I was the bloodline he needed. That was why my mother couldn't say it, because knowing would expose it to Obsidian...and then...

"Aw, how does it feel to be the only one who can raise Arcadyus?"

"We don't know that..." I said.

"No, but something tells me you're about to find out." Her laugh echoed around me, and I felt the pull back to the other side to return to my body. Persephone noticed and her vile demeanor faded as worry blanketed her. "Wait! You promised to set me free! I gave you everything I had!"

I smiled through the craze still surging within and met her gaze. "And what made you believe I'd actually do it?" Anger flared to life in her eyes, giving me at least a small ounce of joy at seeing her break once again. "Goodbye, Persephone."

She screamed and ran towards me. My eyes closed, taking a deep inhale. My eyes shot open, and I sat up, breathing heavily as I stared into my friends' gazes locked on me.

Evren dropped to the floor within the circle, grabbing onto me. "Dy!"

"What happened?" I looked around, taking in the room in shambles. The desk was flipped over and shelves were broken, scattering books on the ground.

Calix was lost in sorrow, matching Levanna's expression as Sorin moved in, helping me up. Maeve was trying to keep her eyes away from me and panic bubbled up.

"Where's Kadeyan?" I looked back, seeing the spelled circle broken on his side, and stepped back.

No… I sent him back here… So, where was he? My eyes connected with the small mirror on the shelf and it swirled for a moment. My stomach twisted into a knot at the sight. There was a protection veil over its power within the glass, trying to keep it suppressed, but with my power firing off within, I sensed it… And I knew who it was.

Obsidian…

"What happened?"

"Obsidian happened," Calix said softly. "His shadows sent out a blast as he appeared in the room, and when we woke up, Kade was…"

I pushed down our bond, expecting to feel him nearby, but I was met with nothing. I couldn't sense Kadeyan at all.

Panic rose from within and it felt like my heart had been ripped from my chest as I took in everyone in the room.

My voice was coated in something beyond this world as I spoke —directed at *him*, wherever he was—and the ground below my feet began to shake.

"Where is my mate?"

CHAPTER 74
DAVYNA

"Davyna, slow down!" Maeve yelled from behind me as I ran down the stairs, feeling the vibration of each step send me into a deep spiral. Something wasn't right. Something felt very wrong, and bile rose into my throat.

Getting to the bottom floor, I walked towards the doors. Faelynn and Dalia rushed over, but I didn't stop. Pressing on the doors that were already moving open, I walked outside, my heartbeat filling my ears.

I needed to find him.

All my friends rushed out behind me, but I barely registered their faces as I glanced around, willing my power to push out over the Lands to feel something… Even just a sliver of our bond.

"What do you need, my Queen?" Calix asked, his voice calm even though I felt his anxiety matching mine.

"Calix, stop! I'm not the Queen!" I yelled, feeling the blood pound through my veins.

"Yes, you are. And that's one order I will never obey because *you* are my Queen! So, tell me, what do you need from me?"

Evren and Sorin moved up beside him. "What do you need from us?" she asked. Turning, I looked at Dalia, Maeve, and Levanna, and brought my hand to my chest, trying to steady my breathing.

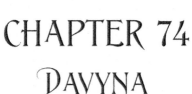

"We need to grab the stones from upstairs." Faelynn vanished with Dalia and I focused. "And we need everyone to start searching because I can't feel him at all... They are blocking him from me again."

Appearing next to us, Faelynn held the two stones in her hand, with Dalia on her shoulder. "Where would you like me to take them?"

"The Mortal Realm... They can't go there." I turned my gaze to Levanna as they vanished. "Levanna, can you get the other stones and take them to Faelynn?" She nodded frantically, and I moved in. "Come here, I need to place a spell over you that will allow you through the barrier I placed on them."

Reaching out, I took her hands in mine and chanted, feeling it wash over her as my gaze fell. Ice instantly met my flesh as I saw through a sheer glamour concealing Levanna's skin, and my heart refused to take another beat. Her hands were decaying, almost entirely grey.

Our eyes collided before her anxiety encircled us, and my own rose. No...I wasn't going to lose her too. Before I could say anything, she gave me a quick nod and purple mist swallowed her whole.

She was sick... And judging by the magic she was using to hide it meant, no one knew.

"Davyna, are you o—" Evren asked.

"No, but you guys need to go. We can't risk losing the other stones. I'm going to go search for Kade."

Magic began to swirl around us, but before I could fall into the void, I was pulled back. Searing pain shot up my arm and into my head, reminding me of *her* power back in Solyus.

"You're not going anywhere, little fae." Wrapping her arm around my throat, Tanith pulled me back and forced me to look into my friends' stunned gazes, slowly filling with rage. "The show is about to begin."

"RUN!" I yelled to them as a blazing white light swallowed us whole and I gritted my teeth as the pain built. Landing on a mountain nearby to overlook the Sky temple, I stumbled away from her.

Tanith smiled as she held the dagger we needed to kill them, inspecting the blade.

"Where is he?" I growled.

"Tell me this first, Davyna." She stepped forward, her pale blonde hair flowing in the breeze. "Did you really think you could beat us?" Smiling, she gazed into my eyes, searching for my acceptance that this was over.

"Does it look like I'm finished yet?" I yelled, causing her to grin and glance towards the temple. "Where is Kadeyan?"

"Probably dead by now. Obsidian had plans for him."

"You fucking cunt!"

She pointed the blade at my heart as I stepped forward. "You know, I had never been stabbed with one of these until you...and it hurt." Pressing the steel to my skin, she tilted her head up, watching as the crimson pooled up and slid down into my leathers. The burning of this blade was just like I remembered from the death ring, when Kadeyan stabbed it into my leg. Strong and unbearable. That pain...made me feel human. "I should just end you."

"But you can't, because he wants something from me, right? Something you can't give him." Her eyes turned feral as she pushed a little harder, causing me to hiss. "Will he kill you like he did to the goddess before you—whose name you inherited—when he finds out who I am?"

Backing away, she turned and faced the temple as her hand gripped tighter around the handle of the dagger. "How do you know about her?"

"I know about her and your sister. I know who your father is and about the uncle you are trying to raise. Arcadyus, right?" Turning, I saw the wrath in her eyes and threw my hands out as my power surged with a vengeance I'd never felt before.

Tanith moved in, clasping chains around both of my wrists, and the magic within me fell just as quickly. I looked down at them, matching the steel of the blade as white and black molded around each other. The same chains the *real Tanith* wore in the dream I saw. My power kept retreating, and I felt weak, as if I was mortal again.

"It's unfortunate, isn't it? Being powerless. Arcadyus brought them from his home. They were for prisoners, spelled heavily with the powers of the stones and other relics to suppress a god's magic." She smiled at me as I glanced up, meeting her cold eyes.

"All you had to do, Davyna, was take the throne. Be Queen of this realm." She sighed, walking around me. "Do you know how many would die to be in that position? And yet, you threw it away. You asked for death and carnage."

"It would have never worked, and you know it."

Leaning over my shoulder, she laughed as she rested her head against mine. "Maybe not...but maybe we could have avoided all of this."

White light boomed from her hand, shaking the ground as it barreled through the air. It slammed into the Sky Court temple, shattering the walls as screams echoed out. My eyes took in the destruction, and I tried to move forward, but she held me back, forcing me to watch.

I fell to my knees, my jaw slack as the building began to crumble in on itself, and the fae inside with it. "What are you doing to them?!" I yelled.

"Holding them in there, of course. You are a selfish child who deserves to watch everything you care for crumble to nothing." She pushed out more power, making the building implode, and my head fell along with tears as the screams no longer rang in my ears.

Tanith walked over to me, sheathing the dagger, before kneeling and showing me the two stones within her hand. The same ones Faelynn just left with. "There is no goddess stronger than me to bring our King home."

"Where are Faelynn and Dalia?" I asked.

She smiled. "They are probably bleeding out inside the gap."

Calix and Maeve appeared next to her, and Calix used his shadows to rip the stones out of her hand.

"You little cunts," Tanith said as she rose from the ground. "Do you want to die too?"

"No one touches our Queen and lives," Calix growled.

"Guys, run!" I screamed, but Maeve's silver eyes beamed bright as she took a step closer towards Tanith.

"I will fall. I will die. And so will you. But at least I'm not afraid of death," she said, steeling her spine as she locked eyes with Tanith.

I thought back to what she said, remembering her vision I was pulled into. She wasn't talking about me...she was talking about herself. A sob bubbled up in my chest as I shook my head, feeling every ounce of fear rise into the thick air coated with debris and smoke.

"Please, Maeve," I begged as the tears streamed down my cheeks before I glanced at Calix. "Go. Now."

Calix shook his head and Maeve's eyes connected with mine, filled with such peace.

"Burn it down," she said as she turned away from me, staring death down with nothing but valor. Tanith raised her hand, and I pushed off the ground, refusing to let them die, no matter what her vision was.

She would not die today, and neither would Calix.

Pulling the blade from her sheath, I sliced into the back of her leg. She screamed and bent down in pain. I threw the dagger towards Maeve, whose shock was plastered on her face, before I headbutted Tanith, knocking her back and causing my own body to sway from the pain.

Calix's shadows wrapped around every inch of her body and he yelled, trying to force more out to keep her down. If they stayed, they were going to die. And I didn't have my power to help them...

Tanith pushed against Calix's shadows, before a beaming light shined through her, evaporating each tendril of smoke.

"Maeve, take it to the Mortal Realm. NOW!" I screamed. She kneeled down and picked the dagger up. Still in shock, she looked up at me before vanishing. "Calix, get back to my sister! That's an order from your Queen!" I screamed and Tanith sat up, her power surging forth from her hands, her eyes turning feral.

Calix fell into the gap just as her power imploded around us, throwing my head back and slamming me against the rocky mountain's edge. My vision spotted with black as her bloody hand wrapped around my throat, pulling me off the ground.

"I thought you were of light..." I choked out.

Tanith tightened her grip, her anger consuming every small detail of her face. "The light was made to be consumed by darkness, Davyna." Digging her fingers into my flesh, she pulled me closer. "And today is the day your light finally goes out."

We fell through the void, and I kept my eyes closed, unsure if I wanted to see what was coming next.

Tanith pushed me forward and my eyes shot open as I fell to the ground. My hands weren't quick enough to catch myself and I rolled, smacking my head against the white and black marble floor. I groaned, wincing from the pain blooming over my body and refusing to fade.

Boots stepped closer to me, and I tilted my head up to see Obsidian kneel down. "Hello, my sweet Davyna." He smiled, brushing the strands of my hair back from my face. "Are you ready?"

"You said I had until the full moon."

"I lied," he said sweetly, as if he wanted his prey to be calm on its way to slaughter.

Pulling back, I got to my knees and narrowed my gaze on him, but Tanith moved forward, wrapping her fingers into my hair before ripping me up off the ground. "Her little friends took the stones and the dagger, but they won't get far with them."

"Where is Kadeyan?" I demanded and Obsidian's lip twitched.

"Tied up at the moment in Valyner... What? Can't feel him, little cinder?" he seethed.

"What did you do to him!?" I yelled, trying to step forward before Tanith's power lunged out. It entered my body, causing me to cry out and stopping me from taking another step.

After a few moments, the pain faded, and I gasped for air.

Obsidian smiled, tilting his head. "Do you want to tell me about your mother...or do you want to die?" His eyes beamed a brighter red.

I thought about what Persephone just told me, her theory about my bloodline to Zaryk. If it was true...he would never raise Arcadyus.

Smiling, I glanced up. "Fuck. You."

His gaze grew more feral as he unsheathed his dagger, the black and white steel glistening in the dim stone room. Darkness began moving in, blurring the edges of the room as he flipped the dagger.

I pulled my hands apart, tightening the chains around my wrists as I took a deep breath.

"What game are you playing here?" he growled.

I kept my mouth shut, waiting for him to deliver the killing blow, while his anger grew with each second.

Tanith moved over. "Obsidian, we talked about this. And you promised me!"

He looked at her, smiling, and my stomach turned. "Oh, Tanith, are you really that blind?"

Shadows lashed out, ripping the chains from my wrists, and with it, my power returned. Fire roared like a beast within, and I glanced over as the blade caught my eye, flying through the air. The dagger buried into Tanith's chest, and I stumbled back, taking in Obsidian's eyes on me.

"What are you doing?" I yelled.

"Doing it myself since you are so fucking stubborn." He turned his gaze back to Tanith as she gasped for air, glancing down at the crimson flowing down her chest. "Nothing personal, love...but I need her, not you."

He pulled the dagger free and her body fell to the ground. My vision swayed, feeling pulled away, similarly to when my father's stone ripped me in. And the world around me faded away, taking me somewhere else.

The cabin was calm, the two sleeping babies in their bassinets as they were last time, and the dark mass of shadows was here. He moved in, picking up the blonde-haired baby, before his magic shot through the air, consuming the other one.

And yet, the image was different this time. The baby with black hair continued to sleep, her little chest rising and falling evenly as the power hovered around her...like something was protecting her.

Obsidian left the cabin, and I moved in, glancing down at the baby. Her little eyes fluttered open, matching the ones I saw in Akari's visions of her. They were golden, shining bright, and I stepped back, trying to catch my breath.

They were my mother's eyes...

Screaming sounded from the woods beyond, growing louder, and a women with black hair and golden eyes entered the cabin, running over to the empty basinet. Her cries filled the cabin, and I looked in the doorway, seeing a male standing there, his head down and his pale blonde hair hiding most of his face.

"This is your fault, Zaryk! You held me back from coming to my daughter. You let him take her!" *she screamed, falling to the ground, her hands gripped onto the empty crib.*

He moved in, dropping by her side as the other baby began to whimper. "I had to make a choice on who to save... I saw what's to come, Evyra... Aesyra will grow and live a long life, I promise you." *He lifted his hands to her face, her sobs still echoing far beyond the small cabin.* "It's Nyna who needs to be protected..."

Pulling out of the vision, I searched for air to fill my lungs as I glanced down at Tanith's still body.

Her name was Aesyra...and she was my aunt.

It was all true. Zaryk needed to protect my mother because I'd be the one who carried Arcadyus' power...making me the key to raising him. Looking over at Obsidian, he smiled wide as I noticed the aura beaming off my skin, swirling with all the colors of the stones and shimmering outward.

I could feel my ties to Valyner deepen, feeling the link fall into place as the new goddess, whether I wanted it or not. I was linked to the fae, and with that, to him.

My stomach turned as he looked me over, biting his bottom lip. "I've been waiting for you, Davyna. And so has Arcadyus."

"I don't know what you are—"

"Stop. Do you think you were the only one seeing that vision? Our connection is stronger now that you are the goddess connected to my realm."

My lip twitched as I steeled my spine. "I will not help you."

My eyes darted to the dagger in his hand before meeting his gaze. I pulled for what made me the monster, letting it devour every inch of my body before throwing out my power to rip the dagger from his hands. He stepped forward, his eyes going hard as I wrapped my fingers around the hilt.

"You are mine now." He took each step slowly. "My property. My weapon. My mate." His chest pressed against mine and I looked away.

"I belong to myself, and *my* mate." I lifted my arm, punching him across the face, and the blade sliced into his cheek. Throwing out my flames, they threw him back, and he yelled before his solid form crashed to the ground.

Dropping to my knee, I pressed my palm into the ground, channeling everything within until the room began to shake and become engulfed in flames.

"You little bitch," he said, standing up and walking back towards me. "What do you think you are doing?"

"I'm going to break our link...and then I'm coming for you." An explosion of magic expelled from me, crumbling his plane.

Sucking in a sharp breath, I began falling through the darkened grey clouds, noticing my wings were out, the tips of the feathers burning. My vision went in and out as I tried to gain control and I pulled for the void, focusing on the only place I wanted to be.

Home.

Falling to the floor, I coughed and looked around to see I was in

Levanna's spell room. I let my head drop and closed my eyes, taking a deep breath to calm my racing heart.

Opening them, I saw Levanna on the floor, with Ravyn crying by her side. And blood...so much blood.

The exhaustion and pain ceased as I jumped up, dropping the dagger in my hands and slid to the floor near her side. The crimson stuck to my leathers and hands as I pulled her up into my lap, the tears falling without pause. "Levanna!" I screamed. "Please... Levanna!"

She opened her eyes, breathing slowly. "B–behind...y–you..." I looked around the room and spotted Sorin, Evren, and Calix on the ground. My stomach instantly dropped, but then, I heard their hearts beating. Slow, but the pulses were there.

"Who did this?"

She coughed, as I laid my hands on her and began healing the wound in her stomach. Once she was breathing normally, I rushed over to the others and did the same, watching their eyes flutter open.

My breathing continued to grow more erratic as I glanced over at Levanna, looking at her hands in shock. The glamour wasn't there, and the grey, decaying skin was also gone. "How is this possible?" she whispered as I helped Evren sit up.

"What happened?" I asked, looking around before I noticed the stones on the table were gone. "Did the stones make it to the Mortal Realm?"

Everything inside froze over, ice stabbing into my organs as I slowly glanced to her, feeling the world slow. I dove into Lev's mind, taking what I needed, and rage was the only thing I felt.

"Dy... He's..." Dropping my head, I saw the scars on my arm turn black, and I knew my eyes were slowly matching, void of mercy.

"I'm going to make him wish he never laid eyes on me...before I send him to a place even the Devil would fear."

CHAPTER 75
KADEYAN

My eyelids felt like heavy weights as I tried to open them, but the pain radiating inside my head begged me to stop. Raising my hands, I only got so far before I felt metal dig into the flesh on my wrists. And regardless of the pain, my eyes shot open.

Glancing around, I took in the dark stone walls, the air heavy with moisture, and tried to stand up. How did I end up here? I pushed myself up but quickly fell back down, hearing the chains rattle against the ground. My eyes darted down, taking in the obsidian metal, and I pulled against them. I surrendered my attempt after a minute and looked around, taking in the black salt circle with the Untouched fae stones surrounding me.

Fuck...

I pulled at the chains again, trying to stand from the ground, but I only got a few inches before my knees slammed back into the stone. "Don't bother. You aren't getting out of here alive." My head snapped up, recognizing that voice. The candlelight glowed on his face as he slowly stepped forward, and I instantly felt my rage rise.

"Alastair," I said as my lip rose, "I thought you were dead?"

"I bet that brought you joy. Sorry to disappoint. That was just one of my wolves that Obsidian forced to skin walk as me...but the words falling from his lips were my own, forcing your little *Dearest* to fall for the story I served to her." He stepped into the circle, grabbing me by my jaw, before looking into my eyes. "And now, I get to finish what I started... What my mother failed to do."

Pulling my head back, I looked him over. Confusion washed

over me as I tried to grasp what he was saying. "What the fuck are you talking about?"

"Oh, so, your mate didn't tell you?" He laughed. "Katarina was never my mother. I've known that for most of my life." Walking around the circle, I kept my face cold. "Davyna was quite sweet in offering her help to find my mother, but your little bitch killed her. And, let's face it, Persephone was never fit to rule anyway."

"Don't you fucking—" I yelled as he came back around.

"Or what? What are you going to do about it?" he taunted, pulling an obsidian dagger from his sheath, and a wicked smile graced his lips. "Today, you and she will die. And the gods and I will restore our world the way it was intended to be."

"You *are* Persephone's son... A fucking psycho who is power hungry."

"And what's the problem with that?" He smiled, showing a side of him I'd never seen in his five hundred years. It was dark, cold... and I didn't know he had it in him.

"Where is Davyna?" I growled.

He flipped the blade around his fingers before glancing down at me. "What, can't feel her anymore?"

I turned away, pulling on the chains until I let out a frustrated yell.

"You know, you should have let me kill her that night in the woods. It would have saved all of us the pain of knowing her."

"I knew you fucking did it... Why? Was it because you thought she was one of the Cursed?" I asked, turning to look into his cold, brown orbs.

"When I first saw her, she was intriguing. Those silver eyes...the heat she gave off." He relished in the memory of her, closing his eyes. "The way she moaned..." I growled and he chuckled. "I did think she was one of the Cursed at first, and we were tasked with killing them when they got out of hand. Although, I didn't care if they were creating chaos or lying low. I did my job and enjoyed it..." His smile slowly grew. "Then, I learned she was Ezekiel's daughter, and my mother wanted that child so badly."

"When did you figure that out?"

"The night I found her with his stone, and the flames pouring from her hands sealed my suspicion." He grinned and my mind went to the ball... "Then, you had to go and fuck everything up when you took her away from the binding spell."

"Marta planned that... And your mother wanted her magic. Why were you willing to kill her before she got it?" I asked.

"Marta did, but who do you think left her all the information to push her to do it?" My stomach turned and he continued. "I mean, I even gave her the poisonous tea before the spell, just in case anything went wrong. But even while choking on her own blood and with me wrapping my fingers so tightly around that pretty, little neck...she just wouldn't die. Then, you showed up."

I burrowed my gaze into him.

"And to answer your other question, it was because Obsidian promised me the throne if I killed her. He cursed Ezekiel, and even he was unsure why a child was born to him. And my mother was determined to become a god. She lost sight of what mattered. So, I became his best ally in Valyner to keep it in order while he carried out his plans."

He sighed, shaking his head. "I thought about keeping her though, to rule with me after that day because, damn...she can get under your skin, can't she? That was until she kept unlocking her powers with you. Why a goddess would be mated to you still has my mind spinning... Because you are nothing."

"When did you become their lap dog?"

He narrowed his eyes on me, smirking at my insult. "I have been serving our makers for a long time now...but more so since I brought her to my Court."

"It was never your Court, Alastair!"

He laughed, moving in and placing the black blade to my chest. "It is because my parents forced me to become a Crescent to hide my father's infidelity... I wanted to be a Crystal." His eyes softened, and he tilted his head to look me over.

"And, let's face it, the Court was mine the day I killed Elias Crescent and ripped the stone from his hands. I forgot he'd even existed until Davyna ended up in my life…and I had to take on someone I wasn't, willing my own mind to give her the version she would trust." He laughed.

"You fucker…" I pulled at the chains again, feeling them rub my skin raw. Alastair dragged the blade across my chest, and I gritted my teeth as blood began to slide down my skin.

"She killed my mother, and that death was supposed to be mine." He cut my arm next, and I hissed as more crimson pooled.

"Do you care about anything but power? What about Jinx?" I seethed.

He laughed. "Davyna did me a favor there, playing right into what I wanted her to do."

I looked up through my lashes. "And what was that?"

"I erased what was in those books for Obsidian, and I couldn't have Davyna figure that out. So, I placed that stain of magic on Jinx."

"How—"

"Shhh." He moved in, placing the flat side of the dagger on my lips. "We aren't to that part in the story yet." He pulled back and began circling me again. "Unfortunately, Persephone was careless with what she wrote down, so some things were in there she wasn't supposed to see. And I couldn't risk her picking up on my emotions or power doing it again." His lip ticked up before shaking his head. "Nonetheless, I made sure the skin walking spell was in Persephone's book, and well, they already hated each other. So, it was only a matter of time.

"See, I covered the Crystal stone with magic and made sure it stood with Jax and Verena, because I knew Davyna would go for it after seeing that spell. And it was a beautiful sight…" He moved in, placing the blade on my cheek and trailing the steel down, making me grind my teeth. "Jinx was nothing but someone to take the fall for me. So no, I didn't give a fuck about her."

"Fuck…you are sick."

"Maybe, but I couldn't have anyone take away what was owed

to me. Not in my kingdom." He smirked. "I assembled my own army to capture her, but she killed most of them, and you killed the others. I had to be right there, pretending to be her friend, when all I wanted to do was fucking gut her."

"Why are you telling me all this?" I asked, glancing up into his vile pools of hatred and deceit.

"Because you won't be here to save her this time. Or anyone you care about. I left all your friends bleeding out and took all the stones from them. I've been watching your little meeting at the Sky Court with the mirror Obsidian gave me; I have been close, watching, and waiting to use what I possess."

Pulling his tunic open, I saw his skin tattooed on his ribs, beaming with the same shimmering black and white scar Davyna had on her arm, but it was a circle. It twisted together, creating all the symbols of the Courts.

"Since I couldn't take the throne and access the power I deserved, they agreed to give me this, along with some of their power after Persephone met her end. They altered it after Davyna returned so it would be harder for her to sense since it was in a fae's body. Although, her skin did heat when we touched. I bet that confused her." He chuckled. "I've been able to sense her. I knew where she was the whole time, Kadeyan... How does that feel?"

Looking away, I felt the pain of his words stab me, pulling me lower to the ground. My eyes caught on the stones and I counted five before looking back. "Why do you need the stones then?"

"They are for Obsidian. He wants them back. I just needed to channel them to keep her from finding you."

"Well, you're missing one." I laughed, making him grow angrier.

"No, I'm not." Glancing at him, I looked at the pale scars I left on his chest, surrounding his heart, and his skin began to glow a bright orange. "One last gift my mother gave me. Well, because Obsidian told her to. Dark magic kept anyone from sensing it...even you, with your hand in my chest." He glanced up, taking a deep breath before meeting my gaze again. "The stone has been right here all along," he whispered.

He stood to his full height and concern fell over his face.

"What? Can't finish what you started? Last time I checked, you usually pull the trigger pretty fast."

He huffed before licking his bottom lip. "No...your mate is close." He walked away, lost in thought.

My heart ached, wanting to scream out through our bond that I was here, and to feel her brush the walls of my mind and send her sweet heat coursing through my body.

"If she is out there without her chains, she is going to be a problem... But maybe she can be yours..." Alastair moved in. "I have a better idea. How would you like to kill your own mate?"

"Are you fucking insane?" I yelled as he punched me. I looked up at him and spit out the blood pooling in my mouth, splattering it across his face.

He hit me again, and again, and my body swayed. I pulled against the chains, but my power refused me, weakening me by the second. Blood continued to fall from my wounds, and a daze set in before I slumped lower to the ground.

"No, but you're about to be."

Alastair continued to cut and slice into my flesh, chanting words as the world began to blur around me once again. And all I could think about was *my heart*—the one person who kept my universe turning. I tried to call for her, over and over again, but it was no use.

I'd never feel her again, not in this life...

A spell fell over my body as darkness surged through my veins, and I knew death would have been more of a comfort, because whatever was coming next was going to make my worst nightmare come true.

I was going to kill her...

CHAPTER 76
DAVYNA

"Davyna, what does this mean?" Evren asked as I paced back and forth in the room, Ravyn keeping pace with me.

"It means I'm the descendant of Zaryk—the maker of the gods. I have both sides of him and his brother because of some curse. I am the key to raising him. And now that Tanith is dead, the realm is attached to me and Obsidian."

"How do you know that?" Calix asked, crossing his arms over his chest.

"I saw Obsidian kill his first mate in my dream, and the power transferred to my aunt... When he killed her, it transferred to me."

"So, what do you want to do?" Levanna touched my arm as she gave me a look filled with compassion surrounding the topic.

"We need to sever the link between me and Obsidian from this realm."

"What will happen to all of us fae? To you?" Evren asked, worry evident on her face.

"I don't know...but you will be free of him siphoning your magic. And if a realm needs two gods to stand, breaking our link should stop that, and then I'll kill him." I ran my fingers through my hair. "We need to find Alastair, and then get all the fae out of Valyner."

"We are going to find him, Davyna," Levanna said, looking over to Sorin as he entered the room.

"Faelynn and Dalia were injured on their way to the Mortal Realm." Sorin clasped his arms behind his back. "I saw to it that one of our friends in the Crystal Court went to them." I took a deep breath and felt some relief fill my heart, before Sorin tilted his head to grab my attention. "What do you need us to get?"

"Get all the dark obsidian that you can find to kill the bastard." Everyone began walking off to the weapons room down the hall, but I pulled Levanna back. "How long were you going to keep it from us? When did it start?"

She glanced down at her hands before looking into my eyes. "It started shortly after you shut everything off. I used my power to cover it, which only made the sickness speed up, since I was depleting my power." She took a deep breath, slowly glancing up to meet my gaze.

"And I would have kept doing it until my heart stopped beating because I wasn't going to stop helping my family." My eyes began to water, and hers followed suit. "After I left you in the Sky Court...it wasn't long after. I felt it pull from my body, and then Alastair..." She closed her eyes and her fury climbed.

"Killing Tanith took away the imbalance of power. If it healed you, that means that anyone infected should be cured."

"Oh my gods... Davyna, then what about the tear in the veil?" I shook my head.

"I cursed it, that's different. I didn't curse all of you. It was our power making the fae sick." I looked at her hands before taking one in mine. "I can't lose one of my best friends."

She smiled. "I can't either...or my Queen." I huffed but she squeezed my hand, pulling my attention back to her. "You are a ruler, Davyna Ember. And I know your mother and father are watching over you, so proud of what you've become."

A tear slipped down my cheek and she lifted her hand to wipe it away as Sorin, Calix, and Evren stepped into the room with weapons in their hands. Ravyn rubbed up against my leg and her eyes beamed with excitement, like she knew it was time to shed blood. And I nodded, watching her snout scrunch up, revealing her sharp fangs.

Pushing my power out around all of us, we fell onto the front lawn of the castle. Evren gave some weapons to Levanna and Calix, before walking over to me.

She handed me two daggers, and her gaze scanned over the lands cast in a light fog below. "Do we know where he is?" Evren asked, her eyes showing concern, and my anxiety resurfaced.

I sheathed the weapons, staring at the dagger strapped to my thigh that I took from Obsidian. "I don't know where he is..." I said softly.

"Davyna, focus," Levanna called out to me. "Think of a memory with him, and let your power do the rest."

Swallowing hard, I felt the emptiness of him growing stronger but kept trying. I closed my eyes, my thoughts drifting to last night, dancing to the music and clothes we wore to the Fallen Ball. I wanted to recreate it, cherish more than I did when he first brought me here. I recalled the comforting memory of him sitting by my bedside in the Salt Court, his hand gently holding mine as I healed from the true siren attack...and when he called me *his Dearest*.

Then, there was the haunting image of the Crystal Court, where I approached him, my attire tainted by the black blood, and his touch on me in the gap. Or how we laid in his bed as tears fell down my cheeks as he shared the tale of my parents. Dancing that night in Hell, and then... That was the night I realized I loved him... I loved him with everything I possessed and then some.

As I reminisced, my heart quickened, and a soothing warmth began to course through my veins.

He changed my life. He made me hate with a force that caused my veins to burn, but also made me love more intensely...bringing me to life...and pulling me back from the darkness. He helped me see who I was when I couldn't.

He never gave up...

A smile rose on my face as I replayed our memories, every moment woven together on a tapestry, telling our story. Behind my eyelids, I could see the light illuminating from me, coloring my vision red...until I saw something. A dark place...water dripping in the distance...and a tunnel I could never forget.

My eyes snapped open, and I gazed into my friend's eyes. "They're in Hell."

Looking around the tunnels, I felt my stomach rise and fall. The memories of this place were good, filled with firsts that I would cherish forever, but they were also now filled with all the people I brought here...and slaughtered like animals. It made bile rise in my throat, still hearing their cries. And maybe some deserved it, but not all.

If Kadeyan hadn't been as persistent as he was to get me back... how many more lives would I have taken? Thousands? And now, I needed to bring him back from whatever he was enduring under Alastair's hand.

But what if we were too late? I still couldn't feel him, and if he was here, alive... Why couldn't I sense that?

Ravyn's hair stood up on end as Levanna, Calix, Evren, and Sorin appeared next to me, weapons across their backs and chest. Their demeanors changed quickly, scanning the tunnel. They were no longer the fae I knew, but soldiers willing to go down for their Lord.

Damn the world and the future if he wasn't in it.

Moving forward, I rolled my shoulders back and let the dark power build in my veins, controlling it to my will as it mixed with the light.

We moved deeper into the tunnels and I kept my eyes straight. "What else is down here other than bedrooms and this area?" I asked, glancing over at Calix.

"There is a staircase that goes to a lower level. It was in case they needed more space or to lock anyone up who was getting stir-crazy," Calix said, and I nodded, following his lead down the hall.

We passed by the room where Kadeyan and I stood, and my eyes drank it in. The door was open, exposing the bed still dressed in reds. My heart stilled in my chest but I pushed onward.

My hands balled into fists as we approached an open door at the end of the hall. I moved forward, seeing the spiral staircase made of dark grey stone and exchanged looks with everyone, before listening in. There was no noise...no heartbeats below, but something felt off.

"Are you sure you saw this place?" Levanna whispered.

Power spiraled up the stairs, coating my skin... It was power I knew all too well now, matching the stones—matching my own. I took off, keeping my feet light on each step as the magic grew stronger, mixing with my wrath. This wasn't a coincidence. If that power was here, it meant he was too.

Stopping at the bottom of the stairs, I saw two double doors at the end of the hall and my magic called me towards it. My friends quietly pulled their weapons free and I took off running as tears filled my eyes. I placed both hands on the doors and pushed them open, not wanting to think about what I would see.

I sucked in a breath and a tear ran down my face, seeing Kadeyan in the middle of the room. He was on his knees and his head hung low with crimson painting his skin.

"Kade!" I ran to him, feeling slight pain as I passed through a barrier, but that didn't matter. Nothing mattered because he was okay and I could now hear it: his heart beating.

Dropping to my knees, I placed my hands on his face, trying to get him to look at me, but he wouldn't. "I'm here, Kade. Look at me. I got you."

My eyes scanned the space, seeing nothing but the dark edges concealing the edges of the room, before my eyes locked on the stones outside the circle. The five of them together must have been enough to block him from me.

"And so, the wolf traps his prey once again... Hello, Davyna." My head slowly turned to see Alastair move from the shadows, smiling.

I noticed everyone else was stuck at the doorframe, trying to get in. Levanna was chanting, her magic battling with the spell keeping them out, and Calix was banging against it. I couldn't hear them and glanced down at the stones... That was why; it was higher magic...and only I could pass through it.

"You bastard!" I stood up, facing him. "What did you do to him?"

"I helped him mend his ways..." He glanced down at Kadeyan before slowly looking back to me and speaking the words of the ancient language. "Venetee." *Kill.*

Turning back to Kade, I barely had time to react. He tackled me to the ground, with his fist crashing down towards my head. I moved over, hearing the stone crack beneath me.

"Kadeyan! Stop!" I yelled, kicking him back.

Pushing off the ground, I jumped up and looked into his eyes. They were all black.

"He can't. Not until you're dead or you kill him, in which case, I'll finish you off," Alastair taunted as Kadeyan lunged at me.

"He can't kill me. He doesn't have the dagger!"

Alastair smiled. "You sure about that?"

Turning back around, my gaze locked with the dagger in Kade's hand, the black and white metal shimmering against the dim room. I glanced down at my empty sheath. Shit!

Kadeyan threw his shadows out, pulling me towards him. He rammed it down, piercing it into my arm, and I cried out. I threw my flames and pushed him back, burning his skin...but it did nothing to stop the insane glint in his eyes that wanted my blood to spill.

"Why are you doing this?" I screamed at him, but Kadeyan was relentless in his attack, moving in on me with no regard to who I was. My heart broke, knowing how he felt now when I was lost to my own dark power. And I understood why Sahar didn't fight Eryx—why she *couldn't*. I could end Kade so easily right now, but that wasn't an option. It would never be one.

He stabbed me again in my leg and warm crimson blood flowed as he pulled it out. I fell to the ground, gripping the wound, and looked up just in time to see the blade coming down towards my heart. I rolled to the side, hearing the metal ring out as it cracked another part of the ground.

"You know I could have loved you, Davyna, but you just wouldn't be who I needed you to be. It's a shame," Alastair said with little emotion laced into his words as Kadeyan's shadows poured out, pulling me towards him again. I broke his hold, throwing him back until he crashed into the wall. "This was always our fate: the love story that ended in glorious tragedy."

"I never loved you, you sick, twisted bastard!" I yelled, looking at him, but he was unfazed. He was always this person...and I gave him a second chance.

Fire roared from my hands and I threw it towards him. He stood still, the flames covering his body, and I took joy in ending him. That was, until he stepped through them, unscathed. He started walking towards Kadeyan and my hands fell in defeat. How was that possible?

"Venetee da." *Kill her.*

Kadeyan wiped the blood from his mouth, walking towards me with a wide grin. Focusing on the magic surrounding us, I stood still and pulled everything from within to the surface to break the barrier. I began siphoning it, feeling it burn my veins as the spell started to crack and lose its hold on the room.

I let out a cry as it shattered and fell to the ground, and Levanna and Calix ran in towards us. Ravyn, Evren, and Sorin went towards Alastair, but he threw them back with a swipe of his wrist. Ravyn recovered, growing triple her size to match what the beasts looked like the day she connected with me. She towered over him, growling so loud that it shook the tunnels around us.

"Get the stones and take them to the Mortal Realm!" I screamed and I threw my fires out at Kade, but he simply dodged each blaze. The spell wasn't breaking on him. Not even looking into his eyes stopped his pursuit. Alastair vanished, his orange mist floating in the air just as Ravyn's jaws opened wide, ready to devour him whole.

He reappeared next to everyone and I pushed off the ground, screaming as his own power brought them down to their knees.

Kade sliced into me, stopping me in my tracks and a cry to fell from my lips. I pushed away from him, searching his eyes for that part of him that was buried away. "Kadeyan, please!" I wept.

The building began to shake above us and everyone stopped. My stomach turned and I glanced up just in time to see the stone give way.

Creatures flooded in, their eyes black as night and their heads nothing but a skull with antlers. They crashed to the floor and let out a piercing scream that sounded like an animal dying. I covered my ears, the sound still echoing around us. They stood tall, like humans, but their legs were those of a beast. They lunged with their bone-like fingers stretched out, ready to devour all of us.

My attention was pulled back to the male I loved, who was pinning me to the floor. I didn't want to fight him... Screams and growls rose into the air, but it all sounded far away as I gazed into his soulless eyes.

A tear escaped and my lip trembled. "Kadeyan..." I called out to him as he raised the blade.

Levanna used her power, pulling the stones to her before placing them in her pocket as another creature came towards her. Ravyn jumped in front of her and ripped it to shreds, throwing the body parts to the ground. I took in the room, watching them fight, and realized...Alastair was gone.

I nodded as Levanna met my gaze, and I saw the pain in her eyes. She didn't want to leave us, but she needed to. "Go. All of you!"

Without a second thought, she pulled everyone in and screamed for Ravyn, who was fighting off two of the creatures before they vanished. Moving my eyes back to Kade, I smiled and pushed through our bond lost in the sea of darkness and called out to him.

"*Come back to me.*"

He stalled and tilted his head just as the blade touched my skin. I could feel him in there, and the connection between us was trying to break through whatever was placed on him.

"I'm right here... Please."

White light began to build around us, keeping the creatures from getting closer. More tears fell down my face and I heard the screams of the beasts, trying to claw their way through the power I was unleashing, but I kept my eyes on my mate.

Taking the dagger from his grip, the cold steel bit into my palm, but I ignored the pain. With my free hand, I pulled him down, pressing my lips fiercely against his.

Light exploded around us and I heard the stone crumbling, but I chose to stay lost in this moment; to savor him how I should have since the day I learned he was mine. I gave him everything I had, lacing it into our kiss. And slowly, he began kissing me back.

Pulling away, I looked into those amber eyes and sobbed. "Davyna?" he cried out and I looked up at the stone falling towards us.

My power shot up and the void welcomed us in like an old friend. The sounds of the stones crashing down started to fade away, destroying the tunnels we once knew, and taking the creatures down with them.

Taking a deep breath, I clung to Kadeyan in the darkness, feeling every broken part of me mend together. My mind, my heart, my soul...

Although, one thought floated around, pulling my attention away from the joy I wanted to stay lost in. And the wrath I imagine only a god could contain began seeping out of me.

Alastair could run...but he couldn't hide from me.

CHAPTER 77
DAVYNA

We landed in the Crescent Court and I sheathed the two-toned dagger I took from Obsidian, before my eyes scanned over the lands. I had a feeling that he was here, wanting me to be on these lands one more time with him. And following the trace of magic he left in his wake confirmed it.

My gaze narrowed on the dense trees behind the ruined estate when a shadowed silhouette stepped into the opening. Alastair stood there, holding a white rose in his hand, and slowly turned to face me. Smiling, he brought his hand out, offering it to me.

Kadeyan stepped by my side, and I didn't need to turn to see his eyes were beaming red. The gap opened behind us and my friends' presences—along with their fury—spun around me. Ravyn stepped up by my side, growling as her small body began to grow in size, ready to fight again.

I started walking towards him and he stood still, not a care in the world, which only made my ire grow. I threw my hand out, sending out black shadows that wrapped around his body, before dragging him through the grass. He laughed as I stood over him, still unamused by this all.

"I should have killed you in the throne room when I had the chance!" I screamed.

"Give it a try now, honey, but you'll fail."

Sending my fires out, I covered his body again, hearing his chuckle over the crackling flames.

Kadeyan pulled me back. "He's channeling Obsidian's power."

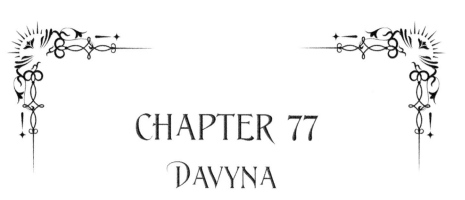

Alastair jumped up, his power wrapping around my throat as he threw me through the air. My back slammed into the ground, and I quickly recovered, seeing him throw crimson flames at Kadeyan.

Shit. If he was channeling Obsidian's power, then his magic was similar to mine. That was what I sensed around the Crystal stone—strong like mine, but different.

It was him.

With a yell, I threw out a searing white bolt of light, stopping the magic from hitting Kadeyan. I pulled him through the gap so that he would stand behind me, and then slowly turned to face Alastair, my chest rising and falling in harsh patterns. My eyes narrowed on the male before me as he began to smile wide. And every lie, every betrayal flashed within my mind, adding to the hatred I felt for him.

Alastair turned, wiping his hands. "Damn, it feels good to use this power. I've had to keep it locked away so that no one knew I had it; so that *you* didn't know I had it. But now, there is nothing keeping me from using it on all of you." He laughed. "Did you think you could beat Tanith and Obsidian, Davyna?"

Darkness took over and I moved forward, his eyes not showing any fear. I sent out my power. It met with his in the middle, creating a surging war of energy that made the air thicken. Yet even with his advantage, I could tell he wasn't as strong as me.

Speeding through the air and the power between us, my hand wrapped around his throat and cut off the air trying to find its way into his lungs. I looked into those honey-brown eyes that used to hold empathy, love, and knew it was all a lie.

"I killed Tanith, Alastair. And now, I'm going to kill you."

He smiled slowly, his hand burying into my chest as his fingers wrapped around my heart. His hand reached down for my dagger, and my yells mixed with everyone's from across the field.

Before I could even blink, they were surrounding him and his hand fell from my waist, the dagger falling back into its sheath. Kadeyan's shadows entered me, removing his hand, and I stumbled back. My heartbeat grew wilder with each passing second as the wound began to heal.

Sorin and Evren shifted, pouncing into the air as their jaws opened wide, ready to rip him apart, but Alastair threw them back. They rolled through the grass before jumping back up, their fur on end as they stalked back towards him.

Levanna began chanting, her magic booming into the air with such authority. The trees began to sway with the growing winds she was creating. Yet, the magic she was using did nothing to pull away from the power in his veins.

Alastair sent out a dark plum mist, laughing as it entered her. "Do you want to die the same way your mate did? What was his name again?"

Levanna fell to the ground, blood pooling from her mouth. I sent my power out, severing his hold on her and placing her in a barrier to recover.

Alastair narrowed his gaze on me.

Kadeyan and Calix moved in, using their shadows to hold his body in place before Kadeyan's fist slammed into Alastair's face. I broke into a run when Alastair turned back around, throwing Calix into the air and taking hold of Kade.

He lifted Kadeyan into the air with tendrils of black vapor and I could see it working its way into his body. "I think it's fitting that shadows consume you from the inside out. Don't you?" he yelled up to him as Kadeyan gritted his teeth, pushing against his hold.

I ran and everything within purged as I let out a scream that shook the ground. Every line of power shot out of me, creating an array of the Court colors blanketing the Lands. The snapping of trees and crumbling stone from the ruined estate filled my ears and I looked at my friends, shielding their eyes from the rays. Alastair fell to the ground, dropping Kadeyan. Just as he stood up, I rushed in, dropping to my knees, and placed my hands on his face.

I felt the power within Alastair and challenged it with my own, and he hissed in response. Chanting silently, I glared at him, my eyes promising pain and suffering as he tried to pull back, finally showing true fear. Kadeyan got behind him and wrapped his arm around his neck. And within my peripheral vision, I could see my friends breathing heavily, waiting to attack if need be.

The spell on him didn't want to leave, reminding me of the magic I expelled on the throne, taking on a life of its own. It wanted to live in its host and feed, but I wouldn't give it that satisfaction. As I began pulling it from him, his screams rose, and I looked back into his eyes.

He glanced up to the sky. "Obsidian!" he cried out.

I pushed harder, ripping every ounce of power I could from his veins, and breaking their connection. He wasn't going to come and save him... Not now. Not when he needed me.

I focused on the power within my veins, tingling and fully entering me, and my skin began to crawl. It was tainted with its vile intent to destroy and it matched Obsidian's will.

Pulling my fingers from Alastair's flesh, I fell back and threw my hands up towards the sky, releasing the magic given to him. I didn't want any power in my veins that was marked with Obsidian's aura.

Iridescent flames shot out behind the magic, consuming it before it exploded. My breathing was ragged, taking in the colorless embers falling around us, and I stood up. I took the deepest breath I could muster and moved over to Kadeyan, both our eyes staying on the male before us.

Kadeyan's shadows seeped from his fingers, ripping Alastair's tunic open and exposing his ribs. Nothing was there, and I glanced up at Kade, hearing his thoughts about the mark Alastair had from Obsidian... I turned back, taking in Alastair's skin again and smiled.

His power was gone.

"Looks like your *god* has forsaken you," Kadeyan said, his voice dropping an octave. "Now you have to deal with me." Shadows poured out of him, their vengeance as clear as the fury Kadeyan held in his eyes.

He ripped Alistair back through the grass before lifting him into the air. A petrified scream fell from his lips as Kade's wings shot out and he flew up after him. Kadeyan hovered in the air as their bodies collided, and he brought his fist down on Alastair's face, the force throwing him back down to the ground. He coughed violently and tried to lift himself up, but his own body refused him. Kadeyan slowly lowered himself and looked at me, nodding his head.

I glanced at my friends, a silent exchange passing between us all that this kill was mine. I looked back to Alastair, his gaze laced with distress.

"Davyna, please... It wasn't me. I didn't know what I was doing. It was all Obsidian!" Alastair cried out. Kadeyan lifted his leg and let his boot crash down on Alastair's back, pressing him back into the grass. "Davyna, please... I didn't—"

"I told you once...if another lie came out of your mouth...I'd rip your tongue out," I growled, narrowing my gaze on him. I walked in slowly and he kept trying to explain himself, but I knew the truth now. I knew everything.

Kadeyan pulled his foot off and grabbed the back of his neck, lifting him to stand before me. His mouth opened again and before he could speak another word—another lie—I pulled the dagger from my hip.

My power surged out, gripping his tongue until it was out of his mouth. The blade sliced through the air, taking it clean off. Blood instantly pooled from his mouth, screams echoing beyond us. Dropping the useless organ from my power's hold, Ravyn jumped forward, catching it in her mouth. She chewed on it, gulping it down before growling like she wanted more.

I placed my hand out, pushing through our connection. She halted, shrinking down to her normal size and obeying my command.

His life was mine.

Turning back, I watched him cough and gag on the blood still pouring from his lips. "I'm sorry, did you want to say something else?" I seethed and his body began to collapse. Taking a few steps back, Kadeyan let him fall to his knees.

I kept my gaze on Alastair as he glanced up at me, the tears and sorrow in his eyes fading as if they were never there. I could see the monster shine through—his true likeness that matched his mother —and chuckled.

There he was... The true Alastair.

Kneeling down, I lifted my hand to the side and allowed my fires to spin off it, growing hotter by the second. "You touched my mate, you killed my uncle... Who knows, you probably had a hand in killing my father as well. And tried to kill me, how many times?" Bringing my hand near his face, his eyes widened. "You are going to burn forever where I'm sending you."

He attempted to yell at me, but I pressed my hand to his flesh and the fires ran over his body. I began visualizing him in agony for eternity, while chanting the spells I used before on Persephone, and smiled. Magic beamed from my skin and I glanced into his eyes. They grew wider, pushing out of his head until they popped and melted under the intense heat that even my friends had to back away from.

Piercing his chest with my hand, I ripped out his heart and pulled myself up, holding it on display. His body fell over, turning to ash, and I glanced back to my palm. Letting my fires back out, I watched them swallow the lifeless organ in my hand. It fell apart and showed me what I needed within.

The Crescent stone was a beautiful orange, matching Evren's hair in the beaming sun, with shimmers running throughout. And I couldn't help but smile as she moved in to examine it.

"To Elias..." I said, looking over to her, and her eyes welled up with tears.

"To our dad," she whispered, and I closed my hand around the stone, placing it in my leather jacket. Looking through the dying flames, Kadeyan's eyes were locked on me and the smile he held was life itself.

Ashes rose from Alastair's body, floating through the destroyed forest, and Kadeyan walked around them. "So...mate, huh?"

"Shut up." I laughed as he brushed his fingers over my cheek.

"About damn time, Dearest." He smirked. His lips crashed down on mine, and I basked in our ice and heat swirling together, wanting to merge into one and create something new—something beautiful and otherworldly.

But this wasn't over... We needed to do one more thing here before taking Obsidian down. Pulling away, I turned and looked at my friends.

"Let's get them all out of here."

CHAPTER 78
DAVYNA

I paced back and forth on the hill where Nesrin and I sat when I first returned, watching the remaining fae in the Ember Lands filter into the field below. Everyone went to the other Courts, calling the fae here, and I couldn't shake the nerves bubbling up. That was, until arms wrapped around my waist, pulling me in.

"You've got this, Davyna. Just speak from your heart."

I thought back to my family, their bravery, and channeled them. Standing tall, I turned around and pulled Kadeyan down, kissing him deeply as our tongues got lost in a dance of passion and lust.

Pulling back, I took a deep breath and closed my eyes. "What if they don't listen?"

His shadows swirled around us, pulling us to the field to stand on the elevated stone before them all. He leaned in, whispering in my ear, "Make them, Your Grace."

Turning, I took in my friends standing off to the sides before Maeve appeared through her white mist. She moved in, hugging me, and I gripped onto her black gown. "Did you bring the dagger to the Mortal Realm?" I asked.

"Yes. But, Davyna...you saved my life. I was supposed to die... Fate deemed it," she whispered, shaking her head.

I smiled, pulling back. "Fate might get some things right," I glanced to Kade, catching his smile as he listened in, "but fuck it if it takes you from this world."

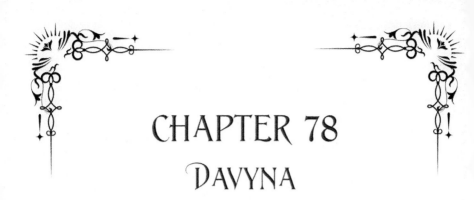

She pulled me back in. "Thank you..." We stood in our embrace for a few more moments before she moved over to join everyone I loved.

I turned, feeling my heart stop as I took in the sea of faces.

The vision Maeve showed me flashed before my eyes, and I remembered what she said—they were going to need *her*...this version of me. I held onto that, pulling myself to stand taller.

I walked forward to the edge of the stone, swallowing hard before saying, "These Lands are your home.... My home." I looked around, taking a moment to memorize their faces, to hold them deep in my heart because I wasn't just fighting for the people standing behind me, but them too. "I have done some horrific things over the last few months, and I will carry that guilt until my dying day...but I don't want any more fae blood to be spilled."

Fae turned to look at each other, confused by my words, some even harboring some anger.

"I want you all to leave Valyner today." Whispers started to flow, and I spoke louder. "As some of you may have witnessed at Saawyn, there was an attack...it was done by the hands of the gods who created this very realm... As the daughter of your former King and the daughter of a goddess, I had the power to kill one: Tanith. But Obsidian is coming! And he has been siphoning you all since my father took the throne."

I took a shaking breath, dropping my head. "You deserve to be freed from him and from the chaos I've created." I glanced back out, my eyes stinging. "And as his equal, this fight is mine and mine alone."

I looked behind me at Sorin, Calix, Maeve, Levanna, and Evren...their eyes locked on me. Although, it was Kadeyan who stole my breath away as his eyes gleamed with pride. He nodded, gesturing his head back up to the crowd, and I turned back to face them.

"The Cursed Lands are still unoccupied in the Mortal Realm. I want you all to grab your things of importance and go there. He can't access your power, or cross over to that realm. When I'm done breaking the link and closing the tear in the veil, you will all be able to come home."

"I will not follow your commands. You are the reason we are in this mess to begin with!" someone yelled, and I took a moment to collect myself, looking over the fae.

I found the male who spoke and steeled my spine before I moved down the platform. The fae's whispers began growing as they moved out of the way, making a clear line straight to him. Kadeyan appeared next to my side, and I glanced over the male, locking my gaze on his forest-green pools.

"You don't have to." I looked around, projecting my voice. "None of you have to like me or respect me. I have created a mess here for you all. I've made you fear, made you hurt, and have even killed... All because I fought who I was. And mark my words, when I kill that bastard, I will not hold back my power on anyone who sides with him. I am fighting for Valyner so you all can have the peace and freedom you deserve." Turning back to the male, I softened my gaze. "Even you."

The whispers died down and everyone's emotions started swarming. They just wanted life to go back to how it was...and I wanted that for them.

We walked back to the platform and Calix moved forward, kneeling before me. "We will follow you, Your Grace." Evren moved by his side, kneeling alongside him before Sorin, Maeve, and Levanna joined.

Kadeyan took my hand, forcing me to look at him before he kneeled, grinning wide. "My one and only Queen," he said, kissing the top of my hand and causing me to smile wide.

Pulling my hand free, I turned and looked out over the sea of faces. One by one, the fae began to kneel. I took a deep breath as the silence fell over the lands and felt a warmth build within.

I didn't deserve this—the respect, the title. I would have to earn it, and be different than my father and his rule. I wanted to be worthy of them.

"Then, as your Queen, I command you all to leave today. Let

me protect you. Let me serve you today and always." I kneeled down, dropping my head in reverence to the people and sensed their eyes on me. I knew it wasn't needed. I knew a Queen was to be looked up to, but I wanted them to see me as *me.*

Even if it was for a short time, I wouldn't stop because this was my fate: saving them. And I could finally see that.

I was born for this...and I wasn't backing down.

CHAPTER 79

DAVYNA

Rising from my knee, I stole another glance of them all before saying, "Please, go grab your things and spread the word to whomever didn't come. Let's get everyone to safety."

They all began vanishing from the field and I turned to Sorin. "I need you to go to the Crescent Court with Evren and help spread the news to whomever wasn't here. And when you both get to the Mortal Realm, I need you to find Drystan. Tell him the fae will be in the Cursed Lands and will not harm the humans."

"Davyna, I'm not leaving you," Evren stated as she stepped in towards me.

"You will...and that's an order. Your people need you, Evren. They need *you*." Her eyes welled up and I buried down my emotions, moving in and clinging to her. After a moment, I pulled her back. "Now go and get them out. I'll be there soon to figure out the stones, okay?"

The Crescent stone was still in my pocket. Part of me didn't want to give it to anyone else because Obsidian would kill them for having it. And if I wasn't near them to protect them...

It was safer with me right now.

She nodded and the tears ran down her cheeks before she took Sorin's hand. They fell into the gap and I memorized her eyes, her face, before I turned to Calix. "Get all the Fallen Court members out now. And then, I need you to go help the Salt Court too."

"Davyna, the army isn't leaving your side."

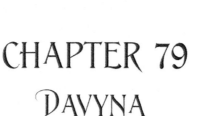

"I need them to watch over the fae in the Mortal Realm." I could sense Calix wanted to push me but stopped, bowing slightly.

Facing Levanna, I saw that her gaze was locked off in the distance, and my own shifted to follow. Anger flowed from two fae, raging into the air, and I shook my head.

"What the fuck are you two doing here?" she yelled as Jax and Verena both let their hands drop and a dark plum power flowed out towards us.

Throwing up a barrier, I looked back to Calix. "GO! We got this!" He nodded before vanishing. I glanced over to Levanna and Kadeyan and smirked, their expressions mirroring mine.

Pushing the barrier out, it devoured their spell before I sent out my shadows and held them in place. Their cries of pain pierced the air and it had an alluring tone to it, causing my power to stir. Rolling my shoulders back, I walked towards them, with Levanna and Kadeyan by my side.

"What are you two doing here?" I asked, tilting my head to take in their pained state from my shadows crushing into them.

"You killed our Lady! You killed Tanith!" Jax yelled. "You fucking bitch!" he screamed, the sound ringing out as I tightened my hold and held back my laugh. Did they really think they could take me on and win?

Turning, I looked at Kadeyan and Levanna as their eyes burrowed into the two people responsible for ripping Silas away. And a shift in their emotions started occurring as they looked at each other, knowing the day was finally here. Smiling with wickedness that had been suppressed for far too long, they glanced at me.

"Are you ready for your revenge?" I asked, taking in their expressions turning cold before they looked back to Levanna's parents.

"More than you know, little Ember."

My power enveloped all of us and we fell into the streets of the Crystal Court. My eyes darted around, and I realized this was the first time I'd seen the town. It was mesmerizing. All different colored crystals were shining through the buildings and walking paths, making it so bright. Although, it was the energy coming off of them that was the true beauty, creating an aura of magic that fed my soul.

Fae walking around glanced at us before coming to a halt. I dropped Verena and Jax to the ground, both coughing violently from the release.

I put them in a barrier for good measure and looked at Levanna. "We need them all here," I whispered.

"Summon them, Dy." Levanna winked.

I turned, closed my eyes, and searched in my mind as my seer ability pulled the words from my lips. The power flowed from my hands, and I opened my eyes to see the mist of purple travel through the streets with a whisper layered within, calling them all to us.

In a matter of minutes, the fae flooded the streets, and we made our way to the town center. A majestic crystal pillar rose high, basking in the sunlight and casting a radiant shimmer upon everything around it.

I looked around at them, seeing there were over a thousand of them trailing back down the roads through town. Their whispers of confusion and anger rose when they saw me, before they saw two of their own locked in my spell. I glanced at Levanna and nodded, stepping back for her to take the lead.

She moved forward. "This Court has been a problem since the beginning of time. Constantly fighting with the other Courts and separating itself to create chaos. That ends today!"

Someone called out, "Where is our leader? She should be weighing in on this."

"She's dead," I retorted, and eyes narrowed on me. Summoning my power to my hands, I showed them each line swirling together, before I let the purple mist shine bright. Many turned away, the light blinding their line of sight as I pushed more out. "I am just like you...and I want this Court to thrive. To join the other Courts and be free to live your life the way you see fit. Not under a tyrant like Persephone or Jinx."

A fae began walking through the crowd, causing the people to part, and I recognized her, along with the other two fae by her side.

Nyx looked around before walking up to me, smiling wide. She stared into my eyes for a long moment before kneeling, and Thea and Nova did the same. As they both rose, Nyx took my hands.

"I thought you were dead..." I said.

"I needed Jinx to believe that so I could help you all. My sister was evil... I learned that while working under Persephone." She shook her head, pushing the pain out of her mind as she glanced over the fae. "The Crystal Court is behind you, Your Grace."

"How did you—"

"I was just in the Ember Court. A few of us were. Who do you think was helping on this side to get you the stone?" She smiled at Levanna before turning to take in her people. "This is the Queen Valyner has always needed. And you will all show her the respect and honor she deserves."

Jax and Verena went to speak, but I sent my shadows out, covering their mouths. Glancing around, I watched as heads bowed and emotions shifted to accept Nyx's declaration.

Thea moved forward, taking my hand. "We can get them all to the Mortal Realm."

"Thank you," I said. They all bowed their heads slightly and walked off to talk to the fae, explaining the plan to get them to safety.

Within minutes, the streets were quickly becoming void of life, and I turned to Levanna and Kadeyan. Their eyes were fixated on Jax and Verena. I dropped my shadows from their mouths and they both began coughing.

"You are all going to fucking die for doing this!" Jax yelled.

"And why is that?" I asked, moving in.

He refused to talk, and I sent out my power. It coursed through his veins, making him grit his teeth together. I willed the truth to pour from his mouth and pushed harder until he cried out, falling to the crystal stone ground.

"Because Obsidian channels our power. If they all leave at once, it will break his hold on them."

"That's exactly what I want." I laughed because I already knew this from what Kade told me when he saw my mother in his dreams. "He will never take another drop of magic from these people."

"Did you know, in the Crystal Court, we do our executions publicly?" Levanna said, moving towards the barrier. She kneeled down, speaking to her parents now. "You took everything from me, and got away with it, painting me as the villain of this Court."

Her sorrow rose into the air, filling the square with the years lost to be a part of her Lands, with her people...with her mate. I knew she loved the Fallen Court like it was her own, but this was her *home,* and she was denied it because she fell in love with someone from another Court.

"You were a disgrace from the moment I looked into your eyes, Levanna. I should have killed you the day you were born," Verena spat out, and I could feel the pain slice into Levanna at her mother's words. It quickly vanished as if she needed to hear it to accept that there would never be a moment in time when love would be offered to her from these people. I knew that feeling... I searched far too long to find it from Hera.

Blood doesn't make you family...love does.

Dropping the barrier, I felt my anger grow and let my shadows lash out, holding them immobile. "Which one of you killed Silas?" I asked, glancing into their blue pools.

Levanna moved in, placing her hands on her mother. "It was her. She did it with her own two hands. My father was just holding him down." She dug her fingertips into her mother's skull and began chanting.

Her power bloomed, intertwining with all her pain, her disappointment, her loss, and even I was amazed by the power emanating from her. Jax began screaming, pulling against my power, but it was no use. He didn't move more than an inch before I tightened my hold.

Kadeyan moved over to Jax, glaring at him with a wrath that could burn the world down, and it made my own skin rise.

Venera's screams echoed down the empty streets, and the darkness within danced to the melody.

Levanna pulled her mother closer, her jaw locking for a moment before saying, "Remember what you said to me when I came home after finding Silas in the woods?" Her mother's chest rose and fell fast from the cries, but Levanna continued. "Stop crying... That was what you said. Are you ready to stop crying, Venera?"

Blood began pouring from her eyes, nose, ears, and mouth, causing her to convulse violently. Jax let out a guttural scream, and hers became softer as she choked on the blood.

Levanna rose, dropping her mother to the ground, and stood taller. It was like the weight of what they did held her down all these years and she was finally free of the burden. Though the loss would never fade, she was free of the constant reminder that Silas' murderers were living their lives without consequence.

That was just the thing, karma would always catch up with you. Be it tomorrow, next month, or a millennium from now...it would inevitably consume you, as it should.

Levanna turned towards me, her eyes filled to the brim, and her lip quivered. And I moved in. Her arms wrapped around me, her nails dug into my leathers, and I met her embrace with the same intensity.

"It's okay, Lev."

Her grief of losing her mate was unreal, forcing me to feel its smothering hold. It was hollow. Empty. And I couldn't for the life of me understand how she was still breathing while living with this pain. How every smile I'd seen her wear looked so effortless. But now I knew...it wasn't.

She was hiding it.

Her father's cries grew as we parted. They were awful. And if it was anyone else, I'd feel bad for him... But that wasn't the case. He pulled against my shadows again, trying to go to his mate, but Kadeyan laughed.

"I think you need to be more concerned with what's about to happen to you." He kneeled down, his hand darting out and burrowing into his chest, cutting off his next scream. Kadeyan let out a breath tainted in pain he'd suppressed all these years, and my heart ached for him.

Ripping his heart out, Kadeyan stood and pushed his body over. It fell by his mate's corpse, and Kade inspected the organ in his hand. Almost like he was making sure it was truly still. After a few seconds, he tilted his hand forward, letting the heart roll out of his palm and onto the ground below.

Looking up, he whispered, "For you, brother." A tear ran down his cheek before he closed his eyes. A small smile graced his lips and I pushed into his mind, seeing him sitting on the rooftop of his castle with his brother. Silas' blue eyes beamed in the darkness of night. His smile was contagious, causing Kade to mirror the expression. I wish I could have met him. Or seen Kade with his family...

My lip quivered and my eyes stung, quickly filling with a layer of droplets wanting to fall. His shoulders relaxed and I sensed the weight of his honor to avenge his brother lift off him, giving him some semblance of peace among the chaos we were living in.

I moved in, wrapping my hands around his waist as he pulled me close. Sniffling, he brought his lips down on my head.

Magic swirled next to us and my skin rose. Turning, I took in Obsidian, his eyes lost in fury. "You told them all to leave! What the fuck do you think you are doing, Davyna?" he yelled, his anger shaking the ground.

Smiling, I placed a barrier around us before opening the void. I pulled the Crescent stone out of my pocket and threw it to Levanna. Pushing her through the gap, I turned back and felt Kadeyan walk up by my side.

"Winning your game," I taunted, smirking.

His anger boomed and shot out at us, but I blocked it. Pulling the gap to us, it ripped us in, and we fell through the darkness.

His wrath followed after us and the heat of his black flames crawled through the void, trying to consume us both. Pushing Kadeyan behind me, I sent out iridescent white flames with a yell as they consumed his. A cry of agony and fury poured from his lips, ringing out in the void before I saw beaming red eyes fade into the darkness. My mind focused on the Mortal Realm and I turned around, grabbing onto Kade.

My stomach rose as our bodies rolled through the soft dirt before we came to a stop. Pushing myself up, I looked over him as he coughed and then laughed. He rolled to his side, looking at me, laughing harder.

"What?" I asked, resting on my knees into the forest floor, and I noticed the dirt sticking to our leathers.

He slowed, looking at me with awe in his eyes as he smiled wide. "How did I get so lucky to have someone like you?"

CHAPTER 80
OBSIDIAN

Hours passed and broken furniture surrounded me in my study, but I couldn't stop. After she made it to the Mortal Lands, I came back to Solyus and the rage I felt only kept growing in power. Picking up a vase, I threw it across the room, watching the glass rain down and chime against the stone floor. Another yell barreled out of me and I felt the spell I placed so long ago weaken more by the second, becoming almost nonexistent... The power they gave me was fading.

They had all the stones. They had the two daggers...

"FUCK!" I yelled and began pacing the room.

The mirror on the desk began to swirl, but I pulled my gaze away, letting my eyes fall to the destruction on the ground.

"What happened?" Arcadyus demanded.

"She fucking found out everything, and took what we need to the Mortal Realm, along with my fae," I gritted through my teeth. "I failed you, my King..." I kneeled, still keeping my head down.

"Mm... Did you try again to undo her curse to the throne?' he asked.

"Yes. I can't... I have no idea what she did."

He began laughing, the sound so light and filled with joy. "That's because it's magic you don't possess...at least not like her. The stones may have given you the magic of my father's Lands...but they are tainted. My mother's, on the other hand...those are pure." He paused, chuckling. "None of you can undo it because my power is in her veins. I guess doing that spell with my brother paid off. Because now, we have her—the key to everything that is to come."

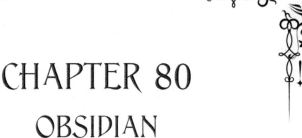

"Your Majesty, I don't think you understand... We don't—"

"No, this is perfect. Let her try and combine the stones..." he stated.

"What do you mean? She—" I asked, but he just chuckled again, cutting me off.

"Obsidian, have I ever steered you wrong? Do you doubt me?" he asked, and I shook my head. "Good, because we will get what we need from her...one way or another."

I walked closer to the table, picking up the chair that was turned over before sitting down. His green eyes beamed through the darkness, and I straightened myself. "Then tell me what you want me to do to my *mate.*"

CHAPTER 81

DAVYNA

Smiling, I stood up and wiped the forest brush and dirt from my leather slacks before moving towards Kade. "We have all the stones now and both daggers. We can—"

"Davyna, slow down." He pushed off the ground and I looked into his amber eyes. "Let's just savor this moment." After a few seconds, I nodded my head, and he pulled me in. "Dy, would you... I mean... Will... Fuck." Apprehension poured from him, and I pulled back, furrowing my brows.

"What?" I asked, sensing his trepidation.

He began pacing, looking out through the woods, and I giggled. I'd never seen him act like this with me. It was cute. He stopped and turned to face me, running his tongue over his bottom lip.

"Why are you nervous?"

"Because I need to ask you something..." He glanced around again, and I followed his gaze. Then, it hit me... I knew exactly where we were.

Pulling my gaze back to him, his eyes were on me. They glistened in the dying rays of the sun peeking through the tall pines surrounding us.

"Ten years ago, I saw you for the first time...in this very clearing." He began walking towards me and my heart sped up. "Elias walked off, but you stood out here, swinging that sword for hours... smiling wide with your hair sticking to your face." He lifted his hand and brushed a piece of my hair back, tucking it behind my ear. "I was lost for what felt like an eternity, Davyna Ember...and meeting you was like coming home. So, what better place to do this..."

"Kade..." My lips trembled before turning up in a smile.

"I don't care that I can't feel our bond anymore, or that you have a fucking god coming after you. I just want to spend every minute I have left tied to you in every way possible." His chest rose and fell faster now. "We will kill him and break the link because..." He pulled back, taking my hands and kneeling down on one knee. "Because my soul yearns for yours and I can't imagine not being tied to you for eternity. You are the woman I chose. The fae I fell in love with. And the goddess I will happily serve until the end of time."

"Kadeyan Fallen..." Dropping to my knees, I placed both of my hands on his cheeks, hearing his thoughts swirl around me. "Yes."

"You didn't even let me ask." He chuckled, pulling me in at my waist.

"Kade, just shut up and bond with me."

His eyes softened before scooping me up off the forest floor, and I laughed. Placing me down, he pulled the dagger from my hip and looked it over. "Are you ready?"

"Yes," I said eagerly, my heart skipping a beat.

Taking my hand, he flipped it over and brought the blade to my skin. Our eyes connected and everything around us faded away, along with the hushed hums of the lush forest. It was just us in this moment. He pulled the blade across my palm, the red blood pooling up instantly. Looking up from it, I watched as he cut his own hand twice as fast before looking into my eyes.

"To our forever," he said as I lifted my hand to join with his.

"To our forever."

Our blood merged together, dripping from our joined hands, and he cleared his throat. "Ves lé untal mer désantos."

Tears formed in my eyes. Picking up on the ancient language from my abilities, I repeated it back: "Until the seas dry up."

"Ves lé matos un tràbum."

"Until the earth withers away."

"De untous val allahi, mur vas duntas." He smiled and the bond grew around us, celebrating as I felt my soul becoming one with his.

"I will be yours, and you, mine."

He stepped closer, and we both spoke the last part together, the words filling my veins and breathing new life into them: "Until the sun burns out and the stars die."

A tear streamed down his face, and I couldn't keep mine back anymore.

"Until death and beyond," we said in unison.

Our eyes connected and everything fell into place as we spoke the last words begging to be set free: "You are mine. Now and forever more."

Power surged through me as I closed my eyes and basked in it. I finally felt whole, like the part of me that was lost and searching came home.

I feared this, feared letting someone in. And my past told me I had reason to always believe I needed to keep people away, but sometimes... It was possible to meet the right person who you could trust with your pain, your victories, and still be exactly who you were meant to be.

Those people would never leave your side.

It was those people who deserved to be let through the impenetrable walls you built. Because you needed them to show you the things you gave up on... To heal old wounds that stood open for far too long.

Smiling wider, I opened my eyes and looked at my mate. The joy surging within slowly shifted as I took him in. He was fine, but the power around him...

"What is happening?" Power was surging from me and into Kadeyan, and he was staring at it in shock.

I focused on my power, feeling it filter out, and shook my head in alarm. "I don't know..." Our hands were still interlaced, and I tried to pull away but couldn't. He wasn't in pain, I could sense that, and the power passing from me to him felt right... But what did it mean?

"Oh my gods," I said as each line of power wrapped around him, encasing him as they wove together to create something new... *Someone* new.

He looked at me, astonished as our hands slowly parted, but I couldn't move. I couldn't speak. He lifted his hand and flames ignited, rolling off his fingertips and back down. Lifting his other hand, he held a small sphere of water, molding it to his will.

"How is this possible?" I whispered and he looked at me, his eyes wide. I finally took a breath, letting out a small laugh.

The power I carried lived within him now and he was everything that I was. My parents were mated, but my father didn't transform into a god... But if Faelynn and Persephone were right about my mother's powers being suppressed as if she didn't have that part of her yet... Then, was this normal?

I went to speak but stopped because fear and worry flooded to the surface. I swallowed hard, my mind moving a mile a minute. If he was like me...then... Was he going to be okay? What did this mean for him when Obsidian found out?

"You don't have to worry about me, Dearest. I'm okay. Better than okay." The smile fell from his face and both of our eyes locked on each other.

"Kade, you..."

His jaw fell open and awe passed over his face as he moved in, placing his hands on my cheeks. "I can hear you again... Davyna..."

"How?" I asked, shaking my head before my mind replayed every day since I came back. He could only pick up on my scent and follow it, but he couldn't read my thoughts or feel me through our bond.

"I think it was because of what you are. It had to be... After you burned the throne, this part of you came out...blocking me. But now, we are both the same, and..." He laughed, smiling wide. "I can feel you, Dy. I can feel our bond again." His lip trembled and I stepped in, wrapping my arms around his middle. A soft cry broke from my lips and his fingers dug into my hair and around my waist. I let out another sob mixed with a laugh.

The air shifted around us, our bond desperate and demanding we finish the last step. Pulling away, I looked into his eyes as they burned a bright amber—melting and swirling like mine did when my fires rose—before blood encased them.

His power lashed out, removing our clothes with the Crystal spell I used on us so many times that I had lost count. He drank me in like it was the first time he saw my bare skin, and I did the same. Sweeping his arms down, he picked me up by my thighs and I wrapped my legs around him. He moved through the woods and slammed my back against a tree.

The air was ripped from my lungs as his cock pressed into my center. His hands ignited and he slid his hands up, grabbing my ass. I moaned, the sound traveling through the trees as the heat engulfed every nerve in my body.

Dropping to his knees, he held me up, placing each leg over his shoulders. "All mine," he said, running his tongue over his bottom lip. "How wet are you, little Ember?" He leaned in, running his tongue up my center and his eyes burrowed into me. "Because I want to drown in you tonight." I bit back the moan as he did it again, but he bit down on my clit, making me release it. His voice entered my mind, and he growled, "*Don't you dare keep those sounds from me. I want to hear every scream...every fucking moan.*"

He caressed and nipped at my clit, sending everything within into a frenzy. I ran my hands over the shaved sides of his head, before gripping onto his hair and pulling him in. I tilted my hips back and forth, taking my pleasure as he moved faster, meeting my intensity.

My body tingled all over from his power twisting around each inch of my skin and pulling me into bliss. I pushed some of mine out and it molded perfectly with his, pushing me further into ecstasy. Every nerve was exposed to him, and my body succumbed to his demand.

Falling over the edge, my flames sparked off my skin with each pulse as I cried out, basking in the inferno within. Kadeyan didn't wait for me to come down before he got up and pulled me to his body. "I need you in bed...now."

Kadeyan used his power before I could respond and the gap swallowed us whole. Within the blink of an eye, we were on the bed in his cabin, with him on top of me. His skin was glowing with an apricot hue, and I trailed my hand down his chest, creating sparks in my wake.

Growling, he took his cock in his hand and ran it down my entrance. Breathtaking chills passed through me. As he did it again, I tilted my hips up, silently begging for him to fill me. "Don't worry, I'm not finished with you... I'll never be," he teased.

Gripping his shoulders, I flipped us over and straddled him. His eyes darkened and I leaned back, rocking my hips over his length.

He moaned, watching the way I moved over him before his hand came up and softly caressed my breast. The heat of his hand made my own fire rise, and I looked down. Flames licked my skin, and he moved his hand lower, causing my breathing to pick up.

He brushed his thumb gently in a circle over my clit and I couldn't help but arch more into his touch. "Take what you want from me... It's yours."

The heat drove me wild with need as I lifted myself and lined his cock up with my entrance. I slowly took in each inch, feeling my walls tighten around him like never before. Moans rang out from the both of us as I began moving up and down.

"Fuck!" he growled, his hands gripping my hips and tilting his own to bury himself deeper into me.

We both got lost in the desire of needing to be one, making it our survival until every line of our power was fused together. His nails dug into my flesh as he sat up, and I pulled him closer, sinking my fangs into his neck.

He groaned and I drank deep and long, savoring the taste of him that was sweeter than ever before. He made me feel stronger as his essence merged with mine, and I became intoxicated in the haze.

Letting go, I watched his blood slide down his chest, matching mine in a melted iron grey. He thrusted his hips up over and over again, hitting that spot within that only heeded his call.

He moved in, biting into my breast. I cried out from the sting of his fangs before a raspy moan passed my lips. Blood traveled down my stomach, and I pulled him closer. "Gods..." I strained and he looked up, running his tongue up and over my nipple.

"No, Dy. God... I'm your *god*..." He moved inside me as I held onto his neck, riding him as I chased my salvation, praying for what he could only fill me with. We were life and death, blending together to create a place that would forever be our home, and it felt right.

It felt...perfect.

Kadeyan's flames began lifting off of him and my own joined in. Within seconds, both of us were fully engulfed in a glorious blaze, burning brighter and devouring the cabin around us. The wood began to crack and sizzle, but I kept moving over him, feeling both our releases chasing towards one another.

The ceiling began to fall around us, but it quickly turned to ash, and I looked up at the night sky through the pines of the forest.

Kadeyan pulled my face down, brushing his tongue against my bottom lip. "Your paradise is right here," he whispered.

I went to speak, but his lips crashed down on mine in a bruising embrace and I fell in. Everything imploded and I pulled back, crying out as my orgasm racked through me. He thrusted once more, pouring himself into me, and I continued to ride out each pulse, lost in the firestorm that was us.

We slowed, our gazes finding each other once again, and it was clear that awe was all we both felt.

It was complete now... We were one in every way you could ever wish to be with a person. And by some miracle—through all the hell we faced—there was only true happiness in this moment.

Smiling, I looked up through the smoke we created, and took in the stars above. "So, what now?" I asked, glancing back down at the smirk plastered to his face.

"Oh, Dearest..." He flipped me to my back, his dick still hard inside me, and I laughed. "We aren't done... Not even close."

CHAPTER 82
KADEYAN

The stars faded from the sky hours ago, but I still couldn't get enough. I fucked her all over the ruined cabin, in the woods, the lake nearby, and I still wanted more. Although, holding her in my arms right now as I watched the sun move in the sky was everything.

Running my fingers through her hair with one hand, I used the other to pull fire to my fingertips, amazed by this. How was it possible? How did I get everything she possessed? With who Davyna was though, maybe I shouldn't be surprised. The granddaughter of Zaryk—the male who created the gods and came from who knows where.

She told me what I missed a little bit ago when we took a small break to eat. I was shocked to hear about Maeve's vision, but glad she was okay. And then the Sky Court, with all the fae who were lost in the destruction of it. I was glad she killed Tanith, but with that, it made everything clear—not only to her, but to Obsidian.

I never made it back to the circle after talking with Persephone, which shocked her. I told her everything Alastair said about working with Obsidian and how far back his deceit went, which didn't surprise her. Obsidian must have been waiting for some disconnect in her magic from our realm to take me away and hand me off to Alastair. But at least his little minion was out of the picture. Finally.

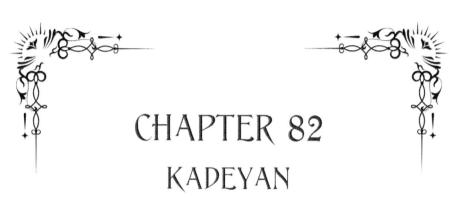

Rubbing her eyes, she opened them and took in the flames at my fingertips, and I grinned at her. Chuckling, she sat up a little, her naked body pressing closer to mine. "You are like a child with a new toy."

"Last time I checked, you liked the new toys and what they made you feel...how they made you come." Smacking my chest, she let out a silent laugh before inching closer to me.

"We need to go to the Cursed Lands..." she said, resting her chin on my chest.

I closed my eyes, soaking in this moment before glancing down at her. "One more time?" Gazing up, her eyes swirled. "I'll make you come fast."

"Fine, but then we need to—"

"I know." Pulling her on top of me, I smiled and felt happiness like never before. Even if we were in the midst of war, I was happy... I was whole.

Walking out of the ruins of my cabin, I interlaced my fingers with hers as she looked up at me. I pulled her into the gap, but not to the Cursed Lands. Our feet landed on the front lawn of the Foster Estate, and I turned to looked at her.

Her eyes glassed over and her heart doubled over as she took in her past. The good and the bad of this place. And I could read her thoughts so clearly about still believing this place would always be cursed.

Lifting my hand, heat traveled through my veins until fire ignited, and I let it shoot out of me. I kept my eyes on her, seeing the flame's glow reflect in her silver pools as one tear fell.

The crackling of wood pierced the still morning air, and heat radiated towards us, brushing up against our skin.

"If I have to come back here every day to make sure they never rebuild this place, I will, Davyna. No one will ever have the stain of loss and pain inflicted on them from living in that house," I whispered. Turning, I took in the white paint charring black, bending in on itself as the boards warped in.

She slowly turned to look at me and I met her gaze, the sounds of the fire roaring and consuming everything within. "Thank you." She stood on her toes, pulling me in by my jacket and I kissed her, lacing my love into the way my lips moved over hers.

I broke our kiss because the bond was still pushing me to have her. And in this moment, I wanted to just hold her and watch this place turn to ash. I should have gotten her out sooner.

"Kade..." She looked up at me, but her eyes were still locked on the blaze. "You did come for me, and I wouldn't be the person I am today without going through what I did. Never feel guilty for that."

I nodded and she rested her head on my chest.

We stood there for a while, taking in the charred wood and thick smoke rising into the air, before I cleared my throat. "You ready?" I looked down and she nodded. The gap swallowed us whole as we fell away from the past and into our future.

Landing in the valley of the mountains in the Cursed Lands, I looked over at Davyna. Her eyes locked on all the fae surrounding us as they walked through the tents scattered over the lands.

As we moved forward, many bowed their heads towards her, and she reciprocated. Grinning, I looked at the larger tents laid out, before spotting my friends lost in conversation with someone.

Sending my shadows out, I tapped on their shoulders, and they all turned. Calix and Levanna's eyes widened, and I could sense their joy to see us.

Lev started running towards us, her eyes glistening as she slammed into my chest. "Fuck! You guys had me scared! Where were you?" she asked, pulling back, but I smiled and looked down at Dy. "Oh my gods, you guys finally..." Her smile was contagious before she covered it with her hands. She lunged forward, pulling Davyna in and they fell into their embrace, their laughs forcing me to smile.

Calix grabbed my shoulder, pulling me in. "You had me worried for a minute."

"Only a minute? And I thought we were friends." Pulling back, I let out a long breath. "We need to talk to you guys…in private."

Calix and Lev looked at me, worry grazing their expressions. Davyna let out a breath, her eyes traveling across the field, and I slowly turned. She was staring at the man standing next to Sorin and Evren, lost in conversation.

"Go, Dearest… Go see your friend," I said through our bond, and she gave me a smile.

She took off running and I began walking towards them.

Drystan turned and looked at her, grinning wide before they locked their arms around one another. Surprisingly, I didn't feel the need to kill him. Well, that was until the hug lasted longer than I cared for.

"Calm down…" Davyna said within my mind, laughing. As they parted, I walked up by her side and gave him a small smile.

"I was just talking to your friend, Sorin, about our armies. We are keeping it under wraps to the general public that any supernatural creatures are here. So, we need them to be discreet if they leave the Cursed Lands. Anything stirring up rumors of fae or the Cursed returning, they will retaliate…and I won't be able to stop them."

"They won't," I assured him.

"Good. If being here is keeping your kind safe, then you are more than welcome to stay." He looked at Davyna, smiling wide. "It's good to see you again, Dy."

"You too," she responded before Evren moved in, hugging her.

"If you don't mind, Drystan, we actually need to discuss something," I said, grabbing his attention.

"No, it's fine. I need to get back home anyway. My wife and son need me." His eyes beamed with love and joy. "But I'm only a letter away if anyone needs me."

Davyna laughed, saying, "Drystan, if we need you, we will just show up where you're at and let you know."

He shook his head, letting out a slight chuckle. "Then, I'll keep an eye out." He glanced over us all in the camp, and I sensed his emotions lost in amazement after all this time that creatures like us existed. That his first love and best friend was one of them. Bowing, he took off, his two men following closely behind him.

"What's going on?" Evren asked, her brows pulling down in worry.

I gestured to the large tent behind her and waited for everyone to enter. Davyna looked at me, her smile faltering.

"Are you ready for this?" she asked through the bond, but I pulled her close, placing a kiss on her forehead.

"Hell yeah. I want to see Calix shit himself," I said back to her, but deep down, I knew what this meant now, and it made my stomach tighten. If three gods threw off the balance in our realm...it would mean the sickness could return and start killing the fae all over again.

Davyna gazed up at me, her eyes screaming that she could sense my worry. There was no more hiding behind a wall anymore...but honestly, I didn't want it any other way.

"Let's go," I said.

Walking in, I looked around at everyone as Davyna took the lead. "So...something happened."

"Same here. I checked in with fae about the sickness, and they all watched it vanish yesterday when mine did," Levanna stated, her eyes beaming until they locked with mine.

"What? And when were you going to tell—"

Davyna pushed into my mind. *"She wasn't going to."*

Shaking my head, I narrowed my gaze on her. "You weren't going to tell us? Me?"

Maeve, Faelynn, and Dalia came in, hugging Davyna before Ravyn pranced up to her. The little beast rubbed her leg before stopping to look at me. She tilted her head for a moment, before bowing, and everyone froze in place.

"Kade?" Evren asked, unsure what to say next.

Pulling my hand up, I focused on the Crystal Court's magic and pulled it forth. Purple swirled off my fingers and Levanna's jaw dropped. I then began to focus on the Salt magic, turning water in my palm, before allowing my hand to shift, showing off the claws. It was insane to feel it, and to know how Davyna lived with all these lines of magic. It was overwhelming but perfect at the same time.

I expected to battle with it last night, like Dy did, but having her near me, our power working together... It was natural. And maybe that was because I lived with fae magic for 1,500 years before her. Or maybe it was because the curse of Zaryk was in her, with Arcadyus' blood...

Everyone's eyes grew wider, but I looked over at Davyna, feeling fire instantly ignite in my palm.

"What the fuck!" Calix yelled, taking a step back before laughing. "Never thought I'd see the day where you become a god and use it to be a hero. It looks weird on you, Kade."

Throwing my fires out towards him, his shadows blocked the small blaze, causing him to laugh harder. "Don't let this fool you... I've still got the hint of a Devil in me." I looked at Davyna and winked.

Evren stepped forward, looking at the both of us. "Is this even possible in a mating bond?" she asked before turning to Maeve.

"No... Never. But Davyna is a goddess. So, I guess anything is possible. Does that mean, you're a..." Maeve stopped herself and I looked at Davyna.

"Yes. He is like me in every way now. And that means there are three gods again... Which means, we need to kill Obsidian or break the link as soon as possible.

"The one benefit we have here is that he can't come to the Mortal Realm. My grandfather blocked them all from coming here, but not me. I think he knew we would need this place to prepare. So, we need to figure out the spell and merge the stones." Dy looked around at everyone, avoiding my gaze. "We have to get this right, because if not..."

She glanced at me and the pressure of our reality set in. He wouldn't kill Davyna... He would come after me, but I wasn't leaving this world. I wasn't going to lose this, not when I just got everything my heart yearned for. And I didn't mean the power. I could give a fuck about that coursing through my veins. I could be made human for all I cared. It was her I refused to lose, to be parted from.

Grinning, I looked at everyone. "So, let's kill our maker."

CHAPTER 83
KADEYAN

We all sat around the tent, night already blanketing over us as we passed around a bottle of whiskey. Laughs were exchanged in the camp with the other fae, but also within our tent. And it felt right, like I could do this for eternity with them.

Davyna sat next to me with her mother's journal, reading intently as I looked over everyone. Levanna was sitting with Maeve, talking to Faelynn and Dalia. All their smiles were wide as Faelynn and Dalia shared stories about the other Courts in the Realms they were from.

Evren giggled, pulling my gaze over to her talking to Calix and Sorin. Calix couldn't rip his eyes from her, and it was a look that made me curious if they might be… No. He would know by now. I was happy for him either way… Happy for all of them for finding joy through all the dark times we faced over the last eight months.

Everyone in this room deserved it.

Davyna's mind was moving a mile a minute, pulling my attention back to her.

We had the weapons, the stones, and knew what to do with them. It was breaking the link that seemed to be the challenge. The spell that Maeve was talking about a while back wasn't going to be enough and something in my blood told me that.

And Davyna nodded. She knew it too.

She flipped to the back of the journal where the unfinished spell was and ran her fingers over it. I silently chanted in my mind, hearing her join me as we got lost in the dialect of the ancient words. Our power molded to one another's, and something sparked in both of us.

Jumping up, she turned and looked at me. "This is it..." All heads popped up and landed on us. "This spell was never to be done alone. It had to be between two gods."

I looked over it again and began seeing how the words needed an extension from one person to another, but you wouldn't know unless you attempted it. Nyna made sure no one could figure it out...until this moment. Did she know that I was going to turn into this too? Did my father?

I smiled, remembering our conversation in the stone when I asked how I could kill them. He said, *It's not your place yet...* He knew and that didn't bring anger or any harsh emotions to the surface—just awe and appreciation for the male who raised me.

"The power can't come from one. It has to go between two." I grinned, pulling her in and kissing her deeply.

"Fuck. You guys are going to be like this for a thousand years, aren't you?" Calix yelled.

Davyna pulled back and looked over her shoulder at him. "If he demands it...then yes."

"I do," I said, bringing my hand to her jaw and turning her to face me. "Let's do it. Right now." She nodded her head and we both rose from the ground.

Davyna and I grabbed the stones and decided to go somewhere farther away from all the fae just in case the power in the stones and us did anything to anyone. Levanna and everyone else used the gap, following after us.

We ended up in another clearing surrounded by mountains, and my eyes scanned it over as Davyna did the same. "I've been here before."

"When?" she asked, moving by my side.

"This is where your mother took me and gave me the dagger." She smiled and turned to me. "Let's make your parents proud and finish what they started." Her eyes glistened as she shook her head before pulling me farther into the field.

We laid the stones around us, joining hands as our friends stood a healthy distance away. "Leave at any sign of this power expanding outward. Do you understand?" I called out, and they took a few extra steps back. I laughed and glanced back to Davyna, sensing her nerves mix together with mine. "Not to sound incompetent, Dearest, but how the hell do I do this?" I whispered.

She looked down and silently chuckled before glancing back into my eyes. She cut her palm with the black and white dagger before taking mine and doing the same.

"It's in your blood. Let it lead you." I arched a brow, wanting to call bullshit, but she sheathed the dagger and took my hands. "Trust me. It will work."

I gripped her hands harder, pulling her closer to me. "Then let's create something new." I brought my head down, resting it against her forehead and started the spell. "La etsa beluiva di tus el notaches."

We said it over and over again, and I could feel my veins tingling as the power between us bounced. It was an intense feeling. One second, I felt powerless, and the next, I was an all-powerful god. Davyna began speaking louder, and I matched her as light beamed from us, the clearing plunging into day.

The stones rose from the ground, circling us slowly at first. They picked up momentum, moving at the speed of light and spinning as they rose into the air above us. Glancing up, I watched each one until they were a blur of colors.

Light beamed from them, painting the clearing and the sky above with purple, blue, orange, red, black, and white. I got lost in the beauty of the words, the stones, and the magic that was given to us. And thought about how my father was right.

It was a gift.

As we chanted the spell once more, the pain invaded my body and I looked to Davyna, feeling hers grow as well. Panic bounced between us, and it took everything in us to say the last word, but we came too far to stop now. It spilled from our lips, and everything went black before the world faded away.

Floating in the darkness, flashes of the throne filled my vision, pulling me to it... It called me and Davyna by name. Reaching out to touch it, I was pulled back just as my body slammed into the ground.

Rolling to my back, I sat up slowly, my head spinning as I focused on where we just stood in the clearing. It threw us back a good twenty feet.

Looking around, I saw the stones were no longer in the sky or blanketing us with their array of hues, and panic rose. I scanned the clearing for Davyna and spotted her on the opposite side from me. I took the deepest breath I could muster, relief washing over me, but there was also an exhaustion I'd never felt before. And it was coming on fast.

Standing, I forced my body to move towards her. "Are you okay?" I called out, but she was already up, moving my way.

"Yeah, are you?"

I nodded, meeting her back where we just stood, where the grass was now fully burned away and covered in ashes. Our friends ran out towards us, even Ravyn as she whined with concern. Their breaths were heavy, looking between me and Davyna.

"Did it work?" Sorin asked.

Davyna glanced down at the ashes before kneeling. She brushed them away, exposing the new stone that laid beneath.

Lifting it up, I stalled and took in the beauty of it. It was half black and the other white with all the colors of the Courts swirling within. It reminded me of what Davyna's power now looked like—what mine would look like. It was enchanting and the power it held was far beyond this world, pulsing into me and Davyna.

Everyone exchanged glances, smiling and soaking in one of the few victories we'd had since this all began. Davyna and I looked at each other, knowing what needed to happen next.

"We have to go back," she said.

"You saw it too?" I asked her through the bond, and she nodded.

"What?" Evren shouted. "No, if you go back to Valyner—"

I cut her off. "We have to be in Valyner to finish this."

"Why?" Calix asked as his brows pulled down, his confusion encasing us all.

Davyna looked to the stone before meeting my gaze, and I swallowed hard. "Because we need to fix the throne."

CHAPTER 84
DAVYNA

Three days passed and me and Kadeyan were still recovering from the spell. After that night, it felt like all the magic in my veins depleted and I was human again. I could barely keep my eyes open as we returned to camp. My muscles ached worse than from any training I'd put my body through in the past, and it traveled deeper, penetrating my bones. Kadeyan crashed on the bed with me, and we slept the first day away. The next two days, it was the same, waking for short periods of time before sleep beckoned us back.

Waking today, I took a deep breath and relished in the ease it came with. My eyes fluttered open and I sensed my power coursing through my veins. It was renewing, giving me exactly what my body needed to feel like myself again.

Sitting up, I took a deep breath and Kadeyan rolled over, smiling at me. "Morning, beautiful."

"Hey..."

He sat up and kissed me, realizing it too. "What the fuck was in that spell?" he asked, pulling away.

"What, you don't like feeling like a sick human?"

"No, fuck that." He laughed before his amber eyes landed on me. "But if I had to, I wouldn't want to feel human with anyone else."

Shaking my head, I leaned forward and rested my arms on my knees. "What if breaking the link kills us?" I questioned, turning my head over my shoulder to look at him.

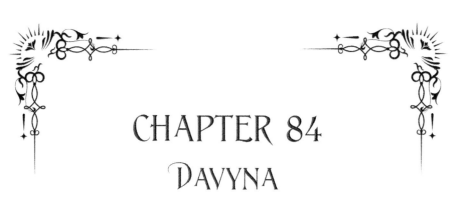

His eyes softened. “I’m okay with that. Because we will be going together.”

“But what if it kills us before we break it? All of Valyner could die.”

He nodded his head, looking off into the distance. “Then we won’t fail them.”

“But what if—”

“Davyna...” he said, pulling me from the spiraling thoughts. “You are compassionate, caring, and always think of others. That’s what makes you who you are. But when we walk into that throne room, you need to give it your all.” My head dropped, but he brought his hand to my chin, making me face the truth in his eyes. “You need to forget everything. Everyone. And let everything inside you take over and fight like hell no matter the outcome.”

“That’s just the thing though, Kade. I’ll go in fighting not only for you but all of them, and I won’t hold back. Because they deserve a better life. I’m just afraid I will fail you all.”

Smiling, he ran his thumb over my cheek. “I know you are going to give it your all...and that alone means you won’t fail. Regardless of the outcome.”

I laughed. “If we don’t win, that is the definition of failing.”

“Is it? Failing is giving up. And maybe you did that before, but look at where you are now... You can’t fail when you refuse to back down from what stands before you.”

We sat for a little longer, talking about our plan to leave for Valyner first thing in the morning before we got up and put on our leathers. As I buttoned my top, I glanced over at the table near me and picked up the stone. Holding it in my hand, my vision began to shift and blur at the edges before it completely went black.

I saw the throne room destroyed. Blood pooled on the ground and a dark shadow stood over someone, and I dropped the stone, the vision vanishing with it.

My heart skipped a beat and Kadeyan walked over to me, concern laced in his gaze. “That’s not going to happen. We won’t let it,” Kadeyan whispered, planting a subtle kiss on my neck.

Nodding, I picked up the stone again and shoved it into my pocket. "Let's go."

Pushing the thick fabric of the tent aside, I took in the fae as they ate and drank together outside. Stopping, I took them all in. Crystals were telling stories to Salt members. And the Crescents laughed, enjoying the company of the Fallens.

My heart ached as I saw only a few Sky members around, knowing many went down that day with the temple. Their veils were off, their crowns nowhere to be found on these lands, and they were coming to life with the other fae.

My shoulders relaxed and I drank in the sight of them all. Fae weren't separated by anything here, and you could feel them coming together as one. And I couldn't help but think maybe that was how it was always supposed to be.

No division. Just unity.

A greater ache took root, realizing not a single Ember was here anymore. I was the last...along with Kadeyan now. And it brought back the rage I needed to channel towards the one who took them from this world.

I moved out, my chest rising and falling. Stopping, I was lost for what to say to them all.

"Everyone! We have something to say!" Kadeyan shouted, moving in by my side. I turned to look up at him before glancing down at his hand. I reached out and interlaced my fingers through his, instantly feeling more courageous and turned to face the masses. *"You've got this, Dy."*

One by one, they began moving closer to us, forming a circle as they waited.

"Tomorrow... Kadeyan and I will go back to Valyner."

Whispers traveled through the camp, but Kade cleared his throat. "Obsidian will more than likely show up while we are there." His voice carried, and worry lifted into the air. "And we need you all to stay here where he can't hurt you."

Kadeyan looked to me and I nodded, projecting my voice as I said, "He has been channeling our power since the beginning, trying to raise a god named Arcadyus from what he called the Abyss." I took a deep breath. "I am the daughter of Nyna and Ezekiel Ember. You knew my father and his power, but like I said back home...my mother was so much more. She was the daughter of a god named Zaryk." A presence washed over me, one that was of peace and love, and I knew it was her... That she was here with me right now.

Tears welled up in my eyes and I looked over the fae again. "This was never your war to fight. It was always mine."

My lip trembled and I directed my voice to her and my father, knowing they needed to hear this more. "And I will gladly take it upon my shoulders now...and make you proud. Not as your Queen, but as someone who has viewed herself as human, fae, and now a goddess. I will fight for Valyner, for the other Realms, and for the humans who live here. Because this world is our home...and it will remain so."

Kadeyan stood tall, looking over everyone. "We both will fight."

The fae before us stood silent for a minute, but one by one they began chanting, "Es val tu rosé. Es val est vertta." Their voices grew louder, echoing into the mountains. and I turned, looking over them all.

My heart beat faster when I saw my sister and Levanna chanting with them, smiling wide. Even Sorin and Calix had their hands over their hearts, their voices carrying through the air with everyone else. And a sense of peace—true peace—washed over me.

Forever our fire Queen.

Forever our shadow King.

My heart was overwhelmed, feeling immense honor, but also sorrow. So many people weren't here who deserved to be. I was fighting for the living, but I knew in this moment...I also needed to fight for the dead. To honor their losses, and to acquire their justice. And I hoped wherever they were, they saw this today and felt the power...felt the union of their people.

Kadeyan entered my mind and I turned to look at him. *"They are here, Dy. Everyone we've lost. They are right here."* He placed his hand over my heart, and I felt a tear slide down my cheek.

Taking a deep breath, I smiled at him. "To raising Hell."
"No, Dearest... To burning it down."

CHAPTER 85
EVREN

I moved through the camp to check in with the fae before nightfall. I wanted to make sure they were good on provisions before we sent out fae in the morning to surrounding areas to get things again. Everyone was in good spirits, but some whispered their concern as I walked by, wondering if they would ever return home...or if they would even have tomorrow.

Wasn't that always the biggest fear...having tomorrow? And yet, regardless of our current circumstance, tomorrow was never guaranteed. Not for a human, a fae, or even a god.

"You okay, Crescent?" Sorin asked, and I turned to see him walking up.

"Yeah. How is everyone?" I asked.

He looked around at the fae for a long minute, his lips turning up to one side. "They are all fine, Evren... They are safe here."

I shook my head, hoping that the illusion of safety would remain... I knew it would here, where Obsidian couldn't get to us. But what about in Valyner? What about Kadeyan and Davyna going back there?

They wouldn't be safe.

Walking towards my tent, Sorin pulled back the thick canvas, gesturing for me to enter first before he followed. I took a deep breath and slowly exhaled. His hands wrapped around my waist from behind, holding me against his solid form.

"I don't like this idea of them going back alone."

"What could any of us do though?" Sorin asked.

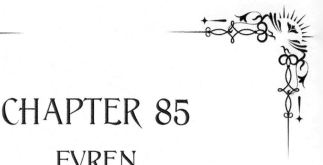

I let my head drop, knowing he was right, but there had to be something. For too long, I sat away from the fights, watching Davyna hold the world on her shoulders. And while I could tell she was in a better place now, it didn't lessen the urge to be by her side when this all went down—even if that meant my death. I was willing to lose it all to fight for what I loved. Just like my father. Just like my sister.

Calix walked in, and I turned, but Sorin kept his hands on me, unfazed by his presence. Calix walked over, took my face between his hands, and searched my eyes before I felt him push into my mind.

"I want to go too, but they won't let us, little wolf." He leaned in, kissing me softly. Sorin let out a low growl, but it only made my core tighten. "Let's just get some rest. It's been a long day." Calix said in a hushed tone.

But it was the last thing I wanted to do.

We weren't mates, but I loved them both. As friends, as protectors, and for who they were. I knew one day, we would all part, and maybe that was next week or in a hundred years, but I knew what I wanted tonight. Even if it would be the only time.

"Would you like me to leave?" Sorin asked.

I swallowed hard, shaking my head. Calix tilted his head, and I knew he was reading my mind as his eyes hardened.

"I want you to stay. Both of you..." I said, glancing back at Sorin, who was shocked, before meeting Calix's cold gaze. I dropped my head, my heartbeat picking up as the blood in my veins tried to keep pace. Waving my hand over the tent, I watched the soft ripples in the air of the privacy barrier falling in place so no one could hear us beyond the tent.

"Then get in bed, little wolf..." Calix said in a low tone, one that forced me to look up into his swirling crimson eyes, erasing the golden brown. Yet, his eyes were on Sorin, and I slowly looked back.

The males before me stood still for a long moment before Sorin nodded.

"Get in bed, Evren," Sorin commanded, and chills cascaded down my spine.

"Are you guys ok—" I was cut off, sucking in a breath, when Calix's hand slid into my leather slacks. Finding the evidence of my arousal, he moaned.

Sorin's hands slowly wrapped around me and moved up, ripping my top open. His hands cupped both my breasts as his thumbs flicked over my nipples, making me bite my lower lip.

Air ceased in my lungs, causing them to ache for my next breath. And I didn't care, not with both of them touching me.

Sorin leaned in, whispering in my ear, and every thought vanished.

"Be our good girl and listen."

The sun's rays were beginning to stretch over the peaks of the mountains, killing off the night, and the nerves within started to rise. What would they be met with when they returned home?

My legs dragged through the camp, sore from shifting with the wolves a few hours ago and running the perimeter of the Cursed Lands. It was a nice distraction from what was happening today, but I still couldn't shake this feeling deep down that this was not Kadeyan and Davyna's fight alone.

I heard someone softly crying, breaking me from my thoughts, and turned. A fae sat on the ground with one hand up as someone moved over and pulled her into his arms. But I saw it, the grey and decaying flesh starting in her fingertips. I swallowed hard.

A hand rested on my shoulder, causing me to jump.

"There are five more cases throughout the camp already," Sorin whispered, pulling me along towards Kadeyan and Davyna's tent.

"That didn't take long to come back," I said, my throat going dry.

"It didn't take long the first time either... But so long as

Obsidian dies or the link is broken, it will go away again before anyone dies."

I nodded, knowing that was true, but it still made my stomach turn. "Can you find Nyx, Nova, or Thea? Have them bring the herbs or cast spells over the sickness to delay it."

Sorin leaned down, kissing my forehead. My eyes slowly closed, taking a deep breath as a quake ran down my spine.

"I'll go now and take care of it." He pulled back. "Go see your sister off."

He took off and I began walking towards Davyna's tent. With each step, my heartbeat quickened.

Pushing the thick canvas back, I took in my sister as she inspected the black and white blade before gripping the gold handle and securing it in her sheath. Moving over, I pulled on her straps to make sure her armor was secured.

When I saw how she slightly trembled, I asked, "Are you sure we can't come? You said all of us leaving broke his hold on using our power, so—"

"Evren...it will be safer here. And with some of the fae... I can't...I..." She paused, and my eyes dropped. She knew about the Fae in the camp already. Clearing her throat, she brought her gaze back up to me. "I don't mean that to undermine your power and ability to fight. I just know Obsidian would kill anyone working with us. And I don't want blood spilled. Not today, not ever."

Kadeyan moved up beside us, sliding his own dagger that matched Davyna's into his sheath before securing a sword on her back. He placed a kiss on her cheek and she leaned back into him, his arms wrapping around her in a loving embrace.

"We will be back soon," he said as he looked up to meet my gaze, smiling. Although, I'd been around both of them long enough to know that the confidence they were emulating was a blanket to hide their fear of this going wrong.

Breaking apart from my sister, he grabbed two daggers off the table and secured them at his hips before moving to exit the tent. Following after them, I breathed in the crisp air before glancing over the morning dew still dressing the grass and casting a sheen on each blade. Everyone in the camp still rested, aside from the tents next to us.

Levanna and Calix walked out, before Maeve, Dalia, and Faelynn joined us. Ravyn stretched her front paws, yawning as she slowly made her way over to lay at Davyna's feet.

Turning, I looked at my sister, my eyes welling up. "I don't want to lose you again." My heart broke because we both knew what it felt like to think the other was dead, never having a goodbye. And somehow, this seemed worse because how could you say everything you needed to say to someone you loved? How did you accept that this could be the last time you saw them?

Pulling her in, I held onto her tighter than ever before, and felt my own soul pull me to this fight. We were born for this pain, for loss...but also for loving more intensely because of it.

"Nothing can ever separate us. I love you, Ev."

"I love you too."

We all exchanged hugs but stood quiet. It was the calm before the storm, and it was eerie, sobering. Kadeyan looked at Davyna, before taking her hand in his.

Magic began to circle around them, blurring the picture I wanted to cherish for eternity until they were nothing but a memory. A harsh exhale fell from my lips, and I knew... Deep down, I knew what I wanted. And I wasn't going to deny the call that rang out deep in my soul.

I turned to everyone, steeling my spine as their eyes locked on me in confusion. "Go through the camp and find anyone willing to go back to Valyner to fight."

"Evren, they said—" Levanna started but I began walking off.

"I know what they said." Stopping, I turned and looked at everyone. "I'm willing to die if it means I fight beside them. Are you?" Everyone exchanged glances and slowly began to smile. "Let's go defend our home and show Obsidian we are not afraid."

CHAPTER 86
DAVYNA

As we fell into Valyner, Kadeyan and I pulled out our wings and began soaring through the sky. Thick fog surrounded us, making it hard to see through, before I realized it wasn't fog…

It was smoke.

Pushing my wings to beat faster, Kadeyan met my pace and we broke through the dense cloud billowing up. I stalled, hovering in the air, and took in the edge of the Fallen Lands. Smoke rose from all over, and the smell of ash was pungent, invading my nostrils.

"He was here," I said, looking over at Kadeyan, his gaze taking in the destruction before us.

"Do you feel him near?" he asked, but I shook my head. "Then let's go." My wings pressed through the thick air, and we began moving towards the Ember Court. Glancing over at Kadeyan, I saw that his gaze was locked on the piles of smoke rising from the northwest.

The Fallen castle.

I changed my direction and went towards what I'd considered my home since arriving there, and my heart drummed against my ribs. After a minute of flying, the town came into view and my jaw fell open. The buildings were all crumbled to the ground, with small embers still burning in the rubble. Kadeyan sped up, heading toward the castle on the highest hill, and I followed after him.

My eyes couldn't stop scanning over the wreckage. Even the Dead Forest was just a wasteland of burned wood. Turning my gaze, I slowed as I took in our home, feeling the air rip from my lungs.

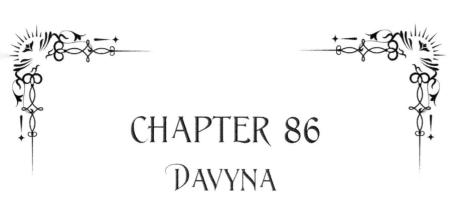

The entire castle was small stones, lying in piles with not a single structure of the building standing tall.

Kadeyan lowered to the ground, his breathing increasing as his eyes scanned over the destruction. His emotions filtered into me, of pain, anger, and sorrow... And it mixed with my own. I slowly landed behind him, my boots digging into the ash and small stones.

"He destroyed my father's home..." Anger rose from him and he dropped his head, allowing his hand to run through the soot and dirt before him.

I knelt down beside him and laid my hand on his shoulder. "I'm sorry, Kade."

We stood there in silence for a few minutes, honoring all that this place was to us, when ice stabbed down my spine. My head snapped up, and I glanced over to where the cliff was. Kadeyan's head slowly rose, and I knew he felt it too.

Black mist crawled up and billowed out onto the charred grounds. Standing, I looked closer at it as shadows began to take on a form, looking like us...but far viler. Power wafted off of them, reminding me of the same energy from Solyus...from the onyx lake. These were the creatures within the water that tried to pull me under.

"Kade..." I stepped back, gripping his leather jacket to stand.

He quickly followed, standing by my side, but he froze. "Umm, Davyna." I turned my head, seeing the black mist rushing towards us in the opposite direction.

Fuck.

Throwing my hands out, I called for the light within my veins and blinding iridescent power flowed out. I burned a line through the creatures, hearing their screams as others gnashed their teeth the closer they got.

"Come on!" I yelled as I grabbed his hand and pushed off the ground. Both of our wings reappeared and we soared through the air as the shadows climbed to reach us. We both shot out our light power and the rays lit up their darkness. The creatures let out haunting screams, but it did little to stop their pursuit of us.

The Ember Court lands came into view quickly, and I turned around, flying backwards. I let out a yell as one of the shadows wrapped around my leg and pulled me down. My calf instantly began burning, and I shot my power at it, forcing it to release me. Kadeyan swooped down, taking me into his arms, and anger rose deep in my soul.

Obsidian did this. He destroyed our home. He sent these things here to prove a point that he had the power... But so did we.

I sent out more light magic that exploded outward, pushing them back.

"Drop down right there!" I yelled.

"Are you crazy?" Kadeyan retorted, looking at me with wide eyes.

"Aren't you?"

He shook his head, smirking as he nosedived towards the ground. The wind ripped my hair back as the ground quickly approached, and I took a deep breath before pushing myself out of his arms. Rolling, I rose quickly and turned to see the sea of shadows roaring greater than any raging storm.

Kadeyan landed and moved by my side, and I turned to face him. "Take my hand."

"What's your plan?" he asked, but then shook his head, smiling.

"If they don't fear the light...then let's give them darkness." Kadeyan took my hand, and we faced the shadows as their faces pressed through the mist, exposing their soulless eyes.

Darkness crept through my veins before I closed my eyes, summoning the power I kept locked away to take over. It obeyed me now, answering my call with celebration and desire to kill. My eyes shot open and a smile rose on my face—one I knew was drenched in evil.

Glancing over at Kade, I watched as his eyes slowly opened, exposing the blacks surrounding his amber irises. He gave me a vile but beautiful grin and we both turned to face them, feeling nothing but pure joy.

Every pore in my body was seeping out with power, but I held it in, waiting for the right moment. Kadeyan held his ground with me as they inched closer, closing the gap between us.

Twenty feet...

Ten...

Five...

Smiling, I looked at him as my other hand went out, his own following my lead. As their shrieks met our ears, we both turned and let out shimmering black flames. I watched in joy as it spread through the lands like wildfire, consuming everything in its path. The screams of the creatures were deeper now, laced in fear as the ones in the back tried to run away. There was no use though—the flames spread for miles, only looking for them.

We sat there and watched until the last bit of shadows was swallowed up by the fire, before it extinguished. It left smoke behind, lifting into the air to merge with what Obsidian left behind.

Dropping Kadeyan's hand, I took a deep breath and commanded the darkness within to rest, and it retreated back to its home within my soul. I looked at Kade, his eyes still black. Placing my hands on his face, I pulled him down slowly and kissed his lips, sending light through me to him. Within a few seconds, he kissed me back, wrapping his arms around my waist.

Drawing back, I watched his eyes slowly open, burning a beautiful amber. "That was... I've never felt power like that."

"I know." Letting him go, I looked around at the Ember Court. It seemed untouched by Obsidian, which confused me. "Come on, let's go close the veil so he can't send anything else. Then we can break the link."

We climbed the hill where the Ember Castle would be, and my stomach twisted. His body stiffened, glancing out at the thousands upon thousands of white roses covered in blood laid around the property.

"What the fuck?" he asked in a hushed tone. At first, I thought of Alastair and how he always offered me a white flower... But now knowing he worked for Obsidian, was it always a sign from him?

I moved forward, trying to focus on what needed to be done.

And yet, I couldn't shake that this was a statement Obsidian wanted me to receive. White roses stood for new beginnings, and I knew that was exactly what he was saying here. The new beginning of Arcadyus ruling this world...with my help. That I was now his and his alone to use.

Kadeyan took my hand and shook his head. "That's not going to happen, Dy."

I nodded, pushing away the quake that wanted to crawl down my spine. As we began walking past the roses, I noticed something happening to them that made my blood pump faster through my veins. They were turning black, wilting into nothing but death. Rage took hold as I narrowed my gaze on the castle. Well, he got something right... He was going to rot away soon.

Entering the throne room, Kade and I stopped to take in the firestorm before us. "So, we have to absorb that back into us?" he asked.

"No...I have to," I said, looking at him as his fear rose.

"The last time you tried, it threw you back," Kadeyan said, his tone laced with concern.

I nodded, glancing back at the flames dancing to their own furious melody.

"I can do this now." Smiling, I moved forward, but I was pulled back into his arms. His breath was heavy, and he slowly rested his head against mine. Our lips brushed and I looked into his eyes. "I can do it," I whispered.

After a moment, he let me go and I took a second to compose myself. Facing the throne, I watched the flames twist and turn in vengeance. They still held onto the anger I felt when I sent them out, showing the fury and pain I held. Something in me said this wasn't going to work—that it needed more from me.

But I had to try.

I took the steps slowly, feeling the heat of the blaze caress my face. I placed my hand into the flames and began chanting within my mind, pulling for all my power to siphon it back into my veins where it needed to be. This magic had become its own, determined to defend its life. Pain bloomed over me, and I pushed harder, visualizing a tear in the darkness.

I couldn't hold back the cries as it began fighting against me. Before I could even lift my head, Kadeyan took my hand and placed his other into the flames. Our eyes connected, and he nodded his head before we both turned to face the inferno.

The pain lessened and my vision went black, showing me the veil beyond. I could see the other fae realms peeking through. They looked similar to ours, but different creatures and fae lived within them. It was beautiful, just like Valyner before all this happened. Our powers were similar...all divided by light and darkness, and something within rang out, feeling my ties to them as well.

Pushing harder, I watched the tear begin to close, like I was stitching it with the thread of my power. I found peace in it and watched the needle of light move faster, closing the hole until the other Realms were nothing but a distant memory.

Opening my eyes, I realized we were on the ground at the back of the throne room. I sat up, my body aching all over before a cough ripped from my lungs. My head spun and I looked over at Kade, who was rolling to his side.

"You good?" I asked him, and he slowly lifted himself up, nodding his head. I took a deep breath, feeling the relief wash over me. "We did it... It's closed."

"Thank fucking gods." He chuckled at his own joke, but it was short-lived as he looked towards the throne. "Umm, Davyna. Why is it still on fire?"

Turning, I saw it, still smothered in the blaze. I went to speak, but I honestly didn't know why. Standing up, I felt something in the pit of my stomach tell me... It wouldn't stop, until I sat upon it.

Maeve warned me about it when I first arrived, and I didn't know if that warning still applied. I controlled both sides now, like the prophecy stated. So, could Obsidian curse me if I took it?

Turning away, I looked out the window and my jaw dropped. "Kadeyan..."

He got up and stood behind me before we both used the gap and landed in the lawn of the castle, feeling lost for words.

Levanna, Calix, Sorin, and Evren were walking towards us, covered in armor and weapons with an army of fae walking behind them. We moved towards them, and a part of me wanted to command them to leave, but Kadeyan entered my mind, telling me to wait.

They all stopped and looked around before glancing at the both of us. Calix moved forward, clearing his throat. "If the plan is to sacrifice ourselves...then count us in."

Evren smacked his arm, giving him a flirtatious smile before she stepped forward. "What he means to say is: If you go down, we go down together." Tears invaded my eyes as I looked over all the fae, before fixing my gaze back on my sister. "Sorry, Your Grace, but we are not leaving. So, what's the plan?"

CHAPTER 87
OBSIDIAN

She was a strong little thing... I'd give her that. But she had no idea what I had planned. And it was taking every fucking ounce of restraint not to go and kill them all for standing behind her.

I was their creator, their maker...

But that was how you won a war: watching and waiting for the right time to strike when their guards were down.

I've been watching them for days from afar as Davyna and Kadeyan trained with the fae, showing them how to control and pull from the light and darkness they possessed.

And my eyes couldn't leave *him.*

He shouldn't have her power.... She shouldn't be mated to a fae. Did Zaryk know this would happen? Did he want this so I would be out of the picture and they could take over Valyner?

That *fucker.*

What they all didn't know yet was this war had been going on for thousands of years, and they were just another small battle I would eradicate. Because I wasn't going to meet my true death anytime soon. Not until Arcadyus killed Zaryk while I held him down with my power...

I needed the daggers, the stone, and her. Stars above, why did it have to be *her?* My little cinder was hell-bent on using them against me... I laughed, looking out the window.

She could use the dagger on me, but it would only send my soul to the Abyss... Mommy must have left out the real way to break the link, and it was quite simple. That stone's capability could do so much more, and it would lead up to the next phase...but I wasn't going to tell her that until it was time.

They wanted freedom, and so did I. I wanted to be free from this form Zaryk forced me to wear. And as much as I viewed the other gods as an annoyance, they were my brothers and sisters. I wanted us back together for what came next. And if they objected, they and their creations would fall.

Turning to my mirror, I watched it as it swirled, showing me what I wanted to see: the Ember Court. "Davyna," I called out to it, and she came into view as if I was standing by her side. She was training with some fae, her power holding back to not hurt them.

I watched her move, memorizing how she danced through the motions. She was quick, graceful, beautiful...

And mine.

Leaning forward, I ran my finger over the mirror, causing the image to ripple. "Oh, my little alyahiia, how you will do grave things soon...and I'll make you love it." I laughed, sitting back as I picked up my glass of blood, swirling it. Bringing it to my lips, I sipped it and watched her go about her day as the sun fell.

They were setting up a bonfire and all her friends joined her. I twisted my hand out, bringing their voices through and focused on the link that grew after Tanith's death.

"When he comes, what is the plan?" asked the one she called *sister.*

"You all need to stay back. He won't hesitate to kill you all to teach me a lesson," Davyna said, and I chuckled. My new bride already knew me so well. "Kadeyan and I will lure him into the throne room. He can't send in any more creatures from the other Realms. His power will be focused on us." I sat forward and tilted my head. "When you see the signal, throw everything you guys have at the castle. Don't hold back."

I smiled, sitting back and drinking down the sweet crimson before slamming the cup down. She thought if they all used their power on me, it would overwhelm my power... *But wouldn't it?*

I would need to do something about that.

Licking my bottom lip, I watched them fall into stories from the past, their laughs growing louder. They seemed to fall back into happiness as they passed around their whiskey, even telling tales of the ones they lost.

Didn't they know it was by my hand that I was giving them this moment, this calm before the storm? She should thank me for this later. I narrowed my gaze on her and felt for her deep down through our link. She turned, looking around as the paranoia returned.

"That's right, Davyna. Be afraid." I smiled. "I'm coming for you soon...and I always get what I want."

CHAPTER 88

DAVYNA

The throne room was in ruins once again, just like it had been every time I saw it from within this dream. The fear of the scene playing out before me was still as if it was the first time. I could see a dark shadow looming over a body, the blood pooling out around it. But everything moved in a blur, and the air was ripped from my lungs as the room began to spin.

Coming to a halt, I turned, breathing heavy, and took in the same room. It was now empty, ashes lying on the ground where the body once was...and the throne was no longer on fire.

What was this?

The throne room doors busted open, and my mother walked in, her eyes gentle on mine. "Mom?" *I stepped forward, allowing the dream to fall away from me. I ran towards her, throwing my arms around her neck in an unbreakable embrace.* "You're here." *I cried and she ran her hand over my hair.* "I'm so sorry."

"Shush now, you have nothing to be sorry for." *She pulled me back, wiping the tears from my face.* "I wish I could have done more to stop any of this from being your burden."

"How did you do all this without your power?" *I asked, my lip trembling.*

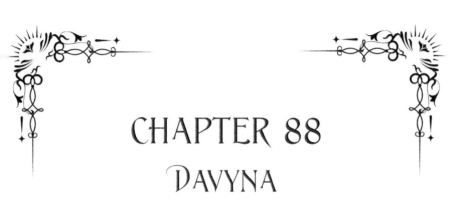

She gave me a weak smile, her own eyes filling to the brim. "I used it once...prior to my death, and it opened the door slightly of the goddess power Zaryk locked away. It was when I passed the magic onto your father to hide his people in the tunnels in Valyner. You did the same when you sent Persephone to the void you created for her. And then, you opened it fully on the throne." *A tear fell down her face.*

"When I was dying, I pushed my power out to your father, so he could finish what I started... And since my goddess power was locked down, the dark obsidian worked. I waited until my heart was beyond the point of healing. I needed to die..."

"So, dark obsidian worked on me before because of your spell?" *I asked.*

"Yes, it was the same one my father used on me. But I altered yours to make you human. To keep you out of Persephone's reach until you were old enough."

"So, everything Dad did...it was with your power?"

She nodded, giving me a broken smile. "I just wish I could have done more for you. But this blood oath with your grandfather... even in death, I still can't say certain things." *Her lip lifted, anger flashing in her eyes.* "I made sure you had what you needed, not what he wanted."

"What do you mean? What did Zaryk want?"

"The gods all have secrets, Davyna. Where do you think this family curse of lies started?"

My stomach tightened, looking into her eyes like they were pleading with me to understand. There was more to Zaryk...but what was he hiding?

"Then how did Kade become like me?" *I asked, still shocked at his transformation.*

"You already know the answer. If I would have gone through my last transformation to become what I truly was before I bonded to your father, the same would have happened to him. A god and a fae bonding changes the fae into the higher being's equal."

Chest tightening, I turned and winced. "Is this all going to happen... Is Kadeyan—" *I choked on the words, feeling my heart split inside my chest at the thought, and my mom pulled me forward.* "Who is on the floor, Mom? Who is going to die?"

"With being a seer, you have the ability to see the possible outcomes. Mine were like yours—in dreams—and it made it harder to see them. But focus on it..." *She smiled and placed her hand on my face.*

When my eyes closed, I saw myself on the ground, and then pushed deeper into the dream. Pain throbbed in my head, shifting the vision and everything within me broke. Because the figure that was blurred before, was now clear.

It was Kadeyan.

"No... No," *I cried.*

"Push further, Davyna." *My mother called out to me, but I couldn't pull my gaze from Kadeyan's vacant eyes. My mother's power shot through my veins, turning the vision before me to mist before a new figure was lying on the ground. My heart rate came down, and my jaw fell open.*

It was Obsidian...dead.

Pulling my eyes open, I gazed into her gentle pools. "Those are the possible outcomes of what is to happen here."

"But if those are alternate endings to this—"

"I know you are worried about Kadeyan, but fate's hands will move in the way they need to. Either way, you can't stop fighting to put Obsidian down before he gets everything he needs to raise Arcadyus."

"I can't lose him, Mom..."

"No one is ever ready to lose their mate..." *She dropped her head, and I knew she was thinking about my father.* "But, sometimes, we just have to make peace with it."

"What if I can protect him?" *I asked, feeling my eyes burrow into her.* "What if I use the new stone to send him back, like you did for me?"

"Davyna, no, you can't," *she said, her expression turning concerned.*

"Why not?"

"You can't... You won't be able to."

I pulled back, feeling anger rise. "Why is that? You did it."

"But are you willing to kill your friend tied to the Fallen line by a blood bond to ensure the spell works?" *she stated, her words hitting me like a ton of bricks. Levanna.* "Your father's death is what made it possible for you to come back. He was your blood and only mine because we bonded. The only loophole to blood magic like this is to sacrifice one whose soul is tethered to the same blood running in Kadeyan's veins. But bringing back a god...it's not that simple."

"Then, what if I link it to myself?"

She shook her head, her worry evident. "Do not dabble in that magic, Davyna. You will fall into the darkness, and it doesn't matter if you succeed because your soul will be forever lost."

"Fuck my soul, Mom. If there is a way to keep him alive..."

A laugh sounded from behind us, and I turned to see Obsidian standing by the throne.

"Well, how sweet. Are you enjoying your mother-daughter bonding, Nyna?" *He leaned against the throne, crossing his arms across his chest.* "Let her do it... It will make it easier to take her away from here."

"You will not touch my daughter!" *she growled and moved forward, standing in front of me.*

"And what will a ghost do to stop me?" *He laughed.* "Have I said how happy I am that I didn't kill you as an infant? You gave me everything I ever wanted."

"You will not win this, Obsidian. You know it and so does Arcadyus."

"Oh, no, on the contrary...we are going to rule over all the Realms with fire and brimstone." *He began walking towards us, and my mother stood her ground, blocking me from him.* "I'm just sorry you won't be around to see it."

His shadows lashed out, grabbing me until I was locked within his toxic embrace. I let out a yell and fought against him, but my power was being drained too fast— No, channeled.

"Obsidian, stop! Let her go."

"No, but you should..." *The line between my mother and I begin to fade, shattering into small splinters, and she started to flicker.*

"MOM!" *I screamed. She looked down at her hands, turning into mist as she tried to summon her power. The connection to her began to fade and I cried out, thrashing in his hold.*

"Goodbye, Nyna. Now you can be with your mate," *Obsidian said. He threw me to the ground and I cried, but he paid me no mind. Pushing myself up, the tears ran down my face as she slowly faded, her wide eyes locked on me.* "And I can be with *mine.*"

"No!" *I screamed as the mist exploded, raining down in a shimmering blue dust. And the world stopped around me.* "You fucking monster! What did you do?" *I sobbed through my anger.*

"I freed you from her... I won't spend our eternity with her in your ear."

"I'm going to fucking kill you!" *I yelled, standing as another tear fell.*

He walked over to me and brought his hand to my face, wiping the tears with his thumb. I refused to back away, staring him down with vengeance. He brought his finger to his mouth, sucking, and groaned.

"And I'm going to kill your mate... Sweet dreams, alyahiia. I'll see you soon."

Jumping up, I felt the air trying to force its way into my lungs, but it wouldn't enter. Taking a look around the room, I realized I was on the floor in the throne room, the flames making the dark room glow bright. When I fell asleep tonight, I was in bed with Kade...

I felt for the sliver of power within that was linked to my mother, but it was gone, like it never existed to begin with. A sob ripped from my throat, and I threw my fist down, the stone cracking below me.

Each second counted in this war with him and I was running out of time, like an hourglass dripping the blood of my other half. But I'd be damned if I let it run out.

I knew what I needed to do... I thought back to the conversation I had with Kadeyan before all this happened, and I didn't know how true it was until now.

My soul was damned anyway.

CHAPTER 89
DAVYNA

Waking, I looked out the window and saw that the sky was still dark. My breath rose into the air as I sat up. What was going on? Jumping up, I looked for Kade but sensed he was outside, his own emotions swaying.

Changing into my leathers, I jumped into the gap and appeared next to him. The frigid air pierced through the thick material, successfully coating my flesh and forcing a quake throughout. Fires burned all over the camp, but the warmth of the flames was void. "What's going on?"

"The sun hasn't risen..." Kadeyan said before giving some orders to the Fallen Court soldiers. Turning towards me, he let out a long breath. "The lands began dying overnight. Water from the streams turned to blood...the trees and grass are wilted, and the fae themselves seem to be feeling an effect on their power weakening."

"It can't be from Obsidian siphoning them... We broke that when they all left."

"I know." He ran his hand over his face, his frustration evident. "Why isn't he coming? This imbalance is going to kill them all before we can even kill him." Defeat rang out in his tone, and I pulled him in, resting my head against his chest.

"I know..." The scent of leathers and pine swirled around me and I soaked it in. Remembering the nightmare last night, it pulled me back to reality. I swallowed hard, feeling my heart double over.

"And what the fuck was that dream last night? Did he invade it?"

"You saw that?" I asked, taking a step back.

"Yeah. And you are not doing that spell. I won't have you lose yourself to save me."

I turned and looked over the fae walking by before pulling him off to the side. "You would do it for me...would you not?" He went to talk but held his tongue. "Exactly. So, don't tell me what I can and can't do."

"Dy...it's not a good idea," he said as he tucked my orange strands behind my ear. "What if—"

"Kadeyan, it's just to protect you if anything goes wrong. And if I lose that part of me, you are the only person who can bring it back. If you have to lock me up and chain me, do it. But let me give us a chance at a future...a life...a family even."

Kadeyan's eyes lit up. "A family, Dearest?"

"Yes...because with you, I want everything."

He pulled me in, kissing me with fervor that made the frozen world around us blur. "You are so damn stubborn, you know that? Our child will probably be just like you."

"Probably..." I gave him a playful smirk. "Now that I have this... us. I won't give it up."

He bit his tongue and averted his gaze, shaking his head as he battled with his own worry. After a moment he turned back, taking my face between his hands. "If anything goes wrong, I'm stopping it. Do you hear me? I won't have you lose anything else or die in the process. Not unless you want me to chase after you and condemn our realm to the same fate."

I nodded. He hesitated before he pulled the stone out of his pocket, looking it over. "I'll be in there soon, and I'll tell Levanna and Evren to head in there to keep an eye on things."

"It's going to be fine." I kept my gaze on him as I gripped the stone. "I can do this, Kadeyan."

"I know you can." He wrapped his fingers around my wrist, pulling me in as his breathing grew heavier. "But go. Before I change my mind."

I pulled myself free and fell into the void, my heart beating faster as I entered the halls of the castle. I sent out my apologies to my mother and a prayer to whomever was out there beyond the gods...

Just this once, please help me to protect the man I love...

A circle of black salt was set in the throne room and I began etching each symbol of the Courts into the ground with my fires. My hands shook while finishing the last one, and I took the deepest breath I could.

A war of emotions filtered through me, contemplating this, but I wouldn't be able to live with myself—soul or not—if I didn't try. Pulling my dagger free, I cut into my palm before I could think about it more. Instantly, the sting bloomed and my crimson blood freely flowed.

I summoned my flames, setting the salt on fire before pulling the stone out of my pocket and placing it in my wounded hand. The blood began flowing up, covering it and something within shifted.

The spell that was created by my mother flooded into my mind and I began speaking it out loud: "Lòs ventrx un veritous. Trébum, le dyaith." Power swirled about me, chilling my body more than the surrounding world, even as flames raged with pulsing heat nearby.

I'd always heard that love makes you do crazy things, but being here right now...I knew they were wrong. There was no insanity when your heart only took its next beat for the person you were meant for. You would kill, destroy, and sacrifice your own life to protect them.

And that wasn't outrageous...it was just untainted love.

The fire around me grew and I looked up as I continued to chant. The flames around me thrashed and I glanced down to see darkness form in the stone, creating a similar void to the one I entered to see my father. Yet it kept flickering...needing something more.

I chanted louder and gripped the stone, pressing it into the wound. But it was denying me. *No...* Anger rose within, and I saw my veins turn black and my skin start to take on a grey hue. Lowering to the ground, I picked up the knife and sliced into my arm. I let out a small scream as the blood ran down to the stone, but it wasn't warm...it was freezing.

The door swung open and I glanced back. Levanna and Evren stood still, stunned by what was happening, but I kept pushing.

"Davyna!" Evren screamed, but I turned away and chanted louder, feeling the darkness come for me.

I was not afraid. I was determined to make it obey me once again.

Dropping the stone to the ground, I cut my other arm and threw the blade down. The flames shot up, billowing off the ceiling. The dark magic was completely captivating. Feeling it pull apart my soul, I knew that was what it needed. It needed a piece of me in that stone to bring him back.

And it could take it...

The grey stones below me began to shake, sending out cracks that traveled through the room and climbed the walls with fury. A scream passed my lips as the pain invaded my heart, sending me to the ground. Levanna screamed something, but it sounded worlds away and I wasn't there anymore with them...with *him.*

My vision went in and out. When it cleared for a moment, I looked up, watching the flames shoot through the stone ceiling. Large pieces fell down to the floor, causing the room to rumble, and the sky slowly shifted from the darkness into a crimson dusk.

My lungs refused to expand, the spell demanding the air from my lungs. Looking down, I watched my skin lose all color, turning a deathly shade of ashen. And before I could even panic, the world around me vanished. I knew I should push away from this feeling. To call for help...but I just felt hollow. Empty.

After a few moments, a blurry world came into view, filled with light and what felt like peace. Everything came to a pause at the veil and I took it in. People were walking around, smiling, and laughing.

A sob worked up my throat as I took them all in, before my mouth fell open in shock. Because I knew him... I knew them.

Elias walked with Akari, lost in conversation, and my eyes couldn't believe it. They looked the same as I last saw them. There was joy held in their eyes and it filled my heart to see it. To know they weren't in pain.

My parents neared them and I froze, taking in my father's silver eyes locked on my mother. I could tell he was happy she was there, but sorrow made them duller. And my mother...she was sad, her golden eyes glistening as she met his gaze, trying to force a smile. I beat against the veil, crying out for them, but my voice was nonexistent.

They continued to walk and tears fell down my face.

I was so close to the family I searched for. That I mourned for... and yet, I couldn't go to them.

My eyes scanned this world, taking in the warmth it was dowsed in. The air ripped from my lungs as I gripped onto the veil, my lip trembling.

Nesrin and Axel walked down a cobblestone road towards Eryx, Sahar, and Priya. They were all here, and they looked so happy...at peace. I couldn't hold back the cries as I let my head drop, wanting to hold them all just one more time...

Lifting my head, I watched them take off in the opposite direction and ripped my gaze back to my parents. Why couldn't I pass over? Why couldn't I go to them?

My mother stopped, her body going rigid as she turned and her eyes locked on mine. My jaw dropped. She could see me. There was a moment of relief before she shook her head, worry filtering back onto her face. One by one, everyone turned, seeing me, and my lip quivered as I pressed my hands to the veil.

I let out a shallow breath, blinking only to see the throne room again, the embers lifting into the air. Everything began to flicker, and the darkness danced in my mind, pulling me away from everything and leaving me with one thought: I was doing this for love...

But would love be enough to bring me back from insanity once again?

Either way, I let the darkness take me as the world faded away into oblivion, and my soul along with it.

CHAPTER 90
KADEYAN

My heart was beating so hard as I lifted her up from the ground. "Fuck, Davyna! Wake up!"

"Why did you let her do this?" Evren screamed next to me.

But I ignored her, biting into my wrist and bringing it to Davyna's mouth. My blood flowed out grey as I placed it to her lips, feeling my heart rip apart and refuse me its next beat. My head dropped, and I felt for her, willing the power in my veins to pull her back to me.

"Come on... Come on!" Pulling my hand back, I looked at her peaceful state and the tears formed in my eyes. Glancing up at the sky above, red lightning began to strike, with thunder rolling over the lands as heavy droplets began falling around us. Leaning in, I kissed her. "Come back to me, Dearest!" I shook her still body as I looked at Levanna, her eyes glassed over.

"I couldn't stop her, Kade. I..." she said, her voice trailing off into a whisper.

The seconds felt like hours as I held her in my arms, breaking me further apart. Glancing down at the blade, I was ready to follow after her, to take my own life because I vowed to never feel this again...to never be parted from her. I wasn't that strong, and I didn't care if that showed weakness.

If that made me pathetic, then that was what I was because I needed her more.

As I went to reach out for the blade, she sucked in a sharp

breath. And I inhaled, too, feeling my own life return to me before pulling her in.

She sobbed, gripping onto me, and her tears mixed with mine as they ran down my face and onto my leathers. "It didn't work. It didn't work..." she got out between her cries, and I held her tighter to my chest.

"I don't care." I pulled her back, looking into the silver eyes that would always be my happily ever after, my saving grace, my universe... "I don't care so long as you are here."

The sky began rumbling again and I looked up, my heart stalling. Screams rang out over the lands as beasts began swarming from the sky. Ones we saw before during attacks, and ones that were new.

The veil was back open... But how?

Davyna pulled away, looking up, before our eyes met.

"He's here," she spoke into my mind, her voice sounding so broken, weak.

"Levanna, get the fae back, and get the Crystals to put up as many barriers as possible to protect them."

"Kade, I'm not leaving you both," she said, tears falling over and flowing down her cheeks.

"Go give them hell, sis," I commanded, feeling her pain before she nodded and fell into the gap. If only she could feel the pain I felt, too...because it was the same. But I needed her and everyone else safe.

Evren looked up, her eyes glowing yellow as she looked down at me and Davyna.

"Rip them apart."

She nodded with a smirk and vanished before us as I picked Davyna up. She stumbled, her fingers digging into my leathers. Fuck, she was weak.

She coughed, glancing up into my eyes. "He waited for this... For me to do this... He knew I would, and that...I'd be—"

"Even on your worst day, Dy, you are a force of nature." I pulled her face up to look at me. "This ends now. This all ends today."

Screams sounded off in the distance, mixed with screeching from the creatures. I felt pulled to the fight, pulled to rip every monster to shreds, but I was faced with a new battle. One I knew would surpass any I'd ever be a part of.

Davyna stood tall, burying down her weakness as she took a deep breath. We both looked over the throne room, and realized it was another part of the dream.

It was happening.

"Kade..." she said, before looking at me with eyes that cried out in fear. Sending out my power I pulled the stone and the blade into my hands before giving her both.

Darkness washed over the room, making both of us stall and our power spin within. Steeling my spine, I slowly turned as the shadowed mass took form, showing Obsidian with a grin on his face.

"Did you miss me, little cinder?"

CHAPTER 91
DAVYNA

"I'm very upset with you, Davyna… Mating with that thing and creating so much more carnage than there needed to be." Obsidian laughed, shaking his head slowly. "Who am I kidding? I love the carnage…"

"Fuck. You!" I gritted my teeth while gripping the stone in my hand.

"Such a temper. It's a turn-on for some…apparently." He looked at Kade, his lip rising into a snarl. "But for me, it's disobedience I don't stand for."

Shadows laced with fire lunged out, and I put up a shield between us. I let out a broken cry as my power faltered, before Kadeyan pushed his own out to help. His power launched across the room, hitting Obsidian and causing him to stumble back. Kade unsheathed his dagger and took off towards him.

Gripping my own dagger, I pushed my body forward and sent out everything within that would come forth. Obsidian ripped the blade from Kade and kicked him in the chest, sending him flying back. His body went over me, and I slid to the ground as Obsidian charged after me. With a roar, I pushed myself up and swung my hand, slicing into his face.

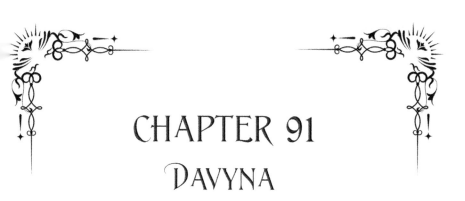

His fires shot out, hitting me in the chest and sending me back towards the throne. Coughing violently, my head spun as I sat up. Kadeyan's shadows wrapped tightly around Obsidian's neck, but he threw the two-toned steel towards Kadeyan, who jumped into the gap and reappeared next to me. The dagger swung through the air and returned to his hand.

Nostrils flaring, he flipped it around and looked us both over. "Did you know, there is only one way to break the link between the gods and their creation? Death. Your mother left that part out! You didn't need that stone to do it. She just wanted me in the Abyss with Arc!" Obsidian shouted, his chest rising and falling as his fury grew.

I looked down at my dagger and smiled, seeing it was stained with his blood. "And what's wrong with that? You belong there."

It was clear now that this stone was something more… It was needed to get to Arc—to the Abyss—but there was something else…

Throwing my dagger down, I dropped to my knees and reeled my arm back, plunging it towards the center of the stone. But Obsidian appeared next to us, grabbing Kadeyan by his throat and placing the dagger that could kill us to his heart. My own dagger stalled, my hand shaking as I took in the two males before me.

"Do it…and watch how fast I kill him," he growled, and my heart refused to take another beat. "Back away from it. Now."

"Fucking do it, Davyna!" Kadeyan yelled as Obsidian pressed the blade deeper into his leathers, making him hiss.

"Yes, please, give me one more reason to kill him."

Every nerve in my body woke up as I stood, trying to evaluate the next move, while the rain pelted down through the opened ceiling my flames created. There were two paths… So, how did we make sure it was him and not Kadeyan?

I looked around and Obsidian began laughing. Using his power, he picked up the stone, and I moved forward towards it. "Ah, careful there, little cinder. You don't want me to kill him before I make you an offer."

"What do you want?"

"What I always wanted: for you to take back the magic you placed on the throne before it continues to spread and combine the realms. I can't have that happen…yet."

Kadeyan tried to free himself, but Obsidian tightened his hold.

"And after, you will break your bond with him...and come with me." At the thought of not being tied to my mate, everything within raged, rejecting the words falling from his mouth. "He can live here while you serve me until Arcadyus has risen and doesn't need you anymore." The stone began spinning through the air, embedding itself into the hilt of his dagger, and my lip twitched. "That's the only offer you are getting from me."

I stood still and narrowed my eyes on him. "I don't believe you."

"Do it. Or I'll use this dagger with the stone to send him to the Abyss. That's how Zaryk did it to Arcadyus. And then, you'll have no choice but to do my bidding to bring *him* back."

My knuckles turned white as I gripped the dagger and walked towards the throne. "Davyna...don't!" Kade yelled, but despite the rage tainting each word, I could sense a different meaning behind them.

My stomach turned as I took the first step, the flames dancing more violently in their anger. I let out a shaky exhale as I took the next step, the darkness within surging through cracks in my mind. And with the last step, all fear and anxiety vanished, turning to mist, because there was only one thing I needed now.

Rage.

"You've got this, Davyna. Do it...and then throw your dagger," Kadeyan said into my mind. I dove into his head for a second to hear his plan, but made sure to keep my body still and show no reaction.

Turning, I took in his crimson eyes. Flames licked at my leathers, and I welcomed it. My fury today matched the madness I unleashed all those months ago. But now, it was stronger, more primal than ever.

"Now! Or more of the fae will die. It's not like I can use them anymore. But I don't need to... I just need you." Obsidian smiled, his eyes drinking me in. The raging war outside the castle was deafening as the fae screamed out in pain.

My eyes slowly glanced up, seeing more creatures appear through the black portals, their roars and screeches piercing my ears. Chills stabbed their way down my spine before I lowered my gaze to Obsidian. The fires within grew, forcing my skin to glow as my eyes locked on him in a warning...my own declaration of war. And my stare turned as cold as ice.

I cautiously lowered myself into the seat, feeling the blaze devour me and the throne's power surge. I took a deep breath as it battled with me, refusing to give up its hold. Slowly, it began to see our ire was the same and listened to my plea for help. Cascading back within where it belonged, it refueled my power and made me feel whole again.

I closed my eyes while each flame licked at my flesh until they started to become mere embers floating around me. Looking up, I saw the fire forming a crown above my head and narrowed my eyes at it. It lowered down, and as it fell into place, I brought my gaze to Obsidian.

He was smiling wide, shaking his head. "Now, was that so hard to obey your god?" He chuckled.

I listened beyond and noticed the creatures were gone, leaving only the heavy breathing and cries of fae who were injured. I glanced down at my scars, seeing them slowly turn to their shimmering black, and smiled.

"You will never be my god." I threw the dagger through the air so fast it was just a mere glimpse as Kadeyan caught it. Flames engulfed his body before he turned and went to bring the dagger down. But Obsidian moved quickly, slamming Kade's body onto the ground with shadows.

I moved forward and threw out both light and dark magic. The contrasting elements spun together, creating something beautiful but deadly. The room shook, and I pushed more out, yelling as sweat trickled down my face. He tried to push back on the power, but it was no use. I had more to lose, more to fight for. And my anger only made me stronger in this moment to push him back.

As I cut off his power, Obsidian arched backward in an unnatural way, screaming out in pain, before I ripped him down to his knees. I smiled and Kadeyan grabbed my dagger from next to him, throwing it at his chest. Obsidian's beaming red eyes widened, his next breath getting lodged in his throat.

I stopped, relief washing over me as he rolled to his side to hide from us like a coward. His hand was coated in crimson blood as he lifted it. He took a shallow breath, and I stepped closer as Kadeyan stood up and moved to my side. Obsidian yelled and coughed while trying to get to his knees, but he failed, stumbling back down.

His heart began to slow, and I smiled, moving over to him to give him one final blow. But he turned fast, his shadows wrapping around my body and completely immobilizing me.

"You missed," he seethed before throwing his dagger through the air. It spun at the speed of light, powered by the stone.

My gaze raised to see it hit its mark and the air was ripped from my lungs. Kadeyan stumbled back a step, gasping for air as his hand went to his chest. His eyes were wide, tethered to mine in shock, before he slowly looked down to see the blade embedded in his chest. The stone in the hilt began glowing, shimmering against his skin that was quickly draining of blood, and my heart stopped beating.

"NOOO!" I screamed, my voice raw and burning.

The world slowed and turned into a blur around me as I ran, feeling Obsidian's shadows fall from me. Kadeyan collapsed on the ground, his eyes locked on the sky above as he softly coughed.

"KADE!" I screamed again, and I couldn't recognize my own voice. Coated in torment and horror, it sounded like nothing I'd ever heard before.

Sliding to the stone floor, I gripped his leather jacket and tried to lift his body, but it was like all the strength within me vanished. "KADEYAN! Come on, stay with me... Stay with ME!" I looked at the blood coating my hands, and they began to tremble as I caught sight of the pool of crimson clinging to my knees. I shook my head, choking on my worst fear becoming a reality.

This wasn't happening...

This wasn't happening.

This wasn't happening!

His eyes slowly glanced over to me as my cries rang out, but I couldn't hear anything... No sounds existed. No presence detected. No magic flourished. Everything felt so far away, as if I was watching someone else experience this pain. This nightmare. It was like I wasn't really here.

I placed my hands around the wound, willing it to stop bleeding, to stop the power of the blade with my own...but it denied me. I tried again, and again, forcing my power into his veins. I asked the fates, the universe itself to take it all. To take me instead. But his blood began turning cold against my flesh.

Tears fell from my face as I pulled my gaze to his, seeing he was fading. "Don't you dare, Kadeyan Fallen! Do you hear me?! You stay right here, with me...please. I–I can't live in this world without you..."

My fires burned out within, almost like they never ignited, never existed. And I became something colder than any winter I had lived through, an icy shell that housed a heart made of frost...

He went to speak, but blood flowed out from the side of his mouth, making him cough harder. My body trembled at the sight, and he entered my mind, his voice sounding so broken. *"Until the seas dry up... Until the earth withers away... I will be yours, and you, mine."*

He choked on the blood, his eyes pleading with me as his skin continued to lose color. *"Don't stop fighting until he is dead. Don't give him what he wants... Okay? You can't. You have to let me go, Dearest... Let me go."*

The emptiness of our bond was beginning to take effect, that part of my soul dying along with him as his eyes began to close.

"I love you. I've...always loved...you..." he said, his voice grounding me to this moment.

Flashes of our past filled my mind, and I realized that he was replaying them in his head and using the last bit of his power to show me. It was like watching someone paint our lives onto a canvas, allowing both of us to see it from the outside.

I saw us in Hell, dancing. In the kitchen when we first kissed. Moments when we bickered and fought. How he would look at me when I stormed away, smiling, but in a way that was filled with so much love that I couldn't see at the time. It all flashed so fast, and I wanted to stay here, I never wanted it to stop.

It all blurred through my mind until it came to a pause in the clearing of the Mortal Lands. Elias was walking away, but I stayed behind, swinging my sword.

Through the vision, my eyes locked on Kade's in the distance, taking in the gentleness in his gaze as he realized what he felt. What he searched for in all of Valyner. And it was found in a mortal girl who held so much power hidden beneath spells.

A girl who feared loving for this exact reason...

Tears coated my lips as I pulled back and brought my blood-stained hands to his cheeks. Leaning down, our lips softly brushed, and I thought back to how I regretted not saying, "I love you" to Elias as he was dying...

And that I couldn't live with that again.

"I love you, Kade... I will always love you."

He tried to muster a smile, but it faded away, his eyes going blank as I pulled back to take him in. My eyes locked on his chest, seeing it slowly exhale, and I couldn't hold back the scream that tore from my throat. The weight of loss crashed down on me, relentless in its attack as it buried me under the waves of sorrow.

Falling forward, I focused past my cries of agony to hear his heartbeat one last time. Yet, it remained still within his chest. The ground began to shake beneath me, as if it, too, felt the pain of my loss. I rested my head against his chest, and his warm blood stuck to my cheek as the wails continued to rip from me.

The ties of our bond ripped apart, shredding every nerve and fiber that made me who and what I was. It was worse than any physical pain I'd endured and surpassed any other loss. It wasn't like before when I couldn't feel him—this was hollowness that no one should ever endure. This was my soul shattering and refusing to mend. And this agony promised it would never weaken, never leave me.

I was empty, broken...and I would forever remain so.

The screams grew louder, and it was something grating, something not of this world. This was only reserved for true pain—true loss—and I unleashed it. I sent it up and let it smear across the lands, tainting it with the anguish ripping through my body. Listening to my cries, my power expelled from me and shot into the sky as my voice gave out.

Dropping my head, the world began to speed up, and the sounds of the lands started to return to me. But I stood numb, feeling just as cold as death itself. Screams invaded my ears, and for a moment, I thought they were my own, still echoing, but they were from the fae...

The rain falling around us was now made of fire, but I couldn't find a reason to care. I couldn't feel anything as I stared into his vacant eyes. My lungs barely expanded as the dagger inside Kadeyan was ripped out by black mist. I pushed back, my breathing coming in rapidly as a trail of red blood followed in my wake, reminding me this was real.

He was gone... He was...

Turning, I looked at Obsidian sheathing the dagger as fire fell over the lands beyond. But I didn't care... It could burn for eternity...

I. Did. Not. Care.

Obsidian kneeled down as I looked away, placing chains on my wrists. Yet, I didn't move... I couldn't as I looked over at the lifeless eyes of the male I loved.

Loved...

He was gone...and so was I.

Maybe that was why I kept seeing my face in those dreams. Because I died today. I died with him...

Obsidian pulled me up by my chains, and I sobbed before he

grabbed my face and dug his fingers into my skin. He forced me to look at him as my tears rolled down onto his charred skin.

"You have taken...everything from me," I whispered, my voice sounding hollower by the second.

"You had a choice, did you not? And you picked the wrong one. You have no one to blame but yourself," he seethed, rubbing at the wound on his chest, and I pinched my eyes closed. "Now his soul is with Arc...and you are with me," he purred and my stomach turned.

Don't give him what he wants... But how was I supposed to honor that when all I wanted was him back?

"Oh, my little alyahiia..." He forced me to look up, and my puffy eyes slowly opened, taking in his vile pools of fury and fire. "You can bring him back..." he said softly, sweet even.

I gritted my teeth together, bile climbing to the back of my throat. "No."

"Really? And here I thought you truly loved him." Obsidian chuckled and then turned my head slowly. He sent out his flames, covering Kadeyan's body. I tried to jump forward, screaming through the pain taking over. But Obsidian's fingers dug into my arms, allowing me to thrash and cry out, yet not get near the inferno he created. "How does that feel, Davyna? Watching the person you *love* burn."

"NO!" The sounds that ripped from my throat were raw, unhinged as my legs gave out. But he forced me to stay standing, holding me tight against his chest and forcing me to watch Kade's body blacken and collapse in on itself. "STOP! Please, stop burning him! Please...stop... Please..." My voice trailed off, the plea lost in the ashes growing before me.

He was nothing but ash...

The remains of my mate floated up, some brushing against my body, and everything within turned to stone. I couldn't move. I couldn't scream. I couldn't do anything as the shock took over.

Obsidian pulled me back to look at him, and I stared into his beaming red eyes as fire fell around us. "If you think this is suffering...you haven't realized what I'm about to do to you is far worse if you don't obey."

I prayed for death. I prayed for the void, Hell, even the Abyss. But I knew none of them would come for me.

Obsidian leaned down, his lips brushing my ear as one last tear fell, accepting that we lost... That *I* lost.

"Now...let's go home."

EPILOGUE

KADEYAN

"*Where the hell are you, Dearest? Where did you go?*" I looked around at the grounds of the Ember Lands. Trepidation and panic seeped into my bones, corrupting them with what I feared.

Her loss.

I couldn't feel her... Why couldn't I feel her anymore? Pins stabbed into my flesh and my breathing picked up as the emptiness grew past the point of pain.

What was going on? Why did it feel like I had been here before though?

The lands slowly became distorted, swirling with onyx mist that disrupted the image before me. I furrowed my brows as the darkness closed in, wrapping around me. What was this?

The emotions rushing through me a moment ago vanished, and I realized I had been here before... I had lived this. But it wasn't happening the same way again... This wasn't her missing. It was me.

I was... I was...

I had always assumed that in death, I would feel nothing...but that wasn't the case.

It tasted of iron, thick and heavy in my throat, as it cut off the air I desperately wanted to swallow down. The smell of ash was growing more pungent, and horrid screams followed me into the darkness that held my soul captive.

And it was cold...

So fucking cold.

Everything slowly began to fade, giving me the relief I craved as I fell away, but it was short-lived. Panic surged through my body, taking root as my mind registered who I left behind.

"Davyna!" I cried, eyes shut tight from despair. But she wasn't there, and the hollowness took root, shattering me beyond repair. Breathing heavily, I opened my eyes, but the next yell that desperately wanted to release was stolen from me.

My mind registered that I was falling, encased in a tunnel and moving at lightning speed. My stomach twisted into a knot, and I frantically looked around. Swirls of magic shimmered through the darkness, matching the Courts' magic. Matching my mate's...and my own.

My brows furrowed and I pulled for my power, refusing death because I wasn't finished. I needed to kill that fucking bastard. I needed him here with me, and away from her.

As the power surged to my fingertips, it was quickly ripped out of my body with a vengeance, causing me to scream out. It filtered into the walls of the tunnel, glowing brighter, and I pulled my eyes shut, gritting my teeth to hold back the tears.

A violent scream echoed out from within the magical walls, matching my own voice for a second before it shifted into another male's voice. It was broken, angry, and it made me want to run far away from it. I glanced up one last time and knew there was no going back.

Because I was...

I was dead.

A shift in power forced me down faster, and I sucked in a breath, falling to what felt like solid ground. I rolled a few times before coming to a stop, groaning. Taking in the eerie silence, I expected my own heartbeat to increase, but it didn't. Because there was nothing beating in my chest, and the realization caused my body to quake.

I slammed my fist down, yelling as I looked up and saw the tunnel I was just in was gone. All that remained was...nothing.

I slowly pushed myself up, taking in the darkness hugging to me like a second skin. My eyes stung, and the tears instantly lined them. Glancing up, everything Obsidian said about the dagger and the stone sending Arc to this place registered.

I wasn't in any normal void...

I was in the Abyss.

Footsteps sounded from behind me, and I closed my eyes, allowing the tears to fall for the life I left behind, and for leaving the love of my life with that fucking monster.

Slowly, the pain consuming me shifted, and my features hardened as I turned. I burrowed my gaze at the male closing in, his green eyes beaming in the darkness.

"You must be Kadeyan," he said, his voice like silk. He pushed his dirty blonde hair back from his eyes, smirking. "Do you know who I am?" He rolled his sleeves up methodically, showcasing the tattoos that covered every inch of his tan skin.

My lip lifted into a snarl, and I narrowed my eyes on him, readying for a fight. Yet, he found amusement in my anger, chuckling softly.

"Arcadyus..." I said.

"Mm, good. You have heard of me." He moved in, and I held my ground. "Now...tell me everything about my precious niece, Davyna."

"Fuck. You," I seethed, which only made him chuckle again. The sound itself made fury bloom over every inch of my soul and my hand balled into a fist. I didn't hesitate, lifting my arm, ready to knock him on his ass. And if I had to, I would beat his face in until the end of time to make sure he never got out of here.

His hand stopped mine, twisting ever so slightly, but immense pain shot up my arm. Wrapping his other hand around my throat, he pulled me closer, and I gritted my teeth.

He looked down, shaking his head slightly before slowly bringing his gaze back to mine. "That's a shame..."

His jaw locked before he tilted his head. His other hand released mine as it buried into my chest, and I gasped. Power that I'd never felt before invaded my soul, and I choked on the cry in my throat.

"We might be dead here, but I can make you wish for things far worse." He threw me to the ground, and I coughed, wondering how that was possible. My power was gone... So, how did he have his?

"She isn't going to free you!" I gritted my teeth through the splintering pain still tearing through me.

Hearing his boots echo off into the Abyss, I looked up into his green pools swirling chaotically as he kneeled by my side.

Staring off into the darkness, he said, "For your sake...I hope she comes soon." He laughed, turning to look at me before gently placing his hand on my chest.

His power shot out again, and my screams bellowed out, filling the void we were prisoners to. I curled in on myself for a long minute, whimpering from the agony as it began to fade, and glanced up into his vile orbs.

"Because, if she doesn't...then our fun is just beginning." He growled before rising and straightening his emerald-green jacket. "So, let's try this again. Tell me everything you know about your mate."

To be continued...

Bonus Chapters

Want to know what happened in those fade to blacks with Evren's POV's? Download the bonus chapter now and find out.

Download here

GLOSSARY

1. Courts in Valyner

Ember court: They are known to be the strongest with their fire abilities. The stronger the bloodline, the more powerful the flames they can summon. They cannot burn.

Fallen Court: They are known for their shadows, feathered wings, and some have the ability to read minds. They can drink blood but don't have to live off of it. It also makes them stronger.

Crystal Court: They are known as the witches of the fae. They can cast spells, hexes, and more.

Crescent Court: They are known as the werewolves of the fae. They can shift at will and are stronger in wolf form. They can also communicate through their minds when they shift.

Salt Court: They are known as the siren fae. They have the ability to summon water as their power. In the water, their eyes become slits and their skin shimmers with scales. Some fae, depending on the bloodline, can even breathe underwater.

Sky Court: This Court was made specifically for Akari by her brother, Ezekiel. She was a seer. But this Court is neutral, studying the fae and gods. They are in charge of the rituals that take place in Valyner. Anyone can give up their Court ability to become a Sky Court member and will be left with the Core abilities of the fae. Very little fae in this Court possess the seer ability, and it either comes with older age or based on the bloodline.

2. **Creatures**- Valyner has various creatures. Some that we meet in *the Dark Curse Series*

Sentores- Mal-afera or known as the dark beasts. They are wolf-like creatures with black glass skin. Very territorial and aggressive.

The Dark Souls a.k.a. Mal-kuya- Fae that have died, and their essence is captured in the Dark Forest. If fae enter the forest, the Dark Souls will try to kill them to have them join their army of the dead. *This curse was broken in Hidden beneath the Embers, by Davyna Ember.*

True sirens a.k.a. Waar Sairini- Only found in the sea. Their bite is lethal unless treated quickly. They are less likely to attack Salt Court members.

The Cursed- Fae who were cursed to lose their fae magic and forced to embrace their Court ability. They were exiled to the Mortal Realm by King Ezekiel when some fae sided with humans in the Great War against his father by supplying dark obsidian to the humans. With the curse placed on them, they went mad over time, becoming more unhinged and attacking the humans they once tried to protect. Some learned control, but not all. Vampires and sirens could not procreate, but witches and werewolves could. **There were no Sky or Embers involved in this curse.*

The Cursed are now referred to as: *Former Cursed fae.*

3. **Dark obsidian**- A material only found in Valyner that can kill the fae. It is an element that was merged into the Realm from one of their creators, Obsidian.

4. **Hell**- This place in Valyner was created by King Ezekiel during his rule to protect the fae of his Court with what was coming. It was

a tunnel system under where the Ember and Fallen Lands meet. The spell was tied to Osiris's life force as a fail-safe when Ezekiel died. After Osiris passed, the spell keeping everyone hidden within transferred to Kadeyan Fallen.

5. **Lords and Ladies of Valyner**
   Ember- Davyna
   Fallen- Kadeyan
   Crystal- Jinx
   Crescent- Alastair
   Salt- Eryx and Sahar
   Sky- Maeve

6. **Planes-** These are holding areas that are created by gods. They can be just outside a realm, but they are still within the atmosphere of that realm. These are used for meeting areas that are more private.

7. **Rituals-**

Lunavas- A ritual to honor the gods who created the fae. It is a yearly tradition where their magic cycles into the lands, and a portion of it goes to the Untouched fae or Ruler over Valyner. The magic also shoots up into the sky as an offering to the gods. Over the years, it has become more depleting for the fae as it strips some of their power. A ritual that took place in Hidden Beneath the Embers.

Saawyn- A ritual to honor the dead fae who have passed on into the afterlife. It occurs every five years in the hope that loved ones will come and visit their living relatives or mates. This ritual (like Lunavas) is performed by the Sky Court. It takes place in the Fallen Court and everyone in attendance makes a sacrifice of blood with a dark obsidian blade before the spell is started. This pulls the dead to the land of the living for a short time to reconnect.

8. Realms

Fae realms- The fae realms were created by the six gods. They came together with their opposites to create the fae.

Valyner- Created by the Goddess of Light; Tanith, and the God of Darkness; Obsidian. Valyner has six Courts, with a small territory in-between each known as No-Man's-Land.

Gelmyra- (formally known as the Unknown Lands) was created by the Goddess of Day; Amara, and the God of Night; Slate. Gelmyra has six Courts: Glint; Alter; Soyl; Pixi; Frost; and Rayn.

Anawyn- (formally known as the Unknown Lands) was created by the Goddess of Death; Onyx, and the God of Life; Bion. Anawyn has six Courts: Hollow; Scaled; Soul; Sage; Vine; and Phantom.

Mortal Realm- There is only one Mortal Realm, and it has always been there. Places in this realm include: Armaros, Qeles, and the Cursed Lands.

Solyus- A realm that was created by the gods when they left their maker; Zaryk. Obsidian banished them shortly after and claimed the land as his own with Tanith, his mate.

The Abyss- A type of realm/holding place created for Arcadyus by his brother Zaryk when they did a spell that joined the six stones (or known as the Untouched stones by the fae). This place has held him captive long before the fae were created.

9. **The ancient language**- Learned in the early days and used mainly by the Sky Court and Crystal Court for spells and rituals. However, other Court members did study it. It is not used as much anymore in Valyner.

10. **Untouched fae-** These were the original six fae created during the first ever Lunavas. The humans came together to call upon the gods to make them more powerful in future wars for more territory. The first humans that were turned into fae in Valyner were: Ezekiel, Elias, Akari, Orla, Persephone, and Osiris.

ABOUT THE AUTHOR

Fay Bec grew up in Massachusetts and moved around before making Florida her home. She is married and has four little ones she couldn't live without. Fay wasn't the biggest reader growing up, but she always wanted to become a writer. She finally took the chance in 2022 with her debut novel and can't wait to continue writing stories that take pieces of her heart. When she isn't writing, she's raising her babies, lost in a TV show, or drawing. She believes Villains do it better, and there is no convincing her otherwise. Keep an eye out for her next book.

Follow her on Instagram and TikTok @faybecbooks,
Goodreads, and her Website

Please consider leaving a review on
Amazon and Goodreads

ACKNOWLEDGMENTS

To my editor, Stevi – I am at a loss for words as I write this because I don't think there are enough pages in the world that could hold just how much I appreciate you. As my editor, you have always gone above and beyond. Seeking was not an easy process, but having you on it made every challenge worth facing. You helped me so much with this story, and all I can say is thank you. As my friend, I love you so much and can't wait to see you thrive in your business and author career!

To proofreading editor and friend Callie – Meeting you this past year and connecting has been such a light in my life. I can't thank you enough for the work you put into seeking and taking the time to brainstorm with me in our writing group. Your support and skills are beyond appreciated, and I couldn't image not having you on future books. I love you, babe, and I can't wait to watch your business thrive either, along with reading your books in the future.

To my cover designer, Emily – Your art will always blow me away! The SBTF cover is exactly what I pictured, and I can't thank you enough for bringing it to life. I can't wait to work together again on the next Dark Curse cover!

To my husband and my family – Thank you for all the love and support during this process of writing Seeking. Whether it was helping with the kids, helping me take a much-needed break, or letting me talk your ear off about the struggles of this book. Your support is something I will always cherish and appreciate. I love you all so much! And to my sweet, amazing children – Never give up on something that sets your soul on fire. And I'll be right here, cheering you on because I know you can do it!

To Ali – my sister, my best friend, and wifey. Where do I even begin? I would be lost without you. Somehow, back in 2022, we met online when we were writing our first books, and now, girl...we are in this for life until we are both in a nursing home. And probably as ghosts, too, knocking our books off shelves to scare the shit out of people. I love you so much and cannot thank you enough for the love and support you have shown me. I will always be here when you need me because your bullshit is my bullshit! Now, let's keep writing books and living this beautiful life together!

To my friends in the bookstagram community – Thea, Ashley, Sydney, Annie, Alex, Deanna, Madi, Sadie, Nicole, Cass, Ash, and anyone else I am missing... I can't thank you all enough for your love and support. Thank you for letting me bounce ideas off of you guys and for always being such amazing people. I love you all so damn much! I can't wait to see what you all achieve in the years to come! I'll be right here, cheering you on!

I want to thank my Alphas, Betas, and ARC readers for taking the time to read and for your advice. There were others along this journey, and even if I didn't name you, this is for you... Thank you for the love and support throughout this all. It meant the world to me.

When I was writing Seeking, this phrase kept coming to mind: "Broken people are not weak." Seeking was not an easy book, as you might now understand why, but so many real-life emotions were added here that it broke me even more. I didn't feel strong enough to overcome some things, and writing this story showed me that it was okay to break. And I'm telling you too: It's okay. It doesn't take away from your strength.

I guess I need to go start the next book now. Get ready. We aren't done with Davyna yet.

XO, Fay

Printed in Great Britain
by Amazon

47144837R00341